"I find myself . . . moved to urge others to read him—critics, science fiction fans, yes, even the general reader. . . . What Stapledon renders better than any other writer I know is the awe, the wonder, the terror, and desperate exhilaration begotten as the tiny microcosm we once thought was all of us there was and the limited macrocosm we were long taught we inhabited have expanded and expanded—until the traditional boundaries between reality and illusion, sanity and madness, self and other blur to indistinction. Once the images in which Stapledon has embodied his vision possess us . . . it is hard to exorcise them, though indeed they may disturb us profoundly. Certainly, since encountering him, I have never been able to stare up into the night sky with the same secure faith that either God exists or he does not; anymore than I have been able between sleeping and walking to be sure that the nighttime 'I' preparing to dream is either identical with or totally different from the conscious 'I' about to surrender its dominion. . . . It is hard, indeed, to think of anyone, with the possible exception of [H. G.] Wells himself, who has inspired so many later authors to the supreme tribute of imitation. Stapledon's vast cosmological point of view widened once and for all the scale and scope of science fiction, opening up for the imagination unlimited time and space—including realms hitherto reserved for the visionary and the mystic; and his unflagging invention created, in passing, plot material which has since been mined and quarried by writers, who turn episodes he dismisses in a paragraph or phrase into whole novels and series of novels."

Leslie Fiedler, *Olaf Stapledon*

STAR MAKER

Also by Olaf Stapledon:

Last and First Men
Odd John
Sirius
Nebula Maker & Four Encounters
Last Men In London
Far Future Calling
A Modern Theory of Ethics
A Man Divided

50th ANNIVERSARY EDITION

STAR MAKER

OLAF STAPLEDON

JEREMY P. TARCHER, INC.
Los Angeles
Distributed by St. Martin's Press
New York

Library of Congress Cataloging in Publication Data

Stapledon, Olaf, 1886–1950.
  Star maker.

  I. Title.
PR6037.T18S7 1987   823'.912   86-29993
ISBN 0-87477-435-7 (pbk.)

Jeremy P. Tarcher, Inc.
9110 Sunset Blvd.
Los Angeles, CA 90069

Design by Tanya Maiboroda

Manufactured in the United States of America

CONTENTS

FOREWORD

Star Maker is the most wonderful novel I have ever read. It retains its wonder on successive readings, and repays study.

To put it at its simplest, the story of the book is the story of a quest, but a quest on a cosmic and superhuman scale. The "I" of the book projects his spirit away from this Earth and "the world's delirium" into the universe, to encounter other worlds, other beings, other classes of beings, finally to confront the creator of the universe itself, the Star Maker, and be permitted communication with it. Nothing could be simpler—or more ambitious.

In his original preface to *Star Maker*, the author states that this is not a novel at all. True, it more resembles an attempt to create myth on the grandest possible scale—a myth for our time that will appease both the scientist and the mystic in us. That is to say, a myth for the two hemispheres of mankind's divided brain. The nobility of this attempt sets *Star Maker* apart from both the modern novel and science fiction, which it superficially resembles. The intention is to instruct as well as to entertain, to imagine as well as to synthesize.

As we might expect, the author of such an astonishing book is himself something of a mystery. William Olaf Stapledon (1886–1950) has been depicted by some critics as a feeble kind of fellow. On the contrary, I believe he was a man of marked character, an athlete in his youth at Oxford, and certainly a brave man to have embarked on an enterprise as considerable as the present book. He may have had his peculiarities, but an ordinary man in the street would hardly create a work like this!

Stapledon was an Englishman whose childhood was divided between England and Egypt, where his father was employed by a shipping line. This pinch of exile probably helped forge the detachment so noticeable in his writing. His first novel (though again the term *novel* is questionable) was *Last and First Men,* published in London in 1930.

That book won enthusiastic critical reviews and remains Stapledon's most famous work. Yet acceptance even of *Last and First Men* is as uncertain as Stapledon's reputation—preserved by science fiction readers, those worldly visionaries. It faded from recognition at one time, to be revived only when the present writer persuaded Penguin Books to reissue it with his Introduction in 1963. Covering as it does the next five billion years, *Last and First Men* is the most thorough and amazing future history ever written. Yet it was to be eclipsed in virtuosity as well as scale seven years later, when *Star Maker* appeared. *Star Maker* is grander in theme, more felicitous in style, subtler in approach—not to mention more overwhelming in imaginative power.

As for Stapledon's courage, at the least he was awarded the Croix de Guerre for his service in World War I, when he worked as an ambulance driver in the mud and muck of Flanders. Ambulance driving was an appropriate occupation, well suited to a man of pacifist inclinations who nevertheless felt compelled to play a part in that ghastly struggle in which the Old Centuries were irrevocably severed from the New.

The quality of aloofness in Stapledon's character was not of his own choosing; whatever difficulties the quality brought him in ordinary life, it made him the kind of writer he became. Much though he feared that the war would undermine civilization—as it undoubtedly did—he appreciated that it gave him the chance to work as one with his fellows. In his strange successor to *Last and First Men,* entitled *Last Men In London,* Stapledon has his protagonist, Paul, say that he entered the war "to accept as far as possible on the one hand the great common agony, and on the other the private loneliness of those who cannot share the deepest passions of their fellows." *Star Maker* is also chock-a-bloc with great common agonies and private lonelinesses—often the private lonelinesses of entire solar communities.

Madness, akin to loneliness, is often in Stapledon's mind. The endless vistas of galaxy after prodigal galaxy threaten the intellect:

> As we searched up and down time and space, discovering more and more of the rare grains called planets, we watched race after race struggle to a certain degree of lucid consciousness, only to succumb to some external accident or, more often, to some flaw in its own nature, we were increasingly oppressed by a sense of the futility, the planlessness of the cosmos.

This somber mood, owing much to the pessimism of Schopenhauer and the conviction that God was dead or an illusion, is more characteristic of the higher thinkers of the late nineteenth century than the optimistic technophiles of the twentieth. There are, however, times when we are reminded that Stapledon explored at a very early date the standby of ambitious science fiction writers from E. E. Smith onward, galactic empires at war:

> Germinating in regions far apart, these empires easily mastered any sub-utopian worlds that lay within reach. Thus they spread from one planetary system to another, till at last empire made contact with empire.
> Then followed wars such as had never before occurred in our galaxy. Fleets of worlds, natural and artificial, manoeuvered among the stars to outwit one another, and destroyed one another with long-range jets of sub-atomic energy. As the tides of battle swung hither and thither through space, whole planetary systems were annihilated. Many a world-spirit found a sudden end. Many a lowly race that had no part in the strife was slaughtered in the celestial warfare that raged around it.

But any similarities between Stapledon's irresistable sweep of events and conventional science fiction is purely coincidental. Stapledon's imagination is omnivorous. After discoursing with the minds of great nebulae, the questing spirit goes on to achieve discourse with the Star Maker itself. The finely sustained climax of the book is the Maker's description of the series of universes with which he is experimenting, of which ours is but one in an almost infinite line. Where does one look in all English prose for a parallel with the magnificent Chapter 15?

An introduction should go no further than this in outlining the many astonishments which the reader is to undergo. But it is worth noting one reason why so many readers are unable to confront Stapledon squarely. He is too challenging for comfort. The scientifically minded mistrust the reverence in the work; the religious shrink from the idea of a creator who neither loves nor has need of love from his creations. To my mind, this intransigent position is in fact the delight of the book, and proves Stapledon's courage. Like his Star Maker, Stapledon inculcates a similar independence in his readers. He is not asking to be loved. He does not love. His work is there. We accept it as we will.

Because of this admirably Parnassian attitude, Stapledon has influenced few writers directly. To show his influence, a writer must have imbibed him when young and demonstrate in his later writing a sense of cosmic process indifferent to the ambitions of humankind. Arthur C. Clarke has claimed to be influenced by Stapledon, and we may believe him. I also came on his writing early, in the middle of a world war, when that dispassionate voice carried the shock of sanity. (*Galaxies Like Grains of Sand* is imitation Stapledon.)

The writers who helped form Stapledon's characteristic utterance are most probably philosophical and political writers. There was also, of course, H. G. Wells, twenty years Stapledon's senior. Otherwise, one might name Dante and the author of *Paradise Lost.* But the most obvious influence appears to be Winwood Reade, the once-celebrated author of *The Martyrdom of Man,* a work published in 1872 and frequently reprinted over the succeeding eighty years. Reade's work ranges freely over the entire history of mankind, and is at once scientific and political. Wells described it as "an extraordinarily inspiring presentation of human history as one consistent process." It would be this view of life as a process that appealed to Stapledon, as it did to Wells.

The Martyrdom of Man roused great antagonism in its time, in the main because of its attack upon religion. Reade did, indeed, put God in his place, as a passage such as the following suggests:

> The arithmetical arrangement of the gods depends entirely upon the intellectual faculties of the people concerned. In the period of thing-worship, as it may be termed, every brook, tree, hill, and star is itself a living creature, benevolent or malignant, asleep or awake. In the next stage every object and phenomenon is inhabited or presided over by a genius or spirit, and with some nations the virtues and the vices are also endowed with personality. As the reasoning powers of men expand their gods diminish in number and rule over larger areas, till finally it is perceived that there is unity in nature, that everything which exists is a part of one harmonious whole. It is then asserted that one being manufactured the world and rules over it supreme. But at first the Great Being is distant and indifferent, "a god sitting outside the universe"; and the old gods become viceroys to whom he has deputed the government of the world. They are afterwards degraded to the rank of messengers or angels, and it is believed that God is everywhere present; that he fills the earth and sky; that from him directly proceeds both the evil and the good. In some systems of belief, however, he is believed to be the author of good alone, and the dominion of evil is assigned to a rebellious angel or a rival god.

This extract is included not only because I hope to find others to share my enthusiasm for Winwood Reade, but because one can see Olaf Stapledon chuckling with appreciation over such downgrading of the deity.

Stapledon takes that thought further. Light years further. Whatever it may be—novel, myth, prose poem, vision—*Star Maker* remains light years ahead, something toward which the rest of us are still travelling.

Brian W. Aldiss

Publisher's Note:

The Star Maker Glossary included in this 50th Anniversary Edition was intended for the original edition of the book.

CHAPTER ONE

THE EARTH

1. The Starting Point

One night when I had tasted bitterness I went out on to the hill. Dark heather checked my feet. Below marched the suburban street lamps. Windows, their curtains drawn, were shut eyes, inwardly watching the lives of dreams. Beyond the sea's level darkness a lighthouse pulsed. Overhead, obscurity.

I distinguished our own house, our islet in the tumultuous and bitter currents of the world. There, for a decade and a half, we two, so different in quality, had grown in and in to one another, for mutual support and nourishment, in intricate symbiosis. There daily we planned our several undertakings, and recounted the day's oddities and vexations. There letters piled up to be answered, socks to be darned. There the children were born, those sudden new lives. There, under that roof, our own two lives, recalcitrant sometimes to one another, were all the while thankfully one, one larger, more conscious life than either alone.

All this, surely, was good. Yet there was bitterness. And bitterness not only invaded us from the world; it welled up also within our own magic circle. For horror at our futility, at our own unreality, and not only at the world's delirium, had driven me out on to the hill.

We were always hurrying from one little urgent task to another, but the upshot was insubstantial. Had we, perhaps, misconceived our whole existence? Were we, as it were, living from false premises? And in particular, this partnership of ours, this seemingly so well-based fulcrum for activity in the world, was it after all nothing but a little eddy of complacent and ingrown domesticity, ineffectively whirling on the surface of the great flux, having in itself no depth of being, and no significance? Had we perhaps after all deceived ourselves? Behind those rapt windows did we, like so many others, indeed live only a dream? In a sick world even the hale are sick. And we two, spinning our little life mostly by rote, seldom with clear cognizance, seldom with firm intent, were products of a sick world.

Yet this life of ours was not all sheer and barren fantasy. Was it not spun from the actual fibres of reality, which we gathered in with all the comings and goings through our door, all our traffic with the suburb and the city and with remoter cities, and with the ends of the earth? And were we not spinning together an authentic expression of our own nature? Did not our life issue daily as more or less firm threads of active living, and mesh itself into the growing web, the intricate, ever-proliferating pattern of mankind?

I considered 'us' with quiet interest and a kind of amused awe. How could I describe our relationship even to myself without either disparaging it or insulting it with the tawdry decoration of sentimentality? For this our delicate balance of dependence and independence, this coolly critical, shrewdly ridiculing, but loving mutual contact, was surely a microcosm of true community, was after all in its simple style an actual and living example of that high goal which the world seeks.

The whole world? The whole universe? Overheard, obscurity unveiled a star. One tremulous arrow of light, projected how many thousands of years ago, now stung my nerves with vision, and my heart with fear. For in such a universe as this what significance could there be in our fortuitous, our frail, our evanescent community?

But now irrationally I was seized with a strange worship, not, surely of the star, that mere furnace which mere distance falsely sanctified, but of something other, which the dire contrast of the star and us signified to the heart. Yet what, what could thus be signified? Intellect, peering beyond the star, discovered no Star Maker, but only darkness; no Love, no Power even, but only Nothing. And yet the heart praised.

Impatiently I shook off this folly, and reverted from the inscrutable to the familiar and the concrete. Thrusting aside worship, and fear also and bitterness, I determined to examine more coldly this remarkable 'us', this surprisingly impressive datum, which to ourselves remained basic to the universe, though in relation to the stars it appeared so slight a thing.

Considered even without reference to our belittling cosmical background, we were after all insignificant, perhaps ridiculous. We were such a commonplace occurrence, so trite, so respectable. We were just a married couple, making shift to live together without undue strain. Marriage in our time was suspect. And ours, with its trivial romantic origin, was doubly suspect.

We had first met when she was a child. Our eyes encountered. She looked at me for a moment with quiet attention; even, I had romantically imagined, with obscure, deep-lying recognition. I, at any rate, recognized in that look (so I persuaded myself in my fever of adolescence) my destiny. Yes! How predestinate had seemed our union! Yet now, in retrospect, how accidental! True, of course, that as a long-married couple we fitted rather neatly, like two close trees whose trunks have grown upwards together as a single shaft, mutually distorting, but mutually supporting. Coldly I now assessed her as merely a useful, but often infuriating adjunct to my personal life. We were on the whole sensible companions. We left one another a certain freedom, and so we were able to endure our proximity.

Such was our relationship. Stated thus it did not seem very significant for the understanding of the universe. Yet in my heart I knew that it was so. Even the cold stars, even the whole cosmos with all its inane immensities could not convince me that this our prized atom of community, imperfect as it was, short-lived as it must be, was not significant.

But could this indescribable union of ours really have any significance at all beyond itself? Did it, for instance, prove that the essential nature of all human beings was to love, rather than to hate and fear? Was it evidence that all men and women the world over, though circumstance might prevent them, were at heart capable of supporting a world-wide, love-knit community? And further, did it, being itself a product of the cosmos, prove that love was in some way basic to the cosmos itself? And did it afford, through its own felt intrinsic excellence, some guarantee that we two, its frail supporters, must in some sense have eternal life? Did it, in fact, prove that love was God, and God awaiting us in his heaven?

No! Our homely, friendly, exasperating, laughter-making, undecorated though most prized community of spirit proved none of these things. It was no certain guarantee of anything but its own imperfect rightness. It was nothing but a very minute, very bright epitome of one out of the many potentialities of existence. I remembered the swarms of the unseeing stars. I remembered the tumult of hate and fear and bitterness which is man's world. I remembered, too, our own not infrequent discordancy. And I reminded myself that we should very soon vanish like the flurry that a breeze has made on still water.

Once more there came to me a perception of the strange contrast of the stars and us. The incalculable potency of the cosmos mysteriously enhanced the rightness of our brief spark of community, and of mankind's brief, uncertain venture. And these in turn quickened the cosmos.

I sat down on the heather. Overhead obscurity was now in full retreat. In its rear the freed population of the sky sprang out of hiding, star by star.

On every side the shadowy hills or the guessed, featureless sea extended beyond sight. But the hawk-flight of imagination followed them as they curved downward below the horizon. I perceived that I was on a little round grain of rock and metal, filmed with water and with air, whirling in sunlight and darkness. And on the skin of that little grain all the swarms of men, generation by generation, had lived in labour and blindness, with intermittent joy and intermittent lucidity of spirit. And all their history, with its folk-wanderings, its empires, its philosophies, its proud sciences, its social revolutions, its increasing hunger for community, was but a flicker in one day of the lives of stars.

If one could know whether among that glittering host there

were here and there other spirit-inhabited grains of rock and metal, whether man's blundering search for wisdom and for love was a sole and insignificant tremor, or part of a universal movement!

2. Earth Among the Stars

Overhead obscurity was gone. From horizon to horizon the sky was an unbroken spread of stars. Two planets stared, unwinking. The more obtrusive of the constellations asserted their individuality. Orion's foursquare shoulders and feet, his belt and sword, the Plough, the zigzag of Cassiopeia, the intimate Pleiades, all were duly patterned on the dark. The Milky Way, a vague hoop of light, spanned the sky.

Imagination completed what mere sight could not achieve. Looking down, I seemed to see through a transparent plant, through heather and solid rock, through the buried graveyards of vanished species, down through the molten flow of basalt, and on into the Earth's core of iron; then on again, still seemingly downwards, through the southern strata to the southern ocean and lands, past the roots of gum trees and the feet of the inverted antipodeans, through their blue, sun-pierced awning of day, and out into the eternal night, where sun and stars are together. For there, dizzyingly far below me, like fishes in the depth of a lake, lay the nether constellations. The two domes of the sky were fused into one hollow sphere, star-peopled, black, even beside the blinding sun. The young moon was a curve of incandescent wire. The completed hoop of the Milky Way encircled the universe.

In a strange vertigo, I looked for reassurance at the little glowing windows of our home. There they still were; and the whole suburb, and the hills. But stars shone through all. It was as though all terrestrial things were made of glass, or of some more limpid, more ethereal vitreosity. Faintly the church clock chimed for midnight. Dimly, receding, it tolled the first stroke.

Imagination was now stimulated to a new, strange mode of perception. Looking from star to star, I saw the heaven no longer as a jewelled ceiling and floor, but as depth beyond flashing depth of suns. And though for the most part the great and familiar lights of the sky stood forth as our near neighbours, some brilliant stars were seen to be in fact remote and mighty, while some dim lamps were visible only because they were so near. On every side the middle distance was crowded with swarms and streams of stars. But even these now seemed near; for the Milky Way had receded into an incomparably greater distance. And through gaps in its nearer parts appeared vista beyond vista of luminous mists, and deep perspectives of stellar populations.

The universe in which fate had set me was no spangled chamber, but a perceived vortex of star-streams. No! It was more. Peering between the stars into the outer darkness, I saw also, as mere flecks and points of light, other such vortices, such galaxies, sparsely scattered in the void, depth beyond depth, so far afield that even the eye of imagination could find no limits to the cosmical, the all-embracing galaxy of galaxies. The universe now appeared to me as a void wherein floated rare flakes of snow, each flake a universe.

Gazing at the faintest and remotest of all the swarm of universes, I seemed, by hypertelescopic imagination, to see it as a population of suns; and near one of those suns was a planet, and on that planet's dark side a hill, and on that hill myself. For our astronomers assure us that in this boundless finitude which we call the cosmos the straight lines of light lead not to infinity but to their source. Then I remembered that, had my vision depended on physical light, and not on the light of imagination, the rays coming thus to me 'round' the cosmos would have revealed, not myself, but events that had ceased long before the Earth, or perhaps even the Sun, was formed.

But now, once more shunning these immensities, I looked again for the curtained windows of our home, which, though star-pierced, was still more real to me than all the galaxies. But our home had vanished, with the whole suburb, and the hills too, and the sea. The very ground on which I had been sitting was gone. Instead there lay far below me an insubstantial gloom. And I myself was seemingly disembodied, for I could neither see nor touch my own flesh. And when I willed to move my limbs, nothing happened. I had no limbs. The familiar inner perceptions of my body, and the headache which had oppressed me since morning, had given way to a vague lightness and exhilaration.

When I realized fully the change that had come over me, I wondered if I had died, and was entering some wholly unexpected new existence. Such a banal possibility at first exasperated me. Then with sudden dismay I understood that if indeed I had died I should not return to my prized, concrete atom of community. The violence of my distress shocked me. But soon I comforted myself with the thought that after all I was probably not dead, but in some sort of trance, from which I might wake at any minute. I resolved, therefore, not to be unduly alarmed by this mysterious change. With scientific interest I would observe all that happened to me.

I noticed that the obscurity which had taken the place of the ground was shrinking and condensing. The nether stars were no longer visible through it. Soon the earth below me was like a huge circular table-top, a broad disc of darkness surrounded by stars. I was apparently soaring away from my native planet at incredible speed. The sun, formerly visible to imagination in the nether heaven, was once more physically eclipsed by the Earth. Though by now I must have been hundreds of miles above the ground, I was not troubled by the absence of oxygen and atmospheric pressure. I experienced only an increasing exhilaration and a delightful effervescence of thought. The extraordinary brilliance of the stars excited me. For, whether through the absence of obscuring air, or through my own increased sensitivity, or both, the sky had taken on an unfamiliar aspect. Every star had seemingly flared up into higher magnitude. The heavens blazed. The major stars were like the headlights of a distant car. The Milky Way, no longer watered down with darkness, was an encircling, granular river of light.

Presently, along the Planet's eastern limb, now far below me, there appeared a faint line of luminosity; which, as I continued to soar, warmed here and there to orange and red. Evidently I was travelling not only upwards but eastwards, and swinging round into the day. Soon the sun leapt into view, devouring the huge crescent of dawn with his brilliance. But as I sped on, sun and planet were seen to drift apart, while the thread of dawn thickened into a misty breadth of sunlight. This increased, like a visibly waxing moon, till half the planet was illuminated. Between the areas of night and day, a belt of shade, warm-tinted, broad as a sub-continent, now marked the area of dawn. As I continued to rise and travel eastwards, I saw the lands swing westward along with the day, till I was over the Pacific and high noon.

The Earth appeared now as a great bright orb hundreds of times larger than the full moon. In its centre a dazzling patch of light was the sun's image reflected in the ocean. The planet's circumference was an indefinite breadth of luminous haze, fading into the surrounding blackness of space. Much of the northern hemisphere, tilted somewhat towards me, was an expanse of snow and cloud-tops. I could trace parts of the outlines of Japan and China, their vague browns and greens indenting the vague blues and greys of the ocean. Towards the equator, where the air was clearer, the ocean was dark. A little whirl of brilliant cloud was perhaps the upper surface of a hurricane. The Philippines and New Guinea were precisely mapped. Australia faded into the hazy southern limb.

The spectacle before me was strangely moving. Personal anxiety was blotted out by wonder and admiration; for the sheer beauty of our planet surprised me. It was a huge pearl, set in spangled ebony. It was nacrous, it was an opal. No, it was far more lovely than any jewel. Its patterned colouring was more subtle, more ethereal. It displayed the delicacy and brilliance, the intricacy and harmony of a live thing. Strange that in my remoteness I seemed to feel, as never before, the vital presence of Earth as of a creature alive but tranced and obscurely yearning to wake.

I reflected that not one of the visible features of this celestial and living gem revealed the presence of man. Displayed before me, though invisible, were some of the most congested centres of human population. There below me lay huge industrial regions, blackening the air with smoke. Yet all this thronging life and humanly momentous enterprise had made no mark whatever on the features of the planet. From this high lookout the Earth would have appeared no different before the dawn of man. No visiting angel, or explorer from another planet, could have guessed that this bland orb teemed with vermin, with world-mastering, self-torturing, incipiently angelic beasts.

CHAPTER TWO

INTERSTELLAR TRAVEL

While I was thus contemplating my native planet, I continued to soar through space. The Earth was visibly shrinking into the distance, and as I raced eastwards, it seemed to be rotating beneath me. All its features swung westwards, till presently sunset and the Mid-Atlantic appeared upon its eastern limb, and then the night. Within a few minutes, as it seemed to me, the planet had become an immense half-moon. Soon it was a misty, dwindling crescent, beside the sharp and minute crescent of its satellite.

With amazement I realized that I must be travelling at a fantastic, a quite impossible rate. So rapid was my progress that I seemed to be passing through a constant hail of meteors. They were invisible till they were almost abreast of me; for they shone only by reflected sunlight, appearing for an instant only, as streaks of light, like lamps seen from an express train. Many of them I met in head-on collision, but they made no impression on me. One huge irregular bulk of rock, the size of a house, thoroughly terrified me. The illuminated mass swelled before my gaze, displayed for a fraction of a second a rough and lumpy surface, and then engulfed me. Or rather, I infer that it must have engulfed me; but so swift was my passage that I had no sooner seen it in the middle distance than I found myself already leaving it behind.

Very soon the Earth was a mere star. I say soon, but my sense of the passage of time was now very confused. Minutes and hours, and perhaps even days, even weeks, were now indistinguishable.

While I was still trying to collect myself, I found that I was already beyond the orbit of Mars, and rushing across the thoroughfare of the asteroids. Some of these tiny planets were now so near that they appeared as great stars streaming across the constellations. One or two revealed gibbous, then crescent forms before they faded behind me.

Already Jupiter, far ahead of me, grew increasingly bright and shifted its position among the fixed stars. The great globe now appeared as a disc, which soon was larger than the shrinking sun. Its four major satellites were little pearls floating beside it. The planet's surface now appeared like streaky bacon, by reason of its cloud-zones. Clouds fogged its whole circumference. Now I drew abreast of it and passed it. Owing to the immense depth of its atmosphere, night and day merged into one another without assignable boundary. I noted here and there on its eastern and unilluminated hemisphere vague areas of ruddy light, which were perhaps the glow cast upwards through dense cloud by volcanic upheavals.

In a few minutes, or perhaps years, Jupiter had become once more a star, and then was lost in the splendour of the diminished but still blazing sun. No other of the outer planets lay near my course, but I soon realized that I must be far beyond the limits of even Pluto's orbit. The sun was now merely the brightest of the stars, fading behind me.

At last I had time for distress. Nothing now was visible but the starry sky. The Plough, Cassiopeia, Orion, the Pleiades, mocked me with their familiarity and their remoteness. The sun was now but one among the other bright stars. Nothing changed. Was I doomed to hang thus for ever out in space, a bodiless viewpoint? Had I died? Was this my punishment for a singularly ineffectual life? Was this the penalty of an inveterate will to remain detached from human affairs and passions and prejudices?

In imagination I struggled back to my suburban hilltop. I saw our home. The door opened. A figure came out into the garden, lit by the hall light. She stood for a moment looking up and down the road, then went back into the house. But all this was imagination only. In actuality, there was nothing but the stars.

After a while I noticed that the sun and all the stars in his neighbourhood were ruddy. Those at the opposite pole of the heaven were of an icy blue. The explanation of this strange phenomenon flashed upon me. I was still travelling, and travelling so fast that light itself was not wholly indifferent to my passage. The overtaking undulations took long to catch me. They therefore affected me as slower pulsations than they normally were, and I saw them therefore as red. Those that met me on my headlong flight were congested and shortened, and were seen as blue.

Very soon the heavens presented an extraordinary appearance, for all the stars directly behind me were now deep red, while those directly ahead were violet. Rubies lay behind me, amethysts ahead of me. Surrounding the ruby constellations there spread an area of topaz stars, and round the amethyst constellations an area of sapphires. Beside my course, on every side, the colours faded into the normal white of the sky's familiar diamonds. Since I was travelling almost in the plane of the galaxy, the hoop of the Milky Way, white on either hand, was violet ahead of me, red behind. Presently the stars immediately before and behind grew dim, then vanished, leaving two starless holes in the heaven, each hole surrounded by a zone of coloured stars. Evidently I was still gathering speed. Light from the forward and the hinder stars now reached me in forms beyond the range of my human vision.

As my speed increased, the two starless patches, before and behind, each with its coloured fringe, continued to encroach upon the intervening zone of normal stars which lay abreast of me on every side. Among these I now detected movement. Through the effect of my own passage the nearer stars appeared to drift across the background of the stars at greater distance. This drifting accelerated, till, for an instant, the whole visible sky was streaked with flying stars. Then everything vanished. Presumably my speed was so great in relation to the stars that light from none of them could take normal effect on me.

Though I was now perhaps travelling faster than light itself, I seemed to be floating at the bottom of a deep and stagnant well. The featureless darkness, the complete lack of all sensation, terrified me, if I may call 'terror' the repugnance and foreboding which I now experienced without any of the bodily accompaniments of terror, without any sensation of trembling, sweating, gasping, or palpitation. Forlornly, and with self-pity, I longed for home, longed to see once more the face that I knew best. With the mind's eye I could see her now, sitting by the fire sewing, a little furrow of anxiety between her brows. Was my body, I wondered, lying dead on the heather? Would they find it there in the morning? How would she confront this great change in her life? Certainly with a brave face; but she would suffer.

But even while I was desperately rebelling against the dissolution of our treasured atom of community, I was aware that something within me, the essential spirit within me, willed very emphatically not to retreat but to press on with this amazing voyage. Not that my longing for the familiar human world could for a moment be counterbalanced by the mere craving for adventure. I was of too home-keeping a kind to seek serious danger and discomfort for their own sake. But timidity was overcome by a sense of the opportunity that fate was giving me, not only to explore the depths of the physical universe, but to discover what part life and mind were actually playing among the stars. A keen hunger now took possession of me, a hunger not for adventure but for insight into the significance of man, or of any manlike beings in the cosmos. This homely treasure of ours, this frank and spring-making daisy beside the arid track of modern life, impelled me to accept gladly my strange adventure; for might I not discover that the whole universe was no mere place of dust and ashes with here and there a stunted life, but actually, beyond the parched terrestrial waste land, a world of flowers?

Was man indeed, as he sometimes desired to be, the growing point of the cosmical spirit, in its temporal aspect at least? Or was he one of many million growing points? Or was mankind of no more importance in the universal view than rats in a cathedral? And again, was man's true function power, or wisdom, or love, or worship, or all of these? Or was the idea of function, of purpose, meaningless in relation to the cosmos? These grave questions I would answer. Also I must learn to see a little more clearly and confront a little more rightly (so I put it to myself) that which, when we glimpse it at all, compels our worship.

I now seemed to my self-important self to be no isolated individual, craving aggrandizement, but rather an emissary of mankind, no, an organ of exploration, a feeler, projected by the living human world to make contact with its fellows in space. At all cost I must go forward, even if my trivial earthly life must come to an untimely end, and my wife and children be left without me. I must go forward; and somehow, some day, even if after centuries of interstellar travel, I must return.

When I look back on that phase of exaltation, now that I have indeed returned to earth after the most bewildering adventures, I am dismayed at the contrast between the spiritual treasure which I aspired to hand over to my fellow men and the paucity of my actual tribute. This failure was perhaps due to the fact that, though I did indeed accept the challenge of the adventure, I accepted it only with secret reservations. Fear and the longing for comfort, I now recognize, dimmed the brightness of my will. My resolution, so boldly formed, proved after all frail. My unsteady courage often gave place to yearnings for my native planet. Over and over again in the course of my travels I had a sense that, owing to my timid and pedestrian nature, I missed the most significant aspects of events.

Of all that I experienced on my travels, only a fraction was clearly intelligible to me even at the time; and then, as I shall tell, my native powers were aided by beings of superhuman development. Now that I am once more on my native planet, and this aid is no longer available, I cannot recapture even so much of the deeper insight as I formerly attained. And so my record, which tells of the most far-reaching of all human explorations, turns out to be after all no more reliable than the rigmarole of any mind unhinged by the impact of experience beyond its comprehension.

To return to my story. How long I spent in debate with myself I do not know, but soon after I had made my decision, the absolute darkness was pierced once more by the stars. I was apparently at rest, for stars were visible in every direction, and their colour was normal.

But a mysterious change had come over me. I soon discovered that, by merely willing to approach a star, I could set myself in motion towards it, and at such a speed that I must have travelled much faster than normal light. This, as I knew very well, was physically impossible. Scientists had assured me that motion faster than the speed of light was meaningless. I inferred that my motion must therefore be in some manner a mental, not a physical phenomenon, that I was enabled to take up successive viewpoints without physical means of locomotion. It seemed to me evident, too, that the light with which the stars were now revealed to me was not normal, physical light; for I noticed that my new and expeditious means of travel took no effect upon the visible colours of the stars. However fast I moved, they retained their diamond hues, though all were somewhat brighter and more tinted than in normal vision.

No sooner had I made sure of my new power of locomotion than I began feverishly to use it. I told myself that I was embarking on a voyage of astronomical and metaphysical research; but already my craving for the Earth was distorting my purpose. It turned my attention unduly towards the search for planets, and especially for planets of the terrestrial type.

At random I directed my course towards one of the brighter of the near stars. So rapid was my advance that certain lesser and still nearer luminaries streamed past me like meteors. I swung close to the great sun, insensitive to its heat. On its mottled surface, in spite of the pervading brilliance, I could see, with my miraculous vision, a group of huge dark sunspots, each one a pit into which a dozen Earths could have been dropped. Round the star's limb the excrescences of the chromosphere looked like fiery trees and plumes and prehistoric monsters, atiptoe or awing, all on a globe too small for them. Beyond these the pale corona spread its films into the darkness. As I rounded the star in hyperbolic flight I searched anxiously for planets, but found none. I searched again, meticulously, tacking and veering near and far. In the wider orbits a small object like the earth might easily be overlooked. I found nothing but meteors and a few insubstantial comets. This was the more disappointing because the star seemed to be of much the same type as the familiar sun. Secretly I had hoped to discover not merely planets but actually the Earth.

Once more I struck out into the ocean of space, heading for another near star. Once more I was disappointed. I approached yet another lonely furnace. This too was unattended by the minute grains that harbour life.

I now hurried from star to star, a lost dog looking for its master. I rushed hither and thither, intent on finding a sun with planets, and among those planets my home. Star after star I searched, but far more I passed impatiently, recognizing at once that they were too large and tenuous and young to be Earth's luminary. Some were vague ruddy giants broader than the orbit of Jupiter; some, smaller and more definite, had the brilliance of a thousand suns, and their colour was blue. I had been told that our Sun was of average type, but I now discovered many more of the great youngsters than of the shrunken, yellowish middle-aged. Seemingly I must have strayed into a region of late stellar condensation.

I noticed, but only to avoid them, great clouds of dust, huge as constellations, eclipsing the star-streams; and tracts of palely glowing gas, shining sometimes by their own light, sometimes by the reflected light of stars. Often these nacrous cloud-continents had secreted within them a number of vague pearls of light, the embryos of future stars.

I glanced heedlessly at many star-couples, trios, and quartets, in which more or less equal partners waltz in close union. Once, and once only, I came on one of those rare couples in which one partner is no bigger than a mere Earth, but massive as a whole great star, and very brilliant. Up and down this region of the galaxy I found here and there a dying star, sombrely smouldering; and here and there the encrusted and extinguished dead. These I could not see till I was almost upon them, and then only dimly, by the reflected light of the whole heaven. I never approached nearer to them than I could help, for they were of no interest to me in my crazy yearning for the

Earth. Moreover, they struck a chill into my mind, prophesying the universal death. I was comforted, however, to find that as yet there were so few of them.

I found no planets. I knew well that the birth of planets was due to the close approach of two or more stars, and that such accidents must be very uncommon. I reminded myself that stars with planets must be as rare in the galaxy as gems among the grains of sand on the sea-shore. What chance had I of coming upon one? I began to lose heart. The appalling desert of darkness and barren fire, the huge emptiness so sparsely pricked with scintillations, the colossal futility of the whole universe, hideously oppressed me. And now, an added distress, my power of locomotion began to fail. Only with a great effort could I move at all among the stars, and then but slowly, and ever more slowly. Soon I should find myself pinned fast in space like a fly in a collection; but lonely, eternally alone. Yes, surely this was my special Hell.

I pulled myself together. I reminded myself that even if this was to be my fate, it was no great matter. The Earth could very well do without me. And even if there was no other living world anywhere in the cosmos, still, the Earth itself had life, and might wake to far fuller life. And even though I had lost my native planet, still, that beloved world was real. Besides, my whole adventure was a miracle, and by continued miracle might I not stumble on some other Earth? I remembered that I had undertaken a high pilgrimage, and that I was man's emissary to the stars.

With returning courage my power of locomotion returned. Evidently it depended on a vigorous and self-detached mentality. My recent mood of self-pity and earthward-yearning had hampered it.

Resolving to explore a new region of the galaxy, where perhaps there would be more of the older stars and a greater hope of planets, I headed in the direction of a remote and populous cluster. From the faintness of the individual members of this vaguely speckled ball of light I guessed that it must be very far afield.

On and on I travelled in the darkness. As I never turned aside to search, my course through the ocean of space never took me near enough to any star to reveal it as a disc. The lights of heaven streamed remotely past me like the lights of distant ships. After a voyage during which I lost all measure of time I found myself in a great desert, empty of stars, a gap between two star-streams, a cleft in the galaxy. The Milky Way surrounded me, and in all directions lay the normal dust of distant stars; but there were no considerable lights, save the thistledown of the remote cluster which was my goal.

This unfamiliar sky disturbed me with a sense of my increasing dissociation from my home. It was almost a comfort to note, beyond the furthest stars of our galaxy, the minute smudges that were alien galaxies, incomparably more distant than the deepest recesses of the Milky Way; and to be reminded that, in spite of all my headlong and miraculous travelling, I was still within my native galaxy, within the same little cell of the cosmos where she, my life's friend, still lived. I was surprised, by the way, that so many of the alien galaxies appeared to the naked eye, and that the largest was a pale, cloudy mark bigger than the moon in the terrestrial sky.

By contrast with the remote galaxies, on whose appearance all my voyaging failed to make impression, the star-cluster ahead of me was now visibly expanding. Soon after I had crossed the great emptiness between the star-streams, my cluster confronted me as a huge cloud of brilliants. Presently I was passing through a more populous area, and then the cluster itself opened out ahead of me, covering the whole forward sky with its congested lights. As a ship approaching port encounters other craft, so I came upon and passed star after star. When I had penetrated into the heart of the cluster, I was in a region far more populous than any that I had explored. On every side the sky blazed with suns, many of which appeared far brighter than Venus in the Earth's sky. I felt the exhilaration of a traveller who, after an ocean crossing, enters harbour by night and finds himself surrounded by the lights of a metropolis. In this congested region, I told myself, many close approaches must have occurred, many planetary systems must have been formed.

Once more I looked for middle-aged stars of the sun's type. All that I had passed hitherto were young giants great as the whole solar system. After further searching I found a few likely stars, but none had planets. I found also many double and triple stars, describing their incalculable orbits; and great continents of gas, in which new stars were condensing.

At last, at last I found a planetary system. With almost insupportable hope I circled among these worlds; but all were greater than Jupiter, and all were molten. Again I hurried from star to star. I must have visited thousands, but all in vain. Sick and lonely I fled out of the cluster. It dwindled behind me into a ball of down, sparkling with dewdrops. In front of me a great tract of darkness blotted out a section of the Milky Way and the neighbouring area of stars, save for a few near lights which lay between me and the obscuring opacity. The billowy edges of this huge cloud of gas or dust were revealed by the glancing rays of bright stars beyond it. The sight moved me with self-pity; on so many nights at home had I seen the edges of dark clouds silvered just so by moonlight. But the cloud which now opposed me could have swallowed not merely whole worlds, not merely countless planetary systems, but whole constellations.

Once more my courage failed me. Miserably I tried to shut out the immensities by closing my eyes. But I had neither eyes nor eyelids. I was a disembodied, wandering viewpoint. I tried to conjure up the little interior of my home, with the curtains drawn and the fire dancing. I tried to persuade myself that all this horror of darkness and distance and barren incandescence was a dream, that I was dozing by the fire, that at any moment I might wake, that she would reach over from her sewing and touch me and smile. But the stars still held me prisoner.

Again, though with failing strength, I set about my search. And after I had wandered from star to star for a period that might have been days or years or aeons, luck or some guardian spirit directed me to a certain sun-like star; and looking outwards from this centre, I caught sight of a little point of light, moving, with my movement, against the patterned sky. As I leapt towards it, I saw another, and another. Here was indeed a planetary system much like my own. So obsessed was I with human standards that I sought out at once the most earth-like of these worlds. And amazingly earth-like it appeared, as its disc swelled before me, or below me. Its atmosphere was evidently less dense than ours, for the outlines of unfamiliar continents and oceans were very plainly visible. As on the earth, the dark sea brilliantly reflected the sun's image. White cloud-tracts lay here and there over the seas and the lands, which, as on my own planet, were mottled green and brown. But even from this height I saw that the greens were more vivid and far more blue than terrestrial vegetation. I noted, also, that on this planet there was less ocean than land, and that the centres of the great continents were chiefly occupied by dazzling creamy-white deserts.

CHAPTER THREE

THE OTHER EARTH

1. On the Other Earth

As I slowly descended towards the surface of the little planet, I found myself searching for a land which promised to be like England. But no sooner did I realize what I was doing than I reminded myself that conditions here would be entirely different from terrestrial conditions, and that it was very unlikely that I should find intelligent beings at all. If such beings existed, they would probably be quite incomprehensible to me. Perhaps they would be huge spiders or creeping jellies. How could I hope ever to make contact with such monsters?

After circling about at random for some time over the filmy clouds and the forests, over the dappled plains and prairies and the dazzling stretches of desert, I selected a maritime country in the temperate zone, a brilliantly green peninsula. When I had descended almost to the ground, I was amazed at the verdure of the countryside. Here unmistakably was vegetation, similar to ours in essential character, but quite unfamiliar in detail. The fat, or even bulbous, leaves reminded me of our desert-flora, but here the stems were lean and wiry. Perhaps the most striking character of this vegetation was its colour, which was a vivid blue-green, like the colour of vineyards that have been treated with copper salts. I was to discover later that the plants of this world had indeed learnt to protect themselves by means of copper sulphate from the microbes and the insect-like pests which formerly devastated this rather dry planet.

I skimmed over a brilliant prairie scattered with Prussian-blue bushes. The sky also attained a depth of blue quite unknown on earth, save at great altitudes. There were a few low yet cirrus clouds, whose feathery character I took to be due to the tenuousness of the atmosphere. This was borne out by the fact that, though my descent had taken place in the forenoon of a summer's day, several stars managed to pierce the almost nocturnal sky. All exposed surfaces were very intensely illuminated. The shadows of the nearer bushes were nearly black. Some distant objects, rather like buildings, but probably mere rocks, appeared to be blocked out in ebony and snow. Altogether the landscape was one of unearthly and fantastical beauty.

I glided with wingless flight over the surface of the planet, through glades, across tracts of fractured rock, along the banks of streams. Presently I came to a wide region covered by neat, parallel rows of fern-like plants, bearing masses of nuts on the lower surfaces of their leaves. It was almost impossible to believe that this vegetable regimentation had not been intelligently planned. Or could it after all be merely a natural phenomenon not known on my own planet? Such was my surprise that my power of locomotion, always subject to emotional interference, now began to fail me. I reeled in the air like a drunk man. Pulling myself together, I staggered on over the ranked crops towards a rather large object which lay some distance from me beside a strip of bare ground. Presently, to my amazement, my stupefaction, this object revealed itself as a plough. It was rather a queer instrument, but there was no mistaking the shape of the blade, which was rusty, and obviously made of iron. There were two iron handles, and chains for attachment to a beast of draught. It was difficult to believe that I was many light-years distant from England. Looking round, I saw an unmistakable cart track, and a bit of dirty ragged cloth hanging on a bush. Yet overhead was the unearthly sky, full noon with stars.

I followed the lane through a little wood of queer bushes, whose large fat drooping leaves had cherry-like fruits along their edges. Suddenly, round a bend in the lane, I came upon —a man. Or so at first he seemed to my astounded and star-weary sight. I should not have been so surprised by the strangely human character of this creature had I at this early stage understood the forces that controlled my adventure. Influences which I shall later describe doomed me to discover first such worlds as were most akin to my own. Meanwhile the reader may well conceive my amazement at this strange encounter.

I had always supposed that man was a unique being. An inconceivably complex conjunction of circumstances had produced him, and it was not to be supposed that such conditions would be repeated anywhere in the universe. Yet here, on the very first globe to be explored, was an obvious peasant. Approaching him, I saw that he was not quite so like terrestrial man as he seemed at a distance; but he was a man for all that. Had God, then, peopled the whole universe with our kind? Did he perhaps in very truth make us in his image? It was incredible. To ask such questions proved that I had lost my mental balance.

As I was a mere disembodied viewpoint, I was able to observe without being observed. I floated about him as he strode along the lane. He was an erect biped, and in general plan definitely human. I had no means of judging his height, but he must have been approximately of normal terrestrial stature, or at least not smaller than a pigmy and not taller than a giant. He was of slender build. His legs were almost like a bird's, and enclosed in rough narrow trousers. Above the waist he was naked, displaying a disproportionately large thorax, shaggy with greenish hair. He had two short but powerful arms, and huge shoulder muscles. His skin was dark and ruddy, and dusted plentifully with bright green down. All his contours were uncouth, for the details of muscles, sinews, and joints were very plainly different from our own. His neck was curiously long and supple. His head I can best describe by saying that most of the brain-pan, covered with a green thatch, seemed to have slipped backwards and downwards over the nape. His two very human eyes peered from under the eaves of hair. An oddly projecting, almost spout-like mouth made him look as though he were whistling. Between the eyes, and rather above them, was a pair of great equine nostrils which were constantly in motion. The bridge of the nose was represented by an elevation in the thatch, reaching from the nostrils backwards over the top of the head. There were no visible ears.

I discovered later that the auditory organs opened into the nostrils.

Clearly, although evolution on this Earth-like planet must have taken a course on the whole surprisingly like that which had produced my own kind, there must also have been many divergencies.

The stranger wore not only boots but gloves, seemingly of tough leather. His boots were extremely short. I was to discover later that the feet of this race, the 'Other Men', as I called them, were rather like the feet of an ostrich or a camel. The instep consisted of three great toes grown together. In place of the heel there was an additional broad, stumpy toe. The hands were without palms. Each was a bunch of three gristly fingers and a thumb.

The aim of this book is not to tell of my own adventures but to give some idea of the worlds which I visited. I shall therefore not recount in detail how I established myself among the Other Men. Of myself it is enough to say a few words. When I had studied this agriculturalist for a while, I began to be strangely oppressed by his complete unawareness of myself. With painful clearness I realized that the purpose of my pilgrimage was not merely scientific observation, but also the need to effect some kind of mental and spiritual traffic with other worlds, for mutual enrichment and community. How should I ever be able to achieve this end unless I could find some means of communication? It was not until I had followed my companion to his home, and had spent many days in that little circular stone house with roof of mudded wicker, that I discovered the power of entering into his mind, of seeing through his eyes, sensing through all his sense organs, perceiving his world just as he perceived it, and following much of his thought and his emotional life. Not till very much later, when I had passively 'inhabited' many individuals of the race, did I discover how to make my presence known, and even to converse inwardly with my host.

This kind of internal 'telepathic' intercourse, which was to serve me in all my wanderings, was at first difficult, ineffective, and painful. But in time I came to be able to live through the experiences of my host with vividness and accuracy, while yet preserving my own individuality, my own critical intelligence, my own desires and fears. Only when the other had come to realize my presence within him could he, by a special act of volition, keep particular thoughts secret from me.

It can well be understood that at first I found these aliens minds quite unintelligible. Their very sensations differed from my familiar sensations in important respects. Their thoughts and all their emotions and sentiments were strange to me. The traditional groundwork of these minds, their most familiar concepts, were derived from a strange history, and expressed in languages which to the terrestrial mind were subtly misleading.

I spent on the Other Earth many 'other years', wandering from mind to mind and country to country, but I did not gain any clear understanding of the psychology of the Other Men and the significance of their history till I had encountered one of their philosophers, an ageing but still vigorous man whose eccentric and unpalatable views had prevented him from attaining eminence. Most of my hosts, when they became aware of my presence within them, regarded me either as an evil spirit or as a divine messenger. The more sophisticated, however, assumed that I was a mere disease, a symptom of insanity in themselves. They therefore promptly applied to the local 'Mental Sanitation Officer'. After I had spent, according to the local calendar, a year or so of bitter loneliness among minds who refused to treat me as a human being, I had the good fortune to come under the philosopher's notice. One of my hosts, who complained of suffering from 'voices', and visions of 'another world', appealed to the old man for help. Bvalltu, for such approximately was the philosopher's name, the 'll' being pronounced more or less as in Welsh, Bvalltu effected a 'cure' by merely inviting me to accept the hospitality of his own mind, where, he said, he would very gladly entertain me. It was with extravagant joy that I made contact at last with a being who recognized in me a human personality.

2. A Busy World

So many important characteristics of this world-society need to be described that I cannot spend much time on the more obvious features of the planet and its race. Civilization had reached a stage of growth much like that which was familiar to me. I was constantly surprised by the blend of similarity and difference. Travelling over the planet I found that cultivation had spread over most of the suitable areas, and that industrialism was already far advanced in many countries. On the prairies huge flocks of mammal-like creatures grazed and scampered. Larger mammals, or quasi-mammals, were farmed on all the best pasture land for food and leather. I say 'quasi-mammal' because, though these creatures were viviparous, they did not suckle. The chewed cud, chemically treated in the maternal belly, was spat into the offspring's mouth as a jet of pre-digested fluid. It was thus also that human mothers fed their young.

The most important means of locomotion on the Other Earth was the steam-train, but trains in this world were so bulky that they looked like whole terraces of houses on the move. This remarkable railway development was probably due to the great number and length of journeys across deserts. Occasionally I travelled on steam-ships on the few and small oceans, but marine transport was on the whole backward. The screw propeller was unknown, its place being taken by paddle wheels. Internal-combustion engines were used in road and desert transport. Flying, owing to the rarified atmosphere, had not been achieved; but rocket-propulsion was already used for long-distance transport of mails, and for long-range bombardment in war. Its application to aeronautics might come any day.

My first visit to the metropolis of one of the great empires of the Other Earth was an outstanding experience. Everything was at once so strange and so familiar. There were streets and many-windowed stores and offices. In this old city the streets were narrow, and so congested was the motor traffic that pedestrians were accommodated on special elevated tracks slung beside the first-storey windows and across the streets. The crowds that streamed along these footpaths were as variegated as our own. The men wore cloth tunics, and trousers surprisingly like the trousers of Europe, save that the crease affected by the respectable was at the side of the leg. The women, breastless and high-nostrilled like the men, were to be distinguished by their more tubular lips, whose biological function it was to project food for the infant. In place of skirts they disported green and glossy silk tights and little gawdy knickers. To my unaccustomed vision the effect was inexpressibly vulgar. In summer both sexes often appeared in the streets naked to the waist; but they always wore gloves.

Here, then, was a host of persons who, in spite of their oddity, were as essentially human as Londoners. They went about their private affairs with complete assurance, ignorant that a spectator from another world found them one and all grotesque, with their lack of forehead, their great elevated quivering nostrils, their startlingly human eyes, their spout-like mouths. There they were, alive and busy, shopping, staring, talking. Children dragged at their mothers' hands. Old men with white facial hair bowed over walking-sticks. Young men eyed young women. The prosperous were easily to be distinguished from the unfortunate by their newer and richer clothes, their confident and sometimes arrogant carriage.

How can I describe in a few pages the distinctive character of a whole teeming and storied world, so different from my own, yet so similar? Here, as on my own planet, infants were being born every hour. Here, as there, they clamoured for food, and very soon for companionship. They discovered what pain was, and what fear, and what loneliness, and love. They grew up, moulded by the harsh or kindly pressure of their fellows, to be either well nurtured, generous, sound, or mentally crippled, bitter, unwittingly vindictive. One and all they desperately craved the bliss of true community; and very few, fewer here, perhaps, than in my own world, found more than the vanishing flavour of it. They howled with the pack and hounded with the pack. Starved both physically and mentally, they brawled over the quarry and tore one another to pieces, mad with hunger, physical or mental. Sometimes some of them paused and asked what it was all for; and there followed a battle of words, but no clear answer. Suddenly they were old and finished. Then, the span from birth to death being an imperceptible instant of cosmical time, they vanished.

This planet, being essentially of the terrestrial type, had produced a race that was essentially human, though, so to speak, human in a different key from the terrestrial. These continents were as variegated as ours, and inhabited by a race as diversified as *Homo Sapiens*. All the modes and facets of the spirit manifested in our history had their equivalents in the history of the Other Men. As with us, there had been dark ages and ages of brilliance, phases of advancement and of retreat, cultures predominantly material, and others in the main intellectual, aesthetic, or spiritual. There were 'Eastern' races and 'Western' races. There were empires, republics, dictatorships. Yet all was different from the terrestrial. Many of the differences, of course, were superficial; but there was also an underlying, deep-lying difference which I took long to understand and will not yet describe.

I must begin by speaking of the biological equipment of the Other Men. Their animal nature was at bottom much like ours. They responded with anger, fear, hate, tenderness, curiosity, and so on, much as we respond. In sensory equipment they were not unlike ourselves, save that in vision they were less sensitive to colour and more to form than is common with us. The violent colours of the Other Earth appeared to me through the eyes of its natives very subdued. In hearing also they were rather ill equipped. Though their auditory organs were as sensitive as ours to faint sounds, they were poor discriminators. Music, such as we know, never developed in this world.

In compensation, scent and taste developed amazingly. These beings tasted not only with their mouths, but with their moist black hands and with their feet. They were thus afforded an extraordinarily rich and intimate experience of their planet.

Tastes of metals and woods, of sour and sweet earths, of the many rocks, and of the innumerable shy or bold flavours of plants crushed beneath the bare running feet, made up a whole world unknown to terrestrial man.

The genitals also were equipped with taste organs. There were several distinctive male and female patterns of chemical characteristics, each powerfully attractive to the opposite sex. These were savoured faintly by contact of hands or feet with any part of the body, and with exquisite intensity in copulation.

This surprising richness of gustatory experience made it very difficult for me to enter fully into the thoughts of the Other Men. Taste played as important a part in their imagery and conception as sight in our own. Many ideas which terrestrial man has reached by way of sight, and which even in their most abstract form still bear traces of their visual origin, the Other Men conceived in terms of taste. For example, our 'brilliant', as applied to persons or ideas, they would translate by a word whose literal meaning was 'tasty'. For 'lucid' they would use a term which in primitive times was employed by hunters to signify an easily runnable taste-trail. To have 'religious illumination' was to 'taste the meadows of heaven'. Many of our non-visual concepts also were rendered by means of taste. 'Complexity' was 'many-flavoured', a word applied originally to the confusion of tastes round a drinking pool frequented by many kinds of beasts. 'Incompatibility' was derived from a word meaning the disgust which certain human types felt for one another on account of their flavours.

Differences of race, which in our world are chiefly conceived in terms of bodily appearance, were for the Other Men almost entirely differences of taste and smell. And as the races of the Other Men were much less sharply localized than our own races, the strife between groups whose flavours were repugnant to one another played a great part in history. Each race tended to believe that its own flavour was characteristic of all the finer mental qualities, was indeed an absolutely reliable label of spiritual worth. In former ages the gustatory and olfactory differences had, no doubt, been true signs of racial differences; but in modern times, and in the more developed lands, there had been great changes. Not only had the races ceased to be clearly localized, but also industrial civilization had produced a crop of genetic changes which rendered the old racial distinctions meaningless. The ancient flavours, however, though they had by now no racial significance at all, and indeed members of one family might have mutually repugnant flavours, continued to have the traditional emotional effects. In each country some particular flavour was considered the true hallmark of the race of that country, and all other flavours were despised, if not actually condemned.

In the country which I came to know best the orthodox racial flavour was a kind of saltness inconceivable to terrestrial man. My hosts regarded themselves as the very salt of the earth. But as a matter of fact the peasant whom I first 'inhabited' was the only genuine pure salt man of orthodox variety whom I ever encountered. The great majority of that country's citizens attained their correct taste and smell by artificial means. Those who were at least approximately salt, with some variety of saltness, though not the ideal variety, were for ever exposing the deceit of their sour, sweet, or bitter neighbours. Unfortunately, though the taste of the limbs could be fairly well disguised, no effective means had been found for changing the flavour of copulation. Consequently newly married couples were apt to make the most shattering discoveries about one another on the wedding night. Since in the great majority of unions neither party had the orthodox flavour, both were willing to pretend to the world that all was well. But often there would turn out to be a nauseating incompatibility between the two gustatory types. The whole population was rotten with neuroses bred of these secret tragedies of marriage. Occasionally, when one party was more or less of the orthodox flavour, this genuinely salt partner would indignantly denounce the impostor. The courts, the news bulletins, and the public would then join in self-righteous protests.

Some 'racial' flavours were too obtrusive to be disguised. One in particular, a kind of bitter-sweet, exposed its possessor to extravagant persecution in all but the most tolerant countries. In past times the bitter-sweet race had earned a reputation of cunning and self-seeking, and had been periodically massacred by its less intelligent neighbours. But in the general biological ferment of modern times the bitter-sweet flavour might crop up in any family. Woe, then, to the accursed infant, and to all its relatives! Persecution was inevitable; unless indeed the family was wealthy enough to purchase from the state 'an honorary salting' (or in the neighbouring land, 'an honorary sweetening'), which removed the stigma.

In the more enlightened countries the whole racial superstition was becoming suspect. There was a movement among the intelligentsia for conditioning infants to tolerate every kind of human flavour, and for discarding the deodorants and degustatants, and even the boots and gloves, which civilized convention imposed.

Unfortunately this movement of toleration was hampered by one of the consequences of industrialism. In the congested and unhealthy industrial centres a new gustatory and olfactory type had appeared, apparently as a biological mutation. In a couple of generations this sour, astringent, and undisguisable flavour dominated in all the most disreputable working-class quarters. To the fastidious palates of the well-to-do it was overwhelmingly nauseating and terrifying. In fact it became for them an unconscious symbol, tapping all the secret guilt and fear and hate which the oppressors felt for the oppressed.

In this world, as in our own, nearly all the chief means of production, nearly all the land, mines, factories, railways, ships, were controlled for private profit by a small minority of the population. These privileged individuals were able to force the masses to work for them on pain of starvation. The tragic farce inherent in such a system was already approaching. The owners directed the energy of the workers increasingly towards the production of more means of production rather than to the fulfilment of the needs of individual life. For machinery might bring profit to the owners; bread would not. With the increasing competition of machine with machine, profits declined, and therefore wages, and therefore effective demand for goods. Marketless products were destroyed, though bellies were unfed and backs unclad. Unemployment, disorder, and stern repression increased as the economic system disintegrated. A familiar story!

As conditions deteriorated, and the movements of charity and state-charity became less and less able to cope with the increasing mass of unemployment and destitution, the new pariah-race became more and more psychologically useful to the hate-needs of the sacred, but still powerful, prosperous. The theory was spread that these wretched beings were the result of secret systematic race-pollution by riff-raff immigrants, and that they deserved no consideration whatever. They were therefore allowed only the basest forms of employment and the harshest conditions of work. When unemployment had become a serious social problem, practically the whole pariah stock was workless and destitute. It was of course easily believed that unemployment, far from being due to the decline of capitalism, was due to the worthlessness of the pariahs.

At the time of my visit the working class had become tainted through and through by the pariah stock, and there was a vigorous movement afoot among the wealthy and the official classes to institute slavery for pariahs and half-pariahs, so that these might be openly treated as the cattle which in fact they were. In view of the danger of continued race-pollution, some politicians urged wholesale slaughter of the pariahs, or, at the least, universal sterilization. Others pointed out that, as a supply of cheap labour was necessary to society, it would be wiser merely to keep their numbers down by working them to an early death in occupations which those of 'pure race' would never accept. This, at any rate, should be done in times of prosperity; but in times of decline, the excess population could be allowed to starve, or might be used up in the physiological laboratories.

The persons who first dared to suggest this policy were scourged by the whips of generous popular indignation. But their policy was in fact adopted; not explicitly but by tacit consent, and in the absence of any more constructive plan.

The first time that I was taken through the poorest quarter of the city I was surprised to see that, though there were large areas of slum property far more squalid than anything in England, there were also many great clean blocks of tenements worthy of Vienna. These were surrounded by gardens, which were crowded with wretched tents and shanties. The grass was worn away, the bushes damaged, the flowers trampled. Everywhere men, women, and children, all filthy and ragged, were idling.

I learned that these noble buildings had been erected before the world-economic-crisis (familiar phrase!) by a millionaire who had made his money in trading an opium-like drug. He presented the buildings to the City Council, and was gathered to heaven by way of the peerage. The more deserving and less unsavoury poor were duly housed; but care was taken to fix the rent high enough to exclude the pariah-race. Then came the crisis. One by one the tenants failed to pay their rent, and were ejected. Within a year the buildings were almost empty.

There followed a very curious sequence of events, and one which, as I was to discover, was characteristic of this strange world. Respectable public opinion, though vindictive towards the unemployed, was passionately tender towards the sick. In falling ill, a man acquired a special sanctity, and exercised a claim over all healthy persons. Thus no sooner did any of the wretched campers succumb to a serious disease than he was carried off to be cared for by all the resources of medical science. The desperate paupers soon discovered how things stood, and did all in their power to fall sick. So successful were they, that the hospitals were soon filled. The empty tenements were therefore hastily fitted out to receive the increasing flood of patients.

Observing these and other farcical events, I was reminded of my own race. But though the Other Men were in many ways so like us, I suspected increasingly that some factor still hidden from me doomed them to a frustration which my own nobler species need never fear. Psychological mechanisms which in our case are tempered with common sense or moral sense stood

out in this world in flagrant excess. Yet it was not true that
Other Man was less intelligent or less moral than man of my
own species. In abstract thought and practical invention he was
at least our equal. Many of his most recent advances in physics
and astronomy had passed beyond our present attainment. I
noticed, however, that psychology was even more chaotic than
with us, and that social thought was strangely perverted.

In radio and television, for instance, the Other Men were
technically far ahead of us, but the use to which they put their
astounding inventions was disastrous. In civilized countries
everyone but the pariahs carried a pocket receiving set. As the
Other Men had no music, this may seem odd; but since they
lacked newspapers, radio was the only means by which the
man in the street could learn the lottery and sporting results
which were his staple mental diet. The place of music, moreover, was taken by taste- and smell-themes, which were trans-
lated into patterns of ethereal undulation, transmitted by all
the great national stations, and restored to their original form
in the pocket receivers and taste-batteries of the population.
These instruments afforded intricate stimuli to the taste organs
and scent organs of the hand. Such was the power of this kind
of entertainment that both men and women were nearly always seen with one hand in a pocket. A special wave length
had been allotted to the soothing of infants.

A sexual receiving set had been put upon the market, and
programmes were broadcast for it in many countries; but not
in all. This extraordinary invention was a combination of ra-
dio-touch, -taste, -odour, and -sound. It worked not through
the sense organs, but by direct stimulation of the appropriate
brain-centres. The recipient wore a specially constructed skull-
cap, which transmitted to him from a remote studio the embraces of some delectable and responsive woman, as they were
then actually being experienced by a male 'love-broadcaster',
or as electromagnetically recorded on a steel tape on some
earlier occasion.

Controversies had arisen about the morality of sexual broadcasting. Some countries permitted programmes for males but
not for females, wishing to preserve the innocence of the purer

sex. Elsewhere the clerics had succeeded in crushing the whole project on the score that radio-sex, even for men alone, would be a diabolical substitute for a certain much desired and jealously guarded religious experience, called the immaculate union, of which I shall tell in the sequel. Well did the priests know that their power depended largely on their ability to induce this luscious ecstasy in their flock by means of ritual and other psychological techniques.

Militarists also were strongly opposed to the new invention; for in the cheap and efficient production of illusory sexual embraces they saw a danger even more serious than contraception. The supply of cannon-fodder would decline.

Since in all the more respectable countries broadcasting had been put under the control of retired soldiers or good churchmen, the new device was at first adopted only in the more commercial and the more disreputable states. From their broadcasting stations the embraces of popular 'radio love-stars' and even of impecunious aristocrats were broadcast along with advertisements of patent medicines, taste-proof gloves, lottery results, savours, and degustatants.

The principle of radio-brain-stimulation was soon developed much further. Programmes of all the most luscious or piquant experiences were broadcast in all countries, and could be picked up by simple receivers that were within the means of all save the pariahs. Thus even the labourer and the factory hand could have the pleasures of a banquet without expense and subsequent repletion, the delights of proficient dancing without the trouble of learning the art, the thrills of motor-racing without danger. In an ice-bound northern home he could bask on tropical beaches, and in the tropics indulge in winter sports.

Governments soon discovered that the new invention gave them a cheap and effective kind of power over their subjects. Slum-conditions could be tolerated if there was an unfailing supply of illusory luxury. Reforms distasteful to the authorities could be shelved if they could be represented as inimical to the national radio-system. Strikes and riots could often be broken by the mere threat to close down the broadcasting studios, or alternatively by flooding the ether at a critical moment with some saccharine novelty.

The fact that the political Left Wing opposed the further development of radio amusements made Governments and the propertied classes the more ready to accept it. The Communists, for the dialectic of history on this curiously earth-like planet had produced a party deserving that name, strongly condemned the scheme. In their view it was pure Capitalist dope, calculated to prevent the otherwise inevitable dictatorship of the proletariat.

The increasing opposition of the Communists made it possible to buy off the opposition of their natural enemies, the priests and soldiers. It was arranged that religious services should in future occupy a larger proportion of broadcasting time, and that a tithe of all licensing fees should be allocated to the churches. The offer to broadcast the immaculate union, however, was rejected by the clerics. As an additional concession it was agreed that all married members of the staffs of Broadcasting Authorities must, on pain of dismissal, prove that they had never spent a night away from their wives (or husbands). It was also agreed to weed out all those B.A. employees who were suspected of sympathy with such disreputable ideals as pacifism and freedom of expression. The soldiers were further appeased by a state-subsidy for maternity, a tax on bachelors, and regular broadcasting of military propaganda.

During my last years on the Other Earth a system was invented by which a man could retire to bed for life and spend all his time receiving radio programmes. His nourishment and all his bodily functions were attended to by doctors and nurses attached to the Broadcasting Authority. In place of exercise he received periodic massage. Participation in the scheme was at first an expensive luxury, but its inventors hoped to make it at no distant date available to all. It was even expected that in time medical and menial attendants would cease to be necessary. A vast system of automatic food-production, and distribution of liquid pabulum by means of pipes leading to the mouths of the recumbent subjects, would be complemented by an intricate sewage system. Electric massage could be applied at will by pressing a button. Medical supervision would be displaced by an automatic endocrine-compensation system. This would enable the condition of the patient's blood to regulate itself automatically by tapping from the communal drugpipes whatever chemicals were needed for correct physiological balance.

Even in the case of broadcasting itself the human element would no longer be needed, for all possible pleasant experiences would have been already recorded from the most exquisite living examples. These would be continuously broadcast in a great number of alternative programmes.

A few technicians and organizers might still be needed to superintend the system; but, properly distributed, their work would entail for each member of the World Broadcasting Authority's staff no more than a few hours of interesting activity each week.

Children, if future generations were required, would be produced ectogenetically. The World Director of Broadcasting would be requested to submit psychological and physiological specifications of the ideal 'listening breed'. Infants produced in accordance with this pattern would then be educated by special radio programmes to prepare them for adult radio life. They would never leave their cots, save to pass by stages to the full-sized beds of maturity. At the latter end of life, if medical science did not succeed in circumventing senility and death, the individual would at least be able to secure a painless end by pressing an appropriate button.

Enthusiasm for this astounding project spread rapidly in all civilized countries, but certain forces of reaction were bitterly opposed to it. The old-fashioned religious people and the militant nationalists both affirmed that it was man's glory to be active. The religious held that only in self-discipline, mortification of the flesh, and constant prayer, could the soul be fitted for eternal life. The nationalists of each country declared that their own people had been given a sacred trust to rule the baser kinds, and that in any case only the martial virtues could ensure the spirit's admittance to Valhalla.

Many of the great economic masters, though they had originally favoured radio-bliss in moderation as an opiate for the
discontented workers, now turned against it. Their craving was
for power; and for power they needed slaves whose labour
they could command for their great industrial ventures. They
therefore devised an instrument which was at once an opiate
and a spur. By every method of propaganda they sought to
rouse the passions of nationalism and racial hatred. They
created, in fact, the 'Other Fascism', complete with lies, with
mystical cult of race and state, with scorn of reason, with praise
of brutal mastery, with appeal at once to the vilest and to the
generous motives of the deluded young.

Opposed to all these critics of radio-bliss, and equally opposed to radio-bliss itself, there was in each country a small
and bewildered party which asserted that the true goal of
human activity was the creation of a world-wide community
of awakened and intelligently creative persons, related by mutual insight and respect, and by the common task of fulfilling
the potentiality of the human spirit on earth. Much of their
doctrine was a re-statement of the teachings of religious seers
of a time long past, but it had also been deeply influenced by
contemporary science. This party, however, was misunder-
stood by the scientists, cursed by the clerics, ridiculed by the
militarists, and ignored by the advocates of radio-bliss.

Now at this time economic confusion had been driving the
great commercial empires of the Other Earth into more and
more desperate competition for markets. These economic rival-
ries had combined with ancient tribal passions of fear and hate
and pride to bring about an interminable series of war scares
each of which threatened universal Armageddon.

In this situation the radio-enthusiasts pointed out that, if
their policy were accepted, war would never occur, and on the
other hand that, if a world-war broke out, their policy would
be indefinitely postponed. They contrived a world-wide peace
movement; and such was the passion for radio-bliss that the
demand for peace swept all countries. An International Broadcasting Authority was at last founded, to propagate the radio

gospel, compose the differences between the empires, and eventually to take over the sovereignty of the world.

Meanwhile the earnestly 'religious' and the sincere militarists, rightly dismayed at the baseness of the motives behind the new internationalism, but in their own manner equally wrong-headed, determined to save the Other Men in spite of themselves by goading the peoples into war. All the forces of propaganda and financial corruption were heroically wielded to foment the passions of nationalism. Even so, the greed for radio-bliss was by now so general and so passionate, that the war party would never have succeeded had it not been for the wealth of the great armourers, and their experience in fomenting strife.

Trouble was successfully created between one of the older commercial empires and a certain state which had only recently adopted mechanical civilization, but was already a Great Power, and a Power in desperate need of markets. Radio, which formerly had been the main force making for cosmopolitanism, became suddenly in each country the main stimulus to nationalism. Morning, noon, and night, every civilized people was assured that enemies, whose flavour was of course subhuman and foul, were plotting its destruction. Armament scares, spy stories, accounts of the barbarous and sadistic behaviour of neighbouring peoples, created in every country such uncritical suspicion and hate that war became inevitable. A dispute arose over the control of a frontier province. During those critical days Bvalltu and I happened to be in a large provincial town. I shall never forget how the populace plunged into almost maniacal hate. All thought of human brotherhood, and even of personal safety, was swept away by a savage blood-lust. Panic-stricken governments began projecting long-range rocket bombs at their dangerous neighbours. Within a few weeks several of the capitals of the Other Earth had been destroyed from the air. Each people now began straining every nerve to do more hurt than it received.

Of the horrors of this war, of the destruction of city after city, of the panic-stricken, starving hosts that swarmed into the open country, looting and killing, of the starvation and

disease, of the disintegration of the social services, of the emergence of ruthless military dictatorships, of the steady or catastrophic decay of culture and of all decency and gentleness in
personal relations, of this there is no need to speak in detail.
Instead, I shall try to account for the finality of the disaster
which overtook the Other Men. My own human kind, in similar circumstances, would never, surely, have allowed itself to
be so completely overwhelmed. No doubt, we ourselves are
faced with the possibility of a scarcely less destructive war;
but, whatever the agony that awaits us, we shall almost certainly recover. Foolish we may be, but we always manage to
avoid falling into the abyss of downright madness. At the last
moment sanity falteringly reasserts itself. Not so with the
Other Men.

3. Prospects of the Race

The longer I stayed on the Other Earth, the more I suspected
that there must be some important underlying difference between this human race and my own. In some sense the difference was obviously one of balance. *Homo Sapiens* was on the
whole better integrated, more gifted with common sense, less
apt to fall into extravagance through mental dissociation.

Perhaps the most striking example of the extravagance of the
Other Men was the part played by religion in their more advanced societies. Religion was a much greater power than on
my own planet; and the religious teachings of the prophets of
old were able to kindle even my alien and sluggish heart with
fervour. Yet religion, as it occurred around me in contemporary
society, was far from edifying.

I must begin by explaining that in the development of religion on the Other Earth gustatory sensation had played a very
great part. Tribal gods had of course been endowed with the
taste-characters most moving to the tribe's own members.
Later, when monotheisms arose, description of God's power,
his wisdom, his justice, his benevolence, were accompanied by
descriptions of his taste. In mystical literature God was often
likened to an ancient and mellow wine; and some reports of

religious experience suggested that this gustatory ecstasy was in many ways akin to the reverent zest of our own wine-tasters, savouring some rare vintage.

Unfortunately, owing to the diversity of gustatory human types, there had seldom been any widespread agreement as to the taste of God. Religious wars had been waged to decide whether he was in the main sweet or salt, or whether his preponderant flavour was one of the many gustatory characters which my own race cannot conceive. Some teachers insisted that only the feet could taste him, others only the hands or the mouth, others that he could be experienced only in the subtle complex of gustatory flavours known as the immaculate union, which was a sensual, and mainly sexual, ecstasy induced by contemplation of intercourse with the deity.

Other teachers declared that, though God was indeed tasty, it was not through any bodily instrument but to the naked spirit that his essence was revealed; and that his was a flavour more subtle and delicious than the flavour of the beloved, since it included all that was most fragrant and spiritual in man, and infinitely more.

Some went so far as to declare that God should be thought of not as a person at all but as actually *being* this flavour. Bvalltu used to say, 'Either God is the universe, or he is the flavour of creativity pervading all things.'

Some ten or fifteen centuries earlier, when religion, so far as I could tell, was most vital, there were no churches or priest-hoods; but every man's life was dominated by religious ideas to an extent which to me was almost incredible. Later, churches and priesthoods had returned, to play an important part in preserving what was now evidently a declining religious consciousness. Still later, a few centuries before the Industrial Revolution, institutional religion had gained such a hold on the most civilized peoples that three-quarters of their total income was spent on the upkeep of religious institutions. The working classes, indeed, who slaved for the owners in return for a mere pittance, gave much of their miserable earnings to the priests, and lived in more abject squalor than need have been.

Science and industry had brought one of those sudden and

extreme revolutions of thought which were so characteristic of the Other Men. Nearly all the churches were destroyed or turned into temporary factories or industrial museums. Atheism, lately persecuted, became fashionable. All the best minds turned agnostic. More recently, however, apparently in horror at the effects of a materialistic culture which was far more cynical and blatant than our own, the most industrialized peoples began to turn once more to religion. A spiritistic foundation was provided for natural science. The old churches were re-sanctified, and so many new religious edifices were built that they were soon as plentiful as cinema houses with us. Indeed, the new churches gradually absorbed the cinema, and provided non-stop picture shows in which sensual orgies and ecclesiastical propaganda were skilfully blended.

At the time of my visit the churches had regained all their lost power. Radio had indeed at one time competed with them, but was successfully absorbed. They still refused to broadcast the immaculate union, which gained fresh prestige from the popular belief that it was too spiritual to be transmitted on the ether. The more advanced clerics, however, had agreed that if ever the universal system of 'radio-bliss' was established, this difficulty might be overcome. Communism, meanwhile, still maintained its irreligious convention; but in the two great Communist countries the officially organized 'irreligion' was becoming a religion in all but name. It had its institutions, its priesthood, its ritual, its morality, its system of absolution, its metaphysical doctrines, which, though devoutly materialistic, were none the less superstitious. And the flavour of deity had been displaced by the flavour of the proletariat.

Religion, then, was a very real force in the life of all these peoples. But there was something puzzling about their devoutness. In a sense it was sincere, and even beneficial; for in very small personal temptations and very obvious and stereotyped moral choices, the Other Men were far more conscientious than my own kind. But I discovered that the typical modern Other Man was conscientious only in conventional situations, and that in genuine moral sensibility he was strangely lacking.

Thus, though practical generosity and superficial comradeship were more usual than with us, the most diabolic mental persecution was perpetrated with a clear conscience. The more sensitive had always to be on their guard. The deeper kinds of intimacy and mutual reliance were precarious and rare. In this passionately social world, loneliness dogged the spirit. People were constantly 'getting together', but they never really got there. Everyone was terrified of being alone with himself; yet in company, in spite of the universal assumption of comradeship, these strange beings remained as remote from one another as the stars. For everyone searched his neighbour's eyes for the image of himself, and never saw anything else. Or if he did, he was outraged and terrified.

Another perplexing fact about the religious life of the Other Men at the time of my visit was this. Though all were devout, and blasphemy was regarded with horror, the general attitude to the deity was one of blasphemous commercialism. Men assumed that the flavour of deity could be bought for all eternity with money or with ritual. Further, the God whom they worshipped with the superb and heart-searching language of an earlier age was now conceived either as a just but jealous employer or as an indulgent parent, or else as sheer physical energy. The crowning vulgarity was the conviction that in no earlier age had religion been so widespread and so enlightened. It was almost universally agreed that the profound teachings of the prophetic era were only now being understood in the sense in which they had originally been intended by the prophets themselves. Contemporary writers and broadcasters claimed to be re-interpreting the scriptures to suit the enlightened religious needs of an age which called itself the Age of Scientific Religion.

Now behind all the complacency which characterized the civilization of the Other Men before the outbreak of the war I had often detected a vague restlessness and anxiety. Of course for the most part people went about their affairs with the same absorbed and self-satisfied interest as on my own planet. They were far too busy making a living, marrying, rearing families, trying to get the better of one another, to spare time for conscious doubt about the aim of life. Yet they had often the air of one who has forgotten some very important thing and is racking his brains to recover it, or of an ageing preacher who uses the old stirring phrases without clear apprehension of their significance. Increasingly I suspected that this race, in spite of all its triumphs, was now living on the great ideas of its past, mouthing concepts that it no longer had the sensibility to understand, paying verbal homage to ideals which it could no longer sincerely will, and behaving within a system of institutions many of which could only be worked successfully by minds of a slightly finer temper. These institutions, I suspected, must have been created by a race endowed not only with much greater intelligence, but with a much stronger and more comprehensive capacity for community than was now possible on the Other Earth. They seemed to be based on the assumption that men were on the whole kindly, reasonable, and self-disciplined.

I had often questioned Bvalltu on this subject, but he had always turned my question aside. It will be remembered that, though I had access to all his thoughts so long as he did not positively wish to withhold them, he could always, if he made a special effort, think privately. I had long suspected that he was keeping something from me, when at last he told me the strange and tragic facts.

It was a few days after the bombardment of the metropolis of his country. Through Bvalltu's eyes and the goggles of his gas-mask I saw the results of that bombardment. We had missed the horror itself, but had attempted to return to the city to play some part in the rescue work. Little could be done. So great was the heat still radiated from the city's incandescent heart, that we could not penetrate beyond the first suburb. Even there, the streets were obliterated, choked with fallen buildings. Human bodies, crushed and charred, projected here and there from masses of tumbled masonry. Most of the population was hidden under the ruins. In the open spaces many lay gassed. Salvage parties impotently wandered. Between the smoke-clouds the Other Sun occasionally appeared, and even a daytime star.

After clambering among the ruins for some time, seeking vainly to give help, Bvalltu sat down. The devastation round about us seemed to 'loosen his tongue', if I may use such a phrase to express a sudden frankness in his thinking towards myself. I had said something to the effect that a future age would look back on all this madness and destruction with amazement. He sighed through his gas-mask, and said, 'My unhappy race has probably now doomed itself irrevocably.' I expostulated; for though ours was about the fortieth city to be destroyed, there would surely some day be a recovery, and the race would at last pass through this crisis and go forward from strength to strength. Bvalltu then told me of the strange matters which, he said, he had often intended to tell me, but somehow he had always shunned doing so. Though many scientists and students of the contemporary world-society had now some vague suspicion of the truth, it was clearly known only to himself and a few others.

The species, he said, was apparently subject to strange and long-drawn-out fluctuations of nature, fluctuations which lasted for some twenty thousand years. All races in all climates seemed to manifest this vast rhythm of the spirit, and to suffer it simultaneously. Its cause was unknown. Though it seemed to be due to an influence affecting the whole planet at once, perhaps it actually radiated from a single starting point, but spread rapidly into all lands. Very recently an advanced scientist had suggested that it might be due to variations in the intensity of 'cosmic rays'. Geological evidence had established that such a fluctuation of cosmical radiation did occur, caused perhaps by variations in a neighbouring cluster of young stars. It was still doubtful whether the psychological rhythm and the astronomical rhythm coincided, but many facts pointed to the conclusion that when the rays were more violent, the human spirit declined.

Bvalltu was not convinced by this theory. On the whole he inclined to the opinion that the rhythmical waxing and waning of human mentality was due to causes nearer home. Whatever the true explanation it was almost certain that a high degree of civilization had been attained many times in the past, and that some potent influence had over and over again damped down the mental vigour of the human race. In the troughs of these vast waves Other Man sank to a state of mental and spiritual dullness more abject than anything which my own race had ever known since it awoke from the sub-human. But at the wave's crest man's intellectual power, moral integrity, and spiritual insight seem to have risen to a pitch that we should regard as superhuman.

Again and again the race would emerge from savagery, and pass through barbarian culture into a phase of world-wide brilliance and sensibility. Whole populations would conceive simultaneously an ever-increasing capacity for generosity, self-knowledge, self-discipline, for dispassionate and pene-trating thought and uncontaminated religious feeling.

Consequently within a few centuries the whole world would blossom with free and happy societies. Average human beings would attain an unprecedented clarity of mind, and by massed action do away with all grave social injustices and private cruelties. Subsequent generations, inherently sound, and blessed with a favourable environment, would create a world-wide utopia of awakened beings.

Presently a general loosening of fibre would set in. The golden age would be followed by a silver age. Living on the achievements of the past, the leaders of thought would lose themselves in a jungle of subtlety, or fall exhausted into mere slovenliness. At the same time moral sensibility would decline. Men would become on the whole less sincere, less self-search-ing, less sensitive to the needs of others, in fact less capable of community. Social machinery, which had worked well so long as citizens attained a certain level of humanity, would be dis-located by injustice and corruption. Tyrants and tyrannical oligarchies would set about destroying liberty. Hate-mad sub-merged classes would give them good excuse. Little by little, though the material benefits of civilization might smoulder on for centuries, the flame of the spirit would die down into a mere flicker in a few isolated individuals. Then would come sheer barbarism, followed by the trough of almost subhuman savagery.

On the whole there seemed to have been a higher achievement on the more recent crests of the wave than on those of the 'geological' past. So at least some anthropologists persuaded themselves. It was confidently believed that the present apex of civilization was the most brilliant of all, that its best was yet to come, and that by means of its unique scientific knowledge it would discover how to preserve the mentality of the race from a recurrence of deterioration.

The present condition of the species was certainly exceptional. In no earlier recorded cycle had science and mechanization advanced to such lengths. So far as could be inferred from the fragmentary relics of the previous cycle, mechanical invention had never passed beyond the crude machinery known in our own mid-nineteenth century. The still earlier cycles, it was believed, stagnated at even earlier stages in their industrial revolutions.

Now though it was generally assumed in intellectual circles that the best was yet to be, Bvalltu and his friends were convinced that the crest of the wave had already occurred many centuries ago. To most men, of course, the decade before the war had seemed better and more civilized than any earlier age. In their view civilization and mechanization were almost identical, and never before had there been such a triumph of mechanization. The benefits of a scientific civilization were obvious. For the fortunate class there was more comfort, better health, increased stature, a prolongation of youth, and a system of technical knowledge so vast and intricate that no man could know more than its outline or some tiny corner of its detail. Moreover, increased communications had brought all the peoples into contact. Local idiosyncrasies were fading out before the radio, the cinema, and the gramophone. In comparison with these hopeful signs it was easily overlooked that the human constitution, though strengthened by improved conditions, was intrinsically less stable than formerly. Certain disin-

tegrative diseases were slowly but surely increasing. In particular, diseases of the nervous system were becoming more common and more pernicious. Cynics used to say that the mental
hospitals would soon outnumber even the churches. But the
cynics were only jesters. It was almost universally agreed that,
in spite of wars and economic troubles and social upheavals,
all was now well, and the future would be better.

The truth, said Bvalltu, was almost certainly otherwise.
There was, as I had suspected, unmistakable evidence that the
average of intelligence and of moral integrity throughout the
world had declined; and they would probably continue to do
so. Already the race was living on its past. All the great seminal
ideas of the modern world had been conceived centuries ago.
Since then, world-changing applications of these ideas had
indeed been made; but none of these sensational inventions
had depended on the extreme kind of penetrating and comprehensive intuition which had changed the whole course of
thought in an earlier age. Recently there had been, Bvalltu
admitted, a spate of revolutionary scientific discoveries and
theories, but not one of them, he said, contained any really
novel principle. They were all re-combinations of familiar
principles. Scientific method, invented some centuries ago, was
so fertile a technique that it might well continue to yield rich
fruit for centuries to come even in the hands of workers incapable of any high degree of originality.

But it was not in the field of science so much as in moral and
practical activity that the deterioration of mental calibre was
most evident. I myself, with Bvalltu's aid, had learnt to appreciate to some extent the literature of that amazing period, many
centuries earlier, when every country seemed to blossom with
art, philosophy, and religion; when people after people had
changed its whole social and political order so as to secure a
measure of freedom and prosperity to all men; when state after
state had courageously disarmed, risking destruction but reap-
ing peace and prosperity; when police forces were disbanded,
prisons turned into libraries or colleges; when weapons and
even locks and keys came to be known only as museum pieces;
when the four great established priesthoods of the world had

exposed their own mysteries, given their wealth to the poor, and led the triumphant campaign for community; or had taken to agriculture, handicrafts teaching, as befitted humble supporters of the new priestless, faithless, Godless religion of world-wide community and inarticulate worship.

After some five hundred years locks and keys, weapons and doctrines, began to return. The golden age left behind it only a lovely and incredible tradition, and a set of principles which, though now sadly misconceived, were still the best influences in a distraught world.

Those scientists who attributed mental deterioration to the increase of cosmic rays affirmed that if the race had discovered science many centuries earlier, when it had still before it the period of greatest vitality, all would have been well. It would soon have mastered the social problems which industrial civilization entails. It would have created not merely a 'medieval' but a highly mechanized utopia. It would almost certainly have discovered how to cope with the excess of cosmic rays and prevent deterioration. But science had come too late.

Bvalltu, on the other hand, suspected that deterioration was due to some factor in human nature itself. He was inclined to believe that it was a consequence of civilization, that in changing the whole environment of the human species, seemingly for the better, science had unwittingly brought about a state of affairs hostile to spiritual vigour. He did not pretend to know whether the disaster was caused by the increase of artificial food, or the increased nervous strain of modern conditions, or interference with natural selection, or the softer upbringing of children, or to some other cause. Perhaps it should be attributed to none of these comparatively recent influences; for evidence did suggest that deterioration had set in at the very beginning of the scientific age, if not even earlier. It might be that some mysterious factor in the conditions of the golden age itself had started the rot. It might even be, he suggested, that genuine community generated its own poison, that the young human being, brought up in a perfected society, in a veritable 'city of God' on earth, must inevitably revolt towards moral and intellectual laziness, towards romantic individualism and sheer devilment; and that, once this disposition had taken root, science and a mechanized civilization had augmented the spiritual decay.

Shortly before I left the Other Earth a geologist discovered a fossil diagram of a very complicated radio set. It appeared to be a lithographic plate which had been made some ten million years earlier. The highly developed society which produced it had left no other trace. This find was a shock to the intelligent world; but the comforting view was spread abroad that some non-human and less hardy species had long ago attained a brief flicker of civilization. It was agreed that man, once he had reached such a height of culture, would never have fallen from it.

In Bvalltu's view man had climbed approximately to the same height time after time, only to be undone by some hidden consequence of his own achievement.

When Bvalltu propounded this theory, among the ruins of his native city, I suggested that some time, if not this time, man would successfully pass this critical point in his career. Bvalltu then spoke of another matter which seemed to indicate that we were witnessing the final act of this long-drawn-out and repetitive drama.

It was known to scientists that, owing to the weak gravitational hold of their world, the atmosphere, already scant, was steadily decreasing. Sooner or later humanity would have to face the problem of stopping this constant leakage of precious oxygen. Hitherto life had successfully adapted itself to the progressive rarefaction of atmosphere, but the human physique had already reached the limit of adaptability in this respect. If the loss were not soon checked, the race would inevitably decline. The only hope was that some means to deal with the atmospheric problem would be discovered before the onset of the next age of barbarism. There had only been a slight possibility that this would be achieved. This slender hope the war had destroyed by setting the clock of scientific research back for a century just at the time when human nature itself was deteriorating and might never again be able to tackle so difficult a problem.

The thought of the disaster which almost certainly lay in wait for the Other Men threw me into a horror of doubt about the universe in which such a thing could happen. That a whole world of intelligent beings could be destroyed was not an unfamiliar idea to me; but there is a great difference between an abstract possibility and a concrete and inescapable danger.

On my native planet, whenever I had been dismayed by the suffering and the futility of individuals, I had taken comfort in the thought that at least the massed effect of all our blind striving must be the slow but glorious awakening of the human spirit. This hope, this certainty, had been the one sure consolation. But now I saw that there was no guarantee of any such triumph. It seemed that the universe, or the maker of the universe, must be indifferent to the fate of worlds. That there should be endless struggle and suffering and waste must of course be accepted; and gladly, for these were the very soil in which the spirit grew. But that all struggle should be finally, absolutely vain, that a whole world of sensitive spirits should fail and die, must be sheer evil. In my horror it seemed to me that Hate must be the Star Maker.

Not so to Bvalltu. 'Even if the powers destroy us,' he said, 'who are we, to condemn them? As well might a fleeting word judge the speaker that forms it. Perhaps they use us for their own high ends, use our strength and our weakness, our joy and our pain, in some theme inconceivable to us, and excellent.' But I protested, 'What theme could justify such waste, such futility? And how can we help judging; and how otherwise can we judge than by the light of our own hearts, by which we judge ourselves? It would be base to praise the Star Maker, knowing that he was too insensitive to care about the fate of his worlds.' Bvalltu was silent in his mind for a moment. Then he looked up, searching among the smoke-clouds for a daytime star. And then he said to me in his mind, 'If he saved all the worlds, but tormented just one man, would you forgive him? Or if he was a little harsh only to one stupid child? What has our pain to do with it, or our failure? Star Maker! It is a good word, though we can have no notion of its meaning. Oh, Star Maker, even if you destroy me, I must praise you. Even if you torture my dearest. Even if you torment and waste all your lovely worlds, the little figments of your imagination, yet I must praise you. For if you do so, it must be right. In me it would be wrong, but in you it *must* be right.'

He looked down once more upon the ruined city, then continued, 'And if after all there is no Star Maker, if the great company of galaxies leapt into being of their own accord, and even if this little nasty world of ours is the only habitation of the spirit anywhere among the stars, and this world doomed, even so, even so, I must praise. But if there is no Star Maker, what can it be that I praise? I do not know. I will call it only the sharp tang and savour of existence. But to call it this is to say little.'

CHAPTER FOUR

I TRAVEL AGAIN

I must have spent several years on the Other Earth, a period far longer than I intended when I first encountered one of its peasants trudging through the fields. Often I longed to be at home again. I used to wonder with painful anxiety how those dear to me were faring, and what changes I should discover if I were ever to return. It was surprising to me that in spite of my novel and crowded experiences on the Other Earth thoughts of home should continue to be so insistent. It seemed but a moment since I was sitting on the hill looking at the lights of our suburb. Yet several years had passed. The children would be altered almost beyond recognition. Their mother? How would she have fared?

Bvalltu was partly responsible for my long spell on the Other Earth. He would not hear of my leaving till we had each attained a real understanding of the other's world. I constantly stimulated his imagination to picture as clearly as possible the life of my own planet, and he had discovered in it much the same medley of the splendid and the ironical as I had discovered in his. In fact he was far from agreeing with me that his world was on the whole the more grotesque.

The call to impart information was not the only consideration that bound me to Bvalltu. I had come to feel a very strong friendship for him. In the early days of our partnership there had sometimes been strains. Though we were both civilized human beings, who tried always to behave with courtesy and generosity, our extreme intimacy did sometimes fatigue us. I used, for instance, to find his passion for the gustatory fine art of his world very wearisome. He would sit by the hour passing his sensitive fingers over the impregnated cords to seize the taste sequences that had for him such great subtlety of form and symbolism. I was at first intrigued, then aesthetically stirred; but in spite of his patient help I was never at this early stage able to enter fully and spontaneously into the aesthetic of taste. Sooner or later I was fatigued or bored. Then again, I was impatient of his periodic need for sleep. Since I was disembodied, I myself felt no such need. I could, of course, disengage myself from Bvalltu and roam the world alone; but I was often exasperated by the necessity of breaking off the day's interesting experiences merely in order to afford my host's body time to recuperate. Bvalltu, for his part, at least in the early days of our partnership, was inclined to resent my power of watching his dreams. For though, while awake, he could withdraw his thoughts from my observation, asleep he was helpless. Naturally I very soon learned to refrain from exercising this power; and he, on his side, as our intimacy developed into mutual respect, no longer cherished this privacy so strictly.

In time each of us came to feel that to taste the flavour of life in isolation from the other was to miss half its richness and subtlety. Neither could entirely trust his own judgement or his own motives unless the other were present to offer relentless though friendly criticism.

We hit upon a plan for satisfying at once our friendship, his interest in my world, and my own longing for home. Why should we not somehow contrive to visit my planet together? I had travelled thence; why should we not both travel thither? After a spell on my planet, we could proceed upon the larger venture, again together.

For this end we had to attack two very different tasks. The technique of interstellar travel, which I had achieved only by accident and in a very haphazard manner, must now be thoroughly mastered. Also we must somehow locate my native planetary system in the astronomical maps of the Other Men.

This geographical, or rather cosmographical, problem proved insoluble. Do what I would, I could provide no data for the orientation. The attempt, however, led us to an amazing, and for me a terrifying discovery. I had travelled not only through space but through time itself. In the first place, it appeared that, in the very advanced astronomy of the Other Men, stars as mature as the Other Sun and as my own Sun were rare. Yet in terrestrial astronomy this type of star was known to be the commonest of all throughout the galaxy. How could this be? Then I made another perplexing discovery. The galaxy as known to the Other Astronomers proved to be strikingly different from my recollection of the galaxy as known to our own astronomers. According to the Other Men the great star-system was much less flattened than we observe it to be. Our astronomers tell us that it is like a circular biscuit five times as wide as it is thick. In their view it was more like a bun. I myself had often been struck by the width and indefiniteness of the Milky Way in the sky of the Other Earth. I had been surprised, too, that the Other Astronomers believed the galaxy to contain much gaseous matter not yet condensed into stars. To our astronomers it seemed to be almost wholly stellar.

Had I then travelled unwittingly much farther than I had supposed, and actually entered some other and younger galaxy? Perhaps in my period of darkness, when the rubies and amethysts and diamonds of the sky had all vanished, I had actually sped across intergalactic space. This seemed at first the only explanation, but certain facts forced us to discard it in favour of one even stranger.

Comparison of the astronomy of the Other Men with my fragmentary recollections of our own astronomy convinced me that the whole cosmos of galaxies known to them differed from the whole cosmos of galaxies known to us. The average form of the galaxies was much more rotund and much more gaseous, in fact much more primitive, for them than for us.

Moreover, in the sky of the Other Earth several galaxies were so near as to be prominent smudges of light even for the naked eye. And astronomers had shown that many of these so-called 'universes' were much closer to the home 'universe' than the nearest known in our astronomy.

The truth that now flashed on Bvalltu and me was indeed bewildering. Everything pointed to the fact that I had somehow travelled up the river of time and landed myself at a date in the remote past, when the great majority of the stars were still young. The startling nearness of so many galaxies in the astronomy of the Other Men could be explained on the theory of the 'expanding universe'. Well I knew that this dramatic theory was but tentative and very far from satisfactory; but at least here was one more striking bit of evidence to suggest that it must be in *some* sense true. In early epochs the galaxies could of course be congested together. There would be no doubt that I had been transported to a world which had reached the human stage very long before my native planet had been plucked from the sun's womb.

The full realization of my temporal remoteness from my home reminded me of a fact, or at least a probability, which, oddly enough, I had long ago forgotten. Presumably I was dead. I now desperately craved to be home again. Home was all the while so vivid, so near. Even though its distance was to be counted in parsecs and in aeons, it was always at hand. Surely if I could only *wake*, I should find myself there on our hill-top again. But there was no waking. Through Bvalltu's eyes I was studying star-maps and pages of outlandish script. When he looked up, I saw standing opposite us a caricature of a human being, with a frog-like face that was scarcely a face at all, and with the thorax of a pouter-pigeon, naked save for greenish down. Red silk knickers crowned the spindle shanks that were enclosed in green silk stockings. This creature, which, to the terrestrial eye, was simply a monster, passed on the Other Earth as a young and beautiful woman. And I myself, observing her through Bvalltu's benevolent eyes, recognized her as indeed beautiful. To a mind habituated to the Other Earth her features and her every gesture spoke of intelligence and wit. Clearly, if I could admire such a woman, I myself must have changed.

It would be tedious to tell of the experiments by which we acquired and perfected the art of controlled flight through interstellar space. Suffice it that, after many adventures, we learned to soar up from the planet whenever we wished, and to direct our course, by mere acts of volition, hither and thither among the stars. We seemed to have much greater facility and accuracy when we worked together than when either ventured into space by himself. Our community of mind seemed to strengthen us even for spatial locomotion.

It was a very strange experience to find oneself in the depth of space, surrounded only by darkness and the stars, yet to be all the while in close personal contact with an unseen companion. As the dazzling lamps of heaven flashed past us, we would think to one another about our experiences, or debate our plans, or share our memories of our native worlds. Sometimes we used my language, sometimes his. Sometimes we needed no words at all, but merely shared the flow of imagery in our two minds.

The sport of disembodied flight among the stars must surely be the most exhilarating of all athletic exercises. It was not without danger; but its danger, as we soon discovered, was psychological, not physical. In our bodiless state, collision with celestial objects mattered little. Sometimes, in the early stages of our adventure, we plunged by accident headlong into a star. Its interior would, of course, be inconceivably hot, but we experienced merely brilliance.

The psychological dangers of the sport were grave. We soon discovered that disheartenment, mental fatigue, fear, all tended to reduce our powers of movement. More than once we found ourselves immobile in space, like a derelict ship on the ocean; and such was the fear roused by this plight that there was no possibility of moving till, having experienced the whole gamut of despair, we passed through indifference and on into philosophic calm.

A still graver danger, but one which trapped us only once, was mental conflict. A serious discord of purpose over our future plans reduced us not only to immobility but to terrifying mental disorder. Our perceptions became confused. Hallucinations tricked us. The power of coherent thought vanished. After a spell of delirium, filled with an overwhelming sense of impending annihilation, we found ourselves back on the Other Earth; Bvalltu in his own body, lying in bed as he had left it, I once more a disembodied view-point floating somewhere over the planet's surface. Both were in a state of insane terror, from which we took long to recover. Months passed before we renewed our partnership and our adventure.

Long afterwards we learned the explanation of this painful incident. Seemingly we had attained such a deep mental accord that, when conflict arose, it was more like dissociation within a single mind than discord between two separate individuals. Hence its serious consequences.

As our skill in disembodied flight increased, we found intense pleasure in sweeping hither and thither among the stars. We tasted the delights at once of skating and of flight. Time after time, for sheer joy, we traced huge figures-of-eight in and out around the two partners of a 'double star'. Sometimes we stayed motionless for long periods to watch at close quarters the waxing and waning of a variable. Often we plunged into a congested cluster, and slid among its suns like a car gliding among the lights of a city. Often we skimmed over billowy and palely luminous surfaces of gas, or among feathery shreds and prominences; or plunged into mist, to find ourselves in a world of featureless dawn light. Sometimes, without warning, dark continents of dust engulfed us, blotting out the universe. Once, as we were traversing a populous region of the heaven, a star suddenly blazed into exaggerated splendour, becoming a 'nova'. As it was apparently surrounded by a cloud of non-luminous gas, we actually saw the expanding sphere of light which was radiated by the star's explosion. Travelling outward at light's speed, it was visible by reflection from the surrounding gas, so that it appeared like a swelling balloon of light, fading as it spread.

These were but a few of the stellar spectacles that delighted us while we easefully skated, as on swallow wings, hither and thither among the neighbours of the Other Sun. This was during our period of apprenticeship to the craft of interstellar flight. When we had become proficient we passed farther afield, and learned to travel so fast that, as on my own earlier and involuntary flight, the forward and the hinder stars took colour, and presently all was dark. Not only so, but we reached to that more spiritual vision, also experienced on my earlier voyage, in which these vagaries of physical light are overcome.

On one occasion our flight took us outwards towards the limits of the galaxy, and into the emptiness beyond. For some time the near stars had become fewer and fewer. The hinder hemisphere of sky was now crowded with faint lights, while in front of us lay starless blackness, unrelieved save by a few isolated patches of scintillation, a few detached fragments of the galaxy, or planetary 'sub-galaxies'. Apart from these the dark was featureless, save for half a dozen of the vague flecks which we knew to be the nearest of the alien galaxies.

Awed by this spectacle, we stayed long motionless in the void. It was indeed a stirring experience to see spread out before us a whole 'universe', containing a billion stars and perhaps thousands of inhabited worlds; and to know that each tiny fleck in the black sky was itself another such 'universe', and that millions more of them were invisible only because of their extreme remoteness.

What was the significance of this physical immensity and complexity? By itself, plainly, it constituted nothing but sheer futility and desolation. But with awe and hope we told ourselves that it promised an even greater complexity and subtlety and diversity of the psychical. This alone could justify it. But this formidable promise, though inspiring, was also terrifying.

Like a nestling that peers over the nest's rim for the first time, and then shrinks back from the great world into its tiny home, we had emerged beyond the confines of that little nest of stars which for so long, but falsely, men called 'the universe'. And now we sank back to bury ourselves once more in the genial precincts of our native galaxy.

As our experiences had raised many theoretical problems which we could not solve without further study of astronomy, we now decided to return to the Other Earth; but after long and fruitless search we realized that we had completely lost our bearings. The stars were all much alike, save that few in this early epoch were as old and temperate as the Other Sun. Searching at random, but at high speed, we found neither Bvalltu's planet nor mine, or any other solar system. Frustrated, we came to rest once more in the void to consider our plight. On every side the ebony of the sky, patterned with diamonds, confronted us with an enigma. Which spark of all this star-dust was the Other Sun? As was usual in the sky of this early epoch, streaks of nebular matter were visible in all directions; but their shapes were unfamiliar, and useless for orientation.

The fact that we were lost among the stars did not distress us. We were exhilarated by our adventure, and each was a cause of good spirits in the other. Our recent experiences had quickened our mental life, still further organizing our two minds together. Each was still at most times conscious of the other and of himself as separate beings; but the pooling or integration of our memories and of our temperaments had now gone so far that our distinctness was often forgotten. Two disembodied minds, occupying the same visual position, possessing the same memories and desires, and often performing the same mental acts at the same time, can scarcely be conceived as distinct beings. Yet, strangely enough, this growing identity was complicated by an increasingly intense mutual realization and comradeship.

Our penetration of one another's minds brought to each not merely addition but multiplication of mental riches; for each knew inwardly not only himself and the other but also the contrapuntal harmony of each in relation to the other. Indeed, in some sense which I cannot precisely describe, our union of minds brought into being a third mind, as yet intermittent, but more subtly conscious than either of us in the normal state. Each of us, or rather both of us together, 'woke up' now and then to be this superior spirit. All the experiences of each took on a new significance in the light of the other; and our two minds together became a new, more penetrating, and more self-conscious mind. In this state of heightened lucidity we, or rather the new I, began deliberately to explore the psychological possibilities of other types of beings and intelligent worlds. With new penetration I distinguished in myself and in Bvalltu those attributes which were essential to the spirit and those mere accidents imposed on each by his peculiar world. This imaginative venture was soon to prove itself a method, and a very potent method, of cosmological research.

We now began to realize more clearly a fact that we had longed suspected. In my previous interstellar voyage, which brought me to the other Earth, I had unwittingly employed two distinct methods of travel, the method of disembodied flight through space and a method which I shall call 'psychical attraction'. This consisted of telepathic projection of the mind directly into some alien world, remote perhaps in time and space, but mentally 'in tune' with the explorer's own mind at the time of the venture. Evidently it was this method that had really played the chief part in directing me to the Other Earth. The remarkable similarities of our two races had set up a strong 'psychical attraction' which had been far more potent than all my random interstellar wanderings. It was this method that Bvalltu and I were now to practise and perfect.

Presently we noticed that we were no longer at rest but slowly drifting. We had also a queer sense that, though we were seemingly isolated in a vast desert of stars and nebulae, we were in fact in some kind of mental proximity with unseen intelligences. Concentrating on this sense of presence, we found that our drift accelerated; and that, if we tried by a violent act of volition to change its course, we inevitably swung back into the original direction as soon as our effort ceased. Soon our drift became a headlong flight. Once more the forward stars turned violet, the hinder red. Once more all vanished.

In absolute darkness and silence we debated our situation. Clearly we were now passing through space more quickly than light itself. Perhaps we were also, in some incomprehensible manner, traversing time. Meanwhile that sense of the proximity of other beings became more and more insistent, though no less confused.

Then once again the stars appeared. Though they streamed past us like flying sparks, they were colourless and normal. One brilliant light lay right ahead of us. It waxed, became a dazzling splendour, then visibly a disc. With an effort of will we decreased our speed, then cautiously we swung round this sun, searching. To our delight, it proved to be attended by several of the grains that may harbour life. Guided by our unmistakable sense of mental presence, we selected one of these planets, and slowly descended towards it.

CHAPTER FIVE

WORLDS INNUMERABLE

1. The Diversity of Worlds

The planet on which we now descended after our long flight among the stars was the first of many to be visited. In some we stayed, according to the local calendar, only a few weeks, in others several years, housed together in the mind of some native. Often when the time came for our departure our host would accompany us for subsequent adventures. As we passed from world to world, as experience was piled upon experience like geological strata, it seemed that this strange tour of worlds was lasting for many lifetimes. Yet thoughts of our own home-planets were constantly with us. Indeed, in my case it was not till I found myself thus exiled that I came to realize fully the little jewel of personal union that I had left behind. I had to comprehend each world as best I could by reference to the remote world where my own life had happened, and above all by the touchstone of that common life that she and I had made together.

Before trying to describe, or rather suggest, the immense diversity of worlds which I entered, I must say a few words about the movement of the adventure itself. After the experiences which I have just recorded it was clear that the method of disembodied flight was of little use. It did indeed afford us extremely vivid perception of the visible features of our galaxy; and we often used to orientate ourselves when we had made some fresh discovery by the method of psychological attraction. But since it gave us freedom only of space and not of time, and since, moreover, planetary systems were so very rare, the method of sheer random physical flight alone was

63

almost infinitely unlikely to produce results. Psychical attraction, however, once we had mastered it, proved very effective. This method depended on the imaginative reach of our own minds. At first, when our imaginative power was strictly limited by experience of our own worlds, we could make contact only with worlds closely akin to our own. Moreover, in this novitiate stage of our work we invariably came upon these worlds when they were passing through the same spiritual crisis as that which underlies the plight of *Homo Sapiens* today. It appeared that, for us to enter any world at all, there had to be a deep-lying likeness or identity in ourselves and our hosts.

As we passed on from world to world we greatly increased our understanding of the principles underlying our venture, and our powers of applying them. Further, in each world that we visited we sought out a new collaborator, to give us insight into his world and to extend our imaginative reach for further exploration of the galaxy. This 'snowball' method by which our company was increased was of great importance, since it magnified our powers. In the final stages of the exploration we made discoveries which might well be regarded as infinitely beyond the range of any single and unaided human mind.

At the outset Bvalltu and I assumed that we were embarking on a purely private adventure; and later, as we gathered helpers, we still believed that we ourselves were the sole initiators of cosmical exploration. But after a while we came in psychical contact with another group of cosmical explorers, natives of worlds as yet unknown to us. With these adventurers, after difficult and often distressing experiments, we joined forces, entering first into intimate community, and later into that strange mental union which Bvalltu and I had already experienced together in some degree on our first voyage among the stars.

When we had encountered many more such groups, we realized that, though each little expedition had made a lonely start, all were destined sooner or later to come together. For, no matter how alien from one another at the outset, each group gradually acquired such far-reaching imaginative power that sooner or later it was sure to make contact with others.

In time it became clear that we, individual inhabitants of a host of worlds, were playing a small part in one of the great movements by which the cosmos was seeking to know itself, and even see beyond itself.

In saying this I do not for a moment claim that, because I have shared in this vast process of cosmical self-discovery, the story which I have to tell is true in a fully literal sense. Plainly it does not deserve to be taken as part of the absolute objective truth about the cosmos. I, the human individual, can only in a most superficial and falsifying way participate in the super-human experience of the communal 'I' which was supported by the innumerable explorers. This book must needs be a ludicrously false caricature of our actual adventure. But further, though we were and are a multitude drawn from a multitude of spheres, we represent only a tiny fraction of the diversity of the whole cosmos. Thus even the supreme moment of our experience, when it seemed to us that we had penetrated to the very heart of reality, must in fact have given us no more than a few shreds of truth, and these not literal but symbolic.

My account of that part of my adventure which brought me into contact with worlds of more or less human type may be fairly accurate; but that which deals with more alien spheres must be far from the truth. The Other Earth I have probably described with little more falsehood than our historians commit in telling of the past ages of *Homo Sapiens*. But of the less human worlds, and the many fantastic kinds of beings which we encountered up and down the galaxy and throughout the whole cosmos, and even beyond it, I shall perforce make statements which, literally regarded, must be almost wholly false. I can only hope that they have the kind of truth that we sometimes find in myths.

Since we were now free of space, we ranged with equal ease over the nearer and the remoter tracts of this galaxy. That we did not till much later make contact with minds in other galaxies was not due to any limitations imposed by space, but seemingly to our own inveterate parochialism, to a strange limitation of our own interest, which for long rendered us inhospitable to the influence of worlds lying beyond the confines of the Milky Way. I shall say more of this curious restriction when I come to describe how we did at last outgrow it.

Along with freedom of space we had freedom of time. Some of the worlds that we explored in this early phase of our adventure ceased to exist long before my native planet was formed; others were its contemporaries; others were not born till the old age of our galaxy, when the Earth had been destroyed, and a large number of the stars had already been extinguished.

As we searched up and down time and space, discovering more and more of the rare grains called planets, as we watched race after race struggle to a certain degree of lucid consciousness, only to succumb to some external accident or, more often, to some flaw in its own nature, we were increasingly oppressed by a sense of the futility, the planlessness of the cosmos. A few worlds did indeed wake to such lucidity that they passed beyond our ken. But several of the most brilliant of these occurred in the earliest epoch of the galactic story; and nothing that we could as yet discover in the later phases of the cosmos suggested that any galaxies, still less the cosmos as a whole, had at last come (or will at last come) more under the sway of the awakened spirit than they were during the epoch of those early brilliant worlds. Not till a much later stage of our inquiry were we fitted to discover the glorious but ironical and heart-rending climax for which this vast proliferation of worlds was but a prologue.

In the first phase of our adventure, when, as I have said, our powers of telepathic exploration were incomplete, every world that we entered turned out to be in the throes of the same spiritual crisis as that which we knew so well on our native planets. This crisis I came to regard as having two aspects. It was at once a moment in the spirit's struggle to become capable of true community on a world-wide scale; and it was a stage in the age-long task of achieving the right, the finally appropriate, the spiritual attitude towards the universe.

In every one of these 'chrysalis' worlds thousands of millions of persons were flashing into existence, one after the other, to drift gropingly about for a few instants of cosmical time before they were extinguished. Most were capable, at least in some humble degree, of the intimate kind of community which is personal affection; but for nearly all of them a stranger was ever a thing to fear and hate. And even their intimate loving was inconstant and lacking in insight. Nearly always they were intent merely on seeking for themselves respite from fatigue or boredom, fear or hunger. Like my own race, they never fully awoke from the primeval sleep of the subman. Only a few here and there, now and then, were solaced, goaded, or tortured by moments of true wakefulness. Still fewer attained a clear and constant vision, even of some partial aspect of truth; and their half-truths they nearly always took to be absolute. Propagating their little partial truths, they bewildered and misdirected their fellow mortals as much as they helped them.

Each individual spirit, in nearly all these worlds, attained at some point in life some lowly climax of awareness and of spiritual integrity, only to sink slowly or catastrophically back into nothingness. Or so it seemed. As in my own world, so in all these others, lives were spent in pursuit of shadowy ends that remained ever just round the corner. There were vast tracts of boredom and frustration, with here and there some rare bright joy. There were ecstasies of personal triumph, of mutual intercourse and love, of intellectual insight, of aesthetic creation. There were also religious ecstasies; but these, like all else in these worlds, were obscured by false interpretations. There were crazy ecstasies of hate and cruelty, felt against individuals and against groups. Sometimes during this early phase of our adventure we were so distressed by the incredible bulk of suffering and of cruelty up and down the worlds that our courage failed, our telepathic powers were disordered, and we slipped towards madness.

Yet most of these worlds were really no worse than our own. Like us, they had reached that stage when the spirit, half awakened from brutishness and very far from maturity, can suffer most desperately and behave most cruelly. And like us, these tragic but vital worlds, visited in our early adventures, were agonized by the inability of their minds to keep pace with changing circumstance. They were always behindhand, always applying old concepts and old ideals inappropriately to novel situations. Like us, they were constantly tortured by their hunger for a degree of community which their condition demanded but their poor, cowardly, selfish spirits could by no means attain. Only in couples and in little circles of companions could they support true community, the communion of mutual insight and respect and love. But in their tribes and nations they conceived all too easily the sham community of the pack, baying in unison of fear and hate.

Particularly in one respect these races were recognizably our kin. Each had risen by a strange mixture of violence and gentleness. The apostles of violence and the apostles of gentleness swayed them this way and that. At the time of our visit many of these worlds were in the throes of a crisis of this conflict. In the recent past, loud lip-service had been paid to gentleness and tolerance and freedom; but the policy had failed, because there was no sincere purpose in it, no conviction of the spirit, no true experience of respect for individual personality. All kinds of self-seeking and vindictiveness had flourished, secretly at first, then openly as shameless individualism. Then at last, in rage, the peoples turned away from individualism and plunged into the cult of the herd. At the same time, in disgust with the failure of gentleness, they began openly to praise violence, and the ruthlessness of the god-sent hero and of the armed tribe. Those who thought they believed in gentleness built up armaments for their tribes against those foreign tribes whom they accused of believing in violence. The highly developed technique of violence threatened to destroy civilization; year by year gentleness lost ground. Few could understand that their world must be saved, not by violence in the short run, but by gentleness in the long run. A still fewer could see that, to be effective, gentleness must be a religion; and that lasting peace can never come till the many have wakened to the lucidity of consciousness which, in all these worlds, only the few could as yet attain.

If I were to describe in detail every world that we explored, this book would develop into a world of libraries. I can give only a few pages to the many types of worlds encountered in this early stage of our adventure, up and down the whole breadth and length and the whole duration of our galaxy. Some of these types had apparently very few instances; others occurred in scores or hundreds.

The most numerous of all classes of intelligent worlds is that which includes the planet familiar to readers of this book. *Homo Sapiens* has recently flattered and frightened himself by conceiving that, though perhaps he is not the sole intelligence in the cosmos, he is at least unique, and that worlds suited to intelligent life of any kind must be extremely rare. This view proves ludicrously false. In comparison with the unimaginable number of the stars intelligent worlds are indeed very rare; but we discovered some thousands of worlds much like the Earth and possessed by beings of essentially human kind, though superficially they were often unlike the type that we call human. The Other Men were among the most obviously human. But in a later stage of our adventure, when our research was no longer restricted to worlds that had reached the familiar spiritual crisis, we stumbled on a few planets inhabited by races almost identical with *Homo Sapiens,* or rather with the creature that *Homo Sapiens* was in the earliest phase of his existence. These most human worlds we had not encountered earlier because, by one accident or another, they were destroyed before reaching the stage of our own mentality.

Long after we had succeeded in extending our research from our peers among the worlds to our inferiors in mental rank we remained unable to make any sort of contact with beings who had passed wholly beyond the attainment of *Homo Sapiens.* Consequently, though we traced the history of many worlds through many epochs, and saw many reach a catastrophic end, or sink into stagnation and inevitable decline, there were a few with which, do what we would, we lost touch just at that moment when they seemed ripe for a leap forward into some more developed mentality. Not till a much later stage of our

adventure, when our corporate being had itself been enriched
by the influx of many superior spirits, were we able to pick up
once more the threads of these most exhalted world-biographies.

2. Strange Mankinds

Though all the worlds which we entered in the first phase of
our adventure were in the throes of the crisis known so well
in our own world, some were occupied by races biologically
similar to man, others by very different types. The more obviously human races inhabited planets of much the same size and
nature as the Earth and the Other Earth. All, whatever the
vagaries of their biological history, had finally been moulded
by circumstance to the erect form which is evidently most
suited to such worlds. Nearly always the two nether limbs
were used for locomotion, the two upper limbs for manipulation. Generally there was some sort of head, containing the
brain and the organs of remote perception, and perhaps the
orifices for eating and breathing. In size these quasi-human
types were seldom larger than our largest gorillas, seldom
much smaller than monkeys; but we could not estimate their
size with any accuracy, as we had no familiar standards of
measurements.

Within this approximately human class there was great variety. We came upon feathered, penguin-like men, descended
from true fliers, and on some small planets we found bird-men
who retained the power of flight, yet were able to carry an
adequate human brain. Even on some large planets, with exceptionally buoyant atmosphere, men flew with their own
wings. Then there were men that had developed from a slug-
like ancestor along a line which was not vertebrate, still less
mammalian. Men of this type attained the necessary rigidity
and flexibility of limb by means of a delicate internal 'basket-
work' of wiry bones.

On one very small but earthlike planet we discovered a
quasi-human race which was probably unique. Here, though
life had evolved much as on earth, all the higher animals dif-

fered remarkably from the familiar type in one obvious re-spect. They were without that far-reaching duplication of or-gans which characterizes all our vertebrates. Thus a man in this world was rather like half a terrestrial man. He hopped on one sturdy, splay-footed leg, balancing himself with a kangaroo tail. A single arm protruded from his chest, but branched into three forearms and prehensile fingers. Above his mouth was a single nostril, above that an ear, and on the top of his head a flexible three-pronged proboscis bearing three eyes.

A very different and fairly common quasi-human kind was sometimes produced by planets rather larger than the Earth. Owing to the greater strength of gravitation, there would first appear, in place of the familiar quadruped, a six-legged type. This would proliferate into little sextuped burrowers, swift and elegant sextuped grazers, a sextuped mammoth, complete with tusks, and many kinds of sextuped carnivora. Man in these worlds sprang usually from some small oppossum-like creature which had come to use the first of its three pairs of limbs for nest-building or for climbing. In time, the forepart of its body thus became erect, and it gradually assumed a form not unlike that of a quadruped with a human torso in place of a neck. In fact it became a centaur, with four legs and two capable arms. It was very strange to find oneself in a world in which all the amenities and conveniences of civilization were fashioned to suit men of this form.

In one of these worlds, rather smaller than the rest, man was not a centaur, though centaurs were among his remote ances-tors. In sub-human stages of evolution the pressure of the environment had telescoped the horizontal part of the cen-taur's body, so that the forelegs and the hind-legs were drawn closer and closer together, till at last they became a single sturdy pair. Thus man and his nearer ancestors were bipeds with very large rumps, reminiscent of the Victorian bustle, and legs whose internal structure still showed their 'centaur' origin.

One very common kind of quasi-human world I must de-scribe in more detail, as it plays an important part in the history of our galaxy. In these worlds man, though varying greatly in form and fortune in particular worlds, had in every case developed from a sort of five-pronged marine animal, rather like a star-fish. This creature would in time specialize one prong for perceiving, four for locomotion. Later it would develop lungs, a complex digestive apparatus, and a well-integrated nervous system. Later still the perceiving limb would produce a brain, the others becoming adapted for running and climbing. The soft spines which covered the body of the ancestral star-fish often developed into a kind of spiky fur. In due season there would arise an erect, intelligent biped equipped with eyes, nostrils, ears, taste-organs, and sometimes organs of electric perception. Save for the grotesqueness of their faces, and the fact that the mouth was generally upon the belly, these creatures were remarkably human. Their bodies, however, were usually covered with the soft spines or fat hairs characteristic of these worlds. Clothes were unknown, save as protection against cold in the arctic regions. Their faces, of course, were apt to be far from human. The tall head often bore a coronet of five eyes. Large single nostrils, used for breathing and smelling and also speaking, formed another circlet below the eyes.

The appearance of these 'Human Echinoderms' belied their nature, for though their faces were inhuman, the basic pattern of their minds was not unlike our own. Their senses were much like ours, save that in some worlds they developed a far more varied colour-sensitivity. Those races that had the electric sense gave us some difficulty; for, in order to understand their thought, we had to learn a whole new gamut of sense qualities and a vast system of unfamiliar symbolism. The electric organs detected very slight differences of electric charge in relation to the subject's own body. Originally this sense had been used for revealing enemies equipped with electric organs of offence. But in man its significance was chiefly social. It gave information about the emotional state of one's neighbours. Beyond this its function was meteorological.

One example of this kind of world, one which clearly illustrates the type, and at the same time presents interesting peculiarities must be described in more detail.

The key to the understanding of this race is, I believe, its strange method of reproduction, which was essentially communal. Every individual was capable of budding a new individual; but only at certain seasons, and only after stimulation by a kind of pollen emanating from the whole tribe and carried on the air. The grains of this ultra-microscopically fine pollen dust were not germ-cells but 'genes', the elementary factors of inheritance. The precincts of the tribe were at all times faintly perfumed by the communal pollen; but on occasions of violent group emotion the pollen cloud became so intensified as to be actually visible as a haze. Only on these rare occasions was conception probable. Breathed out by every individual, the pollen was breathed in by those who were ripe for fertilization. By all it was experienced as a rich and subtle perfume, to which each individual contributed his peculiar odour. By means of a curious physical and physiological mechanism the individual in heat was moved to crave stimulation by the full perfume of the tribe, or of the great majority of its members; and indeed, if the pollen clouds were insufficiently complex, conception would not occur. Cross-fertilization between tribes happened in inter-tribal warfare and in the ceaseless coming and going between tribes in the modern world.

In this race, then, every individual might bear children. Every child, though it had an individual as its mother, was fathered by the tribe as a whole. Expectant parents were sacred, and were tended communally. When the baby 'Echinoderm' finally detached itself from the parental body, it also was tended communally along with the rest of the tribe's juvenile population. In civilized societies it was handed over to professional nurses and teachers.

I must not pause to tell of the important psychological effects of this kind of reproduction. The delights and disgusts which we feel in contact with the flesh of our kind were unknown. On the other hand, individuals were profoundly moved by the ever-changing tribal perfume. It is impossible to describe the strange variant of romantic love which each individual periodically felt for the tribe. The thwarting, the repression, the perversion of this passion was the source at once of the loftiest and the most sordid achievements of the race.

Communal parenthood gave to the tribe a unity and strength quite unknown in more individualistic races. The primitive tribes were groups of a few hundred or a few thousand individuals, but in modern times their size greatly increased. Always, however, the sentiment of tribal loyalty, if it was to remain healthy, had to be based on the personal acquaintance of its members. Even in the larger tribes, everyone was at least 'the friend of a friend's friend' to every other member. Telephone, radio, and television enabled tribes as large as our smaller cities to maintain a sufficient degree of personal intercourse among their members.

But always there was some point beyond which further growth of the tribe was unwholesome. Even in the smallest and most intelligent tribes there was a constant strain between the individual's natural passion for the tribe and his respect for individuality in himself and his fellows. But whereas in the small tribes and healthy larger tribes the tribal spirit was kept sweet and sane by the mutual-respect and self-respect of the individuals, in the largest and imperfectly sane tribes the hypnotic influence of the tribe was all too apt to drown personality. The members might even lose all awareness of themselves and their fellows as persons, and become mere mindless organs of the tribe. Thus the community would degenerate into an instinctive animal herd.

Throughout history the finer minds of the race had realized that the supreme temptation was the surrender of individuality to the tribe. Prophets had over and over again exhorted men to be true to themselves, but their preaching had been almost wholly vain. The greatest religions of this strange world were not religions of love but religions of self. Whereas in our world men long for the utopia in which all men shall love one another, the 'Echinoderms' were apt to exalt the religious hunger for strength to 'be oneself' without capitulation to the tribe. Just as we compensate for our inveterate selfishness by religious veneration of the community, so this race compensated

for inveterate 'gregism' by religious veneration of the individual.

In its purest and most developed form, of course, the religion
of self is almost identical with the religion of love at its best.
To love is to will the self-fulfilment of the beloved, and to find,
in the very activity of loving, an incidental but vitalizing increase of oneself. On the other hand, to be true to oneself, to
the full potentiality of the self, involves the activity of love. It
demands the discipline of the private self in service of a greater
self which embraces the community and the fulfilment of the
spirit of the race.

But the religion of self was no more effective with the
'Echinoderms' than the religion of love with us. The precept,
'Love thy neighbour as thyself,' breeds in us most often the
disposition to see one's neighbour merely as a poor imitation
of oneself, and to hate him if he proves different. With them
the precept, 'Be true to thyself,' bred the disposition merely to
be true to the tribal fashion of mentality.

Modern industrial civilization caused many tribes to swell
beyond the wholesome limit. It also introduced artificial
'super-tribes' or 'tribes of tribes', corresponding to our nations
and social classes. Since the economic unit was the internally
communistic tribe, not the individual, the employing class was
a small group of small and prosperous tribes, and the working
class was a large group of large and impoverished tribes. The
ideologies of the super-tribes exercised absolute power over all
individual minds under their sway.

In civilized regions the super-tribes and the overgrown natural tribes created an astounding mental tyranny. In relation to
his natural tribe, at least if it was small and genuinely civilized,
the individual might still behave with intelligence and imagination. Along with his actual tribal kinsmen he might support
a degree of true community unknown on Earth. He might in
fact be a critical, self-respecting and other-respecting person.
But in all matters connected with the super-tribes, whether
national or economic, he behaved in a very different manner.
All ideas coming to him with the sanction of nation or class

would be accepted uncritically and with fervour by himself and all his fellows. As soon as he encountered one of the symbols or slogans of his super-tribe he ceased to be a human personality and became a sort of de-cerebrate animal, capable only of stereotyped reactions. In extreme cases his mind was absolutely closed to influences opposed to the suggestion of the super-tribe. Criticism was either met with blind rage or actually not heard at all. Persons who in the intimate community of their small native tribe were capable of great mutual insight and sympathy might suddenly, in response to tribal symbols, be transformed into vessels of crazy intolerance and hate directed against national or class enemies. In this mood they would go to any extreme of self-sacrifice for the supposed glory of the super-tribe. Also they would show great ingenuity in contriving means to exercise their lustful vindictiveness upon enemies who in favourable circumstances could be quite as kindly and intelligent as themselves.

At the time of our visit to this world it seemed that mob passions would destroy civilization completely and irrevocably. The affairs of the world were increasingly conducted under the sway of the spreading mania of super-tribalism; conducted, in fact, not intelligently but according to the relative emotional compulsions of almost meaningless slogans.

I must not stay to describe how, after a period of chaos, a new way of life at last began to spread over this distressed world. It could not do so till the super-tribes had been disintegrated by the economic forces of mechanized industry, and by their own frenzied conflict, then at last the individual mind became once more free. The whole prospect of the race now changed.

It was in this world that we first experienced that tantalizing loss of contact with the natives just at that point where, having established something like a social utopia throughout their planet, they were beset by the first painful stirrings of the spirit before advancement to some mental plane beyond our reach, or at least beyond such comprehension as we then had.

Of the other 'Echinoderm' worlds in our galaxy, one, more promising than the average, rose early to brilliance, but was destroyed by astronomical collision. Its whole solar system encountered a tract of dense nebula. The surface of every planet was fused. In several other worlds of this type we saw the struggle for the more awakened mentality definitely fail. Vindictive and superstitious herd-cults exterminated the best minds of the race, and drugged the rest with customs and principles so damaging that the vital sources of sensitivity and adaptability on which all mental progress depends were destroyed for ever.

Many thousands of other quasi-human worlds, besides those of the 'Echinoderm' type, came to an untimely end. One, which succumbed to a curious disaster, perhaps deserves brief notice. Here we found a race of very human kind. When its civilization had reached a stage and character much like our own, a stage in which the ideals of the masses are without the guidance of any well-established tradition, and in which natural science is enslaved to individualistic industry, biologists discovered the technique of artificial insemination. Now at this time there happened to be a widespread cult of irrationalism, of instinct, of ruthlessness, and of the 'divine' primitive 'brute-man'. This figure was particularly admired when he combined brutishness with the power of the mob-controller. Several countries were subjected to tyrants of this type, and in the so-called democratic states the same type was much favoured by popular taste.

In both kinds of country, women craved 'brute-men' as lovers, and as fathers for their children. Since in the 'democratic' countries women had attained great economic independence, their demand for fertilization by 'brute-men' caused the whole matter to be commercialized. Males of the desirable type were taken up by syndicates, and graded in five ranks of desirability. At a moderate charge, fixed in relation to the grade of the father, any woman could obtain 'brute-man' fertilization. So cheap was the fifth grade that only the most abject paupers were debarred from its services. The charge for actual copulation with even the lowest grade of selected male was, of course, much higher, since perforce the supply was limited.

In the non-democratic countries events took a different turn. In each of these regions a tyrant of the fashionable type gathered upon his own person the adoration of the whole population. He was the god-sent hero. He was himself divine. Every woman longed passionately to have him, if not as a lover, at least as father of her children. In some lands artificial insemination from the Master was permitted only as a supreme distinction for women of perfect type. Ordinary women of every class, however, were entitled to insemination from the authorized aristocratic stud of 'brute-men'. In other countries the Master himself condescended to be the father of the whole future population.

The result of this extraordinary custom, of artificial fatherhood by 'brute-men', which was carried on without remission in all countries for a generation, and in a less thorough manner for a very much longer period, was to alter the composition of the whole quasi-human race. In order to maintain continued adaptability to an ever-changing environment a race must at all costs preserve in itself its slight but potent salting of sensibility and originality. In this world the precious factor now became so diluted as to be ineffective. Henceforth the desperately complex problems of the world were consistently bungled. Civilization decayed. The race entered on a phase of what might be called pseudo-civilized barbarism, which was in essence sub-human and incapable of change. This state of affairs continued for some millions of years, but at last the race was destroyed by the ravages of a small rat-like animal against which it could devise no protection.

I must not stay to notice the strange fortunes of all the many other quasi-human worlds. I will mention only that in some, though civilization was destroyed in a succession of savage wars, the germ of recovery precariously survived. In one, the agonizing balance of the old and the new seemed to prolong itself indefinitely. In another, where science had advanced too far for the safety of an immature species, man accidentally blew up his planet and his race. In several, the dialectical process of history was broken short by invasion and conquest on the part of inhabitants of another planet. These and other disasters, to be described in due course, decimated the galactic population of worlds.

In conclusion I will mention that in one or two of these quasi-human worlds a new and superior biological race emerged naturally during the typical world crisis, gained power by sheer intelligence and sympathy, took charge of the planet, persuaded the aborigines to cease breeding, peopled the whole planet with its own superior type, and created a human race which attained communal mentality, and rapidly advanced beyond the limits of our exploring and over-strained understanding. Before our contact failed, we were surprised to observe that, as the new species superseded the old and took over the vast political and economic activity of that world, it came to realize with laughter the futility of all this feverish and aimless living. Under our eyes the old order began to give place to a new and simpler order, in which the world was to be peopled by a small 'aristocratic' population served by machines, freed alike from drudgery and luxury and intent on exploration of the cosmos and the mind.

This change-over to a simpler life happened in several other worlds not by the intervention of a new species, but simply by the victory of the new mentality in its battle against the old.

3. Nautiloids

As our exploration advanced and we gathered more and more helpers from the many worlds that we entered, our imaginative insight into alien natures increased. Though our research was still restricted to races which were in the throes of the familiar spiritual crisis, we gradually acquired the power of making contact with beings whose minds were very far from human in texture. I must now try to give some idea of the main types of these 'non-human' intelligent worlds. In some cases the difference from humanity, though physically striking, and even mentally very remarkable, was not nearly so far-reaching as the cases to be described in the next chapter.

In general the physical and mental form of conscious beings

is an expression of the character of the planet on which they live. On certain very large and aqueous planets, for instance, we found that civilization had been achieved by marine organisms. On these huge globes no land-dwellers as large as a man could possibly thrive, for gravitation would have nailed them to the ground. But in the water there was no such limitation to bulk. One peculiarity of these big worlds was that, owing to the crushing action of gravitation, there were seldom any great elevations and depressions in their surface. Thus they were usually covered by a shallow ocean, broken here and there by archipelagos of small, low islands.

I shall describe one example of this kind of world, the greatest planet of a mighty sun. Situated, if I remember rightly, near the congested heart of the galaxy, this star was born late in galactic history, and it gave birth to planets when already many of the older stars were encrusted with smouldering lava. Owing to the violence of solar radiation its nearer planets had (or will have) stormy climates. On one of them a mollusc-like creature, living in the coastal shallows, acquired a propensity to drift in its boatlike shell on the sea's surface, thus keeping in touch with its drifting vegetable food. As the ages passed, its shell became better adapted to navigation. Mere drifting was supplemented by means of a crude sail, a membrane extending from the creature's back. In time this nautiloid type proliferated into a host of species. Some of these remained minute, but some found size advantageous, and developed into living ships. One of these became the intelligent master of this great world.

The hull was a rigid, stream-lined vessel, shaped much as the nineteenth-century clipper in her prime, and larger than our largest whale. At the rear a tentacle or fin developed into a rudder, which was sometimes used also as a propeller, like a fish's tail. But though all these species could navigate under their own power to some extent, their normal means of long-distance locomotion was their great spread of sail. The simple membranes of the ancestral type had become a system of parchment-like sails and bony masts and spars, under voluntary muscular control. Similarity to a ship was increased by the downward-looking eyes, one on each side of the prow. The mainmast-head also bore eyes, for searching the horizon. An organ of magnetic sensitivity in the brain afforded a reliable means of orientation. At the fore end of the vessel were two long manipulatory tentacles, which during locomotion were folded snugly to the flanks. In use they formed a very serviceable pair of arms.

It may seem strange that a species of this kind should have developed human intelligence. In more than one world of this type, however, a number of accidents combined to produce this result. The change from a vegetarian to a carnivorous habit caused a great increase of animal cunning in pursuit of the much speedier submarine creatures. The sense of hearing was wonderfully developed, for the movements of fish at great distances could be detected by the underwater ears. A line of taste-organs along either bilge responded to the ever-changing composition of the water, and enabled the hunter to track his prey. Delicacy of hearing and of taste combined with omnivorous habits, and with great diversity of behaviour and strong sociality, to favour the growth of intelligence.

Speech, that essential medium of the developed mentality, had two distinct modes in this world. For short-range communication, rhythmic underwater emissions of gas from a vent in the rear of the organism were heard and analysed by means of underwater ears. Long-distance communication was carried on by means of semaphore signals from a rapidly agitating tentacle at the mast head.

The organizing of communal fishing expeditions, the invention of traps, the making of lines and nets, the practice of agriculture, both in the sea and along the shores, the building of stone harbours and workshops, the use of volcanic heat for smelting metals, and of wind for driving mills, the projection of canals into the low islands in search of minerals and fertile ground, the gradual exploration and mapping of a huge world, the harnessing of solar radiation for mechanical power, these and many other achievements were at once a product of intelligence and an opportunity for its advancement.

It was a strange experience to enter the mind of an intelligent ship, to see the foam circling under one's own nose as the vessel plunged through the waves to taste the bitter or delicious currents streaming past one's flanks, to feel the pressure of air on the sails as one beat up against the breeze, to hear beneath the water-line the rush and murmur of distant shoals of fishes, and indeed actually to *hear* the sea-bottom's configuration by means of the echoes that it cast up to the underwater ears. It was strange and terrifying to be caught in a hurricane, to feel the masts straining and the sails threatening to split, while the hull was battered by the small but furious waves of that massive planet. It was strange, too, to watch other great living ships, as they ploughed their way, heeled over, adjusted the set of their yellow or russet sails to the wind's variations; and very strange it was to realize that these were not man-made objects but themselves conscious and purposeful.

Sometimes we saw two of the living ships fighting, tearing at one another's sails with snake-like tentacles, stabbing at one another's soft 'decks' with metal knives, or at a distance firing at one another with cannon. Bewildering and delightful it was to feel in the presence of a slim female clipper the longing for contact, and to carry out with her on the high seas the tacking and yawing, the piratical pursuit and overhauling, the delicate, fleeting caress of tentacles, which formed the love-play of this race. Strange, to come up alongside, close-hauled, grapple her to one's flank, and board her with sexual invasion. It was charming, too, to see a mother ship attended by her children. I should mention, by the way, that at birth the young were launched from the mother's decks like little boats, one from the port side, one from the starboard. Thenceforth they were suckled at her flanks. In play they swam about her like ducklings, or spread their immature sails. In rough weather and for long voyaging they were taken aboard.

At the time of our visit natural sails were beginning to be aided by a power unit and propeller which were fixed to the stern. Great cities of concrete docks had spread along many of the coasts, and were excavated out of the hinterlands. We were delighted by the broad water-ways that served as streets in these cities. They were thronged with sail and mechanized traffic, the children appearing as tugs and smacks among the gigantic elders.

It was in this world that we found in its most striking form a social disease which is perhaps the commonest of all world-diseases—namely, the splitting of the population into two mutually unintelligible castes through the influence of economic forces. So great was the difference between adults of the two castes that they seemed to us at first to be distinct species, and we supposed ourselves to be witnessing the victory of a new and superior biological mutation over its predecessor. But this was far from the truth.

In appearance the masters were very different from the workers, quite as different as queen ants and drones from the workers of their species. They were more elegantly and accurately stream-lined. They had a greater expanse of sail, and were faster in fair weather. In heavy seas they were less seaworthy, owing to their finer lines; but on the other hand they were the more skilful and venturesome navigators. Their manipulatory tentacles were less muscular, but capable of finer adjustments. Their perception was more delicate. While a small minority of them perhaps excelled the best of the workers in endurance and courage, most were much less hardy, both physically and mentally. They were subject to a number of disintegrative diseases which never affected the workers, chiefly diseases of the nervous system. On the other hand, if any of them contracted one of the infectious ailments which were endemic to the workers, but seldom fatal, he would almost certainly die. They were also very prone to mental disorders, and particularly to neurotic self-importance. The whole organization and control of the world was theirs. The workers, on the other hand, though racked by disease and neurosis bred of their cramping environment, were on the whole psychologically more robust. They had, however, a crippling sense of inferiority. Though in handicrafts and all small-scale operations they were capable of intelligence and skill, they were liable, when faced with tasks of wider scope, to a strange paralysis of mind.

The mentalities of the two castes were indeed strikingly different. The masters were more prone to individual initiative and to the vices of self-seeking. The workers were more addicted to collectivism and the vices of subservience to the herd's hypnotic influence. The masters were on the whole more prudent, far-seeing, independent, self-reliant; the workers were more impetuous, more ready to sacrifice themselves in a social cause, often more clearly aware of the right aims of social activity, and incomparably more generous to individuals in distress.

At the time of our visit certain recent discoveries were throwing the world into confusion. Hitherto it had been supposed that the natures of the two castes were fixed unalterably, by divine law and by biological inheritance. But it was now certain that this was not the case, and that the physical and mental differences between the classes were due entirely to nurture. Since time immemorial, the castes had been recruited in a very curious manner. After weaning, all children born on the port side of the mother, no matter what the parental caste, were brought up to be members of the master caste; all those born on the starboard side were brought up to be workers. Since the master class had, of course, to be much smaller than the working class, this system gave an immense superfluity of potential masters. The difficulty was overcome as follows. The starboard-born children of workers and the port-born children of masters were brought up by their own respective parents; but the port-born, potentially aristocratic children of workers were mostly disposed of by infant sacrifice. A few only were exchanged with the starboard-born children of masters.

With the advance of industrialism, the increasing need for large supplies of cheap labour, the spread of scientific ideas and the weakening of religion, came the shocking discovery that port-born children, of both classes, if brought up as workers, became physically and mentally indistinguishable from workers. Industrial magnates in need of plentiful cheap labour now developed moral indignation against infant sacrifice, urging that the excess of port-born infants should be mercifully brought up as workers. Presently certain misguided scientists made the even more subversive discovery that starboard-born children brought up as masters developed the fine lines, the great sails, the delicate constitution, the aristocratic mentality of the master caste. An attempt was made by the masters to prevent this knowledge from spreading to the workers, but certain sentimentalists of their own caste bruited it abroad, and preached a new-fangled and inflammatory doctrine of social equality.

During our visit the world was in terrible confusion. In backward oceans the old system remained unquestioned, but in all the more advanced regions of the planet a desperate struggle was being waged. In one great archipelago a social revolution had put the workers in power, and a devoted though ruthless dictatorship was attempting so to plan the life of the community that the next generation should be homogeneous and of a new type, combining the most desirable characters of both workers and masters. Elsewhere the masters had persuaded their workers that the new ideas were false and base, and certain to lead to universal poverty and misery. A clever appeal was made to the vague but increasing suspicion that 'materialistic science' was misleading and superficial, and that mechanized civilization was crushing out the more spiritual potentialities of the race. Skilled propaganda spread the ideal of a kind of corporate state with 'port and starboard flanks' correlated by a popular dictator, who, it was said, would assume power 'by divine right and the will of the people'.

I must not stay to tell of the desperate struggle which broke out between these two kinds of social organizations. In the world-wide campaigns many a harbour, many an ocean current, flowed red with slaughter. Under the pressure of a war to the death, all that was best, all that was most human and gentle on each side was crushed out by military necessity. On the one side, the passion for a unified world, where every individual should live a free and full life in service of the world community, was overcome by the passion to punish spies, traitors, and heretics. On the other, vague and sadly misguided yearnings for a nobler, less materialistic life were cleverly transformed by the reactionary leaders into vindictiveness against the revolutionaries.

Very rapidly the material fabric of civilization fell to pieces. Not till the race had reduced itself to an almost subhuman savagery, and all the crazy traditions of a diseased civilization had been purged away, along with true culture, could the spirit of these 'ship-men' set out again on the great adventure of the spirit. Many thousands of years later it broke through on to that higher plane of being which I have still to suggest, as best I may.

INTIMATIONS OF THE STAR MAKER

It must not be supposed that the normal fate of intelligent races in the galaxy is to triumph. So far I have spoken mainly of those fortunate Echinoderm and Nautiloid worlds which did at last pass triumphantly into the more awakened state, and I have scarcely even mentioned the hundreds, the thousands, of worlds which met disaster. This selection was inevitable because my space is limited, and because these two worlds, together with the even stranger spheres that I shall describe in the next chapter, were to have great influence on the fortunes of the whole galaxy. But many other worlds of 'human' rank were quite as rich in history as those which I have noticed. Individual lives in them were no less varied than lives elsewhere, and no less crowded with distress and joy. Some triumphed; some in their last phase suffered a downfall, swift or slow, which lent them the splendour of tragedy. But since these worlds play no special part in the main story of the galaxy, they must be passed over in silence, along with the still greater host of worlds which never attained even to 'human' rank. If I were to dwell upon their fortunes I should commit the same error as a historian who should try to describe every private life and neglect the pattern of the whole community.

I have already said that, as our experience of the destruction of worlds increased, we were increasingly dismayed by the wastefulness and seeming aimlessness of the universe. So many worlds, after so much distress, attained so nearly to social peace and joy, only to have the cup snatched from them for ever. Often disaster was brought by some trivial flaw of temperament or biological nature. Some races had not the intelligence, some lacked the social will, to cope with the problems of a unified world-community. Some were destroyed by an upstart bacterium before their medical science was mature. Others succumbed to climatic change, many to loss of atmosphere. Sometimes the end came through collision with dense clouds of dust or gas, or with swarms of giant meteors. Not a few worlds were destroyed by the downfall of a satellite. The lesser body, ploughing its way, age after age, through the extremely rarefied but omnipresent cloud of free atoms in interstellar space, would lose momentum. Its orbit would contract, at first slowly, then rapidly. It would set up prodigious tides in the oceans of the larger body, and drown much of its civilization. Later, through the increasing stress of the planet's attraction, the great moon would begin to disintegrate. First it would cast its ocean in a deluge on men's heads, then its mountains, and then the titanic and fiery fragments of its core. If in none of these manners came the end of the world, then inevitably, though perhaps not till the latter days of the galaxy, it must come in another way. The planet's own orbit, fatally contracting, must bring every world at last so close to its sun that conditions must pass beyond the limit of life's adaptability, and age by age all living things must be parched to death and roasted.

Dismay, terror, horror many a time seized us as we witnessed these huge disasters. An agony of pity for the last survivors of these worlds was part of our schooling.

The most developed of the slaughtered worlds did not need our pity, since their inhabitants seemed capable of meeting the end of all that they cherished with peace, even a strange unshakable joy which we in this early stage of our adventure could by no means comprehend. But only a few, very few, could reach this state. And only a few out of the great host of worlds could win through even to the social peace and fullness towards which all were groping. In the more lowly worlds, moreover, few were the individuals who won any satisfaction of life even within the narrow bounds of their own imperfect nature. No doubt one or two, here and there, in almost every world, found not merely happiness but the joy that passes all understanding. But to us, crushed now by the suffering and futility of a thousand races, it seemed that this joy itself, this ecstasy, whether it was supported by scattered individuals or by whole worlds, must after all be condemned as false, and that those who had found it must after all have been drugged by their own private and untypical well-being of spirit. For surely it had made them insensitive to the horror around them.

The sustaining motive of our pilgrimage had been the hunger which formerly drove men on Earth in search of God. Yes, we had one and all left our native planets in order to discover whether, regarding the cosmos as a whole, the spirit which we all in our hearts obscurely knew and haltingly prized, the spirit which on Earth we sometimes call humane, was Lord of the Universe, or outlaw; almighty, or crucified. And now it was becoming clear to us that if the cosmos had any lord at all, he was not that spirit but some other, whose purpose in creating the endless fountain of worlds was not fatherly towards the beings that he had made, but alien, inhuman, dark.

Yet while we felt dismay, we felt also increasingly the hunger to see and to face fearlessly whatever spirit was indeed the spirit of this cosmos. For as we pursued our pilgrimage, passing again and again from tragedy to farce, from farce to glory, from glory often to a final tragedy, we felt increasingly the sense that some terrible, some holy, yet at the same time unimaginably outrageous and lethal, secret lay just beyond our reach. Again and again we were torn between horror and fascination, between moral rage against the universe (or the Star Maker) and unreasonable worship.

This same conflict was to be observed in all those worlds that were of our own mental stature. Observing these worlds and the phases of their past growth, and groping as best we might towards the next plane of spiritual development, we came at last to see plainly the first stages of any world's pilgrimage. Even in the most primitive ages of every normal intelligent world there existed in some minds the impulse to seek and to praise some universal thing. At first this impulse was confused with the craving for protection by some mighty power. Inevitably the beings theorized that the admired thing must be

Power, and that worship was mere propitiation. Thus they came to conceive the almighty tyrant of the universe, with themselves as his favoured children. But in time it became clear to their prophets that mere Power was not what the praiseful heart adored. Then theory enthroned Wisdom, or Law, or Righteousness. And after an age of obedience to some phantom lawgiver, or to divine legality itself, the beings found that these concepts too were inadequate to describe the indescribable glory that the heart confronted in all things, and mutely prized in all things.

But now, in every world that we visited, alternative ways opened out before the worshippers. Some hoped to come face to face with their shrouded god solely by inward-searching meditation. By purging themselves of all lesser, all trivial desires, by striving to see everything dispassionately and with universal sympathy, they hoped to identify themselves with the spirit of the cosmos. Often they travelled far along the way of self-perfecting and awakening. But because of this inward absorption most of them became insensitive to the suffering of their less-awakened fellows and careless of the communal enterprise of their kind. In not a few worlds this way of the spirit was thronged by all the most vital minds. And because the best attention of the race was given wholly to the inner life, material and social advancement was checked. The sciences of physical nature and of life never developed. Mechanical power remained unknown, and medical and biological power also. Consequently these worlds stagnated, and sooner or later succumbed to accidents which might well have been prevented.

There was a second way of devotion, open to creatures of a more practical temperament. These, in all the worlds, gave delighted attention to the universe around them, and chiefly they found the worshipped thing in the persons of their fellow-beings, and in the communal bond of mutual insight and love between persons. In themselves and in each other they prized above all things love.

And their prophets told them that the thing which they had always adored, the universal spirit, the Creator, the Almighty, the All-wise, was also the All-loving. Let them therefore worship in practical love of one another, and in service of the Love-God. And so for an age, short or long, they strove feebly to love and to become members one of another. They spun theories in defence of the theory of the Love-God. They set up priesthoods and temples in service of Love. And because they hungered for immortality they were told that to love was the way to attain eternal life. And so love, which seeks no reward, was misconceived.

In most worlds these practical minds dominated over the meditators. Sooner or later practical curiosity and economic need produced the material sciences. Probing every region with these sciences, the beings found nowhere, neither in the atom nor in the galaxy, nor for that matter in the heart of 'man' either, any signature of the Love-God. And what with the fever of mechanization, and the exploitation of slaves by masters, and the passions of inter-tribal warfare, and the increasing neglect or coarsening of all the more awakened activities of the spirit, the little flame of praise in their hearts sank lower than it had ever been in any earlier age, so low that they could no longer recognize it. And the flame of love, long fanned by the forced draught of doctrine, but now suffocated by the general obtuseness of the beings to one another, was reduced to an occasional smouldering warmth, which was most often mistaken for mere lust. With bitter laughter and rage the tortured beings now dethroned the image of the Love-God in their hearts.

And so without love and without worship the unhappy beings faced the increasingly formidable problems of their mechanized and hate-racked world.

This was the crisis which we in our own worlds knew so well. Many a world up and down the galaxy never surmounted it. But in a few, some miracle, which we could not yet clearly envisage, raised the average minds of these worlds to a higher plane of mentality. Of this I shall speak later. Meanwhile I will say only that in the few worlds where this happened, we noticed invariably, before the minds of that world passed beyond our reach, a new feeling about the universe, a feeling which it was very difficult for us to share. Not till we had learned to conjure in ourselves something of this feeling could we follow the fortunes of these worlds.

But, as we advanced on our pilgrimage, our own desires began to change. We came to wonder whether, in demanding lordship of the universe for the divinely humane spirit that we prized most in ourselves and in our fellow-mortals in all the worlds, we were perhaps impious. We came less and less to require that Love should be enthroned behind the stars; more and more we desired merely to pass on, opening our hearts to accept fearlessly whatever of the truth might fall within our comprehension.

There was a moment, late in this early phase of our pilgrimage, when, thinking and feeling in unison, we said to one another, 'If the Star Maker is Love, we know that this must be right. But if he is not, if he is some other, some inhuman spirit, *this* must be right. And if he is nothing, if the stars and all else are not his creatures but self-subsistent, and if the adored spirit is but an exquisite creature of our minds, then *this* must be right, this and no other possibility. For we cannot know whether the highest place for love is on the throne or on the cross. We cannot know what spirit rules, for on the throne sits darkness. We know, we have seen, that in the waste of stars love is indeed crucified; and rightly, for its own proving, and for the throne's glory. Love and all that is humane we cherish in our hearts. Yet also we salute the throne and the darkness upon the throne. Whether it be Love or not Love, our hearts praise it, out-soaring reason.'

But before our hearts could be properly attuned to this new, strange feeling, we had still far to go in the understanding of worlds of human rank, though diverse. I must now try to give some idea of several kinds of worlds very different from our own, but not in essentials more mature.

MORE WORLDS

1. A Symbiotic Race

On certain large planets, whose climates, owing to the proximity of a violent sun, were very much hotter than our tropics, we sometimes found an intelligent fish-like race. It was bewildering to us to discover that a submarine world could give rise to mentality of human rank, and to that drama of the spirit which we had now so often encountered.

The very shallow and sun-drenched oceans of these great planets provided an immense diversity of habitats and a great wealth of living things. Green vegetation, which could be classified as tropical, subtropical, temperate, and arctic, basked on the bright ocean floors. There were submarine prairies and forests. In some regions the giant weeds stretched from the sea-bottom to the waves. In these jungles the blue and blinding light of the sun was reduced almost to darkness. Immense coral-like growths, honeycombed with passages and swarming with all manner of live-things, lifted their spires and turrets to the surface. Innumerable kinds of fish-like creatures of all sizes from sprat to whale inhabited the many levels of the waters, some gliding on the bottom, some daring an occasional leap into the torrid air. In the deepest and darkest regions hosts of sea-monsters, eyeless or luminous, browsed on the ceaseless rain of corpses which sank from the upper levels. Over their deep world lay other worlds of increasing brightness and colour, where gaudy populations basked, browsed, stalked, or hunted with arrowy flight.

Intelligence in these planets was generally achieved by some unimposing social creature, neither fish nor octopus nor crustacean, but something of all three. It would be equipped with manipulatory tentacles, keen eyes, and subtle brain. It would

make nests of weed in the crevices of the coral, or build strong-
holds of coral masonry. In time would appear traps, weapons,
tools, submarine agriculture, the blossoming of primitive art,
the ritual of primitive religion. Then would follow the typical
fluctuating advance of the spirit from barbarism to civilization.

One of these submarine worlds was exceptionally interesting. Early in the life of our galaxy, when few of the stars had
yet condensed from the 'giant' to the solar type, when very few
planetary births had yet occurred, a double star and a single
star in a congested cluster did actually approach one another,
reach fiery filaments towards one another, and spawn a planet
brood. Of these worlds, one, an immense and very aqueous
sphere, produced in time a dominant race which was not a
single species but an intimate symbiotic partnership of two
very alien creatures. The one came of a fish-like stock. The
other was in appearance something like a crustacean. In form
it was a sort of paddle-footed crab or marine spider. Unlike our
crustaceans, it was covered not with a brittle carapace but with
a tough pachydermatous hide. In maturity this serviceable jer-
kin was more or less rigid, save at the joints; but in youth it
was very pliant to the still-expanding brain. This creature lived
on the coasts and in the coastal waters of the many islands of
the planet. Both species were mentally of human rank, though
each had specific temperament and ability. In primitive times
each had attained by its own route and in its own hemisphere
of the great aqueous planet to what might be called the last
stage of the subhuman mentality. The two species had then
come into contact, and had grappled desperately. Their battle-
ground was the shallow coastal water. The 'crustaceans',
though crudely amphibian, could not spend long under the sea;
the 'fish' could not emerge from it.

The two races did not seriously compete with one another
in economic life, for the 'fish' were mainly vegetarian, the
'crustaceans' mainly carnivorous; yet neither could tolerate the
presence of the other. Both were sufficiently human to be
aware of one another as rival aristocrats in a subhuman world,
but neither was human enough to realize that for each race the

way of life lay in cooperation with the other. The fish-like creatures, which I shall call 'ichthyoids', had speed and range of travel. They had also the security of bulk. The crab-like or spider-like 'crustaceans', which I shall call 'arachnoids', had greater manual dexterity, and had also access to the dry land. Co-operation would have been very beneficial to both species, for one of the staple foods of the arachnoids was parasitic to the ichthyoids.

In spite of the possibility of mutual aid, the two races strove to exterminate one another, and almost succeeded. After an age of blind mutual slaughter, certain of the less pugnacious and more flexible varieties of the two species gradually discovered profit in fraternization with the enemy. This was the beginning of a very remarkable partnership. Soon the arachnoids took to riding on the backs of the swift ichthyoids, and thus gained access to more remote hunting grounds.

As the epochs passed, the two species moulded one another to form a well-integrated union. The little arachnoid, no bigger than a chimpanzee, rode in a snug hollow behind the great 'fish's' skull, his back being stream-lined with the contours of the larger creature. The tentacles of the ichthyoid were special- ized for large-scale manipulation, those of the arachnoid for minute work. A biochemical interdependence also evolved. Through a membrane in the ichthyoid's pouch an exchange of endocrine products took place. This mechanism enabled the arachnoid to become fully aquatic. So long as it had frequent contact with its host, it could stay under water for any length of time and descend to any depth. A striking mental adaptation also occurred in the two species. The ichthyoids became on the whole more introvert, the arachnoids more extravert.

Up to puberty the young of both species were free-living individuals; but, as their symbiotic organization developed, each sought out a partner of the opposite species. The union which followed was life-long, and was interrupted only by brief sexual matings. The symbiosis itself constituted a kind of contrapuntal sexuality; but a sexuality that was purely mental, since, of course, for copulation and reproduction each individ- ual had to seek out a partner belonging to his or her own

species. We found, however, that even the symbiotic partnership consisted invariably of a male of one species and a female
of the other; and the male, whichever his species, behaved with
parental devotion to the young of his symbiotic partner.

I have not space to describe the extraordinary mental reciprocity of these strange couples. I can only say that, though in
sensory equipment and in temperament the two species were
very different, and though in abnormal cases tragic conflicts
did occur, the ordinary partnership was at once more intimate
than human marriage and far more enlarging to the individual
than any friendship between members of distinct human races.
At certain stages of the growth of civilization malicious minds
had attempted to arouse widespread interspecific conflict, and
had met with temporary success; but the trouble seldom went
as deep even as our 'sex war', so necessary was each species to
the other. Both had contributed equally to the culture of their
world, though not equally at all times. In creative work of
every kind one of the partners provided most of the originality,
the other most of the criticism and restraint. Work in which
one partner was entirely passive was rare. Books, or rather
scrolls, which were made from pulped seaweed, were nearly
always signed by couples. On the whole the arachnoid partners
dominated in manual skill, experimental science, the plastic
arts, and practical social organization. The ichthyoid partners
excelled in theoretical work, in literary arts, in the surprisingly
developed music of that submarine world, and in the more
mystical kind of religion. This generalization, however, should
not be interpreted very strictly.

The symbiotic relationship seems to have given the dual race
a far greater mental flexibility than ours, and a quicker aptitude
for community. It passed rapidly through the phase of inter-
tribal strife, during which the nomadic shoals of symbiotic
couples harried one another like hosts of submarine cavalry;
for the arachnoids, riding their ichthyoid mates, attacked the
enemy with bone spears and swords, while their mounts wres-
tled with powerful tentacles. But the phase of tribal warfare
was remarkably brief. When a settled mode of life was at-

tained, along with submarine agriculture and coral-built cities, strife between leagues of cities was the exception, not the rule. Aided no doubt by its great mobility and ease of communication, the dual race soon built up a world-wide and unarmed federation of cities. We learned also with wonder that at the height of the pre-mechanical civilization of this planet, when in our worlds the cleavage into masters and economic slaves would already have become serious, the communal spirit of the city triumphed over all individualistic enterprise. Very soon this world became a tissue of interdependent but independent municipal communes.

At this time it seemed that social strife had vanished for ever. But the most serious crisis of the race was still to come.

The submarine environment offered the symbiotic race no great possibilities of advancement. All sources of wealth had been tapped and regularized. Population was maintained at an optimum size for the joyful working of the world. The social order was satisfactory to all classes, and seemed unlikely to change. Individual lives were full and varied. Culture, founded on a great tradition, was now concerned entirely with detailed exploration of the great fields of thought that had long ago been pioneered by the revered ancestors, under direct inspiration, it was said, of the symbiotic deity. Our friends in this submarine world, our mental hosts, looked back on this age from their own more turbulent epoch sometimes with yearning, but often with horror; for in retrospect it seemed to them to display the first faint signs of racial decay. So perfectly did the race fit its unchanging environment that intelligence and acuity were already ceasing to be precious, and might soon begin to fade. But presently it appeared that fate had decreed otherwise.

In a submarine world the possibility of obtaining mechanical power was remote. But the arachnoids, it will be remembered, were able to live out of the water. In the epochs before the symbiosis their ancestors had periodically emerged upon the islands, for courtship, parenthood, and the pursuit of prey. Since those days the air-breathing capacity had declined, but it had never been entirely lost. Every arachnoid still emerged for sexual mating, and also for certain ritual gymnastic exercises. It was in this latter connection that the great discovery was made which changed the course of history. At a certain tournament the friction of stone weapons, clashing against one another, produced sparks, and fire among the sun-scorched grasses.

In startlingly quick succession came smelting, the steam engine, the electric current. Power was obtained first from the combustion of a sort of peat formed on the coasts by congested marine vegetation, later from the constant and violent winds, later still from photochemical light traps which absorbed the sun's lavish radiation. These inventions were of course the work of arachnoids. The ichthyoids, though they still played a great part in the systematization of knowledge, were debarred from the great practical work of scientific experiment and mechanical invention above the seas. Soon the arachnoids were running electric cables from the island power-stations to the submarine cities. In this work, at least, the ichthyoids could take part, but their part was necessarily subordinate. Not only in experience of electrical engineering but also in native practical ability they were eclipsed by their arachnoid partners.

For a couple of centuries or more the two species continued to co-operate, though with increasing strain. Artificial lighting, mechanical transport of goods on the ocean floor, and large-scale manufacture, produced an immense increase in the amenities of life in the submarine cities. The islands were crowded with buildings devoted to science and industry. Physics, chemistry, and biology made great progress. Astronomers began to map the galaxy. They also discovered that a neighbouring planet offered wonderful opportunities for settlement by arachnoids, who might without great difficulty, it was hoped, be conditioned to the alien climate, and to divorce from their symbiotic partners. The first attempts at rocket flight were leading to mingled tragedy and success. The directorate of extra-marine activities demanded a much increased arachnoid population.

Inevitably there arose a conflict between the two species, and in the mind of every individual of either species. It was at the height of this conflict, and in the spiritual crisis in virtue of which these beings were accessible to us in our novitiate stage, that we first entered this world. The ichthyoids had not yet succumbed biologically to their inferior position, but psychologically they were already showing signs of deep mental decay. A profound disheartenment and lassitude attacked them, like that which so often undermines our primitive races when they find themselves struggling in the flood of European civilization. But since in the case of the symbiotics the relation between the two races was extremely intimate, far more so than that between the most intimate human beings, the plight of the ichthyoids deeply affected the arachnoids. And in the minds of the ichthyoids the triumph of their partners was for long a source of mingled distress and exultation.

Every individual of both species was torn between conflicting motives. While every healthy arachnoid longed to take part in the adventurous new life, he or she longed also, through sheer affection and symbiotic entanglement, to assist his or her ichthyoid mate to have an equal share in that life. Further, all arachnoids were aware of subtle dependence on their mates, a dependence at once physiological and psychological. It was the ichthyoids who mostly contributed to the mental symbiosis the power of self-knowledge and mutual insight, and the contemplation which is so necessary to keep action sweet and sane. That this was so was evident from the fact that already among the arachnoids internecine strife had appeared. Island tended to compete with island, and one great industrial organization with another.

I could not help remarking that if this deep cleavage of interests had occurred on my own planet, say between our two sexes, the favoured sex would have single-mindedly trampled the other into servitude. Such a 'victory' on the part of the arachnoids did indeed nearly occur. More and more partnerships were dissolved, each member attempting by means of drugs to supply his or her system with the chemicals normally provided by the symbiosis. For mental dependence, however, there was no substitute, and the divorced partners were subject to serious mental disorders, either subtle or flagrant. Nevertheless, there grew up a large population capable of living after a fashion without the symbiotic intercourse.

Strife now took a violent turn. The intransigents of both species attacked one another, and stirred up trouble among the moderates. There followed a period of desperate and confused warfare. On each side a small and hated minority advocated a 'modernized symbiosis', in which each species should be able to contribute to the common life even in a mechanized civilization. Many of these reformers were martyred for their faith.

Victory would in the long run have gone to the arachnoids, for they controlled the sources of power. But it soon appeared that the attempt to break the symbiotic bond was not as successful as it had seemed. Even in actual warfare, commanders were unable to prevent widespread fraternization between the opposed forces. Members of dissolved partnerships would furtively meet to snatch a few hours or moments of each other's company. Widowed or deserted individuals of each species would timidly but hungrily venture towards the enemy's camps in search of new mates. Whole companies would surrender for the same purpose. The arachnoids suffered more from neuroses than from the weapons of the enemy. On the islands, moreover, civil wars and social revolutions made the manufacture of munitions almost impossible.

The most resolute faction of the arachnoids now attempted to bring the struggle to an end by poisoning the ocean. The islands in turn were poisoned by the millions of decaying corpses that rose to the sea's surface and were cast up on the shores. Poison, plague, and above all neurosis, brought war to a standstill, civilization to ruin, and the two species almost to extinction. The deserted sky-scrapers that crowded the islands began to crumble into heaps of wreckage. The submarine cities were invaded by the submarine jungle and by shark-like subhuman ichthyoids of many species. The delicate tissue of knowledge began to disintegrate into fragments of superstition.

Now at last came the opportunity of those who advocated a modernized symbiosis. With difficulty they had maintained a secret existence and their individual partnerships in the more remote and inhospitable regions of the planet. They now came boldly forth to spread their gospel among the unhappy remnants of the world's population. There was a rage of interspecific mating and remating. Primitive submarine agriculture and hunting maintained the scattered people while a few of the coral cities were cleared and rebuilt, and the instruments of a lean but hopeful civilization were refashioned. This was a temporary civilization, without mechanical power, but one which promised itself great adventures in the 'upper world' as soon as it had established the basic principles of the reformed symbiosis.

To us it seemed that such an enterprise was doomed to failure, so clear was it that the future lay with a terrestrial rather than a marine creature. But we were mistaken. I must not tell in detail of the heroic struggle by which the race refashioned its symbiotic nature to suit the career that lay before it. The first stage was the reinstatement of power stations on the islands, and the careful reorganization of a purely submarine society equipped with power. But this reconstruction would have been useless had it not been accompanied by a very careful study of the physical and mental relations of the two species. The symbiosis had to be strengthened so that interspecific strife should in future be impossible. By means of chemical treatment in infancy the two kinds of organism were made more interdependent, and in partnership more hardy. By a special psychological ritual, a sort of mutual hypnosis, all newly joined partners were henceforth brought into indissoluble mental reciprocity. This interspecific communion, which every individual knew in immediate domestic experience, became in time the basic experience of all culture and religion.

The symbiotic deity, which figured in all the primitive my-
thologies, was reinstated as a symbol of the dual personality
of the universe, a dualism, it was said, of creativity and wisdom, unified as the divine spirit of love. The one reasonable
goal of social life was affirmed to be the creation of a world of
awakened, of sensitive, intelligent, and mutually understanding personalities, banded together for the common purpose of
exploring the universe and developing the 'human' spirit's
manifold potentialities. Imperceptibly the young were led to
discover for themselves this goal.

Gradually and very cautiously all the industrial operations
and scientific researches of an earlier age were repeated, but
with a difference. Industry was subordinated to the conscious
social goal. Science, formerly the slave of industry, became the
free colleague of wisdom.

Once more the islands were crowded with buildings and
with eager arachnoid workers. But all the shallow coastal waters were filled with a vast honeycomb of dwelling-houses,
where the symbiotic partners took rest and refreshment with
their mates. In the ocean depths the old cities were turned into
schools, universities, museums, temples, palaces of art and of
pleasure. There the young of both kinds grew up together.
There the full-grown of both species met constantly for recrea-
tion and stimulation. There, while the arachnoids were busy on
the islands, the ichthyoids performed their work of education
and of refashioning the whole theoretical culture of the world.
For it was known clearly by now that in this field their temperament and talents could make a vital contribution to the common life. Thus literature, philosophy, and non-scientific education were carried out chiefly in the ocean; while on the
islands industry, scientific inquiry, and the plastic arts were
more prominent.

Perhaps, in spite of the close union of each couple, this
strange division of labour would have led in time to renewed
conflict, had it not been for two new discoveries. One was the
development of telepathy. Several centuries after the Age of
War it was found possible to establish full telepathic intercourse between the two members of each couple. In time this

intercourse was extended to include the whole dual race. The first result of this change was a great increase in the facility of communication between individuals all over the world, and therewith a great increase in mutual understanding and in unity of social purpose. But before we lost touch with this rapidly advancing race we had evidence of a much more far-reaching effect of universal telepathy. Sometimes, so we were told, telepathic communion of the whole race caused something like the fragmentary awakening of a communal world-mind in which all individuals participated.

The second great innovation of the race was due to genetic research. The arachnoids, who had to remain capable of active life on dry land and on a massive planet, could not achieve any great improvement in brain weight and complexity; but the ichthyoids, who were already large and were buoyed up by the water, were not subject to this limitation. After long and often disastrous experiment a race of 'super-ichthyoids' was produced. In time the whole ichthyoid population came to consist of these creatures. Meanwhile the arachnoids, who were by now exploring and colonizing other planets of their solar system, were genetically improved not in respect of general brain complexity but in those special brain centres which afforded telepathic intercourse. Thus, in spite of their simpler brain-structure, they were able to maintain full telepathic community even with their big-brained mates far away in the oceans of the mother-planet. The simple brains and the complex brains formed now a single system, in which each unit, however simple its own contribution, was sensitive to the whole.

It was at this point, when the original ichthyoid race had given place to the super-ichthyoids, that we finally lost touch. The experience of the dual race passed completely beyond our comprehension. At a much later stage of our adventure we came upon them again, and on a higher plane of being. They were by then already engaged upon the vast common enterprise which, as I shall tell, was undertaken by the Galactic Society of Worlds. At this time the symbiotic race consisted of an immense host of arachnoid adventurers scattered over many planets, and a company of some fifty thousand million super-ichthyoids living a life of natatory delight and intense mental activity in the ocean of their great native world. Even at this stage physical contact between the symbiotic partners had to be maintained, though at long intervals. There was a constant stream of space-ships between the colonies and the mother-world. The ichthyoids, together with their teeming colleagues on a score of planets, supported a racial mind. Though the threads of the common experience were spun by the whole symbiotic race, they were woven into a single web by the ichthyoids alone in their primeval oceanic home, to be shared by all members of both races.

2. Composite Beings

Sometimes in the course of our adventure we came upon worlds inhabited by intelligent beings, whose developed personality was an expression not of the single individual organism but of a group of organisms. In most cases this state of affairs had arisen through the necessity of combining intelligence with lightness of the individual body. A large planet, rather close to its sun, or swayed by a very large satellite, would be swept by great ocean tides. Vast areas of its surface would be periodically submerged and exposed. In such a world, flight was very desirable, but owing to the strength of gravitation only a small creature, a relatively small mass of molecules, could fly. A brain large enough for complex 'human' activity could not have been lifted.

In such worlds the organic basis of intelligence was often a swarm of avian creatures no bigger than sparrows. A host of individual bodies were possessed together by a single individual mind of human rank. The body of this mind was multiple, but the mind itself was almost as firmly knit as the mind of a man. As flocks of dunlin or redshank stream and wheel and soar and quiver over our estuaries, so above the great tide-flooded cultivated regions of these worlds the animated clouds

of avians manoeuvred, each cloud a single centre of consciousness. Presently, like our own winged waders, the little avians
would settle, the huge volume of the cloud shrinking to a mere
film upon the ground, a sort of precipitate along the fringe of
the receding tide.

Life in these worlds was rhythmically divided by the tides.
During the nocturnal tides the bird-clouds all slept on the
waves. During the daytime tides they indulged in aerial sports
and religious exercises. But twice a day, when the land was dry,
they cultivated the drenched ooze, or carried out in their cities
of concrete cells all the operations of industry and culture. It
was interesting to us to see how ingeniously, before the tide's
return, all the instruments of civilization were sealed from the
ravages of the water.

We supposed at first that the mental unity of these little
avians was telepathic, but in fact it was not. It was based on
the unity of a complex electro-magnetic field, in fact on 'radio'
waves permeating the whole group. Radio, transmitted and
received by every individual organism, corresponded to the
chemical nerve current which maintains the unity of the
human nervous system. Each brain reverberated with the
ethereal rhythms of its environment; and each contributed its
own peculiar theme to the complex pattern of the whole. So
long as the flock was within a volume of about a cubic mile,
the individuals were mentally unified, each serving as a specialized centre in the common 'brain'. But if some were separated from the flock, as sometimes happened in stormy
weather, they lost mental contact and became separate minds
of very low order. In fact each degenerated for the time being
into a very simple instinctive animal or a system of reflexes, set
wholly for the task of restoring contact with the flock.

It may easily be imagined that the mental life of these composite beings was very different from anything which we had
yet encountered. Different and yet the same. Like a man, the
bird-cloud was capable of anger and fear, hunger and sexual
hunger, personal love and all the passions of the herd; but the
medium of these experiences was so different from anything
known to us that we found great difficulty in recognizing them.

Sex, for instance, was very perplexing. Each cloud was bisexual, having some hundreds of specialized male and female avian units, indifferent to one another, but very responsive to the presence of other bird-clouds. We found that in these strange multiple beings the delight and shame of bodily contact were obtained not only through actual sexual union of the specialized sexual members but, with the most exquisite subtlety, in the aerial interfusion of two flying clouds during the performance of courtship gymnastics in the air.

More important for us than this superficial likeness to ourselves was an underlying parity of mental rank. Indeed, we should not have gained access to them at all had it not been for the essential similarity of their evolutionary stage with that which we knew so well in our own worlds. For each one of these mobile minded clouds of little birds was in fact an individual approximately of our own spiritual order, indeed a very human thing, torn between the beast and the angel, capable of ecstasies of love and hate towards other such bird-clouds, capable of wisdom and folly, and the whole gamut of human passions from swinishness to ecstatic contemplation.

Probing as best we could beyond the formal similarity of spirit which gave us access to the bird-clouds, we discovered painfully how to see with a million eyes at once, how to feel the texture of the atmosphere with a million wings. We learned to interpret the composite percepts of mud-flats and marshes and great agricultural regions, irrigated twice daily by the tide. We admired the great tide-driven turbines and the system of electric transport of freight. We discovered that the forests of high concrete poles or minarets, and platforms on stilts, which stood in the shallowest of the tidal areas, were nurseries where the young were tended till they could fly.

Little by little we learned to understand something of the alien thought of these strange beings, which was in its detailed texture so different from our own, yet in general pattern and significance so similar. Time presses, and I must not try even to sketch the immense complexity of the most developed of these worlds. So much else has still to be told. I will say only that, since the individuality of these bird-clouds was more precarious than human individuality, it was apt to be better understood and more justly valued. The constant danger of the bird-clouds was physical and mental disintegration. Consequently the ideal of the coherent self was very prominent in all their cultures. On the other hand, the danger that the self of the bird-cloud would be psychically invaded and violated by its neighbours, much as one radio station may interfere with another, forced these beings to guard more carefully than ourselves against the temptations of the herd, against drowning the individual cloud's self in the mob of clouds. But again, just because this danger was effectively guarded against, the ideal of the world-wide community developed without any life-and-death struggle with mystical tribalism, such as we know too well. Instead the struggle was simply between individualism and the twin ideals of the world community and the world-mind.

At the time of our visit world-wide conflict was already breaking out between the two parties in every region of the planet. The individualists were stronger in one hemisphere, and were slaughtering all adherents of the world-mind ideal, and mustering their forces for attack on the other hemisphere. Here the party of the world-mind dominated, not by weapons but by sheer radio-bombardment, so to speak. The pattern of ethereal undulations issuing from the party imposed itself by sheer force on all recalcitrants. All rebels were either mentally disintegrated by radio-bombardment or were absorbed intact into the communal radio system.

The war which ensued was to us astounding. The individualists used artillery and poison gas. The party of the world-mind used these weapons far less than the radio, which they, but not their enemies, could operate with irresistible effect. So greatly was the radio system strengthened, and so adapted to the physiological receptivity of the avian units, that before the individualists had done serious harm, they found themselves engulfed, so to speak, in an overwhelming torrent of radio stimulation. Their individuality crumbled away. The avian units that made up their composite bodies were either destroyed (if they were specialized for war), or reorganized into new clouds, loyal to the world-mind.

Shortly after the defeat of the individualists we lost touch with this race. The experience and the social problems of the young world-mind were incomprehensible to us. Not till a much later stage of our adventure did we regain contact with it.

Others of the world inhabited by races of bird-clouds were less fortunate. Most, through one cause or another, came to grief. In many of them the stresses of industrialism or of social unrest brought about a plague of insanity, or disintegration of the individual into a swarm of mere reflex animals. These miserable little creatures, which had not the power of independent intelligent behaviour, were slaughtered in myriads by natural forces and beasts of prey. Presently the stage was clear for some worm or amoeba to reinaugurate the great adventure of biological evolution towards the human plane.

In the course of our exploration we came upon other types of composite individuals. For instance, we found that very large dry planets were sometimes inhabited by populations of insect-like creatures each of whose swarms or nests was the multiple body of a single mind. These planets were so large that no mobile organism could be bigger than a beetle, no flying organism bigger than an ant. In the intelligent swarms that fulfilled the part of men in these worlds, the microscopic brains of the insect-like units were specialized for microscopic functions within the group, much as the members of an ant's nest are specialized for working, fighting, reproduction, and so on. All were mobile, but each class of the units fulfilled special 'neurological' functions in the life of the whole. In fact they acted as though they were special types of cells in a nervous system.

In these worlds, as in the worlds of the bird-clouds, we had to accustom ourselves to the unified awareness of a huge swarm of units. With innumerable hurrying feet we crept along Lilliputian concrete passages, with innumerable manipulatory antennae we took part in obscure industrial or agricultural operations, or in the navigation of toy ships on the canals and lakes of these flat worlds. Through innumerable many-faceted eyes we surveyed the plains of moss-like vegetation or studied the stars with minute telescopes and spectroscopes.

So perfectly organized was the life of the minded swarm that all routine activities of industry and agriculture had become, from the point of view of the swarm's mind, unconscious, like the digestive processes of a human being. The little insectoid units themselves carried on these operations consciously, though without understanding their significance; but the mind of the swarm had lost the power of attending to them. Its concern was almost wholly with such activities as called for unified conscious control, in fact with practical and theoretical invention of all kinds and with physical and mental exploration.

At the time of our visit to the most striking of these insectoid worlds the world-population consisted of many great nations of swarms. Each individual swarm had its own nest, its Lilliputian city, an area of about an acre, in which the ground was honeycombed to a depth of two feet with chambers and passages. The surrounding district was devoted to the cultivation of the moss-like food-plants. As the swarm increased in size, colonies might be founded beyond the range of the physiological radio system of the parent swarm. Thus arose new group-individuals. But neither in this race, nor in the race of bird-clouds, was there anything corresponding to our successive generations of individual minds. Within the minded group, the insectoid units were ever dying off and giving place to fresh units, but the mind of the group was potentially immortal. The units succeeded one another; the group-self persisted. Its memory reached back past countless generations of units, fading as it receded, and finally losing itself in that archaic time when the 'human' was emerging from the 'subhuman'. Thus the civilized swarms had vague and fragmentary memories of every historical period.

Civilization had turned the old disorderly warrens into carefully planned subterranean cities; had turned the old irrigation channels into a widespread mesh of waterways for the transport of freight from district to district; had introduced mechanical power, based on the combustion of vegetable matter; had smelted metals from outcrops and alluvial deposits; had produced the extraordinary tissue of minute, almost microscopic machinery which had so greatly improved the comfort and health of the more advanced regions; had produced also myriads of tiny vehicles, corresponding to our tractors, trains, ships; had created class distinctions between those group-individuals that remained primarily agricultural, those that were mainly industrial, and those that specialized in intelligent co-ordination of their country's activities. These last became in time the bureaucratic tyrants of the country.

Owing to the great size of the planet and the extreme difficulty of long-distance travel by creatures so small as the insectoid units, civilizations had developed independently in a score of insulated regions; and when at last they came in contact, many of them were already highly industrialized, and equipped with the most 'modern' weapons. The reader may easily imagine what happened when races that were in most cases biologically of different species, and anyhow were completely alien in customs, thought, and ideals, suddenly found themselves in contact and in conflict. It would be wearisome to describe the insane warfare which ensued. But it is of interest to note that we, the telepathic visitors from regions remote in time and space, could communicate with these warring hosts more easily than one host could communicate with another. And through this power we were actually able to play an important part in the history of this world. Indeed, it was probably through our mediation that these races were saved from mutual destruction. Taking up positions in 'key' minds on each side of the conflict, we patiently induced in our hosts some insight into the mentality of the enemy. And since each of these races had already passed far beyond the

level of sociality known on the Earth, since in relation to the
life of his own race a swarm-mind was capable of true community, the realization of the enemy as being not monstrous
but essentially humane, was enough to annihilate the will to
fight.

The 'key' minds on either side, enlightened by 'divine mes-
sengers', heroically preached peace. And though many of them
were hastily martyred, their cause triumphed. The races made
terms with each other; all save two formidable and culturally
rather backward peoples. These we could not persuade; and
as they were by now highly specialized for war, they were a
very serious menace. They regarded the new spirit of peace as
mere weakness on the part of the enemy, and they were determined to take advantage of it, and to conquer the rest of that
world.

But now we witnessed a drama which to terrestrial man
must surely seem incredible. It was possible in this world only
because of the high degree of mental lucidity which had already been attained within the bounds of each race. The pacific
races had the courage to disarm. In the most spectacular and
unmistakable manner they destroyed their weapons and their
munition factories. They took care, too, that these events
should be witnessed by enemy-swarms that had been taken
prisoner. These captives they then freed, bidding them report
their experiences to the enemy. In reply the enemy invaded the
nearest of the disarmed countries and set about ruthlessly imposing the military culture upon it, by means of propaganda
and persecution. But in spite of mass executions and mass
torture, the upshot was not what was expected. For though the
tyrant races were not appreciably more developed in sociality
than *Homo Sapiens*, the victims were far superior. Repression
only strengthened the will for passive resistance. Little by little
the tyranny began to waver. Then suddenly it collapsed. The
invaders withdrew, taking with them the infection of pacifism.
In a surprisingly short time that world became a federation,
whose members were distinct species.

With sadness I realized that on the Earth, though all civilized
beings belong to one and the same biological species, such a

happy issue of strife is impossible, simply because the capacity for community in the individual mind is still too weak. I wondered, too, whether the tyrant races of insectoids would have had greater success in imposing their culture on the invaded country if there had been a distinct generation of juvenile malleable swarms for them to educate.

When this insectoid world had passed through its crisis, it began to advance so rapidly in social structure and in development of the individual mind that we found increasing difficulty in maintaining contact. At last we lost touch. But later, when we ourselves had advanced, we were to come upon this world again.

Of the other insectoid worlds, I shall say nothing, for not one of them was destined to play an important part in the history of the galaxy.

To complete the picture of the races in which the individual mind had not a single, physically continuous, body, I must refer to a very different and even stranger kind. In this the individual body is a cloud of ultramicroscopic sub-vital units, organized in a common radio-system. Of this kind is the race which now inhabits our own planet Mars. As I have already in another book described these beings and the tragic relations which they will have with our own descendants in the remote future, I shall say no more of them here; save that we did not make contact with them till a much later stage of our adventure, when we had acquired the skill to reach out to beings alien to ourselves in spiritual condition.

3. Plant Men and Others

Before passing on to tell the story of our galaxy as a whole (so far as I can comprehend it) I must mention another and a very alien kind of world. Of this type we found few examples, and few of these survived into the time when the galactic drama was at its height; but one at least had (or will have) a great influence on the growth of the spirit in that dramatic era.

On certain small planets, drenched with light and heat from

a near or a great sun, evolution took a very different course from that with which we are familiar. The vegetable and animal functions were not separated into distinct organic types. Every organism was at once animal and vegetable.

In such worlds the higher organisms were something like gigantic and mobile herbs; but the violent flood of solar radiation rendered the tempo of their life much more rapid than that of our plants. To say that they looked like herbs is perhaps misleading, for they looked equally like animals. They had a definite number of limbs and a definite form of body; but all their skin was green, or streaked with green, and they bore here or there, according to their species, great masses of foliage. Owing to the slight power of gravitation on these small planets, the plant-animals often supported vast superstructures on very slender trunks or limbs. In general those that were mobile were less generously equipped with leaves than those that were more or less sedentary.

In these small hot worlds the turbulent circulation of water and atmosphere caused rapid changes in the condition of the ground from day to day. Storm and flood made it very desirable for the organisms of these worlds to be able to move from place to place. Consequently the early plants, which owing to the wealth of solar radiation could easily store themselves with energy for a life of moderate muscular activity, developed powers of perception and locomotion. Vegetable eyes and ears, vegetable organs of taste, scent, and touch, appeared on their stems or foliage. For locomotion, some of them simply withdrew their primitive roots from the ground and crept hither and thither with a kind of caterpillar action. Some spread their foliage and drifted on the wind. From these in the course of ages arose true fliers. Meanwhile the pedestrian species turned some of their roots into muscular legs, four or six, or centipedal. The remaining roots were equipped with boring instruments, which on a new site could rapidly proliferate into the ground. Yet another method of combining locomotion and roots was perhaps more remarkable. The aerial portion of the organism would detach itself from its embedded roots, and wander off by land or air to strike root afresh in virgin soil.

When the second site was exhausted the creature would either go off in search of a third, and so on, or return to its original bed, which by now might have recovered fertility. There, it would attach itself once more to its old dormant roots and wake them into new activity.

Many species, of course, developed predatory habits, and special organs of offence, such as muscular boughs as strong as pythons for constriction, or talons, horns, and formidable serrated pincers. In these 'carnivorous' creatures the spread of foliage was greatly reduced, and all the leaves could be tucked snugly away along the back. In the most specialized beasts of prey the foliage was atrophied and had only decorative value. It was surprising to see how the environment imposed on these alien creatures forms suggestive of our tigers and wolves. And it was interesting, too, to note how excessive specialization and excessive adaptation to offence or defence ruined species after species; and how, when at length 'human' intelligence appeared, it was achieved by an unimposing and inoffensive creature whose sole gifts were intelligence and sensibility towards the material world and towards its fellows.

Before describing the efflorescence of 'humanity' in this kind of world I must mention one grave problem which faces the evolving life of all small planets, often at an early stage. This problem we had already come across on the Other Earth. Owing to the weakness of gravitation and the disturbing heat of the sun, the molecules of the atmosphere very easily escape into space. Most small worlds, of course, lose all their air and water long before life can reach the 'human' stage, sometimes even before it can establish itself at all. Others, less small, may be thoroughly equipped with atmosphere in their early phases, but at a much later date, owing to the slow but steady contraction of their orbits, they may become so heated that they can no longer hold down the furiously agitated molecules of their atmosphere. On some of these planets a great population of living forms develops in early aeons only to be parched and suffocated out of existence through the long-drawn denudation and desiccation of the planet. But in more favourable cases life is able to adapt itself progressively to the increasingly severe conditions. In some worlds, for instance, a biological mechanism appeared by which the remaining atmosphere was imprisoned within a powerful electromagnetic field generated by the world's living population. In others the need of atmosphere was done away with altogether; photosynthesis and the whole metabolism of life were carried on by means of liquids alone. The last dwindling gases were captured in solution, stored in huge tracts of spongy growths among the crowded roots, and covered with an impervious membrane.

Both these natural biological methods occurred in one or other of the plant-animal worlds that reached the 'human' level. I have space only to describe a single example, the most significant of these remarkable worlds. This was one in which all free atmosphere had been lost long before the appearance of intelligence.

To enter this world and experience it through the alien senses and alien temperament of its natives was an adventure in some ways more bewildering than any of our earlier explorations. Owing to the complete absence of atmosphere, the sky, even in full sunlight, was black with the blackness of interstellar space; and the stars blazed. Owing to the weakness of gravitation and the absence of the moulding action of air and water and frost on the planet's shrinking and wrinkled surface, the landscape was a mass of fold-mountains, primeval and extinct volcanoes, congealed floods and humps of lava, and craters left by the impact of giant meteors. None of these features had ever been much smoothed by atmospheric and glacial influences. Further, the ever-changing stresses of the planet's crust had shattered many of the mountains into the fantastic forms of ice-bergs. On our own earth, where gravity, that tireless hound, pulls down its quarry with so much greater strength, these slender, top-heavy crags and pinnacles could never have stood. Owing to the absence of atmosphere the exposed surfaces of the rock were blindingly illuminated; the crevasses and all the shadows were black as night.

Many of the valleys had been turned into reservoirs, seem-

ingly of milk; for the surfaces of these lakes were covered with
a deep layer of a white glutinous substance, to prevent loss by
evaporation. Round about clustered the roots of the strange
people of this world, like tree-stumps where a forest has been
felled and cleared. Each stump was sealed with the white glue.
Every stretch of soil was in use; and we learned that, though
some of this soil was the natural result of past ages of action
by air and water, most was artificial. It had been manufactured
by great mining and pulverizing processes. In primitive times,
and indeed throughout all 'pre-human' evolution, the compet-
itive struggle for a share of the rare soil of this world of rock
had been one of the main spurs to intelligence.

The mobile plant-men themselves were to be seen by day
clustered in the valleys, their foliage spread to the sun. Only
by night did we observe them in action, moving over the bare
rock or busy with machines and other artificial objects, instruments of their civilization. There were no buildings, no roofed
weatherproof enclosures; for there was no weather. But the
plateaux and terraces of the rock were crowded with all manner of artifacts unintelligible to us.

The typical plant-man was an erect organism, like ourselves.
On his head he bore a vast crest of green plumes, which could
be either folded together in the form of a huge, tight, cos
lettuce, or spread out to catch the light. Three many-faceted
eyes looked out from under the crest. Beneath these were three
arm-like manipulatory limbs, green and serpentine, branching
at their extremities. The slender trunk, pliable, encased in hard
rings which slid into one another as the body bowed, was
divided into three legs for locomotion. Two of the three feet
were also mouths, which could either draw sap from the root
or devour foreign matter. The third was an organ of excretion.
The precious excrement was never wasted, but passed through
a special junction between the third foot and the root. The feet
contained taste-organs, and also ears. Since there was no air,
sound was not propagated above ground.

By day the life of these strange beings was mainly vegetable,
by night animal. Every morning, after the long and frigid night,
the whole population swarmed to its rooty dormitories. Each

individual sought out his own root, fixed himself to it, and stood throughout the torrid day, with leaves outspread. Till sunset he slept, not in a dreamless sleep, but in a sort of trance, the meditative and mystical quality of which was to prove in future ages a well of peace for many worlds. While he slept, the currents of sap hastened up and down his trunk, carrying chemicals between roots and leaves, flooding him with a concentrated supply of oxygen, removing the products of past catabolism. When the sun had disappeared once more behind the crags, displaying for a moment a wisp of fiery prominences, he would wake, fold up his leaves, close the passages to his roots, detach himself, and go about the business of civilized life. Night in this world was brighter than moonlight with us, for the stars were unobscured, and several great clusters hung in the night sky. Artificial light, however, was used for delicate operations. Its chief disadvantage was that it tended to send the worker to sleep.

I must not try even to sketch the rich and alien social life of these beings. I will only say that here as elsewhere we found all the cultural themes known on earth, but that in this world of mobile plants all was transposed into a strange key, a perplexing mode. Here as elsewhere we found a population of individuals deeply concerned with the task of keeping themselves and their society in being. Here we found self-regard, hate, love, the passions of the mob, intellectual curiosity, and so on. And here, as in all the other worlds that we had thus far visited, we found a race in the throes of the great spiritual crisis which was the crisis familiar to us in our own worlds, and formed the channel by which we had telepathic access to other worlds. But here the crisis had assumed a style different from any that we had yet encountered. We had, in fact, begun to extend our powers of imaginative exploration.

Leaving all else unnoticed, I must try to describe this crisis, for it is significant for the understanding of matters which reached far beyond this little world.

We did not begin to have insight into the drama of this race till we had learned to appreciate the mental aspect of its dual, animal-vegetable nature. Briefly, the mentality of the plant-men in every age was an expression of the varying tension between the two sides of their nature, between the active, assertive, objectively inquisitive, and morally positive animal nature and the passive, subjectively contemplative, and devoutly acquiescent vegetable nature. It was of course through animal prowess and practical human intelligence that the species had long ago come to dominate its world. But at all times this practical will had been tempered and enriched by a kind of experience which among men is very rare. Every day, throughout the ages, these beings had surrendered their fever-ish animal nature not merely to unconscious or dream-racked sleep, such as animals know, but to the special kind of aware-ness which (we learned) belongs to plants. Spreading their leaves, they had absorbed directly the essential elixir of life which animals receive only at second hand in the mangled flesh of their prey. Thus they seemingly maintained immediate physical contact with the source of all cosmical being. And this state, though physical, was also in some sense spiritual. It had a far-reaching effect on all their conduct. If theological lan-guage were acceptable, it might well be called a spiritual con-tact with God. During the busy night-time they went about their affairs as insulated individuals, having no present imme-diate experience of their underlying unity; but normally they were always preserved from the worst excesses of individual-ism by memory of their day-time life.

It took us long to understand that their peculiar day-time state did not consist simply in being united as a group mind, whether of tribe or race. Theirs was not the condition of the avian units in the bird-cloud, nor yet of the telepathically constituted world-minds which, as we were later to discover, had a very great part to play in galactic history. The plant-man did not in his day-time life come into possession of the per-cepts and thoughts of his fellow plant-men, and thereby waken into a more comprehensive and discriminate awareness of the environment and of the multiple body of the race. On the contrary, he became completely unresponsive to all objective conditions save the flood of sunlight drenching his spread leaves. And this experience afforded him an enduring ecstasy whose quality was almost sexual, an ecstasy in which subject and object seemed to become identical, an ecstasy of subjective union with the obscure source of all finite being. In this state the plant-man could meditate upon his active, night-time life, and could become aware, far more clearly than by day, of the intricacies of his own motives. In this day-time mode he passed no moral judgements on himself or others. He mentally reviewed every kind of human conduct with detached contemplative joy, as a factor in the universe. But when night came again, bringing the active nocturnal mood, the calm, day-time insight into himself and others was lit with a fire of moral praise and censure.

Now throughout the career of this race there had been a certain tension between the two basic impulses of its nature. All its finest cultural achievements had been made in times when both had been vigorous and neither predominant. But, as in so many other worlds, the development of natural science and the production of mechanical power from tropical sunlight caused grave mental confusion. The manufacture of innumerable aids to comfort and luxury, the spread of electric railways over the whole world, the development of radio communication, the study of astronomy and mechanistic biochemistry, the urgent demands of war and social revolution, all these influences strengthened the active mentality and weakened the contemplative. The climax came when it was found possible to do away with the day-time sleep altogether. The products of artificial photosynthesis could be rapidly injected into the living body every morning, so that the plant-man could spend practically the whole day in active work. Very soon the roots of the peoples were being dug up and used as raw material in manufacture. They were no longer needed for their natural purpose.

I must not spend time in describing the hideous plight into which this world now fell. Seemingly, artificial photosynthesis, though it could keep the body vigorous, failed to produce some essential vitamin of the spirit. A disease of robotism, of purely mechanical living, spread throughout the population. There was of course a fever of industrial activity. The plant-men careered round their planet in all kinds of mechanically propelled vehicles, decorated themselves with the latest synthetic products, tapped the central volcanic heat for power, expended great ingenuity in destroying one another, and in a thousand other feverish pursuits pushed on in search of a bliss which ever eluded them.

After untold distresses they began to realize that their whole way of life was alien to their essential plant nature. Leaders and prophets dared to inveigh against mechanization and against the prevalent intellectualistic scientific culture, and against artificial photosynthesis. By now nearly all the roots of the race had been destroyed; but presently biological science was turned to the task of generating, from the few remaining specimens, new roots for all. Little by little the whole population was able to return to natural photosynthesis. The industrial life of the world vanished like frost in sunlight. In returning to the old alternating life of animal and vegetable, the plant-men, jaded and deranged by the long fever of industrialism, found in their calm day-time experience an overwhelming joy. The misery of their recent life intensified by contrast the ecstasy of the vegetal experience. The intellectual acuity that their brightest minds had acquired in scientific analysis combined with the special quality of their revived plant life to give their whole experience a new lucidity. For a brief period they reached a plane of spiritual lucidity which was to be an example and a treasure for the future aeons of the galaxy.

But even the most spiritual life has its temptations. The extravagant fever of industrialism and intellectualism had so subtly poisoned the plant-men that when at last they rebelled against it they swung too far, falling into the snare of a vegetal life as one-sided as the old animal life had been. Little by little they gave less and less energy and time to 'animal' pursuits, until at last their nights as well as their days were spent wholly as trees, and the active, exploring, manipulating, animal intelligence died in them for ever.

For a while the race lived on in an increasingly vague and confused ecstasy of passive union with the universal source of being. So well established and automatic was the age-old biological mechanism for preserving the planet's vital gases in solution that it continued long to function without attention. But industrialism had increased the world population beyond the limits within which the small supply of water and gases could easily fulfil its function. The circulation of material was dangerously rapid. In time the mechanism was over-strained. Leakages began to appear, and no one repaired them. Little by little the precious water and other volatile substances escaped from the planet. Little by little the reservoirs ran dry, the spongy roots were parched, the leaves withered. One by one the blissful and no longer human inhabitants of that world passed from ecstasy to sickness, despondency, uncomprehending bewilderment, and on to death.

But, as I shall tell, their achievement was not without effect on the life of our galaxy.

'Vegetable humanities', if I may so call them, proved to be rather uncommon occurrences. Some of them inhabited worlds of a very curious kind which I have not yet mentioned. As is well known, a small planet close to its sun tends, through the sun's tidal action upon it, to lose its rotation. Its days become longer and longer, till at last it presents one face constantly towards its luminary. Not a few planets of this type, up and down the galaxy, were inhabited; and several of them by 'vegetable humanities'.

All these 'non-diurnal' worlds were very inhospitable to life, for one hemisphere was always extravagantly hot, the other extravagantly cold. The illuminate face might reach the temperature of molten lead; on the dark face, however, no substances could retain the liquid state, for the temperature would remain but a degree or two above absolute zero. Between the two hemispheres there would lie a narrow belt, or rather a mere ribbon, which might be called temperate. Here the immense and incendiary sun was always partly hidden by the horizon. Along the cooler side of this ribbon, hidden from the murderous rays of the sun's actual disc, but illuminated by his corona, and warmed by the conduction of heat from the sunward ground, life was not invariably impossible.

Inhabited worlds of this kind had always reached a fairly high stage of biological evolution long before they had lost their diurnal rotation. As the day lengthened, life was forced to adapt itself to more extreme temperatures of day and night. The poles of these planets, if not too much inclined towards the ecliptic, remained at a fairly constant temperature, and were therefore citadels whence the living forms ventured into less hospitable regions. Many species managed to spread towards the equator by the simple method of burying themselves and 'hibernating' through the day and the night, emerging only for dawn and sunset to lead a furiously active life. As the day lengthened into months, some species, adapted for swift locomotion, simply trekked round the planet, following the sunset and the dawn. Strange it was to see the equatorial and most agile of these species sweeping over the plains in the level sunlight. Their legs were often as tall and slender as a ship's masts. Now and then they would swerve, with long necks extended to snatch some scurrying creature or pluck some bunch of foliage. Such constant and rapid migration would have been impossible in worlds less rich in solar energy.

Human intelligence seems never to have been attained in any of these worlds unless it had been attained already before night and day became excessively long, and the difference of these temperatures excessively great. In worlds where plant-men or other creatures had achieved civilization and science before rotation had become seriously retarded, great efforts were made to cope with the increasing harshness of the environment. Sometimes civilization merely retreated to the poles, abandoning the rest of the planet. Sometimes subterranean settlements were established in other regions, the inhabitants issuing only at dawn and sunset to cultivate the land. Sometimes a system of railways along the parallels of latitude carried a migratory population from one agricultural centre to another, following the twilight.

Finally, however, when rotation had been entirely lost, a

settled civilization would be crowded along the whole length of the stationary girdle between night and day. By this time, if not before, the atmosphere would have been lost also. It can well be imagined that a race struggling to survive in these literally straightened circumstances would not be able to maintain any richness and delicacy of mental life.

CHAPTER EIGHT

CONCERNING
THE EXPLORERS

Bvalltu and I, in company with the increasing band of our fellow explorers, visited many worlds of many strange kinds. In some we spent only a few weeks of the local time; in others we remained for centuries, or skimmed from point to point of history as our interest dictated. Like a swarm of locusts we would descend upon a new-found world, each of us singling out a suitable host. After a period of observation, long or short, we would leave, to alight again, perhaps, on the same world in another of its ages; or to distribute our company among many worlds, far apart in time and in space.

This strange life turned me into a very different being from the Englishman who had at a certain date of human history walked at night upon a hill. Not only had my own immediate experience increased far beyond the normal range, but also, by means of a peculiarly intimate union with my fellows, I myself had been, so to speak, multiplied. For in a sense I was now as much Bvalltu and each one of my colleagues as I was that Englishman.

This change that had come over us deserves to be carefully described, not merely for its intrinsic interest, but also because it afforded us a key for understanding many cosmical beings whose nature would otherwise have been obscure to us.

In our new condition our community was so perfected that the experiences of each were available to all. Thus I, the new I, participated in the adventures of that Englishman and of Bvalltu and the rest with equal ease. And I possessed all their memories of former, separate existence in their respective native worlds.

Some philosophically minded reader may ask, 'Do you mean that the many experiencing individuals became a single individual, having a single stream of experience? Or do you mean that there remained many experiencing individuals, having numerically distinct but exactly similar experiences?' The answer is that I do not know. But this I know. I, the Englishman, and similarly each of my colleagues, gradually 'woke' into possession of each other's experience, and also into more lucid intelligence. Whether, as experients, we remained many or became one, I do not know. But I suspect that the question is one of those which can never be truly answered because in the last analysis it is meaningless.

In the course of my communal observation of the many worlds, and equally in the course of my introspection of my own communal mental processes, now one and now another individual explorer, and now perhaps a group of explorers, would form the main instrument of attention, affording through their particular nature and experience material for the contemplation of all. Sometimes, when we were exceptionally alert and eager, each awakened into a mode of perception and thought and imagination and will more lucid than any experiencing known to any of us as individuals. Thus, though each of us became in a sense identical with each of his friends, he also became in a manner of mind of higher order than any of us in isolation. But in this 'waking' there seemed to be nothing more mysterious in kind than in those many occasions in normal life when the mind delightedly relates together experiences that have hitherto been insulated from one another, or discovers in confused objects a pattern or a significance hitherto unnoticed.

It must not be supposed that this strange mental community blotted out the personalities of the individual explorers. Human speech has no accurate terms to describe our peculiar relationship. It would be as untrue to say that we had lost our individuality, or were dissolved in a communal individuality, as to say that we were all the while distinct individuals.

Though the pronoun 'I' now applied to us all collectively, the pronoun 'we' also applied to us. In one respect, namely unity of consciousness, we were indeed a single experiencing individual; yet at the same time we were in a very important and delightful manner distinct from one another. Though there was only the single, communal 'I', there was also, so to speak, a manifold and variegated 'us', an observed company of very diverse personalities, each of whom expressed creatively his own unique contribution to the whole enterprise of cosmical exploration, while all were bound together in a tissue of subtle personal relationships.

I am well aware that this account of the matter must seem to my readers self-contradictory, as indeed it does to me. But I can find no other way of expressing the vividly remembered fact that I was at once a particular member of a community and the possessor of the pooled experience of that community.

To put the matter somewhat differently, though in respect of our identity of awareness we were a single individual, in respect of our diverse and creative idiosyncrasies we were distinct persons observable by the common 'I'. Each one, as the common 'I', experienced the whole company of individuals, including his individual self, as a group of actual persons, differing in temperament and private experience. Each one of us experienced all as a real community, bound together by such relations of affection and mutual criticism as occurred, for instance, between Bvalltu and myself. Yet on another plane of experience, the plane of creative thought and imagination, the single communal attention could withdraw from this tissue of personal relationships. Instead, it concerned itself wholly with the exploration of the cosmos. With partial truth it might be said that, while for love we were distinct, for knowledge, for wisdom, and for worship we were identical. In the following chapters, which deal with the cosmical experiences of this communal 'I', it would be logically correct to refer to the exploring mind always in the singular, using the pronoun 'I', and saying simply, 'I did so and so, and thought so and so'; nevertheless the pronoun 'we' will still be generally employed so as to preserve the true impression of a communal enterprise, and to avoid the false impression that the explorer was just the human author of this book.

Each one of us had lived his individual active life in one or other of the many worlds. And for each one, individually, his own little blundering career in his remote native world retained a peculiar concreteness and glamour, like the vividness which mature men find in childhood memories. Not only so, but individually he imputed to his former private life an urgency and importance which, in his communal capacity, was overwhelmed by matters of greater cosmical significance. Now this concreteness and glamour, this urgency and importance of each little private life, was of great moment to the communal 'I' in which each of us participated. It irradiated the communal experience with its vividness, its pathos. For only in his own life as a native in some world had each of us actually fought, so to speak, in life's war as a private soldier at close grips with the enemy. It was the recollection of this fettered, imprisoned, blindfold, eager, private individuality, that enabled us to watch the unfolding of cosmical events not merely as a spectacle but with a sense of the poignancy of every individual life as it flashed and vanished.

Thus I, the Englishman, contributed to the communal mind my persistently vivid recollections of all my ineffectual conduct in my own troubled world; and the true significance of that blind human life, redeemed by its little imperfect jewel of community, became apparent to me, the communal 'I', with a lucidity which the Englishman in his primaeval stupor could never attain and cannot now recapture. All that I can now remember is that, as the communal 'I', I looked on my terrestrial career at once more critically and with less guilt than I do in the individual state; and on my partner in that career at once with clearer, colder understanding of our mutual impact and with more generous affection.

One aspect of the communal experience of the explorers I have still to mention. Each of us had originally set out upon the great adventure mainly in the hope of discovering what part was played by community in the cosmos as a whole. This question had yet to be answered; but meanwhile another question was becoming increasingly insistent. Our crowded experiences in the many worlds, and our new lucidity of mind, had bred in each of us a sharp conflict of intellect and feeling. Intellectually the idea that some 'deity', distinct from the cosmos itself, had made the cosmos now seemed to us less and less credible. Intellectually we had no doubt that the cosmos was self-sufficient, a system involving no logical ground and no creator. Yet increasingly, as a man may feel the psychical reality of a physically perceived beloved or a perceived enemy, we felt in the physical presence of the cosmos the psychical presence of that which we had named the Star Maker. In spite of intellect, we knew that the whole cosmos was infinitely less than the whole of being, and that the whole infinity of being underlay every moment of the cosmos. And with unreasoning passion we strove constantly to peer behind each minute particular event in the cosmos to see the very features of that infinity which, for lack of a truer name, we had called the Star Maker. But, peer as we might, we found nothing. Though in the whole and in each particular thing the dread presence indubitably confronted us, its very infinity prevented us from assigning to it any features whatever.

Sometimes we inclined to conceive it as sheer Power, and symbolized it to ourselves by means of all the myriad power-deities of our many worlds. Sometimes we felt assured that it was pure Reason, and that the cosmos was but an exercise of the divine mathematician. Sometimes Love seemed to us its essential character, and we imagined it with the forms of all the Christs of all the worlds, the human Christs, the Echinoderm and Nautiloid Christs, the dual Christ of the Symbiotics, the swarming Christ of the Insectoids. But equally it appeared to us as unreasoning Creativity, at once blind and subtle, tender and cruel, caring only to spawn and spawn the infinite variety of beings, conceiving here and there among a thousand inanities a fragile loveliness. This it might for a while foster with maternal solicitude, till in a sudden jealousy of the excellence of its own creature, it would destroy what it had made.

But we knew well that all these fictions were very false. The felt presence of the Star Maker remained unintelligible, even though it increasingly illuminated the cosmos, like the splendour of the unseen sun at dawn.

CHAPTER NINE

THE COMMUNITY OF WORLDS

1. Busy Utopias

There came a time when our new-found communal mind attained such a degree of lucidity that it was able to maintain contact even with worlds that had passed far beyond the mentality of terrestrial man. Of these lofty experiences I, who am once more reduced to the state of a mere individual human being, have only the most confused memory. I am like one who, in the last extremity of mental fatigue, tries to recapture the more penetrating intuitions that he achieved in his lost freshness. He can recover only faint echoes and a vague glamour. But even the most fragmentary recollections of the cosmical experiences which befell me in that lucid state deserve recording.

The sequence of events in the successfully waking world was generally more or less as follows. The starting point, it will be remembered, was a plight like that in which our own Earth now stands. The dialectic of the world's history had confronted the race with a problem with which the traditional mentality could never cope. The world-situation had grown too complex for lowly intelligences, and it demanded a degree of individual integrity in leaders and in led, such as was as yet possible only to a few minds. Consciousness had already been violently awakened out of the primitive trance into a state of excruciating individualism, of poignant but pitifully restricted self-awareness. And individualism, together with the traditional tribal spirit, now threatened to wreck the world. Only after a long-drawn agony of economic distress and maniac warfare, haunted by an increasingly clear vision of a happier world, could the second stage of waking be achieved. In most cases it was not achieved. 'Human nature', or its equivalent in the many worlds, could not change itself; and the environment could not remake it.

But in a few worlds the spirit reacted to its desperate plight with a miracle. Or, if the reader prefers, the environment miraculously refashioned the spirit. There occurred a widespread and almost sudden waking into a new lucidity of consciousness and a new integrity of will. To call this change miraculous is only to recognize that it could not have been scientifically predicted even from the fullest possible knowledge of 'human nature' as manifested in the earlier age. To later generations, however, it appeared as no miracle but as a belated wakening from an almost miraculous stupor into plain sanity.

This unprecedented access of sanity took at first the form of a widespread passion for a new social order which should be just and should embrace the whole planet. Such a social fervour was not, of course, entirely new. A small minority had long ago conceived it, and had haltingly tried to devote themselves to it. But now at last, through the scourge of circumstance and the potency of the spirit itself, this social will became general. And while it was still passionate, and heroic action was still possible to the precariously awakened beings, the whole social structure of the world was reorganized, so that within a generation or two every individual on the planet could count upon the means of life, and the opportunity to exercise his powers fully, for his own delight and for the service of the world community. It was now possible to bring up the new generations to a sense that the world-order was no alien tyranny but an expression of the general will, and that they had indeed been born into a noble heritage, a thing for which it was good to live and suffer and die. To readers of this book such a change may well seem miraculous, and such a state utopian.

Those of us who had come from less fortunate planets found it at once a heartening and yet a bitter experience to watch world after world successfully emerge from a plight which seemed inescapable, to see a world-population of frustrated and hate-poisoned creatures give place to one in which every

individual was generously and shrewdly nurtured and therefore not warped by unconscious envy and hate. Very soon,
though no change had occurred in the biological stock, the new
social environment produced a world-population which might
well have seemed to belong to a new species. In physique, in
intelligence, in mental independence and social responsibility,
the new individual far outstripped the old, as also in mental
wholesomeness and in integrity of will. And though it was
sometimes feared that the removal of all sources of grave mental conflict might deprive the mind of all stimulus to creative
work, and produce a mediocre population, it was soon found
that, far from stagnating, the spirit of the race now passed on
to discover new fields of struggle and triumph. The world-
population of 'aristocrats', which flourished after the great
change, looked back with curiosity and incredulity into the
preceding age, and found great difficulty in conceiving the
tangled, disreputable and mostly unwitting motives which
were the mainsprings of action even in the most fortunate
individuals among their ancestors. It was recognized that the
whole pre-revolutionary population was afflicted with serious
mental diseases, with endemic plagues of delusion and obsession, due to mental malnutrition and poisoning. As psychological insight advanced, the same kind of interest was aroused by
the old psychology as is wakened in modern Europeans by
ancient maps which distort the countries of the world almost
beyond recognition.

We were inclined to think of the psychological crisis of the
waking worlds as being the difficult passage from adolescence
to maturity; for in essence it was an outgrowing of juvenile
interests, a discarding of toys and childish games, and a discovery of the interests of adult life. Tribal prestige, individual
dominance, military glory, industrial triumphs lost their obsessive glamour, and instead the happy creatures delighted in
civilized social intercourse, in cultural activities, and in the
common enterprise of world-building.

During the phase of history which followed the actual sur-
mounting of the spiritual crisis in a waking world the attention

of the race was of course still chiefly occupied with social reconstruction. Many heroic tasks had to be undertaken. There was need not only for a new economic system but for new systems of political organization, of world-law, of education. In many cases this period of reconstruction under the guidance of the new mentality was itself a time of serious conflict. For even beings who are sincerely in accord about the goal of social activity may disagree violently about the way. But such conflicts as arose, though heated, were of a very different kind from the earlier conflicts which were inspired by obsessive individualism and obsessive group-hatreds.

We noted that the new world-orders were very diverse. This was, of course, to be expected, since biologically, psychologically, culturally, these worlds were very different. The perfected world-order of an Echinoderm race had of course to be different from that of the symbiotic Ichthyoids and Arachnoids; and this from that of a Nautiloid world, and so on. But we noted also in all these victorious worlds a remarkable identity. For instance, in the loosest possible sense, all were communistic; for in all of them the means of production were communally owned, and no individual could control the labour of others for private profit. Again, in a sense all these world-orders were democratic, since the final sanction of policy was world-opinion. But in many cases there was no democratic machinery, no legal channel for the expression of world-opinion. Instead, a highly specialized bureaucracy, or even a world-dictator, might carry out the business of organizing the world's activity with legally absolute power, but under constant supervision by popular will expressed through the radio. We were amazed to find that in a truly awakened world even a dictatorship could be in essence democratic. We observed with incredulity situations in which the 'absolute' world-government, faced with some exceptionally momentous and doubtful matter of policy, had made urgent appeals for a formal democratic decision, only to receive from all regions the reply, 'We cannot advise. You must decide as your professional experience suggests. We will abide by your decision.'

Law in these worlds was based on a very remarkable kind

of sanction which could not conceivably work successfully on Earth. There was never any attempt to enforce the law by violence, save against dangerous lunatics, such as sometimes occurred as throw-backs to an earlier age. In some worlds there was a complex body of 'laws' regulating the economic and social life of groups, and even the private affairs of individuals. It seemed to us at first that freedom had vanished from such worlds. But later we discovered that the whole intricate system was regarded as we should regard the rules of a game or the canons of an art, or the innumerable extra-legal customs of any long-established society. In the main, everyone kept the law because he had faith in its social value as a guide to conduct. But if ever the law seemed inadequate he would without hesitation break it. His conduct might cause offence or inconvenience or even serious hardship to his neighbours. They would probably protest vigorously. But there was never question of compulsion. If those concerned failed to persuade him that this behaviour was socially harmful, his case might be tried by a sort of court of arbitration, backed by the prestige of the world-government. If the decision went against the defendant, and yet he persisted in his illegal behaviour, none would restrain him. But such was the power of public censure and social ostracism that disregard of the court's decision was very rare. The terrible sense of isolation acted on the law-breaker like an ordeal by fire. If his motive was at bottom base, he would sooner or later collapse. But if his case had merely been misjudged, or if his conduct sprang from an intuition of value beyond the range of his fellows, he might persist in his course till he had won over the public.

I mention these social curiosities only to give some illustration of the far-reaching difference between the spirit of these utopian worlds and the spirit which is familiar to readers of this book. It may be easily imagined that in our wanderings we came upon a wonderful diversity of customs and institutions, but I must not pause to describe even the most remarkable of them. I must be content to outline the activities of the typical waking worlds, so as to be able to press on to tell a story not merely of particular worlds but of our galaxy as a whole.

When a waking world had passed through the phase of radical social reconstruction, and had attained a new equilibrium, it would settle into a period of steady economic and cultural advancement. Mechanism, formerly a tyrant over body and mind, but now a faithful servant, would secure for every individual a fullness and diversity of life far beyond anything known on Earth. Radio communication and rocket travel would afford to each mind intimate knowledge of every people. Labour-saving machinery would reduce the work of maintaining civilization; all mind-crippling drudgery would vanish, and the best energy of every one of the world-citizens would be freely devoted to social service that was not unworthy of a well-grown intelligent being. And 'social service' was apt to be interpreted very broadly. It seemed to permit many lives to be given over wholly to freakish and irresponsible self-expression. The community could well afford a vast amount of such wastage for the sake of the few invaluable jewels of originality which occasionally emerged from it.

This stable and prosperous phase of the waking worlds, which we came to call the utopian phase, was probably the happiest of all the ages in the life of any world. Tragedy of one sort or another there would still be, but never widespread and futile distress. We remarked, moreover, that, whereas in former ages tragedy had been commonly thought of in terms of physical pain and premature death, now it was conceived more readily as resulting from the clash and mutual yearning and mutual incompatibility of diverse personalities; so rare had the cruder kind of disaster become, and on the other hand so much more subtle and sensitive were the contacts between persons. Widespread physical tragedy, the suffering and annihilation of whole populations, such as we experience in war and plague, were quite unknown, save in those rare cases when a whole race was destroyed by astronomical accident, whether through loss of atmosphere or the bursting of its planet or the plunging of its solar system into some tract of gas or dust.

In this happy phase, then, which might last for a few centuries or for many thousands of years, the whole energy of the world would be devoted to perfecting the world-community and raising the calibre of the race by cultural and by eugenical means.

Of the eugenical enterprise of these worlds I shall report little, because much of it would be unintelligible without a minute knowledge of the biological and biochemical nature of each of these non-human world-populations. It is enough to say that the first task of the eugenists was to prevent the perpetuation of inheritable disease and malformation of body and mind. In days before the great psychological change even this modest work had often led to serious abuses. Governments would attempt to breed out all those characters, such as independence of mind, which were distasteful to governments. Ignorant enthusiasts would advocate ruthless and misguided interference in the choice of mates. But in the more enlightened age these dangers were recognized and avoided. Even so, the eugenical venture did often lead to disaster. One splendid race of intelligent avians we saw reduced to the sub-human level by an attempt to extirpate susceptibility to a virulent mental disease. The liability to this disease happened to be genetically linked in an indirect manner with the possibility of normal brain development in the fifth generation.

Of positive eugenical enterprises I need only mention improvements of sensory range and acuity (chiefly in sight and touch), the invention of new senses, improvements in memory, in general intelligence, in temporal discrimination. These races came to distinguish ever more minute periods of duration, and at the same time to extend their temporal grasp so as to apprehend ever longer periods as 'now'.

Many of the worlds at first devoted much energy to this kind of eugenical work, but later decided that, though it might afford them some new richness of experience, it must be postponed for the sake of more important matters. For instance, with the increasing complexity of life it soon appeared very necessary to retard the maturing of the individual mind, so as to enable it to assimilate its early experience more thoroughly. 'Before life begins,' it was said, 'there should be a lifetime of childhood.' At the same time efforts were made to prolong maturity to three or four times its normal extent, and to reduce senility. In every world that had gained full eugenical power there arose sooner or later a sharp public discussion as to the most suitable length of individual life. All were agreed that life must be prolonged; but, while one party wished to multiply it only three or four times, another insisted that nothing less than a hundred times the normal life-span could afford the race that continuity and depth of experience which all saw to be desirable. Another party even advocated deathlessness, and a permanent race of never-aging immortals. It was argued that the obvious danger of mental rigidity, and the cessation of all advancement, might be avoided by contriving that the permanent physiological state of the deathless population should be one of very early maturity.

Different worlds found different solutions for this problem. Some races assigned to the individual a period no longer than three hundred of our years. Others allowed him fifty thousand. One race of Echinoderms decided on potential immortality, but endowed themselves with an ingenious psychological mechanism by which, if the ancient began to lose touch with changing conditions, he could not fail to recognize the fact, and would thereupon crave and practise euthanasia, gladly yielding his place to a successor of more modern type.

Many other triumphs of eugenical experiment we observed up and down the worlds. The general level of individual intelligence was, of course, raised far beyond the range of *Homo Sapiens*. But also that super-intelligence which can be attained only by a psychically unified community was greatly developed on the highest practicable plane, that of the conscious individuality of a whole world. This, of course, was impossible till the social cohesion of individuals within the world-community had become as close-knit as the integration of the elements of a nervous system. It demanded also a very great advance of telepathy. Further, it was not possible till the great majority of individuals had reached a breadth of knowledge unknown on earth.

The last and most difficult power to be attained by these worlds in the course of their utopian phase was psychical freedom of time and space, the limited power to observe directly, and even contribute to, events remote from the spatio-temporal location of the observer. Throughout our exploration we had been greatly perplexed by the fact that we, most of whom were beings of a very humble order, should have been able to achieve this freedom, which, as we now discovered, these highly developed worlds found so difficult to master. The explanation was now given us. No such venture as ours could have been undertaken by our unaided selves. Throughout our exploration we had unwittingly been under the influence of a system of worlds which had attained this freedom only after aeons of research. Not one step could we have taken without the constant support of those brilliant Ichthyoid and Arachnoid Symbiotics who played a leading part in the history of our galaxy. They it was who controlled our whole adventure, so that we might report our experiences in our primitive native worlds.

The freedom of space and time, the power of cosmical exploration and of influence by means of telepathic contact, was at once the most potent and the most dangerous asset of the fully awakened utopian worlds. Through the unwise exercise of it many a glorious and single-minded race came to disaster. Sometimes the adventuring world-mind failed to maintain its sanity in face of the welter of misery and despair that now flooded in upon it telepathically from all the regions of the galaxy. Sometimes the sheer difficulty of comprehending the subtleties that were revealed to it flung it into a mental breakdown from which there was no recovery. Sometimes it became so enthralled by its telepathic adventures that it lost touch with its own life upon its native planet, so that the world-community, deprived of its guiding communal mind, fell into disorder and decay, and the exploring mind itself died.

2. Intermundane Strife

Of the busy utopias which I have been describing, a few were already established even before the birth of the Other Earth, a larger number flourished before our own planet was formed, but many of the most important of these worlds are temporally located in an age far future to us, an age long after the destruction of the final human race. Casualties among these awakened worlds are of course much less common than among more lowly and less competent worlds. Consequently, though fatal accidents occurred in every epoch, the number of awakened worlds in our galaxy steadily increased as time advanced. The actual births of planets, due to the chance encounters of mature but not aged stars, reached (or will reach) a maximum fairly late in the history of our galaxy, and then declined. But since the fluctuating progress of a world from bare animality to spiritual maturity takes, on the average, several thousands of millions of years, the maximum population of utopian and fully awakened worlds occurred very late, when physically the galaxy was already somewhat past its prime. Further, though even in early epochs the few awakened worlds did sometimes succeed in making contact with one another, either by interstellar travel or by telepathy, it was not till a fairly late stage of galactic history that intermundane relations came to occupy the main attention of the wakened worlds.

Throughout the progress of a waking world there was one grave, subtle, and easily overlooked danger. Interest might be 'fixated' upon some current plane of endeavour, so that no further advance could occur. It may seem strange that beings whose psychological knowledge so far surpassed the attainment of man should have been trapped in this manner. Apparently at every stage of mental development, save the highest of all, the mind's growing point is tender and easily misdirected. However this may be, it is a fact that a few rather highly developed worlds, even with communal mentality, were disastrously perverted in a strange manner, which I find very difficult to understand. I can only suggest that in them, seemingly, the hunger for true community and true mental lucidity itself became obsessive and perverse, so that the behaviour of these exalted perverts might deteriorate into something very like tribalism and religious fanaticism. The disease would soon lead to the stifling of all elements which seemed recalcitrant to the generally accepted culture of the world-society. When such worlds mastered interstellar travel, they might conceive a fanatical desire to impose their own culture throughout the galaxy. Sometimes their zeal became so violent that they were actually driven to wage ruthless religious wars on all who resisted them.

Obsessions derived from one stage or another of the progress towards utopia and lucid consciousness, even if they did not bring violent disaster, might at any stage side-track the waking world into futility. Superhuman intelligence, courage, and constancy on the part of the devoted individuals might be consecrated to misguided and unworthy world purposes. Thus it was that, in extreme cases, even a world that remained socially utopian and mentally a super-individual, might pass beyond the bounds of sanity. With a gloriously healthy body and an insane mind it might do terrible harm to its neighbours.

Such tragedy did not become possible till after interplanetary and interstellar travel had been well established. Long ago, in an early phase of the galaxy, the number of planetary systems had been very small, and only half a dozen worlds had attained utopia. These were scattered up and down the galaxy at immense distances from one another. Each lived its life in almost complete isolation, relieved only by precarious telepathic intercourse with its peers. In a somewhat later but still early period, when these eldest children of the galaxy had perfected their society and their biological nature, and were on the threshold of super-individuality, they turned their attention to interplanetary travel. First one and then another achieved rocket-flight in space, and succeeded in breeding specialized populations for the colonization of neighbouring planets.

In a still later epoch, the middle period of galactic history, there were many more planetary systems than in the earlier ages, and an increasing number of intelligent worlds were successfully emerging from the great psychological crisis which so many worlds never surmount. Meanwhile some of the elder 'generation' of awakened worlds were already facing the immensely difficult problems of travel on the interstellar and not merely the interplanetary scale. This new power inevitably changed the whole character of galactic history. Hitherto, in spite of tentative telepathic exploration on the part of the most awakened worlds, the life of the galaxy had been in the main the life of a number of isolated worlds which took no effect upon one another. With the advent of interstellar travel the many distinct themes of the world-biographies gradually became merged in an all-embracing drama.

Travel within a planetary system was at first carried out by rocket-vessels propelled by normal fuels. In all the early ventures one great difficulty had been the danger of collision with meteors. Even the most efficient vessel, most skilfully navigated and travelling in regions that were relatively free from these invisible and lethal missiles, might at any moment crash and fuse. The trouble was not overcome till means had been found to unlock the treasure of sub-atomic energy. It was then possible to protect the ship by means of a far-flung envelope of power which either diverted or exploded the meteors at a distance. A rather similar method was with great difficulty devised to protect the space ships and their crews from the constant and murderous hail of cosmic radiation.

Interstellar, as opposed to interplanetary, travel was quite impossible until the advent of sub-atomic power. Fortunately this source of power was seldom gained until late in a world's development, when mentality was mature enough to wield this most dangerous of all physical instruments without inevitable disaster. Disasters, however, did occur. Several worlds were accidentally blown to pieces. In others civilization was temporarily destroyed. Sooner or later, however, most of the minded worlds tamed this formidable djin, and set it to work upon a titanic scale, not only in industry, but in such great enterprises as the alteration of planetary orbits for the improvement of climate. This dangerous and delicate process was effected by firing a gigantic sub-atomic rocket-apparatus at such times and places that the recoil would gradually accumulate to divert the planet's course in the desired direction.

Actual interstellar voyaging was first effected by detaching a planet from its natural orbit by a series of well-timed and well-placed rocket impulsions, and thus projecting it into outer space at a speed far greater than the normal planetary and stellar speeds. Something more than this was necessary, since life on a sunless planet would have been impossible. For short interstellar voyages the difficulty was sometimes overcome by the generation of sub-atomic energy from the planet's own substance; but for longer voyages, lasting for many thousands of years, the only method was to form a small artificial sun, and project it into space as a blazing satellite of the living world. For this purpose an uninhabited planet would be brought into proximity with the home planet to form a binary system. A mechanism would then be contrived for the controlled disintegration of the atoms of the lifeless planet, to provide a constant source of light and heat. The two bodies, revolving round one another, would be launched among the stars.

This delicate operation may well seem impossible. Had I space to describe the age-long experiments and world-wrecking accidents which preceded its achievement, perhaps the reader's incredulity would vanish. But I must dismiss in a few sentences whole protracted epics of scientific adventure and personal courage. Suffice it that, before the process was perfected, many a populous world was either cast adrift to freeze in space, or was roasted by its own artificial sun.

The stars are so remote from one another that we measure their distances in light years. Had the voyaging worlds travelled only at speeds comparable with those of the stars themselves, even the shortest of interstellar voyages would have lasted for many millions of years. But since interstellar space offers almost no resistance to a travelling body, and therefore momentum is not lost, it was possible for the voyaging world, by prolonging the original rocket-impulsion for many years, to increase its speed far beyond that of the fastest star. Indeed, though even the early voyages by heavy natural planets were by our standards spectacular, I shall have to tell at a later stage of voyages by small artificial planets travelling at almost half the speed of light. Owing to certain 'relativity effects' it was impossible to accelerate beyond this point. But even such a rate of travel made voyages to the nearer stars well worth undertaking if any other planetary system happened to lie within this range. It must be remembered that a fully awakened world had no need to think in terms of such short periods as a human lifetime. Though its individuals might die, the minded world was in a very important sense immortal. It was accustomed to lay its plans to cover periods of many million years.

In early epochs of the galaxy, expeditions from star to star were difficult, and rarely successful. But at a later stage, when there were already many thousands of worlds inhabited by intelligent races, and hundreds that had passed the utopian stage, a very serious situation arose. Interstellar travel was by now extremely efficient. Immense exploration vessels, many miles in diameter, were constructed out in space from artificial materials of extreme rigidity and lightness. These could be projected by rocket action and with cumulative acceleration till their speed was almost half the speed of light. Even so, the journey from end to end of the galaxy could not be completed under two hundred thousand years. However, there was no reason to undertake so long a voyage. Few voyages in search of suitable systems lasted for more than a tenth of that time. Many were much shorter. Races that had attained and secured a communal consciousness would not hesitate to send out a number of such expeditions. Ultimately they might project their planet itself across the ocean of space to settle in some remote system recommended by the pioneers.

The problem of interstellar travel was so enthralling that it sometimes became an obsession even to a fairly well-developed utopian world. This could only occur if in the constitution of that world there was something unwholesome, some secret and unfulfilled hunger impelling the beings. The race might then become travel-mad.

Its social organization would be refashioned and directed with Spartan strictness to the new communal undertaking. All its members, hypnotized by the common obsession, would gradually forget the life of intense personal intercourse and of creative mental activity which had hitherto been their chief concern. The whole venture of the spirit, exploring the universe and its own nature with critical intelligence and delicate

sensibility, would gradually come to a standstill. The deepest
roots of emotion and will, which in the fully sane awakened
world were securely within the range of introspection, would
become increasingly obscured. Less and less, in such a world,
could the unhappy communal mind understand itself. More
and more it pursued its phantom goal. Any attempt to explore
the galaxy telepathically was now abandoned. The passion of
physical exploration assumed the guise of a religion. The communal mind persuaded itself that it must at all costs spread the
gospel of its own culture throughout the galaxy. Though culture itself was vanishing, the vague idea of culture was cherished as a justification of world-policy.

Here I must check myself, lest I gave a false impression. It
is necessary to distinguish sharply between the mad worlds of
comparatively low mental development and those of almost
the highest order. The humbler kinds might become crudely
obsessed by sheer mastery or sheer travel, with its scope for
courage and discipline. More tragic was the case of those few
very much more awakened worlds whose obsession was seemingly for community itself and mental lucidity itself, and the
propagation of the kind of community and the special mode of
lucidity most admired by themselves. For them travel was but
the means to cultural and religious empire.

I have spoken as though I were confident that these formidable worlds were indeed mad, aberrant from the line of mental
and spiritual growth. But their tragedy lay in the fact that,
though to their opponents they seemed to be either mad or at
heart wicked, to themselves they appeared superbly sane,
practical, and virtuous. There were times when we ourselves,
the bewildered explorers, were almost persuaded that this was
the truth. Our intimate contact with them was such as to give
us insight, so to speak, into the inner sanity of their insanity,
or the core of rightness in their wickedness. This insanity or
wickedness I have to describe in terms of simple human crazi-
ness and vice; but in truth it was in a sense superhuman, for
it included the perversion of faculties above the range of
human sanity and virtue.

When one of these 'mad' worlds encountered a sane world,

it would sincerely express the most reasonable and kindly intentions. It desired only cultural intercourse, and perhaps economic co-operation. Little by little it would earn the respect of the other for its sympathy, its splendid social order, and its dynamic purpose. Each world would regard the other as a noble, though perhaps an alien and partly incomprehensible, instrument of the spirit. But little by little the normal world would begin to realize that in the culture of the 'mad' world there were certain subtle and far-reaching intuitions that appeared utterly false, ruthless, aggressive, and hostile to the spirit, and were the dominant motives of its foreign relations. The 'mad' world, meanwhile, would regretfully come to the conclusion that the other was after all gravely lacking in sensibility, that it was obtuse to the very highest values and most heroic virtues, in fact that its whole life was subtly corrupt, and must, for its own sake, be changed, or else destroyed. Thus each world, though with lingering respect and affection, would sadly condemn the other. But the mad world would not be content to leave matters thus. It would at length with holy fervour attack, striving to destroy the other's pernicious culture, and even exterminate its population.

It is easy for me now, after the event, after the final spiritual downfall of these mad worlds, to condemn them as perverts, but in the early stages of their drama we were often desperately at a loss to decide on which side sanity lay.

Several of the mad worlds succumbed to their own foolhardiness in navigation. Others, under the strain of age-long research, fell into social neurosis and civil strife. A few, however, succeeded in attaining their end, and after voyages lasting for thousands of years were able to reach some neighbouring planetary system. The invaders were often in a desperate plight. Generally they had used up most of the material of their little artificial sun. Economy had forced them to reduce their ration of heat and light so far that when at last they discovered a suitable planetary system their native world was almost wholly arctic. On arrival, they would first take up their position in a suitable orbit, and perhaps spend some centuries in recuperating. Then they would explore the neighbouring worlds, seek out the most hospitable, and begin to adapt themselves or their descendants to life upon it. If, as was often the case, any of the planets was already inhabited by intelligent beings, the invaders would inevitably come sooner or later into conflict with them, either in a crude manner over the right to exploit a planet's resources, or more probably over the invaders' obsession for propagating their own culture. For by now the civilizing mission, which was the ostensible motive of all their heroic adventures, would have become a rigid obsession. They would be quite incapable of conceiving that the native civilization, though less developed than their own, might be more suited to the natives. Nor could they realize that their own culture, formerly the expression of a gloriously awakened world, might have sunk, in spite of their mechanical powers and crazy religious fervour, below the simpler culture of the natives in all the essentials of mental life.

Many a desperate defence did we see, carried out by some world of the low rank of *Homo Sapiens* against a race of mad supermen, armed not only with the invincible power of sub-atomic energy but with overwhelmingly superior intelligence, knowledge, and devotion, and moreover with the immense advantage that all its individuals participated in the unified mind of the race. Though we had come to cherish above all things the advancement of mentality, and were therefore prejudiced in favour of the awakened though perverted invaders, our sympathies soon became divided, and then passed almost wholly to the natives, however barbaric their culture. For in spite of their stupidity, their ignorance, and superstition, their endless internecine conflicts, their spiritual obtuseness and grossness, we recognized in them a power which the others had forfeited, a naïve but balanced wisdom, an animal shrewdness, a spiritual promise. The invaders, on the other hand, however brilliant, were indeed perverts. Little by little we came to regard the conflict as one in which an untamed but promising urchin had been set upon by an armed religious maniac.

When the invaders had exploited every world in the new-found planetary system, they would again feel the lust of proselytization. Persuading themselves that it was their duty to advance their religious empire throughout the galaxy, they would detach a couple of planets and dispatch them into space with a crew of pioneers. Or they would break up the whole planetary system, and scatter it abroad with missionary zeal. Occasionally their travel brought them into contact with another race of mad superiors. Then would follow a war in which one side or the other, or possibly both, would be exterminated.

Sometimes the adventurers came upon worlds of their own rank which had not succumbed to the mania of religious empire. Then the natives, though they would at first meet the invaders with courtesy and reason, would gradually realize that they were confronted with lunatics. They themselves would hastily convert their civilization for warfare. The issue would depend on superiority of weapons and military cunning; but if the contest was long and grim, the natives, even if victorious, might be so damaged mentally by an age of warfare that they would never recover their sanity.

Worlds that suffered from the mania of religious imperialism would seek interstellar travel long before economic necessity forced it upon them. The saner world-spirits, on the other hand, often discovered sooner or later a point beyond which increased material development and increased population were unnecessary for the exercise of their finer capacities. These were content to remain within their native planetary systems, in a state of economic and social stability. They were thus able to give most of their practical intelligence to telepathic exploration of the universe. Telepathic intercourse between worlds was now becoming much more precise and reliable. The galaxy had emerged from the primitive stage when any world could remain solitary, and live out its career in splendid isolation. In fact, just as, in the experience of *Homo Sapiens,* the Earth is now 'shrinking' to the dimensions of a country, so, in this critical period of the life of our galaxy, the whole galaxy was 'shrinking' to the dimensions of a world. Those world spirits that had been most successful in telepathic exploration had by now constructed a fairly accurate 'mental map' of the whole galaxy, though there still remained a number of eccentric worlds with which no lasting contact could yet be made. There was also one very advanced system of worlds, which had mysteriously 'faded out' of telepathic intercourse altogether. Of this I shall tell more in the sequel.

The telepathic ability of the mad worlds and systems was by now greatly reduced. Though they were often under telepathic observation by the more mature world-spirits, and were even influenced to some extent, they themselves were so self-complacent that they cared not to explore the mental life of the galaxy. Physical travel and sacred imperial power were for them good enough means of intercourse with the surrounding universe.

In time there grew up several great rival empires of the mad worlds, each claiming to be charged with some sort of divine mission for the unifying and awakening of the whole galaxy. Between the ideologies of these empires there was little to choose, yet each was opposed to the others with religious fervour. Germinating in regions far apart, these empires easily mastered any sub-utopian worlds that lay within reach. Thus they spread from one planetary system to another, till at last empire made contact with empire.

Then followed wars such as had never before occurred in our galaxy. Fleets of worlds, natural and artificial, manoeuvred among the stars to outwit one another, and destroyed one another with long-range jets of sub-atomic energy. As the tides of battle swept hither and thither through space, whole planetary systems were annihilated. Many a world-spirit found a sudden end. Many a lowly race that had no part in the strife was slaughtered in the celestial warfare that raged around it.

Yet so vast is the galaxy that these intermundane wars, terrible as they were, could at first be regarded as rare accidents, mere unfortunate episodes in the triumphant march of civilization. But the disease spread. More and more of the sane worlds, when they were attacked by the mad empires, reorganized themselves for military defence. They were right in believing that the situation was one with which non-violence alone could not cope; for the enemy, unlike any possible group of human beings, was too thoroughly purged of 'humanity' to be susceptible to sympathy. But they were wrong in hoping that arms could save them. Even though, in the ensuing war, the defenders might gain victory in the end, the struggle was generally so long and devastating that the victors themselves were irreparably damaged in spirit.

In a later and perhaps the most terrible phase of our galaxy's life I was forcibly reminded of the state of bewilderment and anxiety that I had left behind me on the Earth. Little by little the whole galaxy, some ninety thousand light-years across, containing more than thirty thousand million stars, and (by this date) over a hundred thousand planetary systems, and actually thousands of intelligent races, was paralysed by the fear of war, and periodically tortured by its outbreak.

In one respect, however, the state of the galaxy was much more desperate than the state of our little world today. None of our nations is an awakened super-individual. Even those peoples which are suffering from the mania of herd glory are composed of individuals who in their private life are sane. A change of fortune might perhaps drive such a people into a less crazy mood. Or skilful propaganda for the idea of human unity might turn the scale. But in this grim age of the galaxy the mad worlds were mad almost down to the very roots of their being. Each was a super-individual whose whole physical and mental constitution, including the unit bodies and minds of its private members, was by now organized through and through for a mad purpose. There seemed to be no more possibility of appealing to the stunted creatures to rebel against the sacred and crazy purpose of their race than of persuading the individual brain-cells of a maniac to make a stand for gentleness.

To be alive in those days in one of the worlds that were sane and awakened, though not of the very highest, most percipient order, was to feel (or will be to feel) that the plight of the galaxy was desperate. These average sane worlds had organized themselves into a League to resist aggression; but since they were far less developed in military organization than the mad worlds, and much less inclined to subject their individual members to military despotism, they were at a great disadvantage.

Moreover, the enemy was now united; for one empire had secured complete mastery over the others, and had inspired all the mad worlds with an identical passion of religious imperialism. Though the 'United Empires' of the mad worlds included only a minority of the worlds of the galaxy, the sane worlds had no hope of a speedy victory; for they were disunited, and unskilled in warfare. Meanwhile war was undermining the mental life of the League's own members. The urgencies and horrors were beginning to blot out from their minds all the more delicate, more developed capacities. They were becoming less and less capable of those activities of personal intercourse and cultural adventure which they still forlornly recognized as the true way of life.

The great majority of the worlds of the League, finding themselves caught in a trap from which, seemingly, there was no escape, came despairingly to feel that the spirit which they had thought divine, the spirit which seeks true community and true awakening, was after all not destined to triumph, and therefore not the essential spirit of the cosmos. Blind chance, it was rumoured, ruled all things; or perhaps a diabolic intelligence. Some began to conceive that the Star Maker had created merely for the lust of destroying. Undermined by this terrible surmise, they themselves sank far towards madness. With horror they imagined that the enemy was indeed, as he claimed, the instrument of divine wrath, punishing them for their own impious will to turn the whole galaxy, the whole cosmos, into a paradise of generous and fully awakened beings. Under the influence of this growing sense of ultimate satanic power and the even more devastating doubt of the rightness of their own ideals, the League members despaired. Some surrendered to the enemy. Others succumbed to internal discord, losing their mental unity. The war of the worlds seemed likely to end in the victory of the insane. And so, indeed, it would have done, but for the interference of that remote and brilliant system of worlds which, as was mentioned above, had for a long while withdrawn itself from telepathic intercourse with the rest of our galaxy. This was the system of worlds which had been founded in the spring-time of the galaxy by the symbiotic Ichthyoids and Arachnoids.

3. A Crisis in Galactic History

Throughout this period of imperial expansion a few world-systems of a very high order, though less awakened than the Symbiotics of the sub-galaxy, had watched events telepathically from afar. They saw the frontiers of empire advancing steadily towards them, and knew that they themselves would soon be implicated. They had the knowledge and power to defeat the enemy in war; they received desperate appeals for help; yet they did nothing. These were worlds that were organized through and through for peace and the activities proper to an awakened world. They knew that, if they chose to re-make their whole social structure and reorientate their minds, they could ensure military victory. They knew also that they would thereby save many worlds from conquest, from oppression and from the possible destruction of all that was best in them. But they knew also that in reorganizing themselves for desperate warfare, in neglecting, for a whole age of struggle, all those activities which were proper to them, they would destroy the best in themselves more surely than the enemy would destroy it by oppression; and that in destroying this they would be murdering what they believed to be the most vital germ in the galaxy. They therefore forswore military action.

When at last one of these more developed world-systems was itself confronted by mad religious enthusiasts, the natives welcomed the invaders, readjusted all their planetary orbits to accommodate the in-coming planets, pressed the foreign power actually to settle part of its population in such of their own planets as afforded suitable climatic conditions; and secretly, gradually, subjected the whole mad race throughout the combined solar system to a course of telepathic hypnotism so potent that its communal mind was completely disintegrated. The invaders became mere uncoordinated individuals, such as we know on Earth. Henceforth they were bewildered, shortsighted, torn by conflicts, ruled by no supreme purpose, obsessed more by self than by community. It had been hoped that, when the mad communal mind had been abolished, the individuals of the invading race would soon be induced to open their eyes and their hearts to a nobler ideal. Unfortunately the telepathic skill of the superior race was not sufficient to delve down to the long-buried chrysalis of the spirit in these beings, to give it air and warmth and light. Since the individual nature of these forlorn individuals was itself the product of a crazy world, they proved incapable of salvation, incapable of sane community. They were therefore segregated to work out their own unlovely destiny in ages of tribal quarrels and cultural decline, ending in the extinction which inevitably overtakes creatures that are incapable of adaptation to new circumstances.

When several invading expeditions had been thus circumvented, there arose among the worlds of the mad United Empires a tradition that certain seemingly pacific worlds were in fact more dangerous than all other enemies, since plainly they had a strange power of 'poisoning the soul'. The imperialists determined to annihilate these terrible opponents. The attacking forces were instructed to avoid all telepathic parley and blow the enemy to pieces at long range. This, it was found, could be most conveniently performed by exploding the sun of the doomed system. Stimulated by a potent ray, the atoms of the photosphere would start disintegrating, and the spreading fury would soon fling the star into the 'nova' state, roasting all his planets.

It was our lot to witness the extraordinary calm, nay the exaltation and joy with which these worlds accepted the prospect of annihilation rather than debase themselves by resistance. Later we were to watch the strange events which saved this galaxy of ours from disaster. But first came tragedy.

From our observation points in the minds of the attackers and the attacked, we observed not once but three times the slaughter of races nobler than any that we had yet encountered by perverts whose own natural mental rank was almost as high. Three worlds, or rather systems of worlds, each possessed by a diversity of specialized races, we saw annihilated. From these doomed planets we actually observed the sun break out with tumultuous eruption, swelling hourly. We actually felt, through the bodies of our hosts, the rapidly increasing heat, and through their eyes the blinding light. We saw the vegetation wither, the seas begin to steam. We felt and heard the furious hurricanes which wrecked every structure and bowled the ruins before them. With awe and wonder we experienced something of that exaltation and inner peace with which the doomed angelic populations met their end. Indeed, it was this experienced angelic exaltation in the hour of tragedy that gave us our first clear insight into the most spiritual attitude to fate. The sheer bodily agony of the disaster soon became intolerable to us, so that we were forced to withdraw ourselves from those martyred worlds. But we left the doomed populations themselves accepting not only this torture but the annihilation of their glorious community with all its infinite hopes, accepting this bitterness as though it were not lethal but the elixir of immortality. Not till almost the close of our own adventure did we grasp for a moment the full meaning of this ecstasy.

It was strange to us that none of these three victims made any attempt to resist the attack. Indeed, not one inhabitant in any of these worlds considered for a moment the possibility of resistance. In every case the attitude to disaster seemed to express itself in such terms as these: 'To retaliate would be to wound our communal spirit beyond cure. We choose rather to die. The theme of spirit that we have created must inevitably be broken short, whether by the ruthlessness of the invader or by our own resort to arms. It is better to be destroyed than to triumph in slaying the spirit. Such as it is, the spirit that we have achieved is fair; and it is indestructibly woven into the tissue of the cosmos. We die praising the universe in which at least such an achievement as ours can be. We die knowing that the promise of further glory outlives us in other galaxies. We die praising the Star Maker, the Star Destroyer.'

4. Triumph in a Sub-Galaxy

It was after the destruction of the third system of worlds, when a fourth was preparing for its end, that a miracle, or a seeming miracle, changed the whole course of events in our galaxy. Before telling of this turn of fortune I must double back the thread of my story and trace the history of the system of worlds which was now to play the leading part in galactic events.

It will be remembered that in an outlying 'island' off the galactic 'continent' there lived the strange symbiotic race of Ichthyoids and Arachnoids. These beings supported almost the oldest civilization in the galaxy. They had reached the 'human' plane of mental development even before the Other Men; and, in spite of many vicissitudes, during the thousands of millions of years of their career they had made great progress. I referred to them last as having occupied all the planets of their system with specialized races of Arachnoids, all of which were in permanent telepathic union with the Ichthyoid population in the oceans of the home planet. As the ages passed, they were several times reduced almost to annihilation, now by too daring physical experiments, now through too ambitious telepathic exploration; but in time they won through to a mental development unequalled in our galaxy.

Their little island universe, their outlying cluster of stars, had come wholly under their control. It contained many natural planetary systems. Several of these included worlds which, when the early Arachnoid explorers visited them telepathically, were found to be inhabited by native races of pre-utopian rank. These were left to work out their own destiny, save that in certain crises of their history the Symbiotics secretly brought to bear on them from afar a telepathic influence that might help them to meet their difficulties with increased vigour. Thus when one of these worlds reached the crisis in which *Homo Sapiens* now stands, it passed with seemingly natural ease straight on to the phase of world-unity and the building of utopia. Great care was taken by the Symbiotic race to keep its existence hidden from the primitives, lest they should lose their independence of mind. Thus, even while the Symbiotics were voyaging among these worlds in rocket vessels and using the mineral resources of neighbouring uninhabited planets, the intelligent worlds of pre-utopian rank were left unvisited. Not till these worlds had themselves entered the full utopian phase and were exploring their neighbour planets were they allowed to discover the truth. By then they were ready to receive it with exultation, rather than disheartenment and fear. Thenceforth, by physical and telepathic intercourse the young utopia would be speedily brought up to the spiritual rank of the Symbiotics themselves, and would co-operate on an equal footing in a symbiosis of worlds.

Some of these pre-utopian worlds, not malignant but incapable of further advance, were left in peace, and preserved, as we preserve wild animals in national parks, for scientific interest. Aeon after aeon, these beings, tethered by their own futility, struggled in vain to cope with the crisis which modern Europe knows so well. In cycle after cycle civilization would emerge from barbarism, mechanization would bring the peoples into uneasy contact, national wars and class wars would breed the longing for a better world-order, but breed it in vain. Disaster after disaster would undermine the fabric of civilization. Gradually barbarism would return. Aeon after aeon, the process would repeat itself under the calm telepathic observation of the Symbiotics, whose existence was never suspected by the primitive creatures under their gaze. So might we ourselves look down into some rock-pool where lowly creatures repeat with naïve zest dramas learned by their ancestors aeons ago.

The Symbiotics could well afford to leave these museum pieces intact, for they had at their disposal scores of planetary systems. Moreover, armed with their highly developed physical sciences and with sub-atomic power, they were able to construct, out in space, artificial planets for permanent habitation. These great hollow globes of artificial super-metals, and artificial transparent adamant, ranged in size from the earliest and smallest structures, which were no bigger than a very small asteroid, to spheres considerably larger than the Earth. They were without external atmosphere, since their mass was generally too slight to prevent the escape of gases. A blanket of repelling force protected them from meteors and cosmic rays. The planet's external surface, which was wholly transparent, encased the atmosphere. Immediately beneath it hung the photosynthesis stations and the machinery for generating power from solar radiation. Part of this outer shell was occupied by astronomical observatories, machinery for controlling the planet's orbit, and great 'docks' for interplanetary liners. The interior of these worlds was a system of concentric spheres supported by girders and gigantic arches. Interspersed between these spheres lay the machinery for atmospheric regulation, the great water reservoirs, the food factories and commodity-factories, the engineering shops, the refuse-conversion tracts, residential and recreational areas, and a wealth of research laboratories, libraries, and cultural centres. Since the Symbiotic race was in origin marine, there was a central ocean where the profoundly modified, the physically indolent and mentally athletic descendants of the original Ichthyoids constituted the 'highest brain tract' of the intelligent world. There, as in the primeval ocean of the home planet, the Symbiotic partners sought one another, and the young of both species were nurtured. Such races of the sub-galaxy as were not in origin marine constructed, of course, artificial planets which, though of the same general type were adapted to their special nature. But all the races found it also necessary to mould their own nature drastically to suit their new conditions.

As the aeons advanced, hundreds of thousands of worldlets were constructed, all of this type, but gradually increasing in size and complexity. Many a star without natural planets came to be surrounded by concentric rings of artificial worlds. In some cases the inner rings contained scores, the outer rings thousands of globes adapted to life at some particular distance from the sun. Great diversity, both physical and mental, would distinguish worlds even of the same ring. Sometimes a comparatively old world, or even a whole ring of worlds, would feel itself outstripped in mental excellence by younger worlds and races, whose structure, physical and biological, embodied increasing skill. Then either the superannuated world would simply continue its life in a sort of backwater of civilization, tolerated, loved, studied by the younger worlds; or it would choose to die and surrender the material of its planet for new ventures.

One very small and rather uncommon kind of artificial world consisted almost wholly of water. It was like a titanic bowl of gold-fish. Beneath its transparent shell, studded with rocket-machinery and interplanetary docks, lay a spherical ocean, crossed by structural girders, and constantly impregnated with oxygen. A small solid core represented the sea-bottom. The population of Ichthyoids and the visiting population of Arachnoids swarmed in this huge encrusted drop. Each Ichthyoid would be visited in turn by perhaps a score of partners whose working life was spent on other worlds. The life of the Ichthyoids was indeed a strange one, for they were at once imprisoned and free of all space. An Ichthyoid never left his native ocean, but he had telepathic intercourse with the whole Symbiotic race throughout the sub-galaxy. Moreover, the one form of practical activity which the Ichthyoids performed was astronomy. Immediately beneath the planet's glassy crust hung observatories, where the swimming astronomers studied the constitution of the stars and the distribution of the galaxies.

These 'gold-fish-bowl' worlds turned out to be transitional. Shortly before the age of the mad empires the Symbiotics began to experiment for the production of a world which should consist of a single physical organism. After ages of experiment they produced a 'gold-fish-bowl' type of world in which the whole ocean was meshed by a fixed network of Ichthyoid individuals in direct neutral connection with one another. This world-wide, living, polyp-like tissue had permanent attachments to the machinery and observatories of the world. Thus it constituted a truly organic world-organism, and since the coherent Ichthyoid population supported together a perfectly unified mentality, each of these worlds was indeed in the fullest sense a minded organism, like a man. One essential link with the past was preserved. Arachnoids, specially adapted to the new symbiosis, would visit from their remote planets and swim along the submarine galleries for union with their anchored mates.

More and more of the stars of the outlying cluster or sub-galaxy came to be girdled with rings of worlds, and an increasing number of these worlds were of the new, organic type. Of the populations of the sub-galaxy most were descendants of the original Ichthyoids or Arachnoids; but there were also many whose natural ancestors were humanesque, and not a few that had sprung from avians, insectoids, or plant-men. Between the worlds, between the rings of worlds, and between the solar systems there was constant intercourse, both telepathic and physical. Small, rocket-propelled vessels plied regularly within each system of planets. Larger vessels or high-speed worldlets voyaged from system to system, explored the whole sub-galaxy, and even ventured across the ocean of emptiness into the main body of the galaxy, where thousands upon thousands of planetless stars awaited encirclement by rings of worlds.

Strangely, the triumphant advance of material civilization and colonization now slowed down and actually came to a standstill. Physical intercourse between worlds of the sub-galaxy was maintained, but not increased. Physical exploration of the neighbouring fringe of the galactic 'continent' was abandoned. Within the sub-galaxy itself no new worlds were founded. Industrial activities continued, but at reduced pressure, and no further advance was made in the standard of material convenience. Indeed, manners and customs began to grow less dependent on mechanical aids. Among the Symbiotic worlds, the Arachnoid populations were reduced in number; the Ichthyoids in their cells of ocean lived in a permanent state of mental concentration and fervour, which of course was telepathically shared by their partners.

It was at this time that telepathic intercourse between the advanced sub-galaxy and the few awakened worlds of the 'continent' was entirely abolished. During recent ages, communication had been very fragmentary. The Sub-Galactics had apparently so far outstripped their neighbours that their interest in those primitives had become purely archaeological, and was gradually eclipsed by the enthralling life of their own community of worlds, and by their telepathic exploration of remote galaxies.

To us, the band of explorers, desperately struggling to maintain contact between our communal mind and the incomparably more developed minds of these worlds, the finest activities of the Sub-Galactics were at present inaccessible. We observed only a stagnation of the more obvious physical and mental activities of these systems of worlds. It seemed at first that this stagnation must be caused by some obscure flaw in their nature. Was it, perhaps, the first stage of irrevocable decline?

Later, however, we began to discover that this seeming stagnation was a symptom not of death but of more vigorous life. Attention had been drawn from material advancement just because it had opened up new spheres of mental discovery and growth. In fact the great community of worlds, whose members consisted of some thousands of world-spirits, was busy digesting the fruits of its prolonged phase of physical progress, and was now finding itself capable of new and unexpected psychical activities. At first the nature of these activities was entirely hidden from us. But in time we learned how to let ourselves be gathered up by these superhuman beings so as to obtain at least an obscure glimpse of the matters which so enthralled them. They were concerned, it seemed, partly with telepathic exploration of the great host of ten million galaxies, partly with a technique of spiritual discipline by which they strove to come to more penetrating insight into the nature of the cosmos and to a finer creativity. This, we learned, was possible because their perfect community of worlds was tentatively waking into a higher plane of being, as a single communal mind whose body was the whole sub-galaxy of worlds. Though we could not participate in the life of this lofty being, we guessed that its absorbing passion was not wholly unlike the longing of the noblest of our own human species to 'come

face to face with God'. This new being desired to have the
percipience and the hardihood to endure direct vision of the
source of all light and life and love. In fact this whole population of worlds was rapt in a prolonged and mystical adventure.

5. The Tragedy of the Perverts

Such was the state of affairs when, in the main galactic 'continent', the mad United Empires concentrated their power upon
the few worlds that were not merely sane but of superior
mental rank. The attention of the Symbiotics and their colleagues in the supremely civilized sub-galaxy had long been
withdrawn from the petty affairs of the 'continent'. It was
given instead to the cosmos as a whole and to the inner discipline of the spirit. But the first of the three murders perpetrated
by the United Empires upon a population far more developed
than themselves seems to have caused a penetrating reverberation to echo, so to speak, through all the loftier spheres of
existence. Even in the full flight of their career, the Sub-Galactics took cognizance. Once more attention was directed telepathically to the neighbouring continent of stars.

While the situation was being studied, the second murder
was committed. The Sub-Galactics knew that they had power
to prevent any further disaster. Yet, to our surprise, our horror
and incomprehension, they calmly awaited the third murder.
Still more strange, the doomed worlds themselves, though in
telepathic communication with the Sub-Galaxy, made no appeal for help. Victims and spectators alike studied the situation
with quiet interest, even with a sort of bright exultation not
wholly unlike amusement. From our lowlier plane this detachment, this seeming levity, at first appeared less angelic than
inhuman. Here was a whole world of sensitive and intelligent
beings in the full tide of eager life and communal activity. Here
were lovers newly come together, scientists in the midst of
profound research, artists intent on new delicacies of apprehension, workers in a thousand practical social undertakings of

which man has no conception, here in fact was all the rich diversity of personal lives that go to make up a highly developed world in action. And each of these individual minds participated in the communal mind of all; each experienced not only as a private individual but as the very spirit of his race. Yet these calm beings faced the destruction of their world with no more distress seemingly than one of us would feel at the prospect of resigning his part in some interesting game. And in the minds of the spectators of this impending tragedy we observed no agony of compassion, but only such commiseration, tinged with humour, as we might feel for some distinguished tennis-player who was knocked out in the first round of a tournament by some trivial accident such as a sprained ankle.

With difficulty we came to understand the source of this strange equanimity. Spectators and victims alike were so absorbed in cosmological research, so conscious of the richness and potentiality of the cosmos, and above all so possessed by spiritual contemplation, that the destruction was seen, even by the victims themselves, from the point of view which men would call divine. Their gay exaltation and their seeming frivolity were rooted in the fact that to them the personal life, and even the life and death of individual worlds, appeared chiefly as vital themes contributing to the life of the cosmos. From the cosmical point of view the disaster was after all a very small though poignant matter. Moreover, if by the sacrifice of another group of worlds, even of splendidly awakened worlds, greater insight could be attained into the insanity of the Mad Empires, the sacrifice was well worth while.

So the third murder was committed. Then came the miracle. The telepathic skill of the Sub-Galaxy was far more developed than that of the scattered superior worlds on the galactic 'continent.' It could dispense with the aid of normal intercourse, and it could overcome every resistance. It could reach right down to the buried chrysalis of the spirit even in the most perverted individual. This was not a merely destructive power, blotting out the communal mind hypnotically; it was a kindling, an awakening power, brought to bear on the sane but dormant core of each individual. This skill was now exercised upon the galactic continent with triumphant but also tragic effect; for even this skill was not omnipotent. There appeared here and there among the mad worlds a strange and spreading 'disease' of the mind. To the orthodox imperialists in those worlds themselves it seemed a madness; but it was in fact a late and ineffectual waking into sanity on the part of beings whose nature had been moulded through and through for madness in a mad environment.

The course of this 'disease' of sanity in a mad world ran generally as follows. Individuals here and there, while still playing their part in the well-disciplined action and communal thought of the world, would find themselves teased by private doubts and disgusts opposed to the dearest assumptions of the world in which they lived, doubts of the worth of record-breaking travel and record-breaking empire, and disgust with the cult of mechanical triumph and intellectual servility and the divinity of the race. As these disturbing thoughts increased, the bewildered individuals would begin to fear for their own 'sanity'. Presently they would cautiously sound their neighbours. Little by little, doubt would become more widespread and more vocal, until at last considerable minorities in each world, though still playing their official part, would lose contact with the communal mind, and become mere isolated individuals; but individuals at heart more sane than the lofty communal mind from which they had fallen. The orthodox majority, horrified at this mental disintegration, would then apply the familiar ruthless methods that had been used so successfully in the uncivilized outposts of empire. The dissentients would be arrested, and either destroyed outright or concentrated upon the most inhospitable planet, in the hope that their torture might prove an effective warning to others.

This policy failed. The strange mental disease spread more and more rapidly, till the 'lunatics' outnumbered the 'sane'. There followed civil wars, mass-martyrdom of devoted pacifists, dissension among the imperialists, a steady increase of 'lunacy' in every world of the empire. The whole imperial organization fell to pieces; and since the aristocratic worlds that formed the backbone of empire were as impotent as soldier-ants to maintain themselves without the service and tribute of the subject worlds, the loss of empire doomed them to death. When almost the whole population of such a world had gone sane, great efforts would be made to reorganize its life for self-sufficiency and peace. It might have been expected that this task, though difficult, would not have defeated a population of beings whose sheer intelligence and social loyalty were incomparably greater than anything known on earth. But there were unexpected difficulties, not economic but psychological. These beings had been fashioned for war, tyranny, and empire. Though telepathic stimulation from superior minds could touch into life the slumbering germ of the spirit in them, and help them to realize the triviality of their world's whole purpose, telepathic influence could not refashion their nature to such an extent that they could henceforth actually live for the spirit and renounce the old life. In spite of heroic self-discipline, they tended to sink into inertia, like wild beasts domesticated; or to run amok, and exercise against one another those impulses of domination which hitherto had been directed upon subject worlds. And all this they did with profound consciousness of guilt.

For us it was heartrending to watch the agony of these worlds. Never did the newly enlightened beings lose their vision of true community and of the spiritual life; but though the vision haunted them, the power to realize it in the detail of action was lost. Moreover, there were times when the change of heart that they had suffered seemed to them actually a change for the worse. Formerly all individuals had been perfectly disciplined to the common will, and perfectly happy in executing that will without the heart-searchings of individual responsibility. But now individuals were mere individuals; and all were tormented by mutual suspicion and by violent propensities for self-seeking.

The issue of this appalling struggle in the minds of these former imperialists depended on the extent to which specialization for empire had affected them. In a few young worlds, in which specialization had not gone deep, a period of chaos was followed by a period of reorientation and world-planning, and in due season by sane utopia. But in most of these worlds no such escape was possible. Either chaos persisted till racial decline set in, and the world sank to the human, the sub-human, the merely animal states; or else, in a few cases only, the discrepancy between the ideal and the actual was so distressing that the whole race committed suicide.

We could not long endure the spectacle of scores of worlds falling into psychological ruin. Yet the Sub-Galactics who had caused these strange events, and continued to use their power to clarify and so destroy these minds, watched their handiwork unflinchingly. Pity they felt, pity such as we feel for a child that has broken its toy; but no indignation against fate.

Within a few thousand years every one of the imperial worlds had either transformed itself or fallen into barbarism or committed suicide.

6. A Galactic Utopia

The events that I have been describing took place, or from the human point of view will take place, at a date as far future to us as we are from the condensation of the earliest stars. The next period of galactic history covers the period from the fall of the mad empires to the achievement of utopia in the whole galactic community of worlds. This transitional period was in itself in a manner utopian; for it was an age of triumphant progress carried out by beings whose nature was rich and harmonious, whose nurture was entirely favourable, and their ever-widening galactic community a wholly satisfying object of loyalty. It was only not utopian in the sense that the galactic society was still expanding and constantly changing its structure to meet new needs, economic and spiritual. At the close of this phase there came a period of full utopia in which the attention of the perfected galactic community was directed mainly beyond itself towards other galaxies. Of this I shall tell in due course; and of the unforeseen and stormy events which shattered this beatitude.

Meanwhile we must glance at the age of expansion. The worlds of the Sub-Galaxy, recognizing that no further great advance in culture was possible unless the population of awakened worlds was immensely increased and diversified, now began to plan an active part in the work of reorganizing the whole galactic continent. By telepathic communication they gave to all awakened worlds throughout the galaxy knowledge of the triumphant society which they themselves had created; and they called upon all to join them in the founding of the galactic utopia. Every world throughout the galaxy, they said, must be an intensely conscious individual; and each must contribute its personal idiosyncrasy and all the wealth of its experience to the pooled experience of all. When at last the community was completed, they said, it must go on to fulfil its function in the far greater community of all galaxies, there to participate in spiritual activities as yet but dimly guessed.

In their earlier age of meditation the Sub-Galactic worlds, or rather the single intermittently awakening mind of the Sub-Galaxy, had evidently made discoveries which had very precise bearing on the founding of the galactic society; for they now put forward the demand that the number of minded worlds in the Galaxy must be increased to at least ten thousand times its present extent. In order that all the potentialities of the spirit should be fulfilled, they said there must be a far greater diversity of world-types, and thousands of worlds of each type. They themselves, in their small Sub-Galactic community, had learned enough to realize that only a very much greater community could explore all the regions of being, some few of which they themselves had glimpsed, but only from afar.

The natural worlds of the galactic continent were bewildered and alarmed by the magnitude of this scheme. They were content with the extant scale of life. The spirit, they affirmed, had no concern for magnitude and multiplicity. To this the reply was made that such a protest came ill from worlds whose own achievement depended on the splendid diversity of their members. Diversity and multiplicity of worlds was as necessary on the galactic plane as diversity and multiplicity of individuals on the world plane and diversity and multiplicity of nerve-cells on the individual plane.

In the upshot the natural worlds of the 'continent' played a decreasing part in the advancing life of the galaxy. Some merely remained at the level of their own unaided achievement. Some joined in the great co-operative work, but without fervour and without genius. A few joined heartily and usefully in the enterprise. One, indeed, was able to contribute greatly. This was a symbiotic race, but of a very different kind from that which had founded the community of the Sub-Galaxy. The symbiosis consisted of two races which had originally inhabited separate planets of the same system. An intelligent avian species, driven to desperation by the desiccation of its native planet, had contrived to invade a neighbouring world inhabited by a manlike species. Here I must not tell how, after ages of alternating strife and co-operation, a thorough economic and psychological symbiosis was established.

The building of the galactic community of worlds lies far beyond the comprehension of the writer of this book. I cannot now remember at all clearly what I experienced of these obscure matters in the state of heightened lucidity which came to me through participation in the communal mind of the explorers. And even in that state I was bewildered by the effort to comprehend the aims of that close-knit community of worlds.

If my memory is to be trusted at all, three kinds of activity occupied the minded worlds in this phase of galactic history. The main practical work was to enrich and harmonize the life of the galaxy itself, to increase the number and diversity and mental unity of the fully awakened worlds up to the point which, it was believed, was demanded for the emergence of a mode of experience more awakened than any hitherto attained. The second kind of activity was that which sought to make closer contact with the other galaxies by physical and telepathic study. The third was the spiritual exercise appropriate to beings of the rank of the world-minds. This last seems to have been concerned (or will be concerned) at once with the deepening of the self-awareness of each individual world-spirit and the detachment of its will from merely private fulfilment. But this was not all. For on this relatively high level of the spirit's ascent, as on our own lowliest of all spiritual planes, there had also to be a more radical detachment from the whole adventure of life and mind in the cosmos. For, as the spirit wakens, it craves more and more to regard all existence not merely with a creature's eyes, but in the universal view, as though through the eyes of the creator.

At first the task of establishing the galactic utopia occupied almost the whole energy of the awakened worlds. More and more of the stars were encircled with concentric hoops of pearls, perfect though artificial. And each pearl was a unique world, occupied by a unique race. Henceforth the highest level of persistent individuality was not a world but a system of scores or hundreds of worlds. And between the systems there was as easy and delightful converse as between human individuals.

In these conditions, to be a conscious individual was to enjoy immediately the united sensory impressions of all the races inhabiting a system of worlds. And as the sense-organs of the worlds apprehended not only 'nakedly' but also through artificial instruments of great range and subtlety, the conscious individual perceived not only the structure of hundreds of planets, but also the configuration of the whole system of planets clustered about its sun. Other systems also it perceived, as men perceive one another; for in the distance the glittering bodies of other 'multi-mundane' persons like itself gyrated and drifted.

Between the minded planetary systems occurred infinite variations of personal intercourse. As between human individuals, there were loves and hates, temperamental sympa-

thies and antipathies, joyful and distressful intimacies, co-
operations and thwartings in personal ventures and in the great
common venture of building the galactic utopia.

Between individual systems of worlds, as between symbiotic
partners, there sometimes occurred relationships with an almost sexual flavour, though actual sex played no part in them.
Neighbouring systems would project travelling worldlets, or
greater worlds, or trains of worlds, across the ocean of space
to take up orbits round each other's suns and play intimate
parts in symbiotic, or rather 'sympsychic' relationships in one
another's private life. Occasionally a whole system would mi-
grate to another system, and settle its worlds in rings between
the rings of the other system.

Telepathic intercourse united the whole galaxy; but telepathy, though it had the great advantage that it was not affected
by distance, was seemingly imperfect in other ways. So far as
possible it was supplemented by physical travel. A constant
stream of touring worldlets percolated through the whole galaxy in every direction.

The task of establishing utopia in the galaxy was not pursued without friction. Different kinds of races were apt to have
different policies for the galaxy. Though war was by now
unthinkable, the sort of strife which we know between individuals or associations within the same state was common.
There was, for instance, a constant struggle between the planetary systems that were chiefly interested in the building of
utopia, those that were most concerned to make contact with
other galaxies, and those whose main preoccupation was
spiritual. Besides these great parties, there were groups of
planetary systems which were prone to put the well-being of
individual world-systems above the advancement of galactic
enterprise. They cared more for the drama of personal intercourse and the fulfilment of the personal capacity of worlds
and systems than for organization or exploration or spiritual
purification. Though their presence was often exasperating to
the enthusiasts, it was salutary, for it was a guarantee against
extravagance and against tyranny.

It was during the age of the galactic utopia that another

salutary influence began to take full effect on the busy worlds. Telepathic research had made contact with the long-extinct Plant-Men, who had been undone by the extravagance of their own mystical quietism. The utopian worlds now learned much from these archaic but uniquely sensitive beings. Henceforth the vegetal mode of experience was thoroughly, but not dangerously, knit into the texture of the galactic mind.

CHAPTER TEN

A VISION
OF THE GALAXY

It seemed to us now that the troubles of the many worlds of
this galaxy were at last over, that the will to support the galactic utopia was now universal, and that the future must bring
glory after glory. We felt assured of the same progress in other
galaxies. In our simplicity we looked forward to the speedy,
the complete and final, triumph of the striving spirit throughout the cosmos. We even conceived that the Star Maker re-
joiced in the perfection of his work. Using such symbols as we
could to express the inexpressible, we imagined that, before
the beginning, the Star Maker was alone, and that for love and
for community he resolved to make a perfect creature, to be his
mate. We imagined that he made her of his hunger for beauty
and his will for love; but that he also scourged her in the
making, and tormented her, so that she might at last triumph
over all adversity, and thereby achieve such perfection as he
in his almightiness could never attain. The cosmos we conceived to be that creature. And it seemed to us in our simplicity
that we had already witnessed the greater part of cosmical
growth, and that there remained only the climax of that
growth, the telepathic union of all the galaxies to become the
single, fully awakened spirit of the cosmos, perfect, fit to be
eternally contemplated and enjoyed by the Star Maker.

All this seemed to us majestically right. Yet we ourselves had
no joy in it. We had been sated with the spectacle of continuous and triumphant progress in the latter age of our galaxy, and
we were no longer curious about the host of the other galaxies.
Almost certainly they were much like our own. We were, in
fact, overwhelmingly fatigued and disillusioned. During so
many aeons we had followed the fortunes of the many worlds.

So often we had lived out their passions, novel to them, but to us for the most part repetitive. We had shared all kinds of suffering, all kinds of glories and shames. And now that the cosmical ideal, the full awakening of the spirit, seemed on the point of attainment, we found ourselves a little tired of it. What matter whether the whole huge drama of existence should be intricately known and relished by the perfected spirit or not? What matter whether we ourselves should complete our pilgrimage or not?

During so many aeons our company, distributed throughout the galaxy, had with difficulty maintained its single communal mentality. At all times 'we', in spite of our severalty, were in fact 'I', the single observer of the many worlds; but the maintaining of this identity was itself becoming a toil. 'I' was overpowered with sleepiness; 'we', severally, longed for our little native worlds, our homes, our lairs; and for the animal obtuseness that had walled us in from all the immensities. In particular, I, the Englishman, longed to be sleeping safely in that room where she and I had slept together, the day's urgencies all blotted out, and nothing left but sleep and the shadowy, the peaceful awareness in each of the other.

But though I was fatigued beyond endurance, sleep would not come. I remained perforce with my colleagues, and with the many triumphant worlds.

Slowly we were roused from our drowsiness by a discovery. It gradually appeared to us that the prevailing mood of these countless utopian systems of worlds was at heart very different from that of triumph. In every world we found a deep conviction of the littleness and impotence of all finite beings, no matter how exalted. In a certain world there was a kind of poet. When we told him our conception of the cosmical goal, he said, 'When the cosmos wakes, if ever she does, she will find herself not the single beloved of her maker, but merely a little bubble adrift on the boundless and bottomless ocean of being.'

What had seemed to us at first the irresistible march of god-like world-spirits, with all the resources of the universe in their hands and all eternity before them, was now gradually revealed in very different guise. The great advance in mental calibre, and the attainment of communal mentality throughout the cosmos, had brought a change in the experience of time. The temporal reach of the mind had been very greatly extended. The awakened worlds experienced an aeon as a mere crowded day. They were aware of time's passage as a man in a canoe might have cognizance of a river which in its upper reaches is sluggish but subsequently breaks into rapids and becomes swifter and swifter, till, at no great distance ahead, it must plunge in a final cataract down to the sea, namely to the eternal end of life, the extinction of the stars. Comparing the little respite that remained with the great work which they passionately desired to accomplish, namely the full awakening of the cosmical spirit, they saw that at best there was no time to spare, and that, more probably, it was already too late to accomplish the task. They had a strange foreboding that unforeseen disaster lay in store for them. It was sometimes said, 'We know not what the stars, even, have in store for us, still less what the Star Maker.' And it was sometimes said, 'We should not for a moment consider even our best-established knowledge of existence as true. It is awareness only of the colours that our own vision paints on the film of one bubble in one strand of foam on the ocean of being.'

The sense of the fated incompleteness of all creatures and of all their achievements gave to the Galactic Society of Worlds a charm, a sanctity, as of some short-lived and delicate flower. And it was with an increasing sense of precarious beauty that we ourselves were now learning to regard the far-flung utopia. In this mood we had a remarkable experience.

We had embarked upon a sort of holiday from exploration, seeking the refreshment of disembodied flight in space. Gathering our whole company together out of all the worlds, we centred ourselves into a single mobile view-point; and then, as one being, we glided and circled among the stars and nebulae. Presently the whim took us to plunge into outer space. We hastened till the forward stars turned violet, the hinder red; till both forward and hinder vanished; till all visible features were extinguished by the wild speed of our flight. In absolute darkness we brooded on the origin and the destiny of the galaxies, and on the appalling contrast between the cosmos and our minute home-lives to which we longed to return.

Presently we came to rest. In doing so we discovered that our situation was not such as we expected. The galaxy whence we had emerged did indeed lie far behind us, no bigger than a great cloud; but it was not the featured spiral that it should have been. After some confusion of mind we realized that we were looking at the galaxy in an early stage of its existence, in fact at a time before it was really a galaxy at all. For the cloud was no cloud of stars, but a continuous mist of light. At its heart was a vague brilliance, which faded softly into the dim outer regions and merged without perceptible boundary into the black sky. Even the sky itself was quite unfamiliar. Though empty of stars, it was densely peopled with a great number of pale clouds. All seemingly were farther from us than that from which we had come, but several bulked as largely as Orion in the Earth's sky. So congested was the heaven that many of the great objects were continuous with one another in their filmy extremities, and many were separated only by mere channels of emptiness, through which loomed vistas of more remote nebulae, some of them so distant as to be mere spots of light.

It was clear that we had travelled back through time to a date when the great nebulae were still near neighbours to one another, before the explosive nature of the cosmos had done more than separate them out from the continuous and congested primal substance.

As we watched, it became obvious that events were unfolding before us with fantastic speed. Each cloud visibly shrank, withdrawing into the distance. It also changed its shape. Each vague orb flattened somewhat, and became more definite. Receding and therefore diminishing, the nebulae now appeared as lens-shaped mists, tilted at all angles. But, even as we watched, they withdrew themselves so far into the depth of space that it became difficult to observe their changes. Only our own native nebula remained beside us, a huge oval stretching across half the sky. On this we now concentrated our attention.

Differences began to appear within it, regions of brighter and of less bright mist, faint streaks and swirls, like the foam on the sea's waves. These shadowy features slowly moved, as wisps of cloud move on the hill. Presently it was clear that the internal currents of the nebula were on the whole set in a common pattern. The great world of gas was in fact slowly rotating, almost as a tornado. As it rotated it continued to flatten. It was now like some blurred image of a streaked and flattish pebble, handy for 'ducks and drakes', held too near the eye to be focused.

Presently we noticed, with our novel and miraculous vision, that microscopic points of intenser light were appearing here and there throughout the cloud, but mainly in its outer regions. As we watched, their number grew, and the spaces between them grew dark. Thus were the stars born.

The great cloud still span and flattened. It was soon a disc of whirling star-streams and strands of uncondensed gas, the last disintegrating tissues of the primal nebula. These continued to move within the whole by their own semi-independent activity, changing their shapes, creeping like living things, extending pseudopodia, and visibly fading as clouds fade; but giving place to new generations of stars. The heart of the nebula was now condensing into a smaller bulk, more clearly defined. It was a huge, congested globe of brilliance. Here and there throughout the disc knots and lumps of light were the embryonic starclusters. The whole nebula was strewn with these balls of thistledown, these feathery, sparkling, fairy decorations, each one in fact pregnant with a small universe of stars.

The galaxy, for such it could now be named, continued visibly to whirl with hypnotic constancy. Its tangled tresses of star-streams were spread abroad on the darkness. Now it was like a huge broad-brimmed white sombrero, the crown a glowing mass, the brim a filmy expanse of stars. It was a cardinal's hat, spinning. The two long whirling tassels on the brim were two long spiralling star-streams. Their frayed extremities had broken away and become sub-galaxies, revolving about the main galactic system. The whole, like a spinning top, swayed; and, as it tilted before us, the brim appeared as an ever narrower ellipse, till presently it was edge-on, and the outermost fringe of it, composed of non-luminous matter, formed a thin, dark, knotted line across the glowing inner substance of nebula and stars.

Peering, straining to see more precisely the texture of this shimmering and nacrous wonder, this largest of all the kinds of objects in the cosmos, we found that our new vision, even while embracing the whole galaxy and the distant galaxies, apprehended each single star as a tiny disc separated from its nearest neighbours much as a cork on the Arctic Ocean would be separated from another cork on the Antarctic. Thus, in spite of the nebulous and opalescent beauty of its general form, the galaxy also appeared to us as a void sprinkled with very sparse scintillations.

Observing the stars more closely, we saw that while they streamed along in companies like shoals of fishes, their currents sometimes interpenetrated. Then seemingly the stars of the different streams, crossing one another's paths, pulled at one another, moving in great sweeping curves as they passed from one neighbour's influence to another. Thus, in spite of their remoteness each from each, the stars often looked curiously like minute living creatures taking cognizance of one another from afar. Sometimes they swung hyperbolically round one another and away, or, more rarely, united to form binaries.

So rapidly did time pass before us that aeons were packed into moments. We had seen the first stars condense from the nebular tissue as ruddy giants, though in the remote view inconceivably minute. A surprising number of these, perhaps through the centrifugal force of their rotation, were burst asunder to form binaries, so that, increasingly, the heaven was peopled by these waltzing pairs. Meanwhile, the giant stars slowly shrank and gathered brightness. They passed from red to yellow, and on to dazzling white and blue. While other young giants condensed around them, they shrank still further, and their colour changed once more to yellow and to smouldering red. Presently we saw the eldest of the stars one by one extinguished like sparks from a fire. The incidence of this mortality increased, slowly but steadily. Sometimes a 'nova' flashed out and faded, outshining for a moment all its myriad neighbours. Here and there a 'variable' pulsated with inconceivable rapidity. Now and again we saw a binary and a third star approach one another so closely that one or other of the group reached out a filament of its substance towards its partner. Straining our supernatural vision, we saw these filaments break and condense into planets. And we were awed by the infinitesimal size and the rarity of these seeds of life among the lifeless host of the stars.

But the stars themselves gave an irresistible impression of vitality. Strange that the movements of these merely physical things, these mere fire-balls, whirling and travelling according to the geometrical laws of their minutest particles, should seem so vital, so questing. But then the whole galaxy was itself so vital, so like an organism, with its delicate tracery of star-streams, like the streams within a living cell; and its extended wreaths, almost like feelers; and its nucleus of light. Surely this great and lovely creature must be alive, must have intelligent experience of itself and of things other than it.

In the tide of these wild thoughts we checked our fancy, remembering that only on the rare grains called planets can life gain foothold, and that all this wealth of restless jewels was but a waste of fire.

With rising affection and longing we directed our attention more minutely towards the earliest planetary grains as they condensed out of the whirling filaments of flame, to become at first molten drops that span and pulsated, then grew rock-encrusted, ocean-filmed, and swathed in atmosphere. Our piercing sight observed their shallow waters ferment with life, which soon spread into their oceans and continents. A few of these early worlds we saw waken to intelligence of human rank; and very soon these were in the throes of the great struggle for the spirit, from which still fewer emerged victorious.

Meanwhile new planetary births, rare among the stars, yet, in all, thousands upon thousands, had launched new worlds and new biographies. We saw the Other Earth, with its recurrent glories and shames, and its final suffocation. We saw the many other humanesque worlds, Echinoderm, Centaurian, and so on. We saw Man on his little Earth blunder through many alternating phases of dullness and lucidity, and again abject dullness. From epoch to epoch his bodily shape changed as a cloud changes. We watched him in his desperate struggle with Martian invaders; and then, after a moment that included further ages of darkness and of light, we saw him driven, by dread of the moon's downfall, away to inhospitable Venus. Later still, after an aeon that was a mere sigh in the lifetime of the cosmos, he fled before the exploding sun to Neptune, there to sink back into mere animality for further aeons again. But then he climbed once more and reached his finest intelligence, only to be burnt up like a moth in a flame by irresistible catastrophe.

All this long human story, most passionate and tragic in the living, was but an unimportant, a seemingly barren and negligible effort, lasting only for a few moments in the life of the galaxy. When it was over, the host of the planetary systems still lived on, with here and there a casualty, and here and there among the stars a new planetary birth, and here and there a fresh disaster.

Before and after man's troubled life we saw other humanesque races rise in scores and hundreds, of which a mere handful was destined to waken beyond man's highest spiritual range, to play a part in the galactic community of worlds. These we now saw from afar on their little Earth-like planets, scattered among the huge drift of the star-streams, struggling to master all those world-problems, social and spiritual, which man in our 'modern' era is for the first time confronting. Similarly, we saw again the many other kinds of races, nautiloid, submarine, avian, composite, and the rare symbiotics, and still rarer plant-like beings. And of every kind only a few, if any, won through to utopia, and took part in the great communal enterprise of worlds. The rest fell by the way.

From our remote look-out we now saw in one of the islanded sub-galaxies the triumph of the Symbiotics. Here at last was the germ of a true community of worlds. Presently the stars of this islet-universe began to be girdled with living pearls, till the whole sub-galaxy was alive with worlds. Meanwhile in the main system arose that flagrant and contagious insanity of empire, which we had already watched in detail. But what had before appeared as a war of titans, in which great worlds manoeuvred in space with inconceivable speed, and destroyed one another's populations in holocausts, was now seen as the jerky motion of a few microscopic sparks, a few luminous animalcules, surrounded by the indifferent stellar hosts.

Presently, however, we saw a star blaze up and destroy its planets. The Empires had murdered something nobler than themselves. There was a second murder, and a third. Then, under the influence of the sub-galaxy, the imperial madness faded, and empire crumbled. And soon our fatigued attention was held by the irresistible coming of utopia throughout the galaxy. This was visible to us chiefly as a steady increase of artificial planets. Star after star blossomed with orbit after crowded orbit of these vital jewels, these blooms pregnant with the spirit. Constellation after constellation, the whole galaxy became visibly alive with myriads of worlds. Each world, peopled with its unique, multitudinous race of sensitive individual intelligences united in true community, was itself a living thing, possessed of a common spirit. And each system of many populous orbits was itself a communal being. And the whole galaxy, knit in a single telepathic mesh, was a single intelligent and ardent being, the common spirit, the 'I', of all its countless, diverse, and ephemeral individuals.

This whole vast community looked now beyond itself towards its fellow galaxies. Resolved to pursue the adventure of life and of spirit in the cosmical, the widest of all spheres, it was in constant telepathic communication with its fellows; and at the same time, conceiving all kinds of strange practical ambitions, it began to avail itself of the energies of its stars upon a scale hitherto unimagined. Not only was every solar system now surrounded by a gauze of light traps, which focused the escaping solar energy for intelligent use, so that the whole galaxy was dimmed, but many stars that were not suited to be suns were disintegrated, and rifled of their prodigious stores of sub-atomic energy.

Suddenly our attention was held by an event which even at a distance was visibly incompatible with utopia. A star encircled by planets exploded, destroying all its rings of worlds, and sinking afterwards into wan exhaustion. Another and another, and yet others in different regions of the galaxy, did likewise.

To inquire into the cause of these startling disasters we once more, by an act of volition, dispersed ourselves to our stations among the many worlds.

CHAPTER ELEVEN

STARS AND VERMIN

1. The Many Galaxies

The Galactic Society of Worlds had sought to perfect its communication with other galaxies. The simpler medium of contact was telepathic; but it seemed desirable to reach out physically also across the huge void between this galaxy and the next. It was in the attempt to send envoys on such voyages that the Society of Worlds brought upon itself the epidemic of exploding stars.

Before describing this series of disasters I shall say something of the conditions of other galaxies as they were known to us through our participation in the experience of our own galaxy.

Telepathic exploration had long ago revealed that at least in some other galaxies there existed minded worlds. And now, after long experiment, the worlds of our galaxy, working for this purpose as a single galactic mind, had attained much more detailed knowledge of the cosmos as a whole. This had proved difficult because of an unsuspected parochialism in the mental attitude of the worlds of each galaxy. In the basic physical and biological constitutions of the galaxies there was no far-reaching difference. In each there was a diversity of races of the same general types as those of our own galaxy. But upon the cultural plane the trend of development in each galactic society had produced important mental idiosyncrasies, often so deep-seated as to be unwitting. Thus it was very difficult at first for the developed galaxies to make contact with one another. Our own galactic culture had been dominated by the culture of the Symbiotics, which had developed in the exceptionally happy sub-galaxy. In spite of the horrors of the imperial age, ours was therefore a culture having a certain blandness which made

telepathic intercourse with more tragic galaxies difficult to establish. Further, the detail of basic concepts and values accepted by our own galactic society was also largely a development of the marine culture that had dominated the sub-galaxy.
Though the 'continental' population of worlds was mainly
humanesque, its native cultures had been profoundly influenced by the oceanic mentality. And since this oceanic mental texture was rare among galactic societies, our galaxy was
rather more isolated than most.

After long and patient work, however, our galactic society
succeeded in forming a fairly complete survey of the cosmical
population of galaxies. It was discovered that at this time the
many galaxies were in many stages of mental, as of physical,
development. Many very young systems, in which nebular
matter still predominated over stars, contained as yet no plan-
DHets. In others, though already there was a sprinkling of the
vital grains, life had nowhere reached the human level. Some
galaxies, though physically mature, were wholly barren of
planetary systems, either through sheer accident or by reason
of the exceptionally sparse distribution of their stars. In several, out of the millions of galaxies, a single intelligent world
had spread its race and its culture throughout the galaxy, organizing the whole as an egg's germ organizes into itself the
whole substance of the egg. In these galaxies, very naturally,
the galactic culture had been based on the assumption that
from the one single germ the whole cosmos was to be peopled.
When telepathic intercourse with other galaxies was at last
stumbled upon, its effect was at first utterly bewildering. There
were not a few galaxies in which two or more such germs had
developed independently and finally come into contact. Sometimes the result was symbiosis, sometimes endless strife or
even mutual destruction. By far the commonest type of galactic
society was that in which many systems of worlds had developed independently, come into conflict, slaughtered one another, produced vast federations and empires, plunged again
and again into social chaos, and struggled between whiles haltingly towards galactic utopia. A few had already attained that
goal, though seared with bitterness. More were still flounder-

ing. Many were so undermined by war that there seemed little prospect of recovery. To such a type our own galaxy would have belonged had it not been for the good fortune of the Symbiotics.

To this account of the galactic survey two points should be added. First, there were certain very advanced galactic societies which had been telepathic spectators of all history in our own and all other galaxies. Secondly, in not a few galaxies the stars had recently begun unexpectedly exploding and destroying their girdles of worlds.

2. Disaster in Our Galaxy

While our Galactic Society of Worlds was perfecting its telepathic vision, and at the same time improving its own social and material structure, the unexpected disasters which we had already observed from afar forced it to attend strictly to the task of preserving the lives of its constituent worlds.

The occasion of the first accident was an attempt to detach a star from its natural course and direct it upon an intergalactic voyage. Telepathic intercourse with the nearest of the foreign galaxies was fairly reliable, but, as I have said, it had been decided that a physical exchange of worlds would be invaluable for mutual understanding and co-operation. Plans were therefore made for projecting several stars with their attendant systems of worlds across the vast ocean of space that separated the two floating islets of civilization. The voyage would of course be thousands of times longer than anything hitherto attempted. At its completion many more of the stars in each galaxy would already have ceased to shine, and the end of all life in the cosmos would already be in sight. Yet it was felt that the enterprise of linking galaxy with galaxy throughout the cosmos in this manner would be well justified by the great increase of mutual insight which it would produce in the galaxies in the last and most difficult phase of cosmical life.

After prodigies of experiment and calculation the first attempt at intergalactic voyaging was undertaken. A certain star, barren of planets, was used as a reservoir of energy, both normal and sub-atomic. By cunning devices far beyond my comprehension this fund of power was directed upon a chosen star with planetary girdles in such a way as to sway it gradually in the direction of the foreign galaxy. The task of securing that its planets should remain in their true orbits during this operation, and during the subsequent acceleration of their sun, was very delicate, but was accomplished without the destruction of more than a dozen worlds. Unfortunately, just as the star was correctly aimed and was beginning to gather speed, it exploded. A sphere of incandescent material, expanding from the sun with incredible speed, swallowed up and destroyed every girdle of planets. The star then subsided.

Throughout the history of the galaxy such sudden effulgence and quiescence of a star had been a very common occurrence. It was known to consist of an explosion of sub-atomic energy from the star's superficial layers. This was caused sometimes by the impact of some small wandering body, often no bigger than an asteroid; sometimes by factors in the star's own physical evolution. In either case the Galactic Society of Worlds could predict the event with great accuracy and take steps either to divert the intruding body or to remove the threatened world-system out of harm's way. But this particular disaster was entirely unforeseen. No cause could be assigned to it. It infringed the established laws of physics.

While the Society of Worlds was trying to understand what had happened, another star exploded. This was the sun of one of the leading world-systems. Attempts had recently been made to increase this star's output of radiation, and it was thought that the disaster must have been due to these experiments. After a while another and yet other stars exploded, destroying all their worlds. In several cases attempts had recently been made either to alter the star's course or tap its stored energy.

The trouble spread. System after system of worlds was destroyed. All tampering with stars had now been abandoned, yet the epidemic of 'novae' continued, even increased. In every case the exploding star was a sun with a planetary system.

The normal 'nova' phase, the explosion caused not by collision but by internal forces, was known to occur only in a star's youth or early maturity, and seldom, if ever, more often than once in each star's career. In this late phase of the galaxy far more stars had passed the natural 'nova' stage than not. It would be possible, therefore, to move whole systems of worlds from the dangerous younger stars and settle them in close orbits round the older luminaries. With immense expense of energy this operation was several times performed. Heroic plans were made for the transformation of the whole galactic society by migration to the safe stars, and the euthanasia of the excess population of worlds that could not be thus accommodated.

While this plan was being carried out it was defeated by a new series of disasters. Stars that had already exploded developed a power of exploding again and again whenever they were girdled with planets. Moreover, yet another kind of disaster now began to occur. Very aged stars, which had long since passed the period when explosion was possible, began to behave in an astounding manner. A plume of incandescent substance would issue from the photosphere, and this, as the star revolved, would sweep outwards as a trailing whirl. Sometimes this fiery proboscis calcined the surface of every planet in every orbit, killing all its life. Sometimes, if the sweep of the proboscis was not quite in the plane of the planetary orbits, a number of planets escaped. But in many cases in which the destruction was not at first complete the proboscis gradually brought itself more accurately into the planetary plane and destroyed the remaining worlds.

It soon became clear that, if the two kinds of stellar activity remained unchecked, civilization would be undermined and perhaps life exterminated throughout the galaxy. Astronomical knowledge provided no clue whatever to the problem. The theory of stellar evolution had seemed perfect, but it had no place for these singular events.

Meanwhile the Society of Worlds had set about the task of artificially exploding all stars that had not yet spontaneously passed through the 'nova' phase. It was hoped thus to render them comparatively safe, and then to use them once more as suns. But now that all kinds of stars had become equally dangerous, this work was abandoned. Instead, arrangements were made to procure the radiation necessary to life from the stars that had ceased to shine. Controlled disintegration of their atoms would turn them into satisfactory suns, at least for a while. Unfortunately the epidemic of fiery plumes was increasing rapidly. System by system, the living worlds were being swept out of existence. Desperate research hit at last on a method of diverting the fiery tentacle away from the plane of the ecliptic. This process was far from reliable. Moreover, if it succeeded, the sun would sooner or later project another filament.

The state of the galaxy was being very rapidly changed. Hitherto there had been an incalculable wealth of stellar energy, but this energy was now being shed like rain from a thunder-cloud. Though a single explosion did not seriously affect the vigour of a star, repetitions became more exhausting as they increased in number. Many young stars had been reduced to decrepitude. The great majority of the stellar population had now passed their prime; multitudes were mere glowing coals or lightless ash. The minded worlds, also, were much reduced in number, for in spite of all ingenious measures of defence, casualties were still heavy. This reduction of the population of the worlds was the more serious because in its prime the Galactic Society of Worlds had been so highly organized. In some ways it was less like a society than a brain. The disaster had almost blotted out certain higher 'brain-centres' and greatly reduced the vitality of all. It had also seriously impaired telepathic intercourse between the systems of worlds by forcing each system to concentrate on its own urgent physical problem of defence against the attacks of its own sun. The communal mind of the Society of Worlds now ceased to operate.

The emotional attitude of the worlds had also changed. The fervour for the establishment of cosmical utopia had vanished, and with it the fervour for the completion of the spirit's adventure by the fulfilment of knowledge and creative capacity. Now that extermination seemed inevitable within a comparatively short time, there was an increasing will to meet fate with religious peace. The desire to realize the far cosmical goal, formerly the supreme motive of all awakened worlds, now seemed to be extravagant, even impious. How should the little creatures, the awakened worlds, reach out to knowledge of the whole cosmos, and of the divine? Instead they must play their own part in the drama, and appreciate their own tragic end with godlike detachment and relish.

This mood of exultant resignation, appropriate to unavoidable disaster, quickly changed under the influence of a new discovery. In certain quarters there had long been a suspicion that the irregular activity of the stars was not merely automatic but purposeful, in fact that the stars were alive, and were striving to rid themselves of the pest of planets. This possibility had at first seemed too fantastic; but it gradually became obvious that the destruction of a star's planetary system was the end which determined the duration of the irregular action. Of course it was possible that in some unexplained but purely mechanical way the presence of many planetary girdles created the explosion, or the fiery limb. Astronomical physics could suggest no mechanism whatever which could have this result.

Telepathic research was now undertaken in order to test the theory of stellar consciousness, and if possible to set up communication with the minded stars. This venture was at first completely barren. The worlds had not the slightest knowledge of the right method of approach to minds which, if they existed at all, must be inconceivably different from their own. It seemed all too probable that no factors in the mentality of the minded worlds were sufficiently akin to the stellar mentality to form a means of contact. Though the worlds used their imaginative powers as best they might, though they explored, so to speak, every subterranean passage and gallery of their own mentality, tapping everywhere in the hope of answer, they received none. The theory of stellar purposefulness began to seem incredible. Once more the worlds began to turn to the consolation, nay the joy, of acceptance.

Nevertheless, a few world-systems that had specialized in

psychological technique persisted in their researches, confident that, if only they could communicate with the stars, some kind of mutual understanding and concord could be brought about between the two great orders of minds in the galaxy.

At long last the desired contact with the stellar minds was affected. It came not through the unaided efforts of the minded worlds of our galaxy but partly through the mediation of another galaxy where already the worlds and the stars had begun to realize one another.

Even to the minds of fully awakened worlds the stellar mentality was almost too alien to be conceived at all. To me, the little human individual, all that is most distinctive in it is now quite incomprehensible. Nevertheless, its simpler aspect I must now try to summarize as best I may, since it is essential to my story. The minded worlds made their first contact with the stars on the higher planes of stellar experience, but I shall not follow the chronological order of their discoveries. Instead I shall begin with aspects of the stellar nature which were haltingly inferred only after intercourse of a sort had become fairly well established. It is in terms of stellar biology and physiology that the reader may most easily conceive something of the mental life of stars.

3. Stars

Stars are best regarded as living organisms, but organisms which are physiologically and psychologically of a very peculiar kind. The outer and middle layers of a mature star apparently consist of 'tissues' woven of currents of incandescent gases. These gaseous tissues live and maintain the stellar consciousness by intercepting part of the immense flood of energy that wells from the congested and furiously active interior of the star. The innermost of the vital layers must be a kind of digestive apparatus which transmutes the crude radiation into forms required for the maintenance of the star's life. Outside this digestive area lies some sort of co-ordinating layer, which may be thought of as the star's brain. The outermost layers, including the corona, respond to the excessively faint stimuli of the star's comical environment, to light from neighbouring stars, to cosmic rays, to the impact of meteors, to tidal stresses caused by the gravitational influence of planets or of other stars. These influences could not, of course, produce any clear impression but for a strange tissue of gaseous sense organs, which discriminate between them in respect of quality and direction, and transmit information to the correlating 'brain' layer.

The sense experience of a star, though so foreign to us, proved after all fairly intelligible. It was not excessively difficult for us to enter telepathically into the star's perception of the gentle titillations, strokings, pluckings, and scintillations that came to it from the galactic environment. It was strange that, though the star's own body was actually in a state of extreme brilliance, none of this outward-flowing light took effect upon its sense organs. Only the faint in-coming light of other stars was seen. This afforded the perception of a surrounding heaven of flashing constellations, which were set not in blackness but in blackness tinged with the humanly inconceivable colour of the cosmic rays. The stars themselves were seen coloured according to their style and age.

But though the sense perception of the stars was fairly intelligible to us, the motor side of stellar life was at first quite incomprehensible. We had to accustom ourselves to an entirely new way of regarding physical events. For the normal voluntary motor activity of a star appears to be no other than the star's *normal* physical movement studied by our science, movement in relation to other stars and the galaxy as a whole. A star must be thought of as vaguely aware of the gravitational influence of the whole galaxy, and more precisely aware of the 'pull' of its near neighbours; though of course their influence would generally be far too slight to be detected by human instruments. To these influences the star responds by voluntary movement, which to the astronomers of the little minded worlds seems purely mechanical; but the star itself unquestioningly and rightly feels this movement to be the freely willed expression of its own psychological nature. Such at least was the almost incredible conclusion forced on us by the research carried out by the Galactic Society of Worlds.

Thus the normal experience of a star appears to consist in perception of its cosmical environment, along with continuous voluntary changes within its own body and in its position in relation to other stars. This change of position consists, of course, in rotation and passage. The star's motor life is thus to be thought of almost as a life of dance, or of figure-skating, executed with perfect skill according to an ideal principle which emerges into consciousness from the depths of the stellar nature and becomes clearer as the star's mind matures.

This ideal principle cannot be conceived by men save as it is manifested in practice as the well-known physical principle of 'least action', or the pursuit of that course which in all the gravitational and other conditions is the least extravagant. The star itself, by means of its purchase on the electromagnetic field of the cosmos, apparently wills and executes this ideal course with all the attention and delicacy of response which a motorist exercises in threading his way through traffic on a winding road, or a ballet-dancer in performing the most intricate movements with the greatest economy of effort. Almost certainly, the star's whole physical behaviour is normally experienced as a blissful, an ecstatic, an ever successful pursuit of formal beauty. This the minded worlds were able to discover through their own most formalistic aesthetic experience. In fact it was through this experience that they first made contact with stellar minds. But the actual perception of the aesthetic (or religious?) rightness of the mysterious canon, which the stars so earnestly accepted, remained far beyond the mental range of the minded worlds. They had to take it, so to speak, on trust. Clearly this aesthetic canon was in some way symbolical of some spiritual intuition that remained occult to the minded worlds.

The life of the individual star is not only a life of physical movement. It is also undoubtedly in some sense a cultural and a spiritual life. In some manner each star is aware of its fellow stars as conscious beings. This mutual awareness is probably intuitive and telepathic, though presumably it is also constantly supported by inference from observation of the behaviour of others. From the psychological relations of star with star sprang a whole world of social experiences which were so alien to the minded worlds that almost nothing can be said of them.

There is perhaps some reason for believing that the free behaviour of the individual star is determined not only by the austere canons of the dance but also by the social will to cooperate with others. Certainly the relation between stars is perfectly social. It reminded me of the relation between the performers in an orchestra, but an orchestra composed of persons wholly intent on the common task. Possibly, but not certainly, each star, executing its particular theme, is moved not only by the pure aesthetic or religious motive but also by a will to afford its partners every legitimate opportunity for self-expression. If so, the life of each star is experienced not only as the perfect execution of formal beauty but also as the perfect expression of love. It would, however, be unwise to attribute affection and comradeship to the stars in any human sense. The most that can safely be said is that it would probably be more false to deny them affection for one another than to assert that they were, indeed, capable of love. Telepathic research suggested that the experience of the stars was through and through of a different texture from that of the minded worlds. Even to attribute to them thought or desire of any kind is probably grossly anthropomorphic, but it is impossible to speak of their experience in any other terms.

The mental life of a star is almost certainly a progress from an obscure infantile mentality to the discriminate consciousness of maturity. All stars, young and old, are mentally 'angelic', in that they all freely and joyfully will the 'good will', the pattern of right action so far as it is revealed to them; but the great tenuous young stars, though they perfectly execute their part in the galactic dance, would seem to be in some manner spiritually naïve or childlike in comparison with their more experienced elders. Thus, though there is normally no such thing as sin among the stars, no deliberate choice of the course known to be wrong for the sake of some end known to be irrelevant, there is ignorance, and consequent aberration from the pattern of the ideal as revealed to stars of somewhat maturer mentality. But this aberration on the part of the young is itself apparently accepted by the most awakened class of the stars as itself a desirable factor in the dance pattern of the galaxy. From the point of view of natural science, as known to the minded worlds, the behaviour of young stars is of course always an exact expression of their youthful nature; and the behaviour of the elder stars an expression of their nature. But, most surprisingly, the physical nature of a star at any stage of its growth is in part an expression of the telepathic influence of other stars. This fact can never be detected by the pure physics of any epoch. Unwittingly scientists derive the inductive physical laws of stellar evolution from data which are themselves an expression not only of normal physical influences but also of the unsuspected psychical influence of star on star.

In early ages of the cosmos the first 'generation' of stars had been obliged to find their way unhelped from infancy to maturity; but later 'generations' were in some manner guided by the experience of their elders so that they should pass more quickly and more thoroughly from the obscure to the fully lucid consciousness of themselves as spirits, and of the spiritual universe in which they dwelt.

Almost certainly, the latest stars to condense out of the primeval nebula advanced (or will advance) more rapidly than their elders had done; and throughout the stellar host it was believed that in due season the youngest stars, when they had attained maturity, would pass far beyond the loftiest spiritual insight of their seniors.

There is good reason to say that the two overmastering desires of all stars are the desire to execute perfectly their part in the communal dance, and the desire to press forward to the attainment of full insight into the nature of the cosmos. The latter desire was the factor in stellar mentality which was most comprehensible to the minded worlds.

The climax of a star's life occurs when it has passed through the long period of its youth, during which it is what human astronomers call a 'red giant'. At the close of this period it shrinks rapidly into the dwarf state in which our sun now is. This physical cataclysm seems to be accompanied by far-reaching mental changes. Henceforth, though the star plays a less dashing part in the dance-rhythms of the galaxy, it is perhaps more clearly and penetratingly conscious. It is interested less in the ritual of the stellar dance, more in its supposed spiritual significance. After this very long phase of physical maturity there comes another crisis. The star shrinks into the minute and inconceivably dense condition in which our astronomers call it a 'white dwarf'. Its mentality in the actual crisis proved almost impervious to the research of the minded worlds. It appeared to be a crisis of despair and of reorientated hope. Henceforth the stellar mind presents increasingly a strain of baffling and even terrifying negativity, an icy, an almost cynical aloofness, which, we suspected, was but the obverse of some dread rapture hidden from us. However that may be, the aged star still continues meticulously to fulfil its part in the dance, but its mood is deeply changed. The aesthetic fervours of youth, the more serene but earnest will of maturity, all maturity's devotion to the active pursuit of wisdom, now fall away. Perhaps the star is henceforth content with its achievement, such as it is, and pleased simply to enjoy the surrounding universe with such detachment and insight as it has attained. Perhaps; but the minded worlds were never able to ascertain whether the aged stellar mind eluded their comprehension through sheer superiority of achievement or through some obscure disorder of the spirit.

In this state of old age a star remains for a very long period, gradually losing energy, and mentally withdrawing into itself, until it sinks into an impenetrable trance of senility. Finally its light is extinguished and its tissues disintegrate in death. Henceforth it continues to sweep through space, but it does so unconsciously, and in a manner repugnant to its still conscious fellows.

Such, very roughly stated, would seem to be the normal life of the average star. But there are many varieties within the general type. For stars vary in original size and in composition, and probably in psychological impact upon their neighbours. One of the commonest of the eccentric types is the double star, two mighty globes of fire waltzing through space together, in some cases almost in contact. Like all stellar relations, these partnerships are perfect, are angelic. Yet it is impossible to be certain whether the members experience anything which could properly be called a sentiment of personal love, or whether they regard one another solely as partners in a common task. Research undoubtedly suggested that the two beings did indeed move on their winding courses in some kind of mutual delight, and delight of close co-operation in the measures of the galaxy. But love? It is impossible to say. In due season, with the loss of momentum, the two stars come into actual contact. Then, seemingly in an agonizing blaze of joy and pain, they merge. After a period of unconsciousness, the great new star generates new living tissues, and takes its place among the angelic company.

The strange Cepheid variables proved the most baffling of all the stellar kinds. It seems that these and other variables of much longer period alternate mentally between fervour and quietism, in harmony with their physical rhythm. More than this it is impossible to say.

One event, which happens only to a small minority of the stars in the course of their dance-life, is apparently of great psychological importance. This is the close approach of two or perhaps three stars to one another, and the consequent projection of a filament from one towards another. In the moment of this 'moth kiss', before the disintegration of the filament and the birth of planets, each star probably experiences an intense but humanly unintelligible physical ecstasy. Apparently the stars which have been through this experience are supposed to have acquired a peculiarly vivid apprehension of the unity of body and spirit. The 'virgin' stars, however, though unblessed by this wonderful adventure, seem to have no desire to infringe the sacred canons of the dance in order to contrive opportunities for such encounters. Each one of them is angelically content to play its allotted part, and to observe the ecstasy of those that fate has favoured.

To describe the mentality of stars is of course to describe the unintelligible by means of intelligible but falsifying human metaphors. This tendency is particularly serious in telling of the dramatic relations between the stars and the minded worlds, for under the stress of these relations the stars seem to have experienced for the first time emotions superficially like human emotions. So long as the stellar community was immune from interference by the minded worlds, every member of it behaved with perfect rectitude and had perfect bliss in the perfect expression of its own nature and of the common spirit. Even senility and death were accepted with calm, for they were universally seen to be involved in the pattern of existence; and what every star desired was not immortality, whether for itself or for the community, but the perfect fruition of stellar nature. But when at last the minded worlds, the planets, began to interfere appreciably with stellar energy and motion, a new and terrible and incomprehensible thing presumably entered into the experiences of the stars. The stricken ones found themselves caught in a distracting mental conflict. Through some cause which they themselves could not detect, they not merely erred but willed to err. In fact they sinned. Even while they still adored the right, they chose the wrong.

I said that the trouble was unprecedented. This is not strictly true. Something not wholly unlike this public shame seems to have occurred in the private experience of nearly every star. But each sufferer succeeded in keeping his shame secret until either with familiarity it became tolerable or else its source was overcome. It was indeed surprising that beings whose nature was in many ways so alien and unintelligible should be in this one respect at least so startlingly 'human'.

In the outer layers of young stars life nearly always appears not only in the normal manner but also in the form of parasites, minute independent organisms of fire, often no bigger than a cloud in the terrestrial air, but sometimes as large as the Earth itself. These 'salamanders' either feed upon the welling energies of the star in the same manner as the star's own organic tissues feed, or simply prey upon those tissues themselves. Here as elsewhere the laws of biological evolution come into force, and in time there may appear races of intelligent flame-like beings. Even when the salamandrian life does not reach this level, its effect on the star's tissues may become evident to the star as a disease of its skin and sense organs, or even of its deeper tissues. It then experiences emotions not wholly unlike human fright and shame, and anxiously and most humanly guards its secret from the telepathic reach of its fellows. The salamandrian races have never been able to gain mastery over their fiery worlds. Many of them succumb, soon or late, either to some natural disaster or to internecine strife or to the self-cleansing activities of their mighty host. Many others survive, but in a relatively harmless state, troubling their stars only with a mild irritation, and a faint shade of insincerity in all their dealings with one another.

In the public culture of the stars the salamandrian pest was completely ignored. Each star believed itself to be the only sufferer and the only sinner in the galaxy. One indirect effect the pest did have on stellar thought. It introduced the idea of purity. Each star prized the perfection of the stellar community all the more by reason of its own secret experience of impurity.

When the minded planets began to tamper seriously with stellar energy and stellar orbits, the effect was not a private shame but a public scandal. It was patent to all observers that the culprit had violated the canons of the dance. The first aberrations were greeted with bewilderment and horror. Among the hosts of the virgin stars it was whispered that if the result of the much prized interstellar contacts, whence the natural planets had sprung, was in the end this shameful ir-regularity, probably the original experience itself had also been sinful. The erring stars protested that they were not sinners, but victims of some unknown influence from the grains which revolved about them. Yet secretly they doubted themselves. Had they long ago, in the ecstatic sweep of star to star, after all infringed the canon of the dance? They suspected, moreover, that in respect of the irregularities which were now creating this public scandal, they could, if they had willed firmly enough, have contained themselves, and preserved their true courses in spite of the irritants that had affected them.

Meanwhile the power of the minded planets increased. Suns were boldly steered to suit the purposes of their parasites. To the stellar population it seemed, of course, that these erring stars were dangerous lunatics. The crisis came, as I have already said, when the worlds projected their first messenger towards the neighbouring galaxy. The hurtling star, terrified at its own maniac behaviour, took the only retaliation that was known to it. It exploded into the 'nova' state, and successfully destroyed its planets. From the orthodox stellar point of view this act was a deadly sin; for it was an impious interference with the divinely appointed order of a star's life. But it secured the desired end, and was soon copied by other desperate stars.

Then followed that age of horror which I have already described from the point of view of the Society of Worlds. From the stellar point of view it was no less terrible, for the condition of the stellar society soon became desperate. Gone was the perfection and beatitude of former days. 'The City of God' had degenerated into a place of hatred, recrimination and despair. Hosts of the younger stars had become premature and embittered dwarfs, while the elders had mostly grown senile. The dance pattern had fallen into chaos. The old passion for the canons of the dance remained, but the conception of the canons was obscured. Spiritual life had succumbed to the necessity of urgent action. The passion for the progress of insight into the nature of the cosmos also remained, but insight itself was obscured. Moreover, the former naïve confidence, common to young and mature alike, the certainty that the cosmos was perfect and that the power behind it was righteous, had given place to blank despair.

4. Galactic Symbiosis

Such was the state of affairs when the minded worlds first attempted to make telepathic contact with the minded stars. I need not tell the stages by which mere contact was developed into a clumsy and precarious kind of communication. In time the stars must have begun to realize that they were at grips, not with mere physical forces, nor yet with fiends, but with beings whose nature, though so profoundly alien, was at bottom identical with their own. Our telepathic research obscurely sensed the amazement which spread throughout the stellar population. Two opinions, two policies, two parties seem to have gradually emerged.

One of these parties was convinced that the pretension of the minded planets must be false, that beings whose history was compact of sin and strife and slaughter must be essentially diabolic, and that to parley with them was to court disaster. This party, at first in a majority, urged that the war should be continued till every planet had been destroyed.

The minority party clamoured for peace. The planets, they affirmed, were seeking in their own way the very same goal as the stars. It was even suggested that these minute beings, with their more varied experience and their long acquaintance with evil, might have certain kinds of insight which the stars, those fallen angels, lacked. Might not the two sorts of being create together a glorious symbiotic society, and achieve together the end that was most dear to both, namely the full awakening of the spirit?

It was a long while before the majority would listen to this counsel. Destruction continued. The precious energies of the galaxy were squandered. System after system of worlds was destroyed. Star after star sank into exhaustion and stupor.

Meanwhile the Society of Worlds maintained a pacific attitude. No more stellar energy was tapped. No more stellar orbits were altered. No stars were artificially exploded.

Stellar opinion began to change. The crusade of extermination relaxed, and was abandoned. There followed a period of 'isolationism' in which the stars, intent on repairing their shattered society, left their former enemies alone. Gradually a fumbling attempt at fraternization began between the planets and their suns. The two kinds of beings, though so alien that they could not at all comprehend each other's idosyncrasies, were too lucid for mere tribal passions. They resolved to overcome all obstacles and enter into some kind of community. Soon it was the desire of every star to be girdled with artificial planets and enter into some sort of 'sympsychic' partnership with its encircling companions. For it was by now clear to the stars that the 'vermin' had much to give them. The experience of the two orders of beings was in many ways complementary. The stars retained still the tenor of the angelic wisdom of their golden age. The planets excelled in the analytic, the microscopic, and in that charity which was bred in them by knowledge of their own weak and suffering forbears. To the stars, moreover, it was perplexing that their minute companions could accept not merely with resignation but with joy a cosmos which evidently was seamed with evil.

In due season a symbiotic society of stars and planetary systems embraced the whole galaxy. But it was at first a wounded society, and ever after an impoverished galaxy. Few only of its million million stars were still in their prime. Every possible sun was now girdled with planets. Many dead stars were stimulated to disintegrate their atoms so as to provide artificial suns. Others were used in a more economical manner. Special races of intelligent organisms were bred or synthetized to inhabit the surfaces of these great worlds. Very soon, upon a thousand stars that once had blazed, teeming populations of innumerable types maintained an austere civilization. These subsisted on the volcanic energies of their huge worlds. Minute, artificially contrived worm-like creatures, they crept laboriously over the plains where oppressive gravitation allowed not so much as a stone to project above the general level. So violent, indeed, was gravitation, that even the little bodies of these worms might be shattered by a fall of half an inch. Save for artificial lighting, the inhabitants of the stellar worlds lived in eternal darkness, mitigated only by the starlight, the glow of volcanic eruption, and the phosphorescence of their own bodies. Their subterranean borings led down to the vast photosynthesis stations which converted the star's imprisoned energy for the uses of life and of mind. Intelligence in these gigantic worlds was of course a function not of the separate individual but of the minded swarm. Like the insectoids, these little creatures, when isolated from the swarm, were mere instinctive animals, actuated wholly by the gregarious craving to return to the swarm.

The need to people the dead stars would not have arisen had not the war reduced the number of minded planets and the number of suns available for new planetary systems dangerously near the minimum required to maintain the communal life in full diversity. The Society of Worlds had been a delicately organized unity in which each element had a special function. It was therefore necessary, since the lost members could not be repeated, to produce new worlds to function in their places at least approximately.

Gradually the symbiotic society overcame the immense difficulties of reorganization, and began to turn its attention to the pursuit of that purpose which is the ultimate purpose of all awakened minds, the aim which they inevitably and gladly espouse because it is involved in their deepest nature. Henceforth the symbiotic society gave all its best attention to the further awakening of the spirit.

But this purpose, which formerly the angelic company of the stars and the ambitious Society of Worlds had each hoped to accomplish in relation not merely to the galaxy but to the cosmos, was now regarded more humbly. Both stars and worlds recognized that not merely the home galaxy but the cosmical swarm of galaxies was nearing its end. Physical energy, once a seemingly inexhaustible fund, was becoming less and less available for the maintenance of life. It was spreading itself more and more evenly over the whole cosmos. Only here and there and with difficulty could the minded organisms intercept it in its collapse from high to low potential. Very soon the universe would be physically senile.

All ambitious plans had therefore to be abandoned. No longer was there any question of physical travel between the galaxies. Such enterprises would use up too many of the pence out of the few pounds of wealth that survived after the extravagance of former aeons. No longer was there any unnecessary coming and going, even within the galaxy itself. The worlds clung to their suns. The suns steadily cooled. And as they cooled, the encircling worlds contracted their orbits for warmth's sake.

But though the galaxy was physically impoverished, it was in many ways utopian. The symbiotic society of stars and worlds was perfectly harmonious. Strife between the two kinds was a memory of the remote past. Both were wholly loyal to the common purpose. They lived their personal lives in zestful co-operation, friendly conflict, and mutual interest. Each took part according to its capacity in the common task of cosmical exploration and appreciation. The stars were now dying off more rapidly than before, for the great host of the mature had become a great host of aged white dwarfs. As they died, they bequeathed their bodies to the service of the society, to be used either as reservoirs of sub-atomic energy, or as artificial suns, or as worlds to be peopled by intelligent populations of worms. Many a planetary system was now centered round an artificial sun. Physically the substitution was tolerable; but beings that had become mentally dependent on partnership with a living star regarded a mere furnace with despondency. Foreseeing the inevitable dissolution of the symbiosis throughout the galaxy, the planets were now doing all in their power to absorb the angelic wisdom of the stars. But after very few aeons the planets themselves had to begin reducing their number. The myriad worlds could no longer all crowd closely enough around their cooling suns. Soon the mental power of the galaxy, which had hitherto been with difficulty maintained at its highest pitch, must inevitably begin to wane.

Yet the temper of the galaxy was not sad but joyful. The symbiosis had greatly improved the art of telepathic communion; and now at last the many kinds of spirit which composed the galactic society were bound so closely in mutual insight that there had emerged out of their harmonious diversity a true galactic mind, whose mental reach surpassed that of the stars and of the worlds as far as these surpassed their own individuals.

The galactic mind, which was but the mind of each individual star and world and minute organism in the worlds, enriched by all its fellows and awakened to finer percipience, saw that it had but a short time to live. Looking back through the ages of galactic history, down temporal vistas crowded with teeming and diversified populations, the mind of our galaxy saw that itself was the issue of untold strife and grief and hope frustrated. It confronted all the tortured spirits of the past not with pity or regret but with smiling content, such as a man may feel towards his own childhood's tribulations. And it said, within the mind of each one of all its members, 'Their suffering, which to them seemed barren evil, was the little price to be paid for my future coming. Right and sweet and beautiful is the whole in which these things happen. For I, I am the heaven in which all my myriad progenitors find recompense, finding their heart's desire. For in the little time that is left me I shall press on, with all my peers throughout the cosmos, to crown the cosmos with perfect and joyful insight, and to salute the Maker of Galaxies and Stars and Worlds with fitting praise.'

CHAPTER TWELVE

A STUNTED COSMICAL SPIRIT

When at last our galaxy was able to make a full telepathic exploration of the cosmos of galaxies it discovered that the state of life in the cosmos was precarious. Very few of the galaxies were now in their youth; most were already far past their prime. Throughout the cosmos the dead and lightless stars far outnumbered the living and luminous. In many galaxies the strife of stars and worlds had been even more disastrous than in our own. Peace had been secured only after both sides had degenerated past hope of recovery. In most of the younger galaxies, however, this strife had not yet appeared; and efforts were already being made by the most awakened galactic spirits to enlighten the ignorant stellar and planetary societies about one another before they should blunder into conflict.

The communal spirit of our galaxy now joined the little company of the most awakened beings of the cosmos, the scattered band of advanced galactic spirits, whose aim it was to create a real cosmical community, with a single mind, the communal spirit of its myriad and diverse worlds and individual intelligences. Thus it was hoped to acquire powers of insight and of creativity impossible on the merely galactic plane.

With grave joy we, the cosmical explorers, who were already gathered up into the communal mind of our own galaxy, now found ourselves in intimate union with a score of other galactic minds. We, or rather I, now experienced the slow drift of the galaxies much as a man feels the swing of his own limbs. From my score of viewpoints I observed the great snow-storm of many million galaxies, streaming and circling, and even withdrawing farther apart from one another with the relentless 'expansion' of space. But though the vastness of space was increasing in relation to the size of galaxies and stars and worlds, to me, with my composite, scattered body, space seemed no bigger than a great vaulted hall.

My experience of time also had changed; for now, as on an earlier occasion, the aeons had become for me as brief as minutes. I conceived the whole life of the cosmos not as an immensely protracted and leisurely passage from a remote and shadowy source to a glorious and a still more remote eternity, but as a brief, a headlong and forlorn, race against galloping time.

Confronted by the many backward galaxies, I seemed to myself to be a lonely intelligence in a wilderness of barbarians and beasts. The mystery, the futility, the horror of existence now bore down upon me most cruelly. For to me, to the spirit of that little band of awakened galaxies, surrounded by unawakened and doomed hordes in the last day of the cosmos, there appeared no hope of any triumph elsewhere. For to me the whole extent, seemingly, of existence was revealed. There could be no 'elsewhere'. I knew with exactness the sum of cosmical matter. And though the 'expansion' of space was already sweeping most of the galaxies apart more swiftly than light could bridge the gulf, telepathic exploration still kept me in touch with the whole extent of the cosmos. Many of my own members were physically divided from one another by the insurmountable gulf created by the ceaseless 'expansion'; but telepathically they were still united.

I, the communal mind of a score of galaxies, seemed now to myself to be the abortive and crippled mind of the cosmos itself. The myriad-fold community that supported me ought surely to have expanded to embrace the whole of existence. In the climax of cosmical history the fully awakened mind of the cosmos ought surely to have won through to the fullness of knowledge and of worship. But this was not to be. For even now, in the late phase of the cosmos, when the physical potency was almost all exhausted, I had reached only to a lowly state of spiritual growth. I was mentally still adolescent, yet my cosmical body was already in decay. I was the struggling embryo in the cosmical egg, and the yolk was already in decay.

Looking back along the vistas of the aeons, I was impressed less by the length of the journey that had led me to my present state than by its haste and confusion, and even its brevity. Peering into the very earliest of the ages, before the stars were born, before the nebulae were formed from chaos, I still failed to see any clear source, but only a mystery as obscure as any that confronts the little inhabitants of the Earth.

Equally, when I tried to probe the depths of my own being, I found impenetrable mystery. Though my self-consciousness was awakened to a degree thrice removed beyond the self-consciousness of human beings, namely from the simple individual to the world-mind, and from the world-mind to the galactic mind, and thence to the abortively cosmical, yet the depth of my nature was obscure.

Although my mind now gathered into itself all the wisdom of all worlds in all ages, and though the life of my cosmical body was itself the life of myriads of infinitely diverse worlds and myriads of infinitely diverse individual creatures, and though the texture of my daily life was one of joyful and creative enterprise, yet all this was as nothing. For around lay the host of the unfulfilled galaxies; and my own flesh was already grievously impoverished by the death of my stars; and the aeons were slipping past with fatal speed. Soon the texture of my cosmical brain must disintegrate. And then inevitably I must fall away from my prized though imperfect state of lucidity, and descend, through all the stages of the mind's second childhood, down to the cosmical death.

It was very strange that I, who knew the whole extent of space and time, and counted the wandering stars like sheep, overlooking none, that I who was the most awakened of all beings, I, the glory which myriads in all ages had given their lives to establish, and myriads had worshipped, should now look about me with the same overpowering awe, the same abashed and tongue-tied worship as that which human travellers in the desert feel under the stars.

CHAPTER THIRTEEN

THE BEGINNING AND THE END

1. Back to the Nebulae

While the awakened galaxies were striving to make full use of the last phase of their lucid consciousness, while I, the imperfect cosmical mind, was thus striving, I began to have a strange new experience. I seemed to be telepathically stumbling upon some being or beings of an order that was at first quite incomprehensible to me.

At first I supposed that I had inadvertently come into touch with sub-human beings in the primitive age of some natural planet, perhaps with some very lowly amoeboid micro-organisms, floating in a primeval sea. I was aware only of crude hungers of the body, such as the lust to assimilate physical energy for the maintenance of life, the lust of movement and of contact, the lust of light and warmth.

Impatiently I tried to dismiss this trivial irrelevance. But it continued to haunt me, become more intrusive and more lucid. Gradually it took on such an intensity of physical vigour and well-being, and such a divine confidence, as was manifested by no spirits up and down the ages since the stars began.

I need not tell of the stages by which I learned at last the meaning of this experience. Gradually I discovered that I had made contact not with micro-organisms, nor yet with worlds or stars or galactic minds, but with the minds of the great nebulae before their substance had disintegrated into stars to form the galaxies.

Presently I was able to follow their history from the time when they first awakened, when they first existed as discrete clouds of gas, flying apart after the explosive act of creation, even to the time when, with the birth of the stellar hosts out of their substance, they sank into senility and death.

In their earliest phase, when physically they were the most tenuous clouds, their mentality was no more than a formless craving for action and a sleepy perception of the infinitely slight congestion of their own vacuous substance.

I watched them condense into close-knit balls with sharper contours, then into lentoid discs, featured with brighter streams and darker chasms. As they condensed, each gained more unity, became more organic in structure. Congestion, though so slight, brought greater mutual influence to their atoms, which still were no more closely packed, in relation to their size, than stars in space. Each nebula was now a single great pool of faint radiation, a single system of all-pervasive waves, spreading from atom to atom.

And now mentally these greatest of all megatheria, these amoeboid titans, began to waken into a vague unity of experience. By human standards, and even by the standards of the minded worlds and the stars, the experience of the nebulae was incredibly slow-moving. For owing to their prodigious size and the slow passage of the undulations to which their consciousness was physically related, a thousand years was for them an imperceptible instant. Periods such as men call geological, containing the rise and fall of species after species, they experienced as we experience the hours.

Each of the great nebulae was aware of its own lentoid body as a single volume compact of tingling currents. Each craved fulfilment of its organic potency, craved easement from the pressure of physical energy welling softly within it, craved at the same time free expression of all its powers of movement, craved also something more.

For though, both in physique and in mentality, these primordial beings were strangely like the primeval micro-organisms of planetary life, they were also remarkably different; or at least they manifested a character which even I, the rudimentary cosmical mind, had overlooked in micro-organisms. This was a will or predilection that I can only by halting metaphor suggest.

Though even at their best these creatures were physically and intellectually very simple, they were gifted with something which I am forced to describe as a primitive but intense religious consciousness. For they were ruled by two longings, both of which were essentially religious. They desired, or rather they had a blind urge towards, union with one another, and they had a blind passionate urge to be gathered up once more into the source whence they had come.

The universe that they inhabited was of course a very simple, even a poverty-stricken universe. It was also to them quite small. For each of them the cosmos consisted of two things, the nebula's own almost featureless body and the bodies of the other nebulae. In this early age of the cosmos the nebulae were very close to one another, for the volume of the cosmos was at this time small in relation to its parts, whether nebulae or electrons. In that age the nebulae, which in man's day are like birds at large in the sky, were confined, as it were, within a narrow aviary. Thus each exercised an appreciable influence on its fellows. And as each became more organized, more of a coherent physical unity, it distinguished more readily between its native wave-pattern and the irregularities which its neighbours' influence imposed upon that pattern. And by a native propensity implanted in it at the time of its emergence from the common ancestral cloud, it interpreted this influence to mean the presence of other minded nebulae.

Thus the nebulae in their prime were vaguely but intensely aware of one another as distinct beings. They were aware of one another; but their communication with each other was very meagre and very slow. As prisoners confined in separate cells give one another a sense of companionship by tapping on their cell walls, and may even in time work out a crude system of signals, so the nebulae revealed to one another their kinship by exercising gravitational stress upon one another, and by long-drawn-out pulsations of their light. Even in the early phase of their existence, when the nebulae were very close to one another, a message would take many thousands of years to spell itself out from beginning to end, and many millions of years to reach its destination. When the nebulae were at their prime, the whole cosmos reverberated with their talk.

In the earliest phase of all, when these huge creatures were still very close to one another and also immature, their parleying was concerned wholly with the effort to reveal themselves to one another. With child-like glee they laboriously communicated their joy in life, their hungers and pains, their whims, their idiosyncrasies, their common passion to be once more united, and to be, as men have sometimes said, at one in God.

But even in early days, when few nebulae were yet mature, and most were still very unclear in their minds, it became evident to the more awakened that, far from uniting, they were steadily drifting apart. As the physical influence of one on another diminished, each nebula perceived its companions shrinking into the distance. Messages took longer and longer to elicit answers.

Had the nebulae been able to communicate telepathically, the 'expansion' of the universe might have been faced without despair. But these beings were apparently too simple to make direct and lucid mental contact with one another. Thus they found themselves doomed to separation. And since their life-tempo was so slow, they seemed to themselves to have scarcely found one another before they must be parted. Bitterly they regretted the blindness of their infancy. For as they reached maturity they conceived, one and all, not merely the passion of mutual delight which we call love, but also the conviction that through mental union with one another lay the way to union with the source whence they had come.

When it had become clear that separation was inevitable, when indeed the hard-won community of these naïve beings was already failing through the increased difficulty of communication, and the most remote nebulae were already receding from one another at high speed, each perforce made ready to face the mystery of existence in absolute solitude.

There followed an aeon, or rather for the slow-living creatures themselves a brief spell, in which they sought, by self-mastery of their own flesh and by spiritual discipline, to find the supreme illumination which all awakened beings must, in their very nature, seek.

But now there appeared a new trouble. Some of the eldest of the nebulae complained of a strange sickness which greatly hampered their meditations. The outer fringes of their tenuous flesh began to concentrate into little knots. These became in time grains of intense, congested fire. In the void between, there was nothing left but a few stray atoms. At first the complaint was no more serious than some trivial rash on a man's skin; but later it spread into the deeper tissues of the nebula, and was accompanied by grave mental troubles. In vain the doomed creatures resolved to turn the plague to an advantage by treating it as a heaven-sent test of the spirit. Though for a while they might master the plague simply by heroic contempt of it, its ravages eventually broke down their will. It now seemed clear to them that the cosmos was a place of futility and horror.

Presently the younger nebulae observed that their seniors, one by one, were falling into a state of sluggishness and confusion which ended invariably in the sleep that men call death. Soon it became evident even to the most buoyant spirit that this disease was no casual accident but a fate inherent in the nebular nature.

One by one the celestial megatheria were annihilated, giving place to stars.

Looking back on these events from my post in the far future, I, the rudimentary cosmical mind, tried to make known to the dying nebulae in the remote past that their death, far from being the end, was but an early stage in the life of the cosmos. It was my hope that I might give them consolation by imparting some idea of the vast and intricate future, and of my own final awakening. But it proved impossible to communicate with them. Though within the sphere of their ordinary experience they were capable of a sort of intellection, beyond that sphere they were almost imbecile. As well might a man seek to comfort the disintegrating germ-cell from which he himself sprang by telling it about his own successful career in human society.

Since this attempt to comfort was vain, I put aside compassion, and was content merely to follow to its conclusion the collapse of the nebular community. Judged by human standards the agony was immensely prolonged. It began with the disintegration of the eldest nebulae into stars, and it lasted (or will last) long after the destruction of the final human race on Neptune. Indeed, the last of the nebulae did not sink into complete unconsciousness till many of the corpses of its neighbours had already been transformed into symbiotic societies of stars and minded worlds. But to the slow-living nebulae themselves the plague seemed a galloping disease. One after the other, each great religious beast found itself at grips with the subtle enemy, and fought a gallant losing fight until stupor overwhelmed it. None ever knew that its crumbling flesh teemed with the young and swifter lives of stars, or that it was already sprinkled here and there with the incomparably smaller, incomparably swifter, and incomparably richer lives of creatures such as men, whose crowded ages of history were all compressed within the last few distressful moments of the primeval monsters.

2. The Supreme Moment Nears

The discovery of nebular life deeply moved the incipient cosmical mind that I had become. Patiently I studied those almost formless megatheria, absorbing into my own composite being the fervour of their simple but deep-running nature. For these simple creatures sought their goal with a single-mindedness and passion eclipsing all the worlds and stars. With such earnest imagination did I enter into their history that I myself, the cosmical mind, was in a manner remade by contemplation of these beings. Considering from the nebular point of view the vast complexity and subtlety of the living worlds, I began to wonder whether the endless divagations of the worlds were really due so much to richness of being as to weakness of

spiritual perception, so much to the immensely varied potentiality of their nature as to sheer lack of any intense controlling
experience. A compass needle that is but feebly magnetized
swings again and again to west and east, and takes long to
discover its proper direction. One that is more sensitive will
settle immediately towards the north. Had the sheer complexity of every world, with its host of minute yet complex members, merely confused its sense of the proper direction of all
spirit? Had the simplicity and spiritual vigour of the earliest,
hugest beings achieved something of highest value that the
complexity and subtlety of the worlds could never achieve?

But no! Excellent as the nebular mentality was, in its own
strange way, the stellar and the planetary mentalities had also
their special virtues. And of all three the planetary must be
most prized, since it could best comprehend all three.

I now allowed myself to believe that I, since I did at last
include in my own being an intimate awareness not only of
many galaxies but also of the first phase of cosmical life, might
now with some justice regard myself as the incipient mind of
the cosmos as a whole.

But the awakened galaxies that supported me were still only
a small minority of the total population of galaxies. By telepathic influence I continued to help on those many galaxies
that were upon the threshold of mental maturity. If I could
include within the cosmical community of awakened galaxies
some hundreds instead of a mere score of members, perhaps I
myself, the communal mind, might be so strengthened as to
rise from my present state of arrested mental infancy to something more like maturity. It was clear to me that even now, in
my embryonic state, I was ripening for some new elucidation;
and that with good fortune I might yet find myself in the
presence of that which, in the human language of this book,
has been called the Star Maker.

At this time my longing for that presence had become an
overmastering passion. It seemed to me that the veil which still
hid the source and goal of all nebulae and stars and worlds was
already dissolving. That which had kindled so many myriad
beings to worship, yet had clearly revealed itself to none, that

towards which all beings had blindly striven, representing it to themselves by the images of a myriad divinities, was now, I felt, on the point of revelation to me, the marred but still growing spirit of the cosmos.

I who had myself been worshipped by hosts of my little members, I whose achievement reached far beyond their dreams, was now oppressed, overwhelmed, by the sense of my own littleness and imperfection. For the veiled presence of the Star Maker already overmastered me with dreadful power. The farther I ascended along the path of the spirit, the loftier appeared the heights that lay before me. For what I had once thought to be the summit fully revealed was now seen to be a mere foot-hill. Beyond lay the real ascent, steep, cragged, glacial, rising into the dark mist. Never, never should I climb that precipice. And yet I must go forward. Dread was overcome by irresistible craving.

Meanwhile under my influence the immature galaxies one by one attained that pitch of lucidity which enabled them to join the cosmical community and enrich me with their special experience. But physically the enfeeblement of the cosmos continued. By the time that half the total population of galaxies had reached maturity it became clear that few more would succeed.

Of living stars, very few were left in any galaxy. Of the host of dead stars, some, subjected to atomic disintegration, were being used as artificial suns, and were surrounded by many thousands of artificial planets. But the great majority of the stars were now encrusted, and themselves peopled. After a while it became necessary to evacuate all planets, since the artificial suns were too extravagant of energy. The planet-dwelling races therefore one by one destroyed themselves, bequeathing the material of their worlds and all their wisdom to the inhabitants of the extinguished stars. Henceforth the cosmos, once a swarm of blazing galaxies, each a swarm of stars, was composed wholly of star-corpses. These dark grains drifted through the dark void, like an infinitely tenuous smoke rising from an extinguished fire. Upon these motes, these gigantic worlds, the ultimate populations had created here and there with their artificial lighting a pale glow, invisible even from the innermost ring of lifeless planets.

By far the commonest type of being in these stellar worlds was the intelligent swarm of minute worms or insectoids. But there were also many races of larger creatures of a very curious kind adapted to the prodigious gravitation of their giant worlds. Each of these creatures was a sort of living blanket. Its under surface bore a host of tiny legs that were also mouths. These supported a body that was never more than an inch thick, though it might be as much as a couple of yards wide and ten yards long. At the forward end the manipulatory 'arms' travelled on their own battalions of legs. The upper surface of the body contained a honeycomb of breathing-pores and a great variety of sense organs. Between the two surfaces spread the organs of metabolism and the vast area of brain. Compared with the worm-swarms and insect-swarms, these tripe-like beings had the advantage of more secure mental unity and greater specialization of organs; but they were more cumbersome, and less adapted to the subterranean life which was later to be forced on all populations.

The huge dark worlds with their immense weight of atmosphere and their incredible breadths of ocean, where the waves even in the most furious storms were never more than ripples such as we know on quick-silver, were soon congested with the honeycomb civilizations of worms and insectoids of many species, and the more precarious shelters of the tripe-like creatures. Life on these worlds was almost like life in a two-dimensional 'flat-land'. Even the most rigid of the artificial elements was too weak to allow of lofty structures.

As time advanced, the internal heat of the encrusted stars was used up, and it became necessary to support civilization by atomic disintegration of the star's rocky core. Thus in time each stellar world became an increasingly hollow sphere supported by a system of great internal buttresses. One by one the populations, or rather the new and specially adapted descendants of the former populations, retired into the interiors of the burnt-out stars.

Each imprisoned in its hollow world, and physically isolated from the rest of the cosmos, these populations telepathically supported the cosmical mind. These were my flesh. In the inevitable 'expansion' of the universe, the dark galaxies had already for aeons been flying apart so rapidly that light itself could not have bridged the gulf between them. But this prodigious disintegration of the cosmos was of less account to the ultimate populations than the physical insulation of star from star through the cessation of all stellar radiation and all interstellar travel. The many populations, teeming in the galleries of the many worlds, maintained their telepathic union. Intimately they knew one another in all their diversity. Together they supported the communal mind, with all its awareness of the whole vivid, intricate past of the cosmos, and its tireless effort to achieve its spiritual goal before increase of entropy should destroy the tissue of civilizations in which it inhered.

Such was the condition of the cosmos when it approached the supreme moment of its career, and the illumination towards which all beings in all ages had been obscurely striving. Strange it was that these latter-day populations, cramped and impoverished, counting their last pence of energy, should achieve the task that had defeated the brilliant hosts of earlier epochs. Theirs was indeed the case of the wren that outsoared the eagle. In spite of their straitened circumstances they were still able to maintain the essential structure of a cosmical community, and a cosmical mentality. And with native insight they could use the past to deepen their wisdom far beyond the range of any past wisdom.

The supreme moment of the cosmos was not (or will not be) a moment by human standards; but by cosmical standards it was indeed a brief instant. When little more than half the total population of many million galaxies had entered fully into the cosmical community, and it was clear that no more were to be expected, there followed a period of universal meditation. The populations maintained their straitened utopian civilizations, lived their personal lives of work and social intercourse, and at the same time, upon the communal plane, refashioned the whole structure of cosmical culture. Of this phase I shall say nothing. Suffice it that to each galaxy and to each world was assigned a special creative mental function, and that all assimilated the work of all. At the close of this period I, the communal mind, emerged re-made, as from a chrysalis; and for a brief moment, which was indeed the supreme moment of the cosmos, I faced the Star Maker.

For the human author of this book there is now nothing left of that age-long, that eternal moment which I experienced as the cosmical mind, save the recollection of a bitter beatitude, together with a few incoherent memories of the experience itself which fired me with that beatitude.

Somehow I must tell something of that experience. Inevitably I face the task with a sense of abysmal incompetence. The greatest minds of the human race through all the ages of human history have failed to describe their moments of deepest insight. Then how dare I attempt this task? And yet I must. Even at the risk of well-merited ridicule and contempt and moral censure, I must stammer out what I have seen. If a shipwrecked seaman on his raft is swept helplessly past marvellous coasts and then home again, he cannot hold his peace. The cultivated may turn away in disgust at his rude accent and clumsy diction. The knowing may laugh at his failure to distinguish between fact and illusion. But speak he must.

3. The Supreme Moment and After

In the supreme moment of the cosmos I, as the cosmical mind, seemed to myself to be confronted with the source and the goal of all finite things.

I did not, of course, in that moment sensuously perceive the infinite spirit, the Star Maker. Sensuously I perceived nothing but what I had perceived before, the populous interiors of many dying stellar worlds. But through the medium which in this book is called telepathic I was now given a more inward perception. I felt the immediate presence of the Star Maker. Latterly, as I have said, I had already been powerfully seized by a sense of the veiled presence of some being other than myself, other than my cosmical body and conscious mind, other than my living members and the swarms of the burnt-out stars. But now the veil trembled and grew half-transparent to the mental vision. The source and goal of all, the Star Maker, was obscurely revealed to me as a being indeed other than my conscious self, objective to my vision, yet as in the depth of my own nature; as, indeed, myself, though infinitely more than myself.

It seemed to me that I now saw the Star Maker in two aspects: as the spirit's particular creative mode that had given rise to me, the cosmos; and also, most dreadfully, as something incomparably greater than creativity, namely as the eternally achieved perfection of the absolute spirit.

Barren, barren and trivial are these words. But not barren the experience.

Confronted with this infinity that lay deeper than my deepest roots and higher than my topmost reach, I, the cosmical mind, the flower of all the stars and worlds, was appalled, as any savage is appalled by the lightning and the thunder. And as I fell abject before the Star Maker, my mind was flooded with a spate of images. The fictitious deities of all races in all worlds once more crowded themselves upon me, symbols of majesty and tenderness, of ruthless power, of blind creativity, and of all-seeing wisdom. And though these images were but the fantasies of created minds, it seemed to me that one and all did indeed embody some true feature of the Star Maker's impact upon the creatures.

As I contemplated the host of deities that rose to me like a smoke cloud from the many worlds, a new image, a new symbol of the infinite spirit, took shape in my mind. Though born of my own cosmical imagination, it was begotten by a greater than I. To the human writer of this book little remains of that vision which so abashed and exalted me as the cosmical mind. But I must thrive to recapture it in a feeble net of words as best I may.

It seemed to me that I had reached back through time to the moment of creation. I watched the birth of the cosmos.

The spirit brooded. Though infinite and eternal, it had limited itself with finite and temporal being, and it brooded on a past that pleased it not. It was dissatisfied with some past creation, hidden from me; and it was dissatisfied also with its own passing nature. Discontent goaded the spirit into fresh creation.

But now, according to the fantasy that my cosmical mind conceived, the absolute spirit, self-limited for creativity, objectified from itself an atom of its infinite potentiality.

This microcosm was pregnant with the germ of a proper time and space, and all the kinds of cosmical beings.

Within this punctual cosmos the myriad but not unnumbered physical centres of power, which men conceive vaguely as electrons, protons, and the rest, were at first coincident with one another. And they were dormant. The matter of ten million galaxies lay dormant in a point.

Then the Star Maker said, 'Let there be light.' And there was light.

From all the coincident and punctual centres of power, light leapt and blazed. The cosmos exploded, actualizing its potentiality of space and time. The centres of power, like fragments of a bursting bomb were hurled apart. But each one retained in itself, as a memory and a longing, the single spirit of the whole; and each mirrored in itself aspects of all others throughout all the cosmical space and time.

No longer punctual, the cosmos was now a volume of inconceivably dense matter and inconceivably violent radiation, constantly expanding. And it was a sleeping and infinitely dissociated spirit.

But to say that the cosmos was expanding is equally to say that its members were contracting. The ultimate centres of power, each at first coincident with the punctual cosmos, themselves generated the cosmical space by their disengagement from each other. The expansion of the whole cosmos was but the shrinkage of all its physical units and of the wavelengths of its light.

Though the cosmos was ever of finite bulk, in relation to its minutiae of light-waves, it was boundless and centre-less. As the surface of a swelling sphere lacks boundary and centre, so the swelling volume of the cosmos was boundless and centreless. But as the spherical surface is centred on a point foreign to it, in a 'third dimension', so the volume of the cosmos was centred in a point foreign to it, in a 'fourth dimension'.

The congested and exploding cloud of fire swelled till it was of a planet's size, a star's size, the size of a whole galaxy, and of ten million galaxies. And in swelling it became more tenuous, less brilliant, less turbulent.

Presently the cosmical cloud was disrupted by the stress of its expansion in conflict with the mutual clinging of its parts, disrupted into many million cloudlets, the swarm of the great nebulae.

For a while these were as close to one another in relation to their bulk as the flocculations of a mottled sky. But the channels between them widened, till they were separated as flowers on a bush, as bees in a flying swarm, as birds migrating, as ships on the sea. More and more rapidly they retreated from one another; and at the same time each cloud contracted, becoming first a ball of down and then a spinning lens and then a featured whirl of star-streams.

Still the cosmos expanded, till the galaxies that were most remote from one another were flying apart so swiftly that the creeping light of the cosmos could no longer bridge the gulf between them.

But I, with imaginative vision, retained sight of them all. It was as though some other, some hypercosmical and instantaneous light, issuing from nowhere in the cosmical space, illuminated all things inwardly.

Once more, but in a new and cold and penetrating light, I watched all the lives of stars and worlds, and of the galactic communities, and of myself, up to the moment wherein now I stood, confronted by the infinity that men call God, and conceive according to their human cravings.

I, too, now sought to capture the infinite spirit, the Star Maker, in an image spun by my own finite though cosmical nature. For now it seemed to me, it seemed, that I suddenly outgrew the three-dimensional vision proper to all creatures, and that I saw with physical sight the Star Maker. I saw, though nowhere in cosmical space, the blazing source of the hypercosmical light, as though it were an overwhelmingly brilliant point, a star, a sun more powerful than all suns together. It seemed to me that this effulgent star was the centre of a four-dimensional sphere whose curved surface was the three-dimensional cosmos. The star of stars, this star that was indeed the Star Maker, was perceived by me, its cosmical creature, for one moment before its splendour seared my vision. And in that moment I knew that I had indeed seen the very source of all cosmical light and life and mind; and of how much else besides I had as yet no knowledge.

But this image, this symbol that my cosmical mind had conceived under the stress of inconceivable experience, broke and was transformed in the very act of my conceiving it, so inadequate was it to the actuality of the experience. Harking back in my blindness to the moment of my vision, I now conceived that the star which was the Star Maker, and the immanent centre of all existence, had been perceived as looking down on me, his creature from the height of his infinitude; and that when I saw him I immediately spread the poor wings of my spirit to soar up to him, only to be blinded and seared and struck down. It had seemed to me in the moment of my vision that all the longing and hope of all finite spirits for union with the infinite spirit were strength to my wings. It seemed to me that the Star, my Maker, must surely stoop to meet me and raise me and enfold me in his radiance. For it seemed to me that I, the spirit of so many worlds, the flower of so many ages, was the Church Cosmical, fit at last to be the bride of God. But instead I was blinded and seared and struck down by terrible light.

It was not only physical effulgence that struck me down in that supreme moment of my life. In that moment I guessed what mood it was of the infinite spirit that had in fact made the cosmos, and constantly supported it, watching its tortured growth. And it was that discovery which felled me.

For I had been confronted not by welcoming and kindly

love, but by a very different spirit. And at once I knew that the Star Maker had made me not to be his bride, nor yet his treasured child, but for some other end.

It seemed to me that he gazed down on me from the height of his divinity with the aloof though passionate attention of an artist judging his finished work; calmly rejoicing in its achievement, but recognizing at last the irrevocable flaws in its initial conception, and already lusting for fresh creation.

His gaze anatomized me with calm skill, dismissing my imperfections, and absorbing for his own enrichment all the little excellence that I had won in the struggle of the ages.

In my agony I cried out against my ruthless maker. I cried out that, after all, the creature was nobler than the creator; for the creature loved and craved love, even from the star that was the Star Maker; but the creator, the Star Maker, neither loved nor had need of love.

But no sooner had I, in my blinded misery, cried out, than I was struck dumb with shame. For suddenly it was clear to me that virtue in the creator is not the same as virtue in the creature. For the creator, if he should love his creature, would be loving only a part of himself; but the creature, praising the creator, praises an infinity beyond himself. I saw that the virtue of the creature was to love and to worship, but the virtue of the creator was to create, and to be the infinite, the unrealizable and incomprehensible goal of worshipping creatures.

Once more, but in shame and adoration, I cried out to my maker. I said, 'It is enough, and far more than enough, to be the creature of so dread and lovely a spirit, whose potency is infinite, whose nature passes the comprehension even of a minded cosmos. It is enough to have been created, to have embodied for a moment the infinite and tumultuously creative spirit. It is infinitely more than enough to have been used, to have been the rough sketch for some perfected creation.'

And so there came upon me a strange peace and a strange joy.

Looking into the future, I saw without sorrow, rather with quiet interest, my own decline and fall. I saw the populations of the stellar worlds use up more and more of their resources for the maintenance of their frugal civilizations. So much of the interior matter of the stars did they disintegrate, that their worlds were in danger of collapse. Some worlds did indeed crash in fragments upon their hollow centres, destroying the indwelling peoples. Most, before the critical point was reached, were re-made, patiently taken to pieces and rebuilt upon a smaller scale. One by one, each star was turned into a world of merely planetary size. Some were no bigger than the moon. The populations themselves were reduced to a mere millionth of their original numbers, maintaining within each little hollow grain a mere skeleton civilization in conditions that became increasingly penurious.

Looking into the future aeons from the supreme moment of the cosmos, I saw the populations still with all their strength maintaining the essentials of their ancient culture, still living their personal lives in zest and endless novelty of action, still practising telepathic intercourse between worlds, still telepathically sharing all that was of value in their respective world-spirits, still supporting a truly cosmical community with its single cosmical mind. I saw myself still preserving, though with increasing difficulty, my lucid consciousness; battling against the onset of drowsiness and senility, no longer in the hope of winning through to any more glorious state than that which I had already known, or of laying a less inadequate jewel of worship before the Star Maker, but simply out of sheer hunger for experience, and out of loyalty to the spirit.

But inevitably decay overtook me. World after world, battling with increasing economic difficulties, was forced to reduce its population below the numbers needed for the functioning of its own communal mentality. Then, like a degenerating brain-centre, it could no longer fulfil its part in the cosmical experience.

Looking forward from my station in the supreme moment of the cosmos, I saw myself, the cosmical mind, sink steadily towards death. But in this my last aeon, when all my powers were waning, and the burden of my decaying body pressed heavily on my enfeebled courage, an obscure memory of past lucidity still consoled me. For confusedly I knew that even in this my last, most piteous age I was still under the zestful though remote gaze of the Star Maker.

Still probing the future, from the moment of my supreme unwithered maturity, I saw my death, the final breaking of those telepathic contacts on which my being depended. Thereafter the few surviving worlds lived on in absolute isolation, and in that barbarian condition which men call civilized. Then in world after world the basic skills of material civilization began to fail; and in particular the techniques of atomic disintegration and photosynthesis. World after world either accidentally exploded its little remaining store of matter, and was turned into a spreading, fading sphere of light-waves in the immense darkness; or else died miserably of starvation and cold. Presently nothing was left in the whole cosmos but darkness and the dark whiffs of dust that once were galaxies. Aeons incalculable passed. Little by little each whiff of dustgrains contracted upon itself through the gravitational influence of its parts; till at last, not without fiery collisions between wandering grains, all the matter in each whiff was concentrated to become a single lump. The pressure of the huge outer regions heated the centre of each lump to incandescence and even to explosive activity. But little by little the last resources of the cosmos were radiated away from the cooling lumps, and nothing was left but rock and the inconceivably faint ripples of radiation that crept in all directions throughout the ever 'expanding' cosmos, far too slowly to bridge the increasing gulfs between the islanded grains of rock.

Meanwhile, since each rocky sphere that had once been a galaxy had been borne beyond every possible physical influence of its fellows, and there were no minds to maintain telepathic contact between them, each was in effect a wholly distinct universe. And since all change had ceased, the proper time of each barren universe had also ceased.

Since this apparently was to be the static and eternal end, I withdrew my fatigued attention back once more to the supreme moment which was in fact my present, or rather my immediate past. And with the whole mature power of my mind

I tried to see more clearly what it was that had been present to me in that immediate past. For in that instant when I had seen the blazing star that was the Star Maker, I had glimpsed, in the very eye of that splendour, strange vistas of being; as though in the depths of the hypercosmical past and the hypercosmical future also, yet coexistent in eternity, lay cosmos beyond cosmos.

CHAPTER FOURTEEN

THE MYTH
OF CREATION

A walker in mountainous country, lost in mist, and groping from rock to rock, may come suddenly out of the cloud to find himself on the very brink of a precipice. Below he sees valleys and hills, plains, rivers, and intricate cities, the sea with all its islands, and overhead the sun. So I, in the supreme moment of my cosmical experience, emerged from the mist of my finitude to be confronted by cosmos upon cosmos, and by the light itself that not only illumines but gives life to all. Then immediately the mist closed in upon me again.

That strange vision, inconceivable to any finite mind, even of cosmical stature, I cannot possibly describe. I, the little human individual, am now infinitely removed from it; and even to the cosmical mind itself it was most baffling. Yet if I were to say nothing whatever of the content of my adventure's crowning moment, I should belie the spirit of the whole. Though human language and even human thought itself are perhaps in their very nature incapable of metaphysical truth, something I must somehow contrive to express, even if only by metaphor.

All I can do is to record, as best I may with my poor human powers, something of the vision's strange and tumultuous after-effect upon my own cosmical imagination when the intolerable lucidity had already blinded me, and I gropingly strove to recollect what it was that had appeared. For in my blindness the vision did evoke from my stricken mind a fantastic reflex of itself, an echo, a symbol, a myth, a crazy dream, contemptibly crude and falsifying, yet, as I believe, not wholly without significance. This poor myth, this mere parable, I shall recount, so far as I can remember it in my merely human state.

More I cannot do. But even this I cannot properly accomplish. Not once, but many times, I have written down an account of my dream, and then destroyed it, so inadequate was it. With a sense of utter failure I stammeringly report only a few of its more intelligible characters.

One feature of the actual vision my myth represented in a most perplexing and inadequate manner. It declared that the supreme moment of my experience as the cosmical mind actually comprised eternity within it, and that within eternity there lay a multiplicity of temporal sequences wholly distinct from one another. For though in eternity all times are present, and the infinite spirit, being perfect, must comprise in itself the full achievement of all possible creations, yet this could not be unless in its finite, its temporal and creative mode, the infinite and absolute spirit conceived and executed the whole vast series of creations. For creation's sake the eternal and infinite spirit entails time within its eternity, contains the whole protracted sequence of creations.

In my dream, the Star Maker himself, as eternal and absolute spirit, timelessly contemplated all his works; but also as the finite and creative mode of the absolute spirit, he bodied forth his creations one after the other in a time sequence proper to his own adventure and growth. And further, each of his works, each cosmos, was itself gifted with its own peculiar time, in such a manner that the whole sequence of events within any single cosmos could be viewed by the Star Maker not only from within the cosmical time itself but also externally, from the time proper to his own life, with all the cosmical epochs co-existing together.

According to the strange dream or myth which took possession of my mind, the Star Maker in his finite and creative mode was actually a developing, an awakening spirit. That he should be so, and yet also eternally perfect, is of course humanly inconceivable; but my mind, overburdened with superhuman vision, found no other means of expressing to itself the mystery of creation.

Eternally, so my dream declared to me, the Star Maker is perfect and absolute; yet in the beginning of the time proper to his creative mode he was an infant deity, restless, eager, mighty, but without clear will. He was equipped with all creative power. He could make universes with all kinds of physical and mental attributes. He was limited only by logic. Thus he could ordain the most surprising natural laws, but he could not, for instance, make twice two equal five. In his early phase he was limited also by his immaturity. He was still in the trance of infancy. Though the unconscious source of his consciously exploring and creating mentality was none other than his own eternal essence, consciously he was at first but the vague blind hunger of creativity.

In his beginning he immediately set about exploring his power. He objectified from himself something of his own unconscious substance to be the medium of his art, and this he moulded with conscious purpose. Thus again and again he fashioned toy cosmos after toy cosmos.

But the creative Star Maker's own unconscious substance was none other than the eternal spirit itself, the Star Maker in his eternal and perfect aspect. Thus it was that, in his immature phases, whenever he evoked from his own depth the crude substance of a cosmos, the substance itself turned out to be not formless but rich in determinate potentialities, logical, physical, biological, psychological. These potentialities were sometimes recalcitrant to the conscious purpose of the young Star Maker. He could not always accommodate, still less fulfil them. It seemed to me that this idiosyncrasy of the medium itself often defeated his plan; but also that it suggested again and again more fertile conceptions. Again and again, according to my myth, the Star Maker learned from his creature, and thereby outgrew his creature, and craved to work upon an ampler plan. Again and again he set aside a finished cosmos and evoked from himself a new creation.

Many times in the early part of my dream I felt doubt as to what the Star Maker was striving to accomplish in his creating. I could not but believe that his purpose was at first not clearly conceived. He himself had evidently to discover it gradually; and often, as it seemed to me, his work was tentative, and his aim confused. But at the close of his maturity he willed to create as fully as possible, to call forth the full potentiality of his medium, to fashion works of increasing subtlety, and of increasingly harmonious diversity. As his purpose became clearer, it seemed also to include the will to create universes each of which might contain some unique achievement of awareness and expression. For the creature's achievement of perception and of will was seemingly the instrument by which the Star Maker himself, cosmos by cosmos, woke into keener lucidity.

Thus it was that, through the succession of his creatures, the Star Maker advanced from stage to stage in the progress from infantile to mature divinity.

Thus it was that in the end he became what, in the eternal view, he already was in the beginning, the ground and crown of all things.

In the typically irrational manner of dreams, this dream-myth which arose in my mind represented the eternal spirit as being at once the cause and the result of the infinite host of finite existents. In some unintelligible manner all finite things, though they were in a sense figments of the absolute spirit, were also essential to the very existence of the absolute spirit. Apart from them it had no being. But whether this obscure relationship represented some important truth or was merely a trivial dream-fiction, I cannot say.

CHAPTER FIFTEEN

THE MAKER
AND HIS WORKS

1. Immature Creating

According to the fantastic myth or dream that was evoked from my mind after the supreme moment of experience, the particular cosmos which I had come to regard as 'myself' falls somewhere neither early nor late in the vast series of creations. It appeared to be in some respects the Star Maker's first mature work; but in comparison with later creations it was in many ways juvenile in spirit.

Though the early creations express the nature of the Star Maker merely in his immature phase, for the most part they fall in important respects aside from the direction of human thought, and therefore I cannot now recapture them. They have left me with little more than a vague sense of the multiplicity and diversity of the Star Maker's works. Nevertheless a few humanly intelligible traces remain and must be recorded.

In the crude medium of my dream the first cosmos of all appeared as a surprisingly simple thing. The infant Star Maker, teased, as it seemed to me, by his unexpressed potency, conceived and objectified from himself two qualities. With these alone he made his first toy cosmos, a temporal rhythm, as it were of sound and silence. From this first simple drumbeat, premonitory of a thousand creations, he developed with infantile but godlike zest a flickering tattoo, a changeful complexity of rhythm. Presently, through contemplation of his creature's simple form, he conceived the possibility of more subtle creating. Thus the first of all creatures itself bred in its creator a need that itself could never satisfy. Therefore the infant Star Maker brought his first cosmos to a close. Regarding it from outside the cosmical time which it had generated, he apprehended its whole career as present, though none the less a flux. And when he had quietly assessed his work, he withdrew his attention from it and brooded for a second creation.

Thereafter, cosmos upon cosmos, each more rich and subtle than the last, leapt from his fervent imagination. In some of his earliest creations he seemed to be concerned only with the physical aspect of the substance which he had objectified from himself. He was blind to its psychical potentiality. In one early cosmos, however, the patterns of physical quality with which he played simulated an individuality and a life which they did not in fact possess. Or did they possess it? In a later creation, certainly, true life broke out most strangely. This was a cosmos which the Star Maker apprehended physically much as men apprehend music. It was a rich sequence of qualities diverse in pitch and in intensity. With this toy the infant Star Maker played delightedly, inventing an infinite wealth of melody and counterpoint. But before he had worked out all the subtleties of pattern implied in this little world of cold, mathematical music, before he had created more than a few kinds of lifeless, musical creatures, it became evident that some of his creatures were manifesting traces of a life of their own, recalcitrant to the conscious purpose of the Star Maker. The themes of the music began to display modes of behaviour that were not in accord with the canon which he had ordained for them. It seemed to me that he watched them with intense interest, and that they spurred him to new conceptions, beyond the creatures' power to fulfil. Therefore he brought this cosmos to completion; and in a novel manner. He contrived that the last state of the cosmos should lead immediately back to the first. He knotted the final event temporally to the beginning, so that the cosmical time formed an endless circlet. After considering his work from outside its proper time, he set it aside, and brooded for a fresh creation.

For the next cosmos he consciously projected something of his own percipience and will, ordaining that certain patterns and rhythms of quality should be the perceivable bodies of perceiving minds. Seemingly these creatures were intended to work together to produce the harmony which he had conceived for this cosmos; but instead, each sought to mould the whole cosmos in accordance with its own form. The creatures fought desperately, and with self-righteous conviction. When they were damaged, they suffered pain. This, seemingly, was something which the young Star Maker had never experienced or conceived. With rapt, surprised interest, and (as it seemed to me) with almost diabolical glee, he watched the antics and the sufferings of his first living creatures, till by their mutual strife and slaughter they had reduced this cosmos to chaos.

Thenceforth the Star Maker never for long ignored his creatures' potentiality for intrinsic life. It seemed to me, however, that many of his early experiments in vital creation went strangely awry, and that sometimes, seemingly in disgust with the biological, he would revert for a while to purely physical fantasies.

I can only briefly describe the host of the early creations. Suffice it that they issued from the divine though still infantile imagination one after the other like bright but trivial bubbles, gaudy with colour, rich with all manner of physical subtleties, lyrical and often tragic with the loves and hates, the lusts and aspirations and communal enterprises of the Star Maker's early experimental conscious beings.

Many of these early universes were non-spatial, though none the less physical. And of these non-spatial universes not a few were of the 'musical' type in which space was strangely represented by a dimension corresponding to musical pitch, and capacious with myriads of tonal differences. The creatures appeared to one another as complex patterns and rhythms of tonal characters. They could move their tonal bodies in the dimension of pitch, and sometimes in other dimensions, humanly inconceivable. A creature's body was a more or less constant tonal pattern, with much the same degree of flexibility and minor changefulness as a human body. Also, it could traverse other living bodies in the pitch dimension much as wave-trains on a pond may cross one another. But though these beings could glide through one another, they could also grapple, and damage one another's tonal tissues. Some, indeed, lived by devouring others; for the more complex needed to integrate into their own vital patterns the simpler patterns that exfoliated throughout the cosmos directly from the creative power of the Star Maker. The intelligent creatures could manipulate for their own ends elements wrenched from the fixed tonal environment, thus constructing artifacts of tonal pattern. Some of these served as tools for the more efficient pursuit of 'agricultural' activities, by which they enhanced the abundance of their natural food. Universes of this non-spatial kind, though incomparably simpler and more meagre than our own cosmos, were rich enough to produce societies capable not only of 'agriculture' but of 'handicrafts', and even a kind of pure art that combined the characteristics of song and dance and verse. Philosophy, generally rather Pythagorean, appeared for the first time in a cosmos of this 'musical' kind.

In nearly all the Star Maker's works, as revealed in my dream, time was a more fundamental attribute than space. Though in some of his earliest creations he excluded time, embodying merely a static design, this plan was soon abandoned. It gave little scope to his skill. Moreover, since it excluded the possibility of life and mind, it was incompatible with all but the earliest phase of his interest.

Space, my dream declared, appeared first as a development of a non-spatial dimension in a 'musical' cosmos. The tonal creatures in this cosmos could move not merely 'up' and 'down' the scale but 'sideways'. In human music particular themes may seem to approach or retreat, owing to variations of loudness and timbre. In a rather similar manner the creatures in this 'musical' cosmos could approach one another or retreat and finally vanish out of earshot. In passing 'sideways' they travelled through continuously changing tonal environments. In a subsequent cosmos this 'sideways' motion of the creatures was enriched with true spatial experience.

There followed creations with spatial characters of several dimensions, creations Euclidean and non-Euclidean, creations exemplifying a great diversity of geometrical and physical principles. Sometimes time, or space-time, was the fundamental reality of the cosmos, and the entities were but fleeting modifications of it; but more often, qualitative events were fundamental, and these were related in spatio-temporal manners. In some cases the system of spatial relations was infinite, in other finite though boundless. In some the finite extent of space was of constant magnitude in relation to the atomic material constituents of the cosmos; in some, as in our own cosmos, it was manifested as in many respects 'expanding'. In others again space 'contracted'; so that the end of such a cosmos, rich perhaps in intelligent communities, was the collision and congestion of all its parts, and their final coincidence and vanishing into a dimensionless point.

In some creations expansion and ultimate quiescence were followed by contraction and entirely new kinds of physical activity. Sometimes, for example, gravity was replaced by antigravity. All large lumps of matter tended to burst asunder, and all small ones to fly apart from each other. In one such cosmos the law of entropy also was reversed. Energy, instead of gradually spreading itself evenly throughout the cosmos, gradually piled itself upon the ultimate material units. I came in time to suspect that my own cosmos was followed by a reversed cosmos of this kind, in which, of course, the nature of living things was profoundly different from anything conceivable to man. But this is a digression, for I am at present describing much earlier and simpler universes.

Many a universe was physically a continuous fluid in which the solid creatures swam. Others were constructed as series of concentric spheres, peopled by diverse orders of creatures. Some quite early universes were quasi-astronomical, consisting of a void sprinkled with rare and minute centres of power.

Sometimes the Star Maker fashioned a cosmos which was without any single, objective, physical nature. Its creatures were wholly without influence on one another; but under the direct stimulation of the Star Maker each creature conceived an illusory but reliable and useful physical world of its own, and peopled it with figments of its imagination. These subjective worlds the mathematical genius of the Star Maker correlated in a manner that was perfectly systematic.

I must not say more of the immense diversity of physical form which, according to my dream, the early creations assumed. It is enough to mention that, in general, each cosmos was more complex, and in a sense more voluminous than the last; for in each the ultimate physical units were smaller in relation to the whole, and more multitudinous. Also, in each the individual conscious creatures were generally more in number, and more diverse in type; and the most awakened in each cosmos reached a more lucid mentality than any creatures in the previous cosmos.

Biologically and psychologically the early creations were very diverse. In some cases there was a biological evolution such as we know. A small minority of species would precariously ascend towards greater individuation and mental clarity. In other creations the species were biologically fixed, and progress, if it occurred, was wholly cultural. In a few most perplexing creations the most awakened state of the cosmos was at the beginning, and the Star Maker calmly watched this lucid consciousness decay.

Sometimes a cosmos started as a single lowly organism with an internal, non-organic environment. It then propagated by fission into an increasing host of increasingly small and increasingly individuated and awakened creatures. In some of these universes evolution would continue till the creatures became too minute to accommodate the complexity of organic structure necessary for intelligent minds. The Star Maker would then watch the cosmical societies desperately striving to circumvent the fated degeneration of their race.

In some creations the crowning achievement of the cosmos was a chaos of mutually unintelligible societies, each devoted to the service of some one mode of the spirit, and hostile to all others. In some the climax was a single utopian society of distinct minds; in others a single composite cosmical mind.

Sometimes it pleased the Star Maker to ordain that each creature in a cosmos should be an inevitable determinate expression of the environment's impact on its ancestors and itself. In other creations each creature had some power of arbitrary choice, and some modicum of the Star Maker's own creativity. So it seemed to me in my dream; but even in my dream I suspected that to a more subtle observer both kinds would have appeared as in fact determinate, and yet both of them also spontaneous and creative.

In general the Star Maker, once he had ordained the basic principles of a cosmos and created its initial state, was content to watch the issue; but sometimes he chose to interfere, either by infringing the natural laws that he himself had ordained, or by introducing new emergent formative principles, or by influencing the minds of the creatures by direct revelation. This according to my dream, was sometimes done to improve a cosmical design; but, more often, interference was included in his original plan.

Sometimes the Star Maker flung off creations which were in effect groups of many linked universes, wholly distinct physical systems of very different kinds, yet related by the fact that the creatures lived their lives successively in universe after universe, assuming in each habitat an indigenous physical form, but bearing with them in their transmigration faint and easily misinterpreted memories of earlier existences. In another way also, this principle of transmigration was sometimes used. Even creations that were not thus systematically linked might contain creatures that mentally echoed in some vague but haunting manner the experience or the temperament of their counterparts in some other cosmos.

One very dramatic device was used in cosmos after cosmos. I mentioned earlier that in my dream the immature Star Maker had seemed to regard the tragic failure of his first biological experiment with a kind of diabolical glee. In many subsequent creations also he appeared to be twi-minded. Whenever his conscious creative plan was thwarted by some unsuspected potentiality of the substance which he had objectified from his unconscious depth, his mood seemed to include not only frustration but also surprised satisfaction, as of some unrecognized hunger unexpectedly satisfied.

This twi-mindedness at length gave rise to a new mode of creating. There came a stage in the Star Maker's growth, as my dream represented it, when he contrived to dissociate himself as two independent spirits, the one his essential self, the spirit that sought positive creation of vital and spiritual forms and ever more lucid awareness, the other a rebellious, destructive and cynical spirit, that could have no being save as a parasite upon the works of the other.

Again and again he dissociated these two moods of himself, objectified them as independent spirits, and permitted them to strive within a cosmos for mastery. One such cosmos, which consisted of three linked universes, was somewhat reminiscent of Christian orthodoxy. The first of these linked universes was inhabited by generations of creatures gifted with varying degrees of sensibility, intelligence, and moral integrity. Here the two spirits played for the souls of the creatures. The 'good' spirit exhorted, helped, rewarded, punished; the 'evil' spirit deceived, tempted, and morally destroyed. At death the creatures passed into one or other of the two secondary universes, which constituted a timeless heaven and a timeless hell. There they experienced an eternal moment either of ecstatic comprehension and worship or of the extreme torment of remorse.

When my dream presented me with this crude, this barbaric figment, I was at first moved with horror and incredulity. How could the Star Maker, even in his immaturity, condemn his creatures to agony for the weakness that he himself had allotted to them? How could such a vindictive deity command worship?

In vain I told myself that my dream must have utterly falsified the reality; for I was convinced that in this respect it was not false, but in some sense true, at least symbolically. Yet, even when I was confronted by this brutal deed, even in the revulsion of pity and horror, I saluted the Star Maker.

To excuse my worship, I told myself that this dread mystery lay far beyond my comprehension, and that in some sense even such flagrant cruelty must, in the Star Maker, be right. Did barbarity perhaps belong to the Star Maker only in his immaturity? Later, when he was fully himself, would he finally outgrow it? No! Already I deeply knew that this ruthlessness was to be manifested even in the ultimate cosmos. Could there, then, be some key fact, overlooked by me, in virtue of which such seeming vindictiveness was justified? Was it simply that all creatures were indeed but figments of the creative power, and that in tormenting his creatures the Star Maker did but torment himself in the course of his adventure of self-expression? Or was it perhaps that even the Star Maker himself, though mighty, was limited in all creation by certain absolute logical principles, and that one of these was the indissoluble bond between betrayal and remorse in half-awakened spirits? Had he, in this strange cosmos, simply accepted and used the ineluctable limitations of his art? Or again, was my respect given to the Star Maker only as the 'good' spirit, not as the 'evil' spirit? And was he in fact striving to eject evil from himself by means of this device of dissociation?

Some such explanation was suggested by the strange evolution of this cosmos. Since its denizens had mostly a very low degree of intelligence and moral integrity, the hell was soon overcrowded, while the heaven remained almost empty. But the Star Maker in his 'good' aspect loved and pitied his creatures. The 'good' spirit therefore entered into the mundane sphere to redeem the sinners by his own suffering. And so at last the heaven was peopled, though the hell was not depopulated.

Was it, then, only the 'good' aspect of the Star Maker that I worshipped? No! Irrationally, yet with conviction, I gave my adoration to the Star Maker as comprising both aspects of his dual nature, both the 'good' and the 'evil', both the mild and terrible, both the humanly ideal and the incomprehensibly inhuman. Like an infatuated lover who denies or excuses the flagrant faults of the beloved, I strove to palliate the inhumanity of the Star Maker, nay positively I gloried in it. Was there then something cruel in my own nature? Or did my heart vaguely recognize that love, the supreme virtue in creatures, must not in the creator be absolute?

This dire and insoluble problem confronted me again and again in the course of my dream. For instance there appeared a creation in which the two spirits were permitted to strive in a novel and more subtle manner. In its early phase this cosmos manifested only physical characters; but the Star Maker provided that its vital potentiality should gradually express itself in certain kinds of living creatures which, generation by generation, should emerge from the purely physical and evolve towards intelligence and spiritual lucidity. In this cosmos he permitted the two spirits, the 'good' and the 'evil', to compete even in the very making of the creatures.

In the long early ages the spirits struggled over the evolution of the innumerable species. The 'good' spirit worked to produce creatures more highly organized, more individual, more delicately related to the environment, more skilled in action, more comprehensively and vividly aware of their world, of themselves, and of other selves. The 'evil' spirit tried to thwart this enterprise.

The organs and tissues of every species manifested throughout their structure the conflict of the two spirits. Sometimes the 'evil' spirit contrived seemingly unimportant but insidious and lethal features for a creature's undoing. Its nature would include some special liability to harbour parasites, some weakness of digestive machinery, some instability of nervous organization. In other cases the 'evil' spirit would equip some lower species with special weapons for the destruction of the pioneers of evolution, so that they should succumb, either to some new disease, or to plagues of the vermin of this particular cosmos, or to the more brutish of their own kind.

A still more ingenious plan the evil spirit sometimes used with great effect. When the 'good' spirit had hit upon some promising device, and from small beginnings had worked up in its favoured species some new organic structure or mode of behaviour, the evil spirit would contrive that the process of evolution should continue long after it had reached perfect adjustment to the creature's needs. Teeth would grow so large that eating became excessively difficult, protective shells so heavy that they hampered locomotion, horns so curved that they pressed upon the brain, the impulse to individuality so imperious that it destroyed society, or the social impulse so obsessive that individuality was crushed.

Thus in world after world of this cosmos, which greatly surpassed all earlier creations in complexity, almost every species came sooner or later to grief. But in some worlds a single species reached the 'human' level of intelligence and of spiritual sensibility. Such a combination of powers ought to have secured it from all possible attack. But both intelligence and spiritual sensibility were most skilfully perverted by the 'evil' spirit. For though by nature they were complementary, they could be brought into conflict; or else one or both could be exaggerated so as to become as lethal as the extravagant horns and teeth of earlier kinds. Thus intelligence, which led on the one hand to the mastery of physical force and on the other to intellectual subtlety, might, if divorced from spiritual sensibility, cause disaster. The mastery of physical force often produced a mania for power, and the dissection of society into two alien classes, the powerful and the enslaved. Intellectual subtlety might produce a mania for analysis and abstraction, with blindness to all that intellect could not expound. Yet sensibility itself, when it rejected intellectual criticism and the claims of daily life, would be smothered in dreams.

2. Mature Creating

According to the myth that my mind conceived when the supreme moment of my cosmical experience had passed, the Star Maker at length entered into a state of rapt meditation in which his own nature suffered a revolutionary change. So at least I judged from the great change that now came over his creative activity.

After he had reviewed with new eyes all his earlier works, dismissing each, as it seemed to me, with mingled respect and impatience, he discovered in himself a new and pregnant conception.

The cosmos which he now created was that which contains the readers and the writer of this book. In its making he used, but with more cunning art, many of the principles which had already served him in earlier creations; and he wove them together to form a more subtle and more capacious unity than ever before.

It seemed to me, in my fantasy that he approached this new enterprise in a new mood. Each earlier cosmos appeared to have been fashioned with conscious will to embody certain principles, physical, biological, psychological. As has already been reported, there often appeared a conflict between his intellectual purpose and the raw nature which he had evoked for his creature out of the depth of his own obscure being. This time, however, he dealt more sensitively with the medium of his creation. The crude spiritual 'material' which he objectified from his own hidden depth for the formation of his new creature was moulded to his still tentative purpose with more sympathetic intelligence, with more respect for its nature and its potentiality, though with detachment from its more extravagant demands.

To speak thus of the universal creative spirit is almost childishly anthropomorphic. For the life of such a spirit, if it exists at all, must be utterly different from human mentality, and utterly inconceivable to man. Nevertheless, since this childish symbolism did force itself upon me, I record it. In spite of its crudity, perhaps it does contain some genuine reflection of the truth, however distorted.

In the new creation there occurred a strange kind of discrepancy between the Star Maker's own time and the time proper to the cosmos itself. Hitherto, though he could detach himself from the cosmical time when the cosmical history had completed itself, and observe all the cosmical ages as present, he could not actually create the later phases of a cosmos before he had created the earlier. In his new creation he was not thus limited.

Thus although this new cosmos was my own cosmos, I regarded it from a surprising angle of vision. No longer did it appear as a familiar sequence of historical events beginning with the initial physical explosion and advancing to the final death. I saw it now not from within the flux of the cosmical time but quite otherwise. I watched the fashioning of the cosmos in the time proper to the Star Maker; and the sequence of the Star Maker's creative acts was very different from the sequence of historical events.

First he conceived from the depth of his own being a something, neither mind nor matter, but rich in potentiality, and in suggestive traits, gleams, hints for his creative imagination. Over this fine substance for a long while he pondered. It was a medium in which the one and the many demanded to be most subtly dependent upon one another; in which all parts and all characters must pervade and be pervaded by all other parts and all other characters; in which each thing must seemingly be but an influence in all other things; and yet the whole must be no other than the sum of all its parts, and each part an all-pervading determination of the whole. It was a cosmical substance in which any individual spirit must be, mysteriously, at once an absolute self and a mere figment of the whole.

This most subtle medium the Star Maker now rough-hewed into the general form of a cosmos. Thus he fashioned a still indeterminate space-time, as yet quite ungeometrized; an amorphous physicality with no clear quality or direction, no intricacy of physical laws; a more distinctly conceived vital trend and epic adventure of mentality; and a surprisingly definite climax and crown of spiritual lucidity. This last, though its situation in the cosmical time was for the most part late, was given a certain precision of outline earlier in the sequence of creative work than any other factor in the cosmos. And it seemed to me that this was so because the initial substance itself so clearly exposed its own potentiality for some such spiritual form. Thus it was that the Star Maker at first almost neglected the physical minutiae of his work, neglected also the earlier ages of cosmical history, and devoted his skill at first almost entirely to shaping the spiritual climax of the whole creature.

Not till he had blocked in unmistakably the most awakened phase of the cosmical spirit did he trace any of the variegated psychological trends which, in the cosmical time, should lead up to it. Not till he had given outline to the incredibly diverse themes of mental growth did he give attention fully to constructing the biological evolutions and the physical and geometrical intricacy which could best evoke the more subtle potentialities of his still rough-hewn cosmical spirit.

But, as he geometrized, he also intermittently turned again to modify and elucidate the spiritual climax itself. Not till the physical and geometrical form of the cosmos was almost completely fashioned could he endow the spiritual climax with fully concrete individuality.

While he was still working upon the detail of the countless, poignant individual lives, upon the fortunes of men, of ichthyoids, of nautiloids, and the rest, I became convinced that his attitude to his creatures was very different from what it had been for any other cosmos. For he was neither cold to them nor yet simply in love with them. In love with them, indeed, he still was; but he had seemingly outgrown all desire to save them from the consequences of their finitude and from the cruel impact of the environment. He loved them without pity. For he saw that their distinctive virtue lay in their finitude, their minute particularity, their tortured balance between dullness and lucidity; and that to save them from these would be to annihilate them.

When he had given the last touches to all the cosmical ages from the supreme moment back to the initial explosion and on to the final death, the Star Maker contemplated his work. And he saw that it was good.

As he lovingly, though critically, reviewed our cosmos in all its infinite diversity and in its brief moment of lucidity, I felt that he was suddenly filled with reverence for the creature that he had made, or that he had ushered out of his own secret depth by a kind of divine self-midwifery. He knew that this creature, though imperfect, though a mere creature, a mere figment of his own creative power, was yet in a manner more real than himself. For beside this concrete splendour what was he but a mere abstract potency of creation? Moreover in another respect the thing that he had made was his superior, and his teacher. For as he contemplated this the loveliest and subtlest of all his works with exultation, even with awe, its impact upon him changed him, clarifying and deepening his will. As he discriminated its virtue and its weakness, his own perception and his own skill matured. So at least it seemed to my bewildered, awe-stricken mind.

Thus, little by little, it came about, as so often before, that the Star Maker outgrew his creature. Increasingly he frowned upon the loveliness that he still cherished. Then, seemingly with a conflict of reverence and impatience, he set our cosmos in its place among his other works.

Once more he sank into deep meditation. Once more the creative urge possessed him.

Of the many creations which followed I must perforce say almost nothing, for in most respects they lay beyond my mental reach. I could not have any cognizance of them save in so far as they contained, along with much that was inconceivable, some features that were but fantastic embodiments of principles which I had already encountered. Thus all their most vital novelty escaped me.

I can, indeed, say of all these creations that, like our own cosmos, they were immensely capacious, immensely subtle; and that, in some alien manner or other, every one of them had both a physical and a mental aspect; though in many the physical, however crucial to the spirit's growth, was more transparent, more patently phantasmal than in our own cosmos. In some cases this was true equally of the mental, for the beings were often far less deceived by the opacity of their individual mental processes, and more sensitive to their underlying unity.

I can say too that in all these creations the goal which, as it seemed to me, the Star Maker sought to realize was richness, delicacy, depth, and harmoniousness of being. But what these words in detail mean I should find it hard to say. It seemed to me that in some cases, as in our own cosmos, he pursued this end by means of an evolutionary process crowned by an awakened cosmical mind, which strove to gather into its own awareness the whole wealth of the cosmical existence, and by creative action to increase it. But in many cases this goal was achieved with incomparably greater economy of effort and suffering on the part of the creatures, and without the huge dead loss of utterly wasted, ineffective lives which is to us so heart-rending. Yet in other creations suffering seemed at least as grave and widespread as in our own cosmos.

In his maturity the Star Maker conceived many strange forms of time. For instance, some of the later creations were designed with two or more temporal dimensions, and the lives of the creatures were temporal sequences in one or other dimension of the temporal 'area' or 'volume'. These beings experienced their cosmos in a very odd manner. Living for a brief period along one dimension, each perceived at every moment of its life a simultaneous vista which, though of course fragmentary and obscure, was actually a view of a whole unique 'transverse' cosmical evolution in the other dimension. In some cases a creature had an active life in every temporal dimension of the cosmos. The divine skill which arranged the whole temporal 'volume' in such a manner that all the infinite spontaneous acts of all the creatures should fit together to produce a coherent system of transverse evolutions far surpassed even the ingenuity of the earlier experiment in 'pre-established harmony'.

In other creations a creature was given only one life, but this was a 'zig-zag line', alternating from one temporal dimension to another according to the quality of the choices that the creature made. Strong or moral choices led in one temporal direction, weak or immoral choices in another.

In one inconceivably complex cosmos, whenever a creature was faced with several possible courses of action, it took them all, thereby creating many distinct temporal dimensions and distinct histories of the cosmos. Since in every evolutionary sequence of the cosmos there were very many creatures, and each was constantly faced with many possible courses, and the combinations of all their courses were innumerable, an infinity of distinct universes exfoliated from every moment of every temporal sequence in this cosmos.

In some creations each being had sensory perception of the whole physical cosmos from many spatial points of view, or even from every possible point of view. In the latter case, of course, the perception of every mind was identical in spatial range, but it varied from mind to mind in respect of penetration or insight. This depended on the mental calibre and disposition of particular minds. Sometimes these beings had not only omnipresent perception but omnipresent volition. They could take action in every region of space, though with varying precision and vigour according to their mental calibre. In a manner they were disembodied spirits, striving over the physical cosmos like chess-players, or like Greek gods over the Trojan Plain.

In other creations, though there was indeed a physical aspect, there was nothing corresponding to the familiar systematic physical universe. The physical experience of the beings was wholly determined by their mutual impact on one another. Each flooded its fellows with sensory 'images', the quality and sequence of which were determined according to psychological laws of the impact of mind on mind.

In other creations the processes of perception, memory, intellection, and even desire and feeling were so different from ours as to constitute in fact a mentality of an entirely different order. Of these minds, though I seemed to catch remote echoes of them, I cannot say anything.

Or rather, though I cannot speak of the alien psychical modes of these beings, one very striking fact about them I can record. However incomprehensible their basic mental fibres and the patterns into which these were woven, in one respect all these beings came fleetingly within my comprehension. However foreign to me their lives, in one respect they were my kin. For all these cosmical creatures, senior to me, and more richly endowed, constantly faced existence in the manner that I myself still haltingly strove to learn. Even in pain and grief, even in the very act of moral striving and of white-hot pity, they met fate's issue with joy. Perhaps the most surprising and heartening fact that emerged from all my cosmical and hypercosmical experience was this kinship and mutual intelligibility of the most alien beings in respect of the pure spiritual experience. But I was soon to discover that in this connection I had still much to learn.

3. *The Ultimate Cosmos and the Eternal Spirit*

In vain my fatigued, my tortured attention strained to follow the increasingly subtle creations which, according to my dream, the Star Maker conceived. Cosmos after cosmos issued from his fervent imagination, each one with a distinctive spirit infinitely diversified, each in its fullest attainment more awakened than the last; but each one less comprehensible to me.

At length, so my dream, my myth, declared, the Star Maker created his ultimate and most subtle cosmos, for which all others were but tentative preparations. Of this final creature I can say only that it embraced within its own organic texture the essences of all its predecessors; and far more besides. It was like the last movement of a symphony, which may embrace, by the significance of its themes, the essence of the earlier movement; and far more besides.

This metaphor extravagantly understates the subtlety and complexity of the ultimate cosmos. I was gradually forced to believe that its relation to each earlier cosmos was approximately that of our own cosmos to a human being, nay to a single physical atom. Every cosmos that I had hitherto observed now turned out to be but a single example of a myriadfold class, like a biological species, or the class of all the atoms of a single element. The internal life of each 'atomic' cosmos had seemingly the same kind of relevance (and the same kind of irrelevance) to the life of the ultimate cosmos as the events within a brain cell, or in one of its atoms, to the life of a human mind. Yet in spite of this huge discrepancy I seemed to sense throughout the whole dizzying hierarchy of creations a striking identity of spirit. In all, the goal was conceived, in the end, to include community and the lucid and creative mind.

I strained my fainting intelligence to capture something of the form of the ultimate cosmos. With mingled admiration and protest I haltingly glimpsed the final subtleties of world and flesh and spirit, and of the community of those most diverse and individual beings, awakened to full self-knowledge and mutual insight. But as I strove to hear more inwardly into that music of concrete spirits in countless worlds, I caught echoes not merely of joys unspeakable, but of griefs inconsolable. For some of these ultimate beings not only suffered, but suffered in darkness. Though gifted with full power of insight, their power was barren. The vision was withheld from them. They suffered as lesser spirits would never suffer. Such intensity of harsh experience was intolerable to me, the frail spirit of a lowly cosmos. In an agony of horror and pity I despairingly stopped the ears of my mind. In my littleness I cried out against my maker that no glory of the eternal and absolute could redeem such agony in the creatures. Even if the misery that I had glimpsed was in fact but a few dark strands woven into the golden tapestry to enrich it, and all the rest was bliss, yet such desolation of awakened spirits, I cried, ought not, ought never to be. By what diabolical malice, I demanded, were these glorious beings not merely tortured but deprived of the supreme consolation, the ecstasy of contemplation and praise which is the birthright of all fully awakened spirits?

There had been a time when I myself, as the communal mind of a lowly cosmos, had looked upon the frustration and sorrow of my little members with equanimity, conscious that the suffering of these drowsy beings was no great price to pay for the lucidity that I myself contributed to reality. But the suffering individuals within the ultimate cosmos, though in comparison with the hosts of happy creatures they were few, were beings, it seemed to me, of my own, cosmical, mental stature, not the frail, shadowy existences that had contributed their dull griefs to my making. And this I could not endure.

Yet obscurely I saw that the ultimate cosmos was nevertheless lovely, and perfectly formed; and that every frustration and agony within it, however cruel to the sufferer, issued finally, without any miscarriage, in the enhanced lucidity of the cosmical spirit itself. In this sense at least no individual tragedy was vain.

But this was nothing. And now, as through tears of compassion and hot protest, I seemed to see the spirit of the ultimate and perfected cosmos face her maker. In her, it seemed, compassion and indignation were subdued by praise. And the Star

Maker, that dark power and lucid intelligence, found in the concrete loveliness of his creature the fulfilment of desire. And in the mutual joy of the Star Maker and the ultimate cosmos was conceived, most strangely, the absolute spirit itself, in which all times are present and all being is comprised; for the spirit which was the issue of this union confronted my reeling intelligence as being at once the ground and the issue of all temporal and finite things.

But to me this mystical and remote perfection was nothing. In pity of the ultimate tortured beings, in human shame and rage, I scorned my birthright of ecstasy in that inhuman perfection, and yearned back to my lowly cosmos, to my own human and floundering world, there to stand shoulder to shoulder with my own half animal kind against the powers of darkness; yes, and against the indifferent, the ruthless, the invincible tyrant whose mere thoughts are sentient and tortured worlds.

Then, in the very act of this defiant gesture, as I slammed and bolted the door of the little dark cell of my separate self, my walls were all shattered and crushed inwards by the pressure of irresistible light, and my naked vision was once more seared by lucidity beyond its endurance. '

Once more? No. I had but reverted in my interpretative dream to the identical moment of illumination, closed by blindness, when I had seemed to spread wing to meet the Star Maker, and was struck down by terrible light. But now I conceived more clearly what it was that had overwhelmed me.

I was indeed confronted by the Star Maker, but the Star Maker was now revealed as more than the creative and therefore finite spirit. He now appeared as the eternal and perfect spirit which comprises all things and all times, and contemplates timelessly the infinitely diverse host which it comprises. The illumination which flooded in on me and struck me down to blind worship was a glimmer, so it seemed to me, of the eternal spirit's own all-penetrating experience.

It was with anguish and horror, and yet with acquiescence, even with praise, that I felt or seemed to feel something of the eternal spirit's temper as it apprehended in one intuitive and timeless vision all our lives. Here was no pity, no proffer of salvation, no kindly aid. Or here were all pity and all love, but mastered by a frosty ecstasy. Our broken lives, our loves, our follies, our betrayals, our forlorn and gallant defences, were one and all calmly anatomized, assessed, and placed. True, they were one and all lived through with complete understanding, with insight and full sympathy, even with passion. But sympathy was not ultimate in the temper of the eternal spirit; contemplation was. Love was not absolute; contemplation was. And though there was love, there was also hate comprised within the spirit's temper, for there was cruel delight in the contemplation of every horror, and glee in the downfall of the virtuous. All passions, it seemed, were comprised within the spirit's temper; but mastered, icily gripped within the cold, clear, crystal ecstasy of contemplation.

That this should be the upshot of all our lives, this scientist's, no, artist's, keen appraisal! And yet I worshipped!

But this was not the worst. For in saying that the spirit's temper was contemplation, I imputed to it a finite human experience, and an emotion; thereby comforting myself, even though with cold comfort. But in truth the eternal spirit was ineffable. Nothing whatever could be truly said about it. Even to name it 'spirit' was perhaps to say more than was justified. Yet to deny it that name would be no less mistaken; for whatever it was, it was more, not less, than spirit, more, not less, than any possible human meaning of that word. And from the human level, even from the level of a cosmical mind, this 'more', obscurely and agonizingly glimpsed, was a dread mystery, compelling adoration.

CHAPTER SIXTEEN

EPILOGUE: BACK TO EARTH

I woke on the hill. The street lamps of our suburb outshone the stars. The reverberation of the clock's stroke was followed by eleven strokes more. I singled out our window. A surge of joy, of wild joy, swept me like a wave. Then peace.

The littleness, but the intensity, of earthly events! Gone, abolished in an instant, was the hypercosmical reality, the wild fountain of creations, and all the spray of worlds. Vanished, transmuted into fantasy, and into sublime irrelevance.

The littleness, but the intensity, of this whole grain of rock, with its film of ocean and of air, and its discontinuous, varie-gated, tremulous film of life; of the shadowy hills, of the sea, vague, horizonless; of the pulsating, cepheid, lighthouse; of the clanking railway trucks. My hand caressed the pleasant harsh-ness of the heather.

Vanished, the hypercosmical apparition. Not such as I had dreamed must the real be, but infinitely more subtle, more dread, more excellent. And infinitely nearer home.

Yet, however false the vision in detail of structure, even perhaps in its whole form, in temper surely it was relevant; in temper perhaps it was even true. The real itself, surely, had impelled me to conceive that image, false in every theme and facet, yet in spirit true.

The stars wanly trembled above the street lamps. Great suns? Or feeble sparks in the night sky? Suns, it was vaguely rumoured. Lights at least to steer by, and to beckon the mind from the terrestrial flurry; but piercing the heart with their cold spears.

Sitting there on the heather, on our planetary grain, I shrank from the abysses that opened up on every side, and in the future. The silent darkness, the featureless unknown, were more dread than all the terrors that imagination had mustered. Peering, the mind could see nothing sure, nothing in all human experience to be grasped as certain, except uncertainty itself; nothing but obscurity gendered by a thick haze of theories. Man's science was a mere mist of numbers; his philosophy but a fog of words. His very perception of this rocky grain and all its wonders was but a shifting and a lying apparition. Even oneself, that seeming-central fact, was a mere phantom, so deceptive, that the most honest of men must question his own honesty, so insubstantial that he must even doubt his very existence. And our loyalties! So self-deceiving, so misinformed and mis-conceived. So savagely pursued and hate-warped! Our very loves, and these in full and generous intimacy, must be condemned as unseeing, self-regarding, and self-gratulatory.

And yet? I singled out our window. We had been happy together! We had found, or we had created, our little treasure of community. This was the one rock in all the welter of experience. This, not the astronomical and hypercosmical immensity, nor even the planetary grain, this, this alone, was the solid ground of existence.

On every side was confusion, a rising storm, great waves already drenching our rock. And all around, in the dark welter, faces and appealing hands, half-seen and vanishing.

And the future? Black with the rising storm of this world's madness, though shot through with flashes of a new and violent hope, the hope of a sane, a reasonable, a happier world. Between our time and that future, what horror lay in store? Oppressors would not meekly give way. And we two, accustomed only to security and mildness, were fit only for a kindly world; wherein, none being tormented, none turns desperate. We were adapted only to fair weather, for the practice of the friendly but not too difficult, not heroical virtues, in a society both secure and just. Instead, we found ourselves in an age of titanic conflict, when the relentless powers of darkness and the ruthless because desperate powers of light were coming to grips for a death struggle in the world's torn heart, when grave choices must be made in crisis after crisis, and no simple or familiar principles were adequate.

Beyond our estuary a red growth of fire sprang from a foundry. At hand, the dark forms of the gorse lent mystery to the suburb's foot-worn moor. In imagination I saw, behind our own hill's top, the farther and unseen hills. I saw the plains and woods and all the fields, each with its myriads of particular blades. I saw the whole land curving down from me, over the planet's shoulder. The villages were strung together on a mesh of roads, steel lines, and humming wires. Mist-drops on a cobweb. Here and there a town displayed itself as an expanse of light, a nebulous luminosity, sprinkled with stars.

Beyond the plains, London, neon-lit, seething, was a microscope-slide drawn from foul water, and crowded with nosing animalcules. Animalcules! In the stars' view, no doubt, these creatures were mere vermin; yet each to itself, and sometimes one to another, was more real than all the stars.

Gazing beyond London, imagination detected the dim stretch of the Channel, and then the whole of Europe, a patchwork of tillage and sleeping industrialism. Beyond poplared Normandy spread Paris, with the towers of Notre-Dame tipped slightly, by reason of Earth's curvature. Farther on, the Spanish night was ablaze with the murder of cities. Away to the left lay Germany, with its forests and factories, its music, its steel helmets. In cathedral squares I seemed to see the young men ranked together in thousands, exalted, possessed, saluting the flood-lit Führer. In Italy too, land of memories and illusions, the mob's idol spell-bound the young.

Far left-wards again, Russia, an appreciably convex segment of our globe, snow-pale in the darkness, spread out under the stars and cloud-tracts. Inevitably I saw the spires of the Kremlin, confronting the Red Square. There Lenin lay, victorious. Far off, at the foot of the Urals, imagination detected the ruddy plumes and smoke-pall of Magnetostroy. Beyond the hills there gleamed a hint of dawn; for day, at my midnight, was already pouring westward across Asia, overtaking with its advancing front of gold and rose the tiny smoke-caterpillar of the Trans-Siberian Express. To the north, the iron-hard Arctic oppressed the exiles in their camps. Far southward lay the rich valleys and plains that once cradled our species. But there I now saw railway lines ruled across the snow. In every village Asiatic children were waking to another school-day, and to the legend of Lenin. South again the Himalayas, snow-clad from waist to crest, looked over the rabble of their foot-hills into crowded India. I saw the dancing cotton plants, and the wheat, and the sacred river that bore the waters of Kamet past ricefields and crocodile-shallows, past Calcutta with its shipping and its offices, down to the sea. From my midnight I looked into China. The morning sun glanced from the flooded fields and gilded the ancestral graves. The Yang Tse, a gleaming, crumpled thread, rushed through its gorge. Beyond the Korean ranges, and across the sea, stood Fujiyama, extinct and formal. Around it a volcanic population welled and seethed in that narrow land, like lava in a crater. Already it spilled over Asia a flood of armies and of trade.

Imagination withdrew and turned to Africa. I saw the man-made thread of water that joins West to East; then minarets, pyramids, the ever-waiting Sphinx. Ancient Memphis itself now echoed with the rumour of Magnetostroy. Far southward, black men slept beside the great lakes. Elephants trampled the crops. Farther still, where Dutch and English profit by the Negro millions, those hosts were stirred by vague dreams of freedom.

Peering beyond the whole bulge of Africa, beyond cloud-spread Table Mountain, I saw the Southern Ocean, black with storms, and then the ice-cliffs with their seals and penguins, and the high snow-fields of the one unpeopled continent. Imagination faced the midnight sun, crossed the Pole, and passed Erebus, vomiting hot lava down his ermine. Northward it sped over the summer sea, past New Zealand, that freer but less conscious Britain, to Australia, where clear-eyed horsemen collect their flocks.

Still peering eastward from my hill, I saw the Pacific, strewn with islands; and then the Americas, where the descendants of

Europe long ago mastered the descendants of Asia, through priority in the use of guns, and the arrogance that guns breed. Beside the farther ocean, north and south, lay the old New World; the River Plate and Rio, the New England cities, radiating centre of the old new style of life and thought. New York, dark against the afternoon sun, was a cluster of tall crystals, a Stonehenge of modern megaliths. Round these, like fishes nibbling at the feet of waders, the great liners crowded. Out at sea also I saw them, and the plunging freighters, forging through the sunset, port holes and decks aglow. Stokers sweated at furnaces, look-out men in crow's-nests shivered, dance music, issuing from opened doors, was drowned by the wind.

The whole planet, the whole rock-grain, with its busy swarms, I now saw as an arena where two cosmical antagonists, two spirits, were already preparing for a critical struggle, already assuming terrestrial and local guise, and coming to grips in our half-awakened minds. In city upon city, in village after village, and in innumerable lonely farmsteads, cottages, hovels, shacks, huts, in all the crevices where human creatures were intent on their little comforts and triumphs and escapes, the great struggle of our age was brewing.

One antagonist appeared as the will to dare for the sake of the new, the longed for, the reasonable and joyful world, in which every man and woman may have scope to live fully, and live in service of mankind. The other seemed essentially the myopic fear of the unknown; or was it more sinister? Was it the cunning will for private mastery, which fomented for its own ends the archaic, reason-hating, and vindictive, passion of the tribe.

It seemed that in the coming storm all the dearest things must be destroyed. All private happiness, all loving, all creative work in art, science, and philosophy, all intellectual scrutiny and speculative imagination, and all creative social building; all, indeed, that man should normally live for, seemed folly and mockery and mere self-indulgence in the presence of public calamity. But if we failed to preserve them, when would they live again?

How to face such an age? How to muster courage, being capable only of homely virtues? How to do this, yet preserve the mind's integrity, never to let the struggle destroy in one's own heart what one tried to serve in the world, the spirit's integrity.

Two lights for guidance. The first, our little glowing atom of community, with all that it signifies. The second, the cold light of the stars, symbol of the hypercosmical reality, with its crystal ecstasy. Strange that in this light, in which even the dearest love is frostily assessed, and even the possible defeat of our half-waking world is contemplated without remission of praise, the human crisis does not lose but gains significance. Strange, that it seems more, not less, urgent to play some part in this struggle, this brief effort of animalcules striving to win for their race some increase of lucidity before the ultimate darkness.

A NOTE
ON MAGNITUDE

Immensity is not itself a good thing. A living man is worth more than a lifeless galaxy. But immensity has indirect importance through its facilitation of mental richness and diversity. Things are of course only large and small in relation to one another. To say that a cosmos is large is only to say that, in relation to it, some of its constituents are small. To say that its career is long is merely to say that many happenings are contained within it. But though the spatial and temporal immensity of a cosmos have no intrinsic merit, they are the ground for psychical luxuriance, which we value. Physical immensity opens up the possibility of vast physical complexity, and this offers scope for complex minded organisms. This is at any rate true of a cosmos like ours in which mind is conditioned by the physical.

The probable size of our cosmos may be very roughly conceived by means of the following analogy, adapted from one given in W. J. Luyten's *The Pageant of the Stars.* Let Wales represent the size of our galaxy, say 100,000 light years. This is said to be surrounded by a system of seven much smaller sub-galaxies and globular clusters, all lying within a diameter of 1,000,000 light years. In our model, they would spread far into the Atlantic and into Europe. Other such systems would lie throughout space at average intervals represented by the distance from Wales to North America. On the same scale the remotest galaxy visible through the great 100-inch telescope, some 500,000,000 light years distant, would lie 60,000 miles off, or a quarter of the distance to the moon. The forth-coming 200-inch telescope will doubtless have a far greater range. The total extent of the cosmos would be represented in this model by a volume about 11,000,000 miles across, or one-eighth the distance from the earth to the sun. The distance between the sun and the nearest star (4.5 light years) would be about thirteen feet. A light year itself would be rather less than three feet. The average speed of stellar motion (20 miles a second) is represented by a rate of about four inches in 100 years. The earth's orbit is one-thousandth of an inch in diameter; the sun's diameter is six-millionths of an inch; the earth is reduced to a grain one-twentieth of a millionth of an inch across.

Time Scale 1

Note—Every item on this scale is placed where it is solely to illustrate the fictitious story of this book. Many scientists would deny that man can be so far from the birth of the stars as I have found it convenient to suppose.

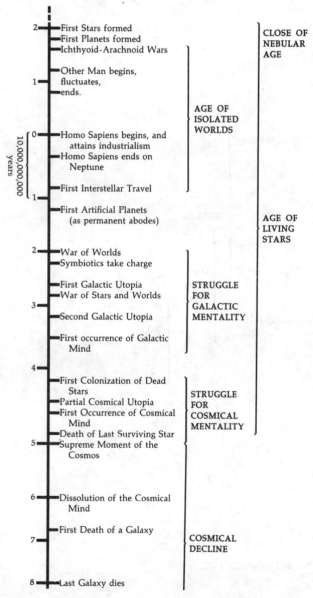

2	First Stars formed First Planets formed Ichthyoid-Arachnoid Wars	CLOSE OF NEBULAR AGE
1	Other Man begins, fluctuates, ends.	
		AGE OF ISOLATED WORLDS
0	Homo Sapiens begins, and attains industrialism Homo Sapiens ends on Neptune	
1	First Interstellar Travel	
	First Artificial Planets (as permanent abodes)	AGE OF LIVING STARS
2	War of Worlds Symbiotics take charge	
3	First Galactic Utopia War of Stars and Worlds Second Galactic Utopia	STRUGGLE FOR GALACTIC MENTALITY
	First occurrence of Galactic Mind	
4	First Colonization of Dead Stars Partial Cosmical Utopia First Occurrence of Cosmical Mind Death of Last Surviving Star	STRUGGLE FOR COSMICAL MENTALITY
5	Supreme Moment of the Cosmos	
6	Dissolution of the Cosmical Mind	
7	First Death of a Galaxy	COSMICAL DECLINE
8	Last Galaxy dies	

10,000,000,000 years

Time Scale 2

Note—This scale makes the present age of the cosmos *very* much greater than it is allowed to be by the current theory of the Expanding Universe. We may be very much nearer the beginning of things than I have imagined in this book.

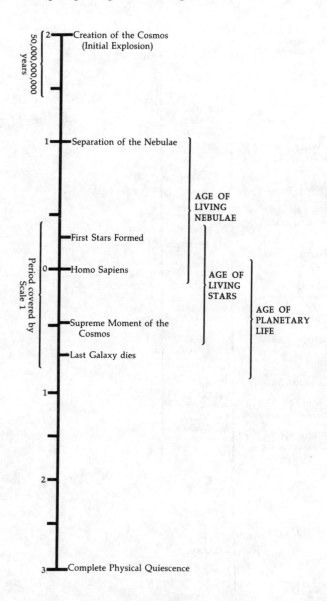

Time Scale 3

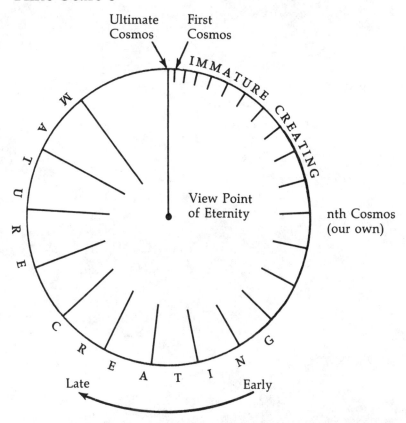

THE circle represents the time proper to the Star Maker as creative. Its upper-most point is the beginning and the end of the Star Maker's time. The passage of time is clockwise. Each 'broken spoke' of the wheel represents a cosmical time. The cosmical times are, of course, incommensurable; but the progress in the Star Maker's creative activity is represented by making the cosmical lines increasingly long as the creation becomes more mature. The increase of length represents the increasing complexity and subtlety of successive creations. The 'View Point of Eternity' represents the Star Maker's 'timeless' apprehension of all existence, in his capacity of eternal and absolute spirit. The goal of the creative spirit is the complete fulfilment of its capacity, and the attainment of the eternal view through the climax of the ultimate cosmos. Earlier creations approach, but do not reach, this climax. Each cosmical history is represented as lying in a dimension at right angles to the Star Maker's own time. He can, of course, 'live through' a cosmical history, but he can also apprehend it all at once. Some of the cosmical histories might have been represented by circles, since the times of some are cyclic. Others might have been areas, since they have more than one temporal dimension. I have only represented a few of the infinite number of creations.

GLOSSARY

Introduction

The Glossary to *Star Maker* was found in two forms in the manuscripts of Olaf Stapledon. The earlier version is found at the end of the hand-written manuscript of *Star Maker* which is now in the Special Collections Department of the Sidney Jones Library, Liverpool University. This hand-written version is not complete. Several cross references are made to definitions which do not actually appear.

Another version, a typed version, of the Glossary was found among the manuscripts held at Simon's Field, West Kirby by Mrs. Agnes Z. Stapledon. This latter version is complete. The definitions missing from the earlier manuscript are found in the typescript.

The typed Glossary was placed on deposit at the Sidney Jones Library, together with many other manuscripts, letters, and books from Olaf Stapledon's library, in 1983.

The Glossary presented here is an accurate reproduction of the typescript discussed above. In particular Stapledon's punctuation has been retained. The brackets which appear in the original have been included. It is probable that the bracketed material was originally marked for deletion if the full Glossary was deemed too lengthy by the publisher of *Star Maker*. As published in 1937 the original edition of *Star Maker* appeared without any definition of terms. "A Note on Magnitude" appended to the book, briefly discusses some of the words which appear in the Glossary, and readers of this booklet who are familiar with the Note on Magnitude will recognize some of the phrases used there.

The publisher would like to thank the Estate of William Olaf Stapledon and the Sidney Jones Library for permission to reproduce this material.

Harvey Satty
Literary Executor to the Estate of
William Olaf Stapledon

[Awake. See 'Waking'.]

Awakened World. A world that has attained communal consciousness. To do this, it has to pass far beyond the present human stage, and through the utopian stage.

Communal Consciousness, or mentality, or mind. This concept is open to serious philosophical objection, but is significant, and may contain a truth which cannot yet be stated coherently. Whether it involves a single, though communal, experiencing mind, or merely identity of 'content' in many minds, does not matter for my purpose, and *may* be a false distinction. In this book communal consciousness, at least in some of its forms, does not necessarily preclude individual differences of experience and temperament; but these must be subordinated to an identical consciousness, shared by all individuals, in respect of all public matters. Further, through this pooling of public experience, each individual mind must be raised to a higher 'power' of mentality. Communal consciousness is thought of as occurring in many degrees, from a fleeting and precarious identity of two individuals to the all-embracing and securely unified consciousness of a minded cosmos.

Community. The word has two senses. (a) Any group of individuals living in relation to one another. In this sense a nation is a community. (b) A group in which all individuals consciously cooperate in a common life approved by all. In this sense no group can be a community if one section has great power and prosperity at the expense of, and against the wishes of, another section. The pattern of all community is the small group in personal contact. Each individual must realise the underlying concord and the unique idiosyncrasy of the others. Each must respect the personality of the others, and recognize them as ends, not mere means to some other end, such as the wealth or glory of the group. Each must enrich, and be enriched by, the mental life of others. Each must prize the communal culture and life-pattern of the group itself, striving to subordinate all conflicts to the well-being of the whole. In larger groups personal contact obviously cannot hold; but the individuals may generalise from personal experience, and act on the principle that all individuals, known or unknown, should be treated as ends.

Cosmos. Any self-complete system of existence; generally with both physical and mental attributes; generally, but not necessarily, containing a number of individual minds, and sometimes a single cosmical mind.

[Create. I have found it convenient to use the mythical notion of a creator, a finite creative spirit, itself an aspect of the infinite and eternal spirit, and the source of all other finite things. The Star Maker is conceived as evoking from his own unconscious nature the raw material of his work, and consciously moulding it to fulfil a conscious purpose.

Creation. (a) The activity of creating. (b) Often used as equivalent to 'cosmos'. 'Creations' is a convenient plural for 'cosmos'.

Creature. Any created thing; but the word is generally used of living things within a cosmos.]

Crisis, The Familiar. The phase of social development through which the human race is now passing. The struggle to emerge from an individualistic, uncoordinated, world-order to one that is consciously planned for world-community.

[Dialectic. I have occasionally used this word to suggest that events give birth to future events according to an inner necessity of their own nature. This necessity includes the psychological connections between mental events.

Eternal. Not merely everlasting in time, but nontemporal, or rather supra-temporal, and comprising time-sequences within it as co-present. If time is absolute as it seems to us, this is nonsense; but there is no reason to suppose that our temporal experience is adequate.]

Expansion of the Universe. This physical theory, though it is open to serious objection, and may well have to be modified out of all recognition or actually abandonned at any moment, has probably more than ephemeral interest. Anyhow, its emotional significance accords with my theme. I have therefore used it, though with the knowledge that in doing so I may have 'dated' this book as flagrantly as I dated an earlier book by missing Fascism. The theory may be roughly described as that according to which the total extent of the finite though boundless physical universe is continually increasing in relation to all objects that are not larger than galaxies.

Galaxy. The largest kind of stellar group short of a whole cosmos. Our solar system is situated somewhere in the middle of our galaxy, which is roughly a lentoid, or bun or biscuit, five times as broad as it is thick. Within our galaxy the stars are so remote from one another that the density of their distribution may be represented by the molecules of a cubic inch of normal air spread over a cube 150 miles each way. The size of our galaxy, which may possibly be a good deal larger than the average of its kind, is such that light, travelling at 186,000 miles a second, takes from 30,000 to 50,000 years to cross it. There may be some ten million galaxies in the cosmos. Of these, only a few million are visible through the greatest extant telescope. The average distance between the galaxies is at least thirty times their average size. (See 'Size'.)

[**Individual.** Though strictly speaking a communal mind may be said to be an 'individual' in virtue of its single consciousness, I incline to reserve the word for a consciousness connected with a single body. Thus a man is an individual. A communal mind may be said to have 'super-individuality'. Even worlds, however, if they have communal minds, may be regarded as individuals in relation to a galactic society of worlds; and even minded galaxies in relation to a cosmical society of galaxies.]

Light Year. The distance travelled by light in one year, approximately six million million miles.

[**Mentality.** Mindedness. Type of mind.

Mind. Any self-contained system of experience. Any unified consciousness, whether of amoeba, man, or cosmos.

Minded. Having a single mind of its own.]

Myth. A story having some far-reaching intellectual and emotional significance. A myth must express symbolically ideas and emotions of importance to the people and the period to which the myth applies. This it must do by means of lesser ideas which are themselves significant to the myth's public. The story need not be fully credible in a literal sense, but the more credible it is, the better. This whole book is a rather crude myth. Chapters XIV and XV constitute a myth within a myth.

Nebula. Two very different senses belong to the word in astronomy. This misfortune is due to the fact that both kinds of nebulae appear as cloudy patches of light. (a) A 'great nebula', or 'spiral nebula', or 'extra-galactic nebula', is either simply a galaxy, or else the cloud of gas from which a galaxy is believed to originate. (b) Any gas-cloud *within* a galaxy is refered to as a nebula. I have never used the word as simply equivalent to 'galaxy'.

Religion. (a) In the mouths of Communists the word means a particular sort of capitalist dope, namely certain doctrines and practices calculated to withdraw attention from the need for revolution, and to fix it upon an unreal world of fantasy, thus relieving the 'religious' person from the moral responsibility of serving the revolution. Some readers may condemn this book as 'religious' in this pejorative sense. (b) In another sense 'religion' includes all that is best in the emotional attitude of Communism itself, namely the resolute will to live devotedly in service of mankind. 'Religion' in this sense includes also a conviction that this will has in some manner not merely terrestrial but also cosmical significance. Further, it includes the feeling that even the will to fight in life's battle against the forces of death should be complemented by an ultimate piety toward something superhuman, and even super-vital, a piety toward fate, or the whole of being, or some inconceivable diety. This attitude, so well expressed by Spinoza, is alien to contemporary Communism; but it is not to be confused with capitalist dope, for those who have felt it most strongly have been amongst the most active in the service of mankind. (See 'Spiritual', and 'Worship'.)

Size. Immensity is not itself of any importance. A living Socrates or Lenin is worth more than a lifeless galaxy. Nevertheless immensity has indirect importance, through facilitation of mental richness and diversity. Size is relative. Things can only be large or small in relation to one another. To say that a cosmos is large is merely to say that, in relation to it, some of its constituents are small. But the spatial and temporal immensity of a cosmos favour psychical complexity. For physical immensity opens up the possibility of vast physical complexity, and this offers scope for complex and diverse minds. This is at any rate true in a cosmos such as ours, in which mind is conditioned by the physical universe.

The probable size of the cosmos and its constituents may be very roughly conceived by means of the following analogy, derived mainly from W.J. Luyten's *The Pagent of the Stars.* Let Wales represent the size of our galaxy, say 50,000 light-years. The speed of light (186,000 miles a second) becomes three feet per year. The average distance between the galaxies becomes about the distance from Wales to Cuba. On the same scale the remotest galaxy visible through the great 100-inch telescope lies 60,000 miles off, or one quarter of the distance to the Moon. The new 200-inch telescope will have a much greater range. The whole cosmos would be represented by a volume about 11,000,000 miles across, or one eighth the distance from the earth to the sun. In this model, in which Wales represents our galaxy, the distance between the sun and the nearest star (4.5 light-years) is about 13 feet. The average speed of stellar motion (20 miles a second) is represented by a rate of about 4 inches in 1,000 years. The earth's orbit is one thousandth of an inch in diameter; the sun's diameter is six millionths of an inch; the earth is reduced to a grain one twenty-millionth of an inch across.

Spirit.   I have used this emotive and dangerously ambiguous word in at least three senses. The sense intended is generally revealed by the context. Where it is not, the ambiguity is intentional. (a) Perhaps the commonest sense is, any experiencing subject, any experient, of what ever rank. I intend no implication that a spirit is a metaphysical substance or soul, or that it is necessarily distinct from other spirits. For all I know, all spirits may be one spirit in diverse states. Nor do I mean by 'spirit' necessarily an eternal spirit, save in the sense that, in the eternal view everything is eternal. (b) The word 'spirit' is also used in a more abstract sense, as in the phrase, 'the advancement of the spirit'. Here 'the spirit' is simply spirit in general, whether in an individual, or in successive generations of individuals, or in minded worlds, or a minded cosmos. In this sense the word implies more than mere consciousness, since the advance consists of progress in or toward 'spirituality'. (See 'Spiritual'.) (c) The third sense is illustrated by such a phrase as 'the spirit of our times', 'the spirit of friendship', where 'spirit' means merely a mental attitude or mode of behaviour on the part of conscious beings.

Spiritual.   In such phrases as 'the spiritual attitude', and 'spiritual sensibility', the adjective obviously distinguishes the noun from other, non-spiritual, though mental, states. Any use of the word 'spiritual' inevitably echoes the old distinction between body, mind, and spirit. I use it to suggest activities at or near the upper limit of human mental capacity. More significantly, it implies a certain direction of interest or attention, and of will; a direction not possible at lower levels of development. It involves detachment from all self-regarding desires, but not necessarily self-mortification. It also involves detachment from all social and racial ends, in fact from all 'creature' ends of every order, not in the sense of refusing to work for them, but in the sense of striving to see all things, as it were, in the universal view, and prizing them in their relation to the whole of things. The spiritual attitude is a mere sham and a snare unless it combines the glad acceptance of fate with heroic championship of our waking humanity. The lives of Spinoza and some Quakers are examples of the sucessful combination of these opposites. I have supposed that spirituality in man is but the first tentative advance in a very far-reaching progress. (See 'Religion', and 'Worship'.)

[Star Maker.   The name applies to (a) the finite and creative spirit, conceived as the source of all existents, and (b) the eternal and absolute spirit, of which the creative spirit is an abstract mode.

Super-Individual.   A group of individuals is said to have attained super-individuality when it has acquired permanent communal mentality.]

Symbiosis.   A close association of two distinct species, resulting in mutual benefit. A mutually profitable 'parasitism', in which structure and function in each species are adapted to the common life.

Telepathy.   Immediate, extra-sensory, contact between minds. A mind's direct access to another mind without physical mediation. Whether such an activity occurs, I know not. There is some striking evidence for it, but it is not yet generally accepted among scientists. I have made great use of this concept, partly for the very reason that it suggests that human science has yet far to go. A distinction may be made between 'one way' telepathy and 'reciprocal' telepathy. In the former, one party alone has access to the other's experience; his own experience remains inaccessible to the other.

Universe. Occasionally used as equivalent to 'cosmos'. The word has unfortunately become ambiguous, since some astronomers have used it as equivalent to 'galaxy'. Possibly it ought to be reserved for the totality of being, including every cosmos as a part.

Utopian Stage, or phase. The happy stage of perfected social order which, with good fortune, a world may win for itself when it has emerged from the 'familiar crisis', and has passed through a long period of economical, political, and educational reconstruction. The 'utopian stage' is for us a goal; but for worlds in which it has been attained it is a brief respite before the struggle for communal mentality.

Waking. I have used this word as practically equivalent to 'mentally developing'. This seems to have three aspects, knowing, feeling, and willing: or in technical language, cognition, affection, and conation. It involves increasing accuracy, penetration, and comprehensiveness of cognition in respect of the physical and social environment and the individual's inner life, and in every possible mode of cognition. It involves the acquiring of increasingly delicate modes and distinctions of feeling *about* the environment and the self. It involves increasing appropriateness of feeling and action to the cognised world and self. In respect of action, this means increasing power of taking all relevant matters into account, allowing due weight to all relevant motives, in such a manner that familiar, easy, and insistent impulses shall not be allowed to over-ride more recently acquired, more difficult, less insistent impulses that happen to be in fact more appropriate to the actual situation. 'Appropriate' raises many philosophical difficulties, but in practice we do recognize that certain actions are appropriate to certain situations. In the final analysis this appropriateness is intuitive. Thus, to take a humble example, we intuit the appropriate act in relation to an empty stomach to be eating.

[World.   (a) Any more or less self-contained system of physical nature thought of as inhabited or habitable. A cosmos, a galaxy, a planet, a sea, a rock pool, a louse-infested or microbe-infested man, are worlds in this sense. (b) I have generally used the word in a more special sense to mean planets, natural and artificial. Stars also are sometimes referred to as 'worlds', either when they are said to be inhabited by native salamandrians, or when, having become cool and encrusted, they are colonised by races derived from planet-dwellers.]

Worship.   At the risk of raising thunder on the Left, I have used this word to designate an emotional attitude or activity which I believe to be extremely important, and to be the essential meaning which the common debased use of the word has obscured. [All emotion is an attitude or activity consequent on valuing something or other either actually enjoyed or merely needed. Sometimes what is valued is a simple bodily activity; sometimes it is something demanding more developed powers of apprehension, for instance, personal triumph, or the well-being of another individual, or of a community. More developed emotion, though always woven of simple emotional responses to primitive situations, such as hunger, and danger, becomes complicated and refined in relation to more subtle situations, such as personal and social relationships, adequately cognised. Now we may adopt, or strive to adopt, an emotional attitude appropriate not merely to personal or social relations but to our relation to our experienced universe as a whole. I suggest that this attitude, when it really is appropriate, is the most significant meaning of the word 'worship'.] I should describe the essence of worship as the attempt to see and feel all experienced things not merely from the private or even the racial point of view but from the universal point of view. It is a prizing of the whole of things (so far as revealed) not as means to personal or racial advancement, but for its own sake. 'The whole of things' needs qualification. Perhaps the activity which I am calling 'worship' is an appreciation not precisely of the whole of experienced things, but rather of an attribute or essence that is experienced as characteristic of all particular existents. Metaphorically this essence might be called the 'spirit of the whole'. (See 'Religion', and see 'Spiritual'.)